The Last Single Couple in America

Martin Sacchetti

Libro Origini Publishing—Albany, NY
ISBN: 979-8-218-34121-3
Library of Congress Control Number: 2024901366
Title: *The Last Single Couple in America*
Author: Martin Sacchetti
Digital distribution | 2024
Paperback | 2024

This is a work of fiction. The characters, names, incidents, places, and dialogue are products of the author's imagination and are not to be construed as real.

Dedication

To my parents who supported.
Joyce Hunt-Bouyea who encouraged and inspired.
David Tassone who believed (even when I didn't).

Chapter One
Mother Nature, Father Time

October 1995

"Nature's run amok!" The frantic voice booming from the answering machine broke Jude Giacolone's bedroom silence. "You have to be there, so pick up," Francine Duffy continued to bellow with dominatrix command.

Jude squinted, trying to focus on his new Swiss Army watch, an early birthday gift from his parents. *Eight thirty! On a Saturday morning! It's too early for calls, especially after Diego, a 24-year-old tsunami of hormonal rage left a scant three hours ago.* Jude grimaced. He twisted under the cocoon of sheets and comforter, landing on his stomach, a naked leg exposed.

"Jude? Please, for God's sake, pick up." The dominatrix was replaced by the plea of a whining child. With his face buried in his down pillow, he felt for his telephone with the maladroit dexterity of a blind person fumbling around unchartered territory. Finally picking up, "This better be good." His voice was rife with somnolence.

"Nature has freaked out."

"Did you find a grey hair? A wrinkle?" He tried to generate moisture in his mouth.

"Don't be glib. I have a real problem. You need to come over right away." The dominatrix was back.

"For Christ's sake, Francine, it's eight o'clock—"

"Eight-thirty."

"Whatever! It's still too early for histrionics."

"I have a kitchen full of wasps. I hardly call that being hysterical!"

"*Wasps?* Your family stopped by unannounced?"

"BEES, SMARTASS! FUCKING BEES!"

Jude bolted upright. Her shrieking voice shattered his ear as if an atomic bomb detonated in his head.

"Christ, Fran! Calm down."

Francine took a deep breath. "Will you please come over and help me?" The pleading child returned. "Unless coming to the aid of your best friend is going to interfere with sleeping the day away, no doubt from an all-night sexual romp, then just forget it."

There was nothing like shaming a friend into acquiescence.

"Okay, okay. I'll be right over." Jude stretched and yawned as he rose from his platform bed. The angled sunlight through the window bathed his naked body. "I'll jump in the shower and—"

"No shower! There's no time. I could be a human pin cushion by the time you shower. Just get over here NOW! And bring your bug spray—the one with no fluorocarbons," Francine added. "Ahhhh! Hurry! I'm getting attacked—" The line went dead as if her kidnapper caught her calling for help.

Jude, completely awake now, went to the bathroom and pissed what seemed like an endless stream. *Come on, penis. I have an angry dominatrix waiting for me!*

Knowing Francine, she probably calculated how long it would take him to get to her apartment. It would take approximately two to three minutes to wait for and ride down the ten floors in the vintage *'Rosemary's Baby'* elevator, as Jude christened it because the sliding wooden door with the small window and the squeaky, folding metal gate reminded him of the one Mia Farrow took to escape the coven of witches in the classic film.

Jude lived in an old brownstone building on State Street opposite Albany's Washington Park entrance. Although his building installed a modern elevator, Jude, a cinema fanatic, liked using the older, rickety one as an homage to one of his favorite movies.

In Jude's mind, Francine, no doubt, rationalized that traffic would be light on a Saturday morning. According to her calculations, Jude projected it should take fifteen minutes—*no more*—to get to her place.

Feeling like a contestant in a game show where they raced against the clock, Jude quickly splashed water on his face, brushed his teeth, and applied moisturizer to his face—*never leave home without it*—then pulled on faded jeans and a tight-fitting T-shirt; his theory was that one never knew who one would encounter in the halls, as some hot guys lived in his building, so he always had to look his most fetching.

He grabbed a baseball cap, the one with the word *Cocks*

emblazoned across the brim in red letters. It was short for *Gamecocks,* the namesake for the University of South Carolina. It was always an attention-getter.

"Some people wear their hearts on their sleeve. I wear my hobby on my hat," Jude told a flirtatious hottie who inquired about it one night at the bar. Jude ended up going home with him, and his *hobby* turned out to be enormous.

Jude grabbed the bug spray in the pump bottle Francine insisted he purchase instead of the aerosol kind from under his kitchen sink and headed out the door. As luck had it, the elevators were right across from his apartment. Francine no doubt considered that in her computation (Jude projected that Francine would presume no one would be up to use the elevators so early in the morning). He checked his watch: eight forty-five. The clock was ticking.

Outside, the warm air swaddled him. It was another in a string of unusually mild days for mid-October. It was as if the summer heat bled into autumn like a rained-on watercolor. At a time when the trees should be nature's fireworks, bursting with fiery crimsons, buttercup yellows, and saffron oranges, a preponderance of green still dominated, suffocating the autumnal shades.

"It's global warming," Francine declared when they went apple picking in Red Hook last weekend. "That's why the leaves haven't changed," Francine said authoritatively, like a Nobel Prize-winning scientist.

With the Catskill Mountains as a backdrop, the drive down the Thruway to the Mid-Hudson region should have been a spectacular kaleidoscope of color. However, this autumn, the landscape looked drab and enervated. Mother Nature needed a massive dose of B-12. Jude was sure to be given another lecture about global warming, given the infestation confronting Francine on this humid, autumnal Saturday morning.

While Francine battled with Mother Nature, Jude had a personal conflict with Father Time. In just over a week, he was turning thirty. The inevitable march toward this dreaded milestone was cause for great consternation. To be gay and thirty was an explosive mix. There wasn't enough vodka in the world to numb the anxiety-producing combo. Francine claimed Jude was not only obsessed with youth but utterly vain. She was right. Jude *was* obsessed with youth *and* the first to admit, unabashedly vain. He argued that society and the media constantly infiltrated people's minds like an IV drip into the subconscious with youth-oriented propaganda. What normal, red-blooded American gay wouldn't be obsessed with youth? Many tried to convince Jude that thirty was hardly old and, more importantly, that he didn't look old. His close childhood friend, Matthew Zyskowski, went so far as to say Jude kept a portrait of himself in his parents' attic. Nevertheless, Jude rationalized those who preached thirty was not old were *over* thirty and would kill to be thirty again, while Jude wanted to kill because he was going to *be* thirty. Like the stubborn leaves resisting change, he was resistant to crossing that threshold from one decade to the next.

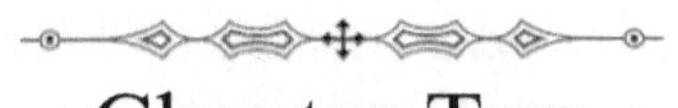

Chapter Two
Koyaanisqatsi

Francine lived in the downstairs apartment in an old pink and white-trimmed Victorian house in Delmar, a suburb of Albany, on a tree-lined street, the kind with no sidewalks. Still working against the clock, Jude trotted up the long walk toward the house. He saw Francine in the window. The sheer curtain fluttered shut as she disappeared upon spotting Jude. He was barely at the door when it opened.

"Thank God you're finally here." She held a fly swatter upright like some military salute in the war against the wasps. The plastic netting contained a few of her smushed victims. "You smell like sex." She turned, heading toward ground zero.

"I bee-lined it over as fast as I could." Jude followed.

Francine turned with Marine-like precision, giving Jude a piercing glare. "Very funny. I'm freaking out, and you're making bad jokes." With an about-face, she continued towards the battlefield.

"Hey, wait a minute." Jude stopped. Francine turned, indignant, placing her free hand on her hip.

"Shouldn't we have some kind of protection besides a fly swatter? I'm not partial to stinging wasps."

Francine commenced walking towards the war zone. "They won't sting you. I discovered they're half dead."

"You got me out of bed on a Saturday morning for a bunch of half-dead wasps?"

This time, Francine stopped and spun around, causing Jude to nearly collide with her. "Listen, Mr. Oh-my-God-there's-a-spider-in-my-bathtub. There are hundreds of wasps in my kitchen. The fact that they are near death does not diminish their unwarranted, unwelcome, *unnatural* presence in my apartment, especially in the sanctity of my beloved kitchen. Now you can help me or go back to your comfy little bed."

There was nothing like the wrath of a friend amid an insect siege to humble a person.

"Sorry, Fran," Jude said. "I accept my mission, face my fate—"

"Oh, shut up." Francine was once again headed to the battle zone when they stopped for a third time.

"Wait."

"What is it now?"

"Well, if there are as many wasps as you say, is one fly swatter enough of a defense? I mean, we're not going to be walking into a scene from an Irwin Allen disaster movie, are we?"

Francine clucked her tongue and headed to the kitchen. "Don't be ridiculous. I told you. They're half dead. If hundreds of aggravated wasps were in my kitchen, would I even be in the house?" She stopped in the doorway. Jude looked cautiously over her shoulder.

"Look at them," she said contemptuously.

For once, Francine's tendency for hyperbole proved to be accurate. There were hordes of wasps, living and dead, everywhere. A swarm so dense on her window allowed sunlight to peek through diaphanous wings and minuscule openings as if a swatch of black lace covered it.

There was a large contingency lining her countertop and stove. They were crawling on her cabinets and refrigerator and blotted out a portion of her framed Charles Greer poster of a half-eaten Oreo cookie on a blue-rimmed plate.

A gallant few attempted to take flight. Drifting in mid-air, some wasps sank like slow-leaking helium balloons, landing on whatever surface was beneath them.

"Jesus! You weren't kidding. It looks like an apiary in here," Jude said.

"I can't tell you how many of the fuckers I killed."

"Where's Cants?" Jude asked.

Cants was short for Cantaloupe, Francine's overweight Tabby she adopted from another teacher at work. Francine christened the cat while on the phone with the vet. When asked the pet's name, she declared confidently, "Cantaloupe," catching sight of the prominent melon in a still-life painting as if she named the cat before the kitten's birth.

"I put her in my bedroom. I didn't want her aggravating the wasps. You know how she gets when other creatures invade her territory."

Abruptly, a wasp sprang from the Oreo cookie poster and crash-landed on the kitchen table where Francine wielded her might, flattening the insect with the fly swatter. "Die, fucker."

"Ooh, I love when you talk butch," Jude said.

"Just start dousing the SOBs with the bug spray."

Jude took the plastic spray bottle he brought and began to spritz the window.

"One bottle?" Francine placed a hand on her hip and pointed to the eco-friendly container with the fly swatter.

"I didn't have time to buy more. You made it sound like you were minutes away from death by stinging. One bottle should be enough."

"There are more wasps than extras in *Gone with the Wind,* and they keep coming. They're multiplying like they're on fertility drugs."

Francine absentmindedly grabbed the bug spray from Jude's hand and replaced it with the fly swatter.

"This is crazy. What's the title of that experimental film you dragged me to that means out of balance? Koy—something."

"*Koyaanisqatsi.* Life out of balance," Jude answered flatly, knowing he was about to be preached to on global warming.

"Yeah, that's it. Well, that's exactly what's going on here. Only it's nature out of balance." Francine frantically soused a cluster of impotent wasps. "I mean, shouldn't they be hibernating or flying south or whatever it is bees do for the winter?"

They were dropping from the window like flies, except they were, indeed, wasps.

It was no surprise to Jude that Francine thought bees hibernated like bears or followed the elderly to Florida for the winter. Jude knew her concern for the earth's ecosystem was not born out of any understanding of scientific knowledge. It wasn't that Francine was unintelligent or didn't grasp the fundamentals of the subject; rather, it manifested from constant media reports about global warming, air pollutants, El Nino's wrath, and right-wing politics. All these unnatural phenomena provided a convenient hook to hang all the world's environmental woes. With this latest anomaly, Stephen Douglas couldn't win a debate against Francine's insistence that smog, extreme wind currents, and Republican politics were responsible for the present state of *Koyaanisqatsi.*

Francine continued to spray everything like a graffiti artist gone berserk while Jude swatted them dead.

"Damn, this is therapeutic. I wish it were this easy with people," Jude said, slapping the swatter crushing a bee.

"The bottle is empty. This better do the trick." Francine's eyes scrutinized her kitchen for any movement among the bee carcasses.

"We'll be lucky if we don't die."

"Never mind. I want to make sure I killed them and any others that come out of hiding. What I want to know is *where* they came from. And where is that landlord of mine? I phoned him after I called you."

When it appeared they had decimated the invaders, they double-checked for signs of life in what looked like an insect's Gettysburg. Jude and Francine began cleaning up the wasp remains.

After they finished, they sat at the 50s-style Formica table Francine inherited from her Aunt Maude and drank reheated coffee that she made earlier before the invasion.

Francine sighed. "I never want to see another wasp as long as I live." She got up and went to the stove. "I was about to make a pie with the apples we picked last week when I heard buzzing behind me. When I turned around, I freaked out." She tossed the now-hardened piecrust into the trash; the abandoned confection was a casualty of the war against the wasps. "That's when I called you."

Jude fanned himself. "Maybe we should open a window. The smell of bug spray is making me nauseous."

"NO!" Francine shrieked. "They could be massing out there."

"This isn't an Alfred Hitchcock movie, Fran. I don't think there's a bee left in New York State."

"I'm not taking any chances. Go outside if you need fresh air."

The dominatrix was back.

When they finished their coffee, Mr. Lattanzio, Francine's landlord, arrived. He was a squat, little man with enough ear hair to compensate for the lack of it on his balding head. Jude and Francine stood outside, watching him investigate the situation. He discovered several hives underneath the kitchen window. Wearing protective gear, he removed them and gingerly placed them in a large garbage bag.

"You're going to get rid of them, aren't you? Like off the property?" Francine asked when they returned inside. Mr. Lattanzio promised to take them home in his truck and incinerate them.

Mr. Lattanzio attributed the *in-a-festasch* to the unusual weather, fueling Francine's ecological theory. She glared at Jude with an *I-told-you-so* look.

She threw the oxidized apple slices into a plastic bag, sprinkled some cinnamon and sugar on them, and handed it to Mr. Lattanzio. "Consider this a low-fat, no-crust apple pie. I promise to make you a real pie for saving my kitchen and my sanity."

They all headed for the door.

Francine and Jude looked out the window and watched Mr. Lattanzio walk to his truck. He swatted at something apparently buzzing around his head. They did not know if it was a wasp.

"Thank you for saving my kitchen, Mr. Lattanzio," Jude mimicked Francine. "What about me? I risked hives killing the bastards, too."

"You know I'm grateful to you, and it being so early on a Saturday morning."

"Not to mention getting very little sleep thanks to a frisky twenty-something."

Francine rolled her eyes. "To show my gratitude, I'll take you to the Coffee Clutch Café and treat you to a piece of their heavenly, though not as heavenly as my apple pie."

"Too fattening. I'll settle for a cup of coffee and a low-fat scone."

"You really are neurotic."

"Only since I've known you."

"What bull. You came out of your mother's womb neurotic—and vain."

Francine applied lipstick and mascara before they headed to the café to celebrate their victory against the wasps.

With the sun ripe in the October sky, the temperature was already in the low 60s. As they drove along a patch of Route 85, they came to a particular stretch Jude always liked driving through because—for him—it showcased a quintessential representation of whatever season it was. In winter, the trees, with their intricate network of naked branches, stood against a frosty sky, and after a snowfall, the barren trees were covered in white as if dipped in batter and dredged through flour. The landscape in spring was like an English garden with its assortment of colorful, wild blooms worthy of a Monet painting. The lush, velvety greens of summer blurred against the thick haze, and at dusk, they came alive with a symphony of cicadas and chirping birds. In autumn, the trees were dappled with rusts, bronzes, and honey colors, trumpeting their last hurrahs before surrendering their leaves to Old Man Winter. But this autumn, the typically breathtaking scenery looked fatigued and anemic.

"I have beautiful, expensive wool sweaters I want to—*should* be wearing. At this rate, I won't have any use for them until Christmas!"

The Last Single Couple in America

As Francine spoke, Jude's mind drifted to his impending thirtieth birthday, which morphed into a thought of Cher: *If I could turn back time.*

Chapter Three
Pencil Dick

As usual, Saturday morning at the Coffee Clutch Café was busy, filled with customers, most as eclectic as its décor. A twenty-something dressed in black, wearing Jackie O sunglasses, sat as if rigor mortis had set in; a steaming, oversized coffee cup sat in front of her. A college student with ash-blonde dreadlocks sat reading a copy of Carlos Castaneda's *Tales* of *Power*. On his feet, he wore Birkenstocks.

"Why must people insist upon exposing their feet in public, especially with nails worthy of Freddy Kreuger?" Jude said after they were out of earshot and over a Shawn Colvin song crooning from the sound system.

They found a table toward the back where Francine sat in an overstuffed wingback chair upholstered in a tiny leopard print; Jude sat on a high-back, Phillipe Starck knock-off.

Though Jude liked the place, as a pragmatic homosexual, he found the lighting, consisting of Halogen bulbs shooting beams in random angles, unflattering. Anyone caught in a laser-like ray had their flaws exposed and highlighted. He firmly believed in the Blanche DuBois school of thought—*avoid direct lighting.* Yet, the tasteful gay in him found the lighting a designer's dream and aesthetically appealing.

A young girl wearing a baby doll dress and sporting short, spiked, bleached hair approached and spoke in a lisp. She introduced herself as *Thara.* It turns out her name was Sarah (according to her name tag), and the cause for her lisp was a recent tongue piercing. She stuck out her tongue, displaying a silver bead, sitting in the middle of her impaled tumescent muscle. Jude gave Francine the eye, who closed hers and looked away.

"Nice. It goes well with your braces," Jude said.

For someone who claimed it was quite painful—as she put it—she saw *'thtars,'* she was rather chatty, informing them she was on a mashed potato diet. She also enlightened them that it was her boyfriend who convinced her to pierce her tongue because it was "great for oral *thex,*" at which point Francine interrupted, "We'd like to order now." *Thara* left to place their order.

"It looked like a pearl in an oyster, except not as pretty," Jude commented on the unwarranted display.

Sarah returned, placing Francine's apple pie and hazelnut coffee on the table etched with a checkerboard pattern. Then, she put Jude's low-fat blueberry scone and French vanilla coffee in front of him before pirouetting like a whirling dervish, remembering to ask if they needed anything else. Francine answered negatively. Sarah twirled again and walked away with a child-like bounce in her step, the flimsy rayon material hanging limply on her tiny frame.

"There's the future of our country." Francine poked at the pie with her fork. Her eyes darted between Jude and the confection on her plate.

Noticing her odd behavior, Jude asked, "If you'll excuse the expression, but do you have a bee in your bonnet?" He stirred cream in his coffee.

"No." She hurried to change the subject. "How's your scone?"

"Delicious." Jude grimaced.

"You know, you're better off getting a regular scone. When they remove the fat, more sugar is pumped in to compensate for the lack of taste, so you're just defeating the purpose of eating to keep trim."

"Now you tell me?" Jude dropped the partially eaten scone onto the plate.

"I've been telling you, but you don't listen."

"Well, you never told me *that.*"

Francine shook her head and thrummed her fingers. Her French tips made a monotonous clickity-clack tapping on the table.

"Are you sending Morse code or trying to drive me insane?"

"Sorry." She stopped rapping her lacquered nails. She twitched in her seat.

"Okay, what's with you? You're generating enough energy to light up the place."

"What? Nothing," she tried to sound casual. "Okay, hear me out before you say no." Francine leaned in closer.

"Oh, Christ. Be afraid, Jude. Be very afraid."

"You sound weird when you talk in the third person," Francine said, rolling her eyes. She cleared her throat. "Um…I was talking to

Chickie, and her brother on Long Island has this…um…artist friend who moved from New York City to open an art gallery in Hudson, and…uh…she thinks he'd be perfect for me."

Chickie was one of Francine's closest friends from college. The others, Horny (aka Hortense) and Ellen, shortened Chiccarelli, her last name, to *Chickie,* and she went by the proclaimed moniker ever since those State University of New York at Albany days.

"And?" Jude was skeptical.

"So, I was thinking, with your birthday coming up…" She hesitated, anticipating Jude's reaction. "I could throw you a party!" She rushed the words out as if shouting vital instructions through closing elevator doors.

"Oh no. Not a birthday party, especially this year." Jude did not want to acknowledge thirty.

Francine sat back in her chair, pouting. "I just thought it would be a perfect opportunity to meet him. You know, size him up and feel him out."

"With the possibility of him feeling you up?" Jude crossed his arms. "A party?" he whined. "You know I hate being the center of attention."

"You're a Scorpio. You love being the center of attention!"

"Leos like being the center of attention. Scorpios like being the center of the orgy. Besides, how are you going to get him to this party?" Jude could tell by the encouraged twinkle in her eyes that she had an answer.

"Naturally, Chickie invites him along as her guest. Problem solved."

"So, if this guy is such a catch, why doesn't Chickie go out with him? Isn't she hot to trot for a man, too?"

"First of all, we are not *hot to trot* for a man—"

Jude interrupted Francine, "Well, by the nose you just grew there, Pinocchio, you won't need a man. You could just bend over—"

Ignoring Jude, she added, "Second of all, it came up in a drunken conversation he's uncircumcised."

"So?"

"You know how Chickie is." Francine leaned back, brushing a tendril out of her eyes. "She's particular about…those things."

"Penises? Oh well, I agree with Chickie. Toss aside a potentially good man because of a flap of skin."

"Excuse me? I recall you're no fan of the uncircumcised penis, either."

Jude would be the first to admit he was not a fan of the *hood,* having experienced a few uncircumcised penises in his day, given his penchant for the male sex organ since age twelve. But if the uncircumcised phallus were attached to the right guy, he wouldn't— as former boyfriend-but-still-dear-friend Michael Antonucci always said—*throw him out of bed for eating crackers.*

"It's only the kind that looks like an ant eater that I am not fond of," Jude explained. "Besides, there are plenty of not-so-nice-looking *circumcised* penises as well."

For Jude, penises were like works of art. Some were DaVinci's or van Gogh's; others were garish, like an Elvis on velvet. And still, some were as bizarre as a Picasso.

"There were a few circumcised penises that I could have done without." Jude absent-mindedly took a bite of his non-fat scone, grimaced, and dropped it back on his plate. "Like that guy I dubbed Pencil Dick."

"Pencil Dick?" Fran's brow furrowed.

"Yeah, remember? I just broke up with Michael Antonucci the day before Thanksgiving back in 1985 and was heading out to the bar—" Jude claimed that going out the night before Thanksgiving was one of the best nights for hitting the gay bars because there was a sea of fresh faces in town for the holiday. "—when Pencil Dick, I don't remember his real name—"

"I'd say *Pencil Dick* is quite memorable enough." Francine sipped her coffee.

"—cruised me as I was walking along Washington Park—"

Sarah pranced over and asked if Jude and Francine wanted coffee refills. Both answered in the positive.

"Let's see, you..." she said, pointing to Jude, "...were French vanilla. And you..." turning to Francine, "were..." Sarah's swollen tongue caused her to struggle with the word, so Francine finished her sentence.

"Hazelnut."

Sarah looked skyward as she shifted to her left foot, and like a car tire that suddenly went flat, her left side dropped an inch. "Right." She flitted away.

"Anyway," Jude continued, "we ended up getting some beer and sat in his jeep in Washington Park. We exchanged pleasantries. He told me he was from New York City, proving my theory about new faces in town for the holiday, and that he worked at MTV. I told him I was getting my degree in Communications. He gave me his card and told me to send him my résumé. He said MTV was always looking for new talent."

Sarah returned with cups of coffee and placed them—wrongly—in front of Jude and Francine before scurrying away.

As they switched cups, Jude went on. "After a few beers, Pencil Dick lunged and started kissing me." Putting a finger to his chin, Jude recalled, "I remember he was an excellent kisser. And then he undid his jeans and took out his…um…dick. If that were a scene in a film, that would be where the shrieking violins filled the soundtrack." Stirring cream into his coffee, he leaned in. "It was the most freakishly thin penis I ever saw."

"So, what did you do?" Fran took a bite of pie.

"I made up an excuse that I wasn't over Michael yet and didn't think I could do anything." Jude sipped his coffee. "He called me a cocktease and threw me out of his Jeep. I asked him—half-joking — if I could still send him my résumé."

"What did he say?"

"He said, by all means, and he'd be sure to wipe his ass with it." Jude took another sip of coffee.

Francine laughed and sat quietly for a moment. "So, what about the party?" Francine took the last bite of her pie. "I heard he has several hot gay friends. I'll make sure he brings one or two, okay? We could both meet the man of our dreams." Francine's pleading look now gave way to panting-dog eagerness. She looked at Jude, grinning and nodding with encouragement. Jude reluctantly gave in to Francine. She arched across the table and kissed Jude. "Oooh, thank you! I'll throw you a wonderful thirtieth birthday party."

"Can we leave the number out of it, please?"

"It's your party."

"And I'll cry if I want to."

"Oh, you." When she settled back in her chair, she crossed her legs and arms. "You changed your mind pretty quickly once I mentioned bringing his hot gay friends. Welcome to Club Hot-To-Trot." Her smile dripped with smug victory.

Jude couldn't deny the prospect of meeting new gay faces was tantalizing. If ten percent of the population was gay, there were limited possibilities among the gay denizens in Albany, so Jude felt it would be nice to expand his options beyond the city limits. Though he didn't want to admit it, Francine piqued his curiosity. She always had a way of hitting a nerve in Jude, like a root canal without Novocain.

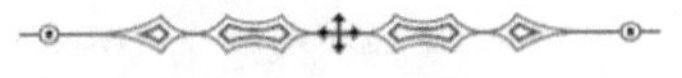

Chapter Four
The Beginning of a Beautiful Friendship

September – October 1983

The fates brought Jude and Francine together one soggy night in early October 1983. Francine was a junior at SUNYA pursuing an education degree; Jude began his studies in the newly established Communications program at the College of Saint Rose.

That rainy evening was Jude's first night as a waiter at the Beverwyck, an upscale Albany eatery, where Francine worked as hostess.

Francine and Sergio, the Hispanic bartender, studied Jude's every move as if he were a microbe under a microscope. They trawled him throughout the night for a glimpse into what his sexual preference might be.

"He's definitely gay." Sergio was confident. His eyes, dark as olives, fixated on the profile view and how Jude's backside filled out his black Chinos, and a lecherous smile morphed under Sergio's thin mustache.

"Wishful thinking, hombre," Francine said, leaning against the bar. "I swear I caught him looking at my cleavage."

"And you didn't hear the innuendo in his voice when he ordered a screwdriver and a Harvey Wallbanger." Sergio trilled his tongue as he sauntered off to make a customer's request for a martini.

At the end of the night, Francine suggested Jude stick around for a drink to ride out the constant downpour. After the last patrons left, the three gathered at the bar, which was made of crackled glass blocks backlit by ice blue lighting, rendering a cozy, atmospheric glow.

"What can I get you, Papi?" Sergio asked Jude.

"Scotch. With lime, please."

Sergio shot Francine a knowing smile. He took a long pull on the vodka stinger he made for himself. She looked quizzically at Sergio.

Francine turned her attention to Jude. "How about that? We both drink scotch," she gloated. Sergio rolled his eyes as he prepared their drinks.

Francine scrunched her face, changing the subject. "What's going on with Hector?"

"He's got my nerves macraméd." Sergio squeezed the citrus wedge into Jude's glass.

Francine turned to Jude, "Hector is Sergio's criminally handsome, manipulative boyfriend, who's been sponging off Sergio since they met two years ago, mostly to support his cocaine habit. Whenever Sergio threatens to leave, Hector turns on his Brazilian charm and seduces the pants off Sergio—literally—and the cycle repeats itself."

"This time, I mean it. I have to leave to save what's left of my sanity—" Sergio lit a cigarette. Smoke swirled up and wreathed his face.

"And what's left of your inheritance," Francine interrupted as she faced Jude. "Sergio inherited a nest egg from a rich relative from which Hector has been constantly mooching."

"I'm sorry you're having boyfriend troubles. It can be very emotional," Jude said before excusing himself to go to the men's room. They observed Jude as he walked away.

"I hate to tell you, Chica, but he's gay. He knows how emotional boyfriend troubles can be…and he puts lime in his scotch."

"That doesn't prove anything. He was just being supportive, and what's so gay about lime in scotch? I'll bet you your tip jar he's straight." There was a slight pause. "Okay, maybe bi."

"Maybe gay," Sergio said defiantly.

When Jude returned, they stared with Cheshire cat grins splayed across their faces.

"What? Did I miss something funny?" Jude was perplexed.

"No." Francine waved her hand dismissively. "We're just discussing Sergio's boyfriend dilemma." Fran turned to Sergio. "Have you told your therapist about your decision to finally leave Hector?"

"Ah, she ran off to Mexico with one of her patients."

"Say the word, and I'll hook you up with my shrink. She's a miracle worker." Francine sipped her scotch.

"You're both in therapy?" Jude was bemused.

"Yes, aren't you?"

Jude saw the dubious look on her face as if it was a rite of passage for everyone to be fucked up. "No, I never—"

"Oh honey, that's not normal." Francine shook her head. "There's a little dysfunction in all of us." She made a sweeping motion with glass in hand as if waving a wand before letting another taste glide down her throat.

"She's the poster child for therapy," Sergio quipped.

"It's true. I've done it all—hypnosis, Scientology, yoga. I practically went hoarse from primal screaming, but there's nothing like a good therapist. Mine did wonders for me. She can do the same for you," Francine said, pointing at Sergio.

"No. I'm through with therapy—and Hector. I mean it this time. He's the reason I'm *in* therapy. I give him up, and my problem is solved." Sergio ingested a lungful of smoke from his cigarette, a look of contentment on his face. He exhaled as if, symbolically, the blue-tinted plume billowing upward was Hector, fading from his life for good.

"Yeah, well, don't make it a Lenten thing and go back after 40 days like you always do. This time, dump the son-of-a-bitch for good."

A while later, the rain finally stopped. Jude swallowed the last of a second scotch and lime. "This has been enlightening, but I have to get up early tomorrow. Gotta hit the gym before classes. Thanks for the drinks, Sergio. I'll see you guys tomorrow." Jude headed for the exit. The second the door closed, Sergio turned to Francine. "See, Chica. He goes to a gym. He's gay."

"Oh, please. Lots of straight guys go to gyms. I'll prove to you he's straight or my name isn't—"

"Delusional?" Sergio interrupted.

***

Francine was ready to claim Sergio's tip jar, despite his prognostication Jude was gay, when a few weeks later, Jude asked Francine, not Sergio, to a screening of the film *Koyaanisqatsi* at the Spectrum Theatre. Before the film, Jude invited Francine to his parents' house for dinner.

"Benvenuti nella mia umile casa. Welcome to my humble home," Dolores Giacolone announced with a smile as warm and inviting as just-baked bread when she greeted Francine at the door. Dolores kissed her on both cheeks before repeating the gesture with Jude. "Son!" she said, more of a declaration than a greeting.

"Dolores."

"Come, make yourself to home."

As they made their way through the living room filled with Italian-crafted furniture, Dolores chatted about the dinner she was making.

Above the sofa was a painting called *Jesus in the Garden of Gethsemane*. Jude's eyes followed Francine's, which gravitated to the portrait.

Passing through the dining room, on a Waterfall-style Art Deco buffet, a ceramic statue of the Virgin Mary stood on a lace runner—a flame in a votive candle burned in front of the pious figurine. Jude noticed Francine, now transfixed on the mini shrine.

They entered the spacious kitchen where a large window in the breakfast nook at the far end overlooked a modest garden and a white trellis covered with tangled vines, like hundreds of tentacles from an alien consuming it, leaving the memory of grapes long gone.

Above the nook's archway was a gold crucifix. Once again, Jude observed Francine eyeing the holy symbol.

"She's a tad religious."

"Hmm, I guess. But if there's ever an apocalypse, I'm coming here," she whispered to Jude. Francine sniffed the aroma permeating the kitchen. "Everything smells delicious."

"My sauce." Dolores puffed out her chest. "I doctor up a few jars of Ragu." The thick tomato sauce roiled like a bubbling marinara mud pit.

"Francine, see these meatballs?" Dolores hoisted one from the pot with a large spoon. "I buy them frozen from the Italian specialty store. They taste as good as the ones I used to make. I just throw them in my doctored-up sauce and let them heat through." Dolores stood proud, boasting about her culinary shortcuts. "They're delicious." She kissed her fingertips, launching them outward as if sprinkling fairy dust—or perhaps Parmesan cheese—in the air.

"Nothing says loving like a home-cooked meal." Jude ripped a piece of Peretti's Italian bread and dipped it into the tampered tomato sauce. Dolores dismissed his sarcasm with a wave of her hand.

Jude's father, Augie, emerged from the basement with a few sprigs of basil grown under a heat lamp. His green eyes twinkled, spotting Jude. "Hey, son," he said, speaking in his customary, cheerful tone.

"Aug, this is my friend, Fran. Fran, my father, Augie."

"Hello, Dolly," Augie chirped.

"Aug, she's not a Broadway musical."

"I call everyone *Dolly*. It's my thing." He handed Dolores the basil, which she immediately started to chiffonade.

"Nice to meet you, Mr. Giacolone."

"Oh, call me Augie, Dolly." His sunny smile radiated genuine warmth.

"Make us all a drink, Augie." Dolores tossed the basil strips into her Ragu where they sat like confetti until she stirred them into the sauce.

"Martinis for everyone?" Augie didn't wait for a response. He went to the cupboard, gathered the ingredients, and started making a round. Jude took over, knowing that vigorously shaking the drinks could aggravate his wrist injury suffered during WWII.

As Jude began to fill the silver cocktail shaker with ice, Augie supervised. "Remember, swirl the vermouth around the ice and throw it out, son."

"I know Augustine. You taught me how to make the perfect martini when I was like ten."

"Do you always call your parents by their first names?" Francine approached the question delicately.

"Yes, it's their name, right Aug? Right Dolores?"

"Right, son," Augie said, laughing.

"My parents would kill me if I called them Frank and Mary." Francine shuddered at the thought. Jude handed her a martini.

Tending to her spruced-up Ragu, Dolores added, "Oh, we know he does it out of affection." She held her martini in one hand and a salt shaker in the other.

"It started as a joke, but I kept it up, and it just stuck. They know I love them." Jude hugged Dolores and kissed her cheek, causing her to drop the salt shaker and her martini to slosh over the rim.

"Ahh, Jude!" She picked up the shaker and shook a little salt over her left shoulder, which did not go unnoticed by Francine, which, in turn, did not go unnoticed by Jude.

"She's as superstitious as she is religious," Jude clarified.

"That's for sure," Augie said. "One time when we were on our way to meet friends for dinner…" pointing to Dolores, "…she made me turn the car around because a black cat crossed in front of us." His smile turned into a laugh.

Dolores looked directly at Francine. "You never cross their path. It's bad luck."

"Then there was the matter of the two peacock wall hangings," Jude began. "According to Dolores, birds in any form in the house are bad luck. Though she can't say who the decrier of that superstition was, but it was writ along with black cats and salt over the shoulder." Jude ripped off another piece of bread and dipped it into the pot of sauce. Dolores smacked his arm. He kissed her cheek.

"Never mind," Dolores said, stirring some grated cheese into her tomato concoction. "You would never have had that tumor if I didn't put those damn things on the wall."

"Tumor? You had cancer?" Francine's voice registered concern.

"It was benign. On my palate," Jude said.

"Thank God." Dolores paused from stirring to make the sign of the cross. She turned to Francine and spoke with heightened dramatics. "It was so rare we had to take him to New York or Boston. My sister, Esther, who's a nurse and an excellent one at that, insisted on Boston." She returned to her stirring.

"So, what did the peacocks have to do with your tumor?" Francine was perplexed.

"Dolores felt because she had the peacocks in the house, they were the cause of my tumor as if they sent out radioactive waves into my head," Jude said as he undulated his extended hand towards Dolores, who batted it away.

"Don't joke. I got rid of them as soon as we returned from Boston."

"She made me take them to the dump," Augie said through laughter.

"I didn't even want them on the premises," Dolores added.

"Hence, the replacement of the *Jesus in the Garden of Gethsemane* painting you admired on your way in." Jude went for another dip of sauce.

After finishing their drinks, they sat down to Dolores' *homemade* dinner. She said grace. "Bless us and bless this food, and thank you for enabling us to share this meal tonight with Jude, our son—"

Jude looked at Francine and whispered, "In case God doesn't know I'm theirs."

"—and with his girlfriend, Francine. Amen."

"Dolores, we're just friends."

"I know. She's a girl, and she's your friend," Dolores rationalized as she ladled extra Ragu over her pasta.

Jude leaned towards Francine. "She'll have us engaged by the end of dessert."

***

"Jesus, what the hell was that?" Francine asked, leaving the Spectrum Theatre after the advanced screening of *Koyaanisqatsi.* She lifted her coat collar before threading her arm through Jude's, pulling him close as a gusty October wind picked up, walking to Jude's car.

"Didn't you like it? I thought it was brilliant."

"It was just a bunch of images put together over a synthesized soundtrack."

"It was more than that," Jude said as he started his car. Francine turned on the heat. "It was an experimental, visual essay about how man's quest for technology is destroying the environment. I thought *you,* of all people, would appreciate it."

"Yeah, I guess I'm just old-fashioned when it comes to movies. Give me *Flashdance* any day over *Koyaanis*—whatever," Francine said, waving her hand.

"Stick with me. I'll turn you into a cineaste."

"Right now, I'll settle for turning into a bar for a drink. Let's pop in on Sergio."

Minutes later, Jude was parking on Lark Street. Near closing, the Beverwyck was almost empty. They saw the owner, Patrick Gallagher, tending bar.

"Hey, Patrick. Where's Sergio? Did he call in sick?" Francine asked as she sat on the chrome and leather barstool, removing her coat.

Patrick's eyes were sullen. He pulled his lips tight as if dams to the tears in his eyes.

"There's no easy way to tell you, so I'm just going to say it. Sergio is dead." Patrick's words echoed dully in Jude's ears. He saw the color drain from Francine's face as she reached for Jude's hand, squeezing it tightly. She tried to speak, but the words remained strangled in her throat. Jude became her voice.

"My God! What happened?"

"I think we could use some drinks," Patrick told them the details as he fixed their cocktails, mostly what he learned from the police report. "Last night, according to neighbors in his building, an argument ensued, and at some point, Hector got a gun and shot Sergio."

Francine's eyes overflowed. She gripped Jude's hand tighter.

"Hector then put the gun to his head and shot himself. It was your classic murder-suicide."

Jude reached out to give Francine a comforting hug.

After several drinks, Francine was still reeling from shock and distress, so Jude volunteered to stay with her so she didn't have to be alone. She was thankful for the offer. They left the Beverwyck and drove to Francine's in numbed silence.

Inside her apartment, Francine stumbled around in the dark until she found the lamp and turned it on. She tossed her coat on the antique rocking chair, landing on a sleeping Cantaloupe who wailed with a shrieking *'meow'* before scampering off.

She headed to the kitchen to get a bottle of wine and some glasses. When she returned, Jude was sitting on the floral print sofa and asked, "What's with the Morticia Addams bouquet?" referring to the vase of withered, lifeless roses, their blooms, a faded reddish-black, hung as if not quite guillotined.

Francine explained as she poured the wine. "Oh, those. I keep meaning to throw them away," she began flatly. "They're the remains of my relationship with Jonathan. It died like the roses."

"What happened?" Cantaloupe returned, jumping on Jude's lap.

"He was up my ass like a suppository. I felt like a mother rather than a girlfriend," she said with her glass poised at her mouth. "So, I gave him the boot." Her words blended in a semi-drunken slur. She sipped her wine. "And he sent these roses as an…I don't know, in hopes of getting back together? A peace offering? A thanks-for-the-memories gesture? Who knows?" She picked up some dried petals off the coffee table. "Ashes to ashes…" and crushed them in her palm. "…dust to dust." She let the crumbles sift through her hand, littering the glass-topped table.

"How long were you together?"

"One hundred fifteen days, sixteen hours, five minutes, ten seconds. I started ticking the days off like a prisoner," Francine said bleakly. "I guess I was like Sergio, unable to end things when I should have." Francine leaned forward, putting her head in her hands. "Poor Sergio," she said, on the verge of tears. "If only he left that bum earlier when he wanted to."

"We can't think about that now." Jude tried to be reassuring.

Francine sat upright, her palms on her thighs, and then took a deep breath and a lengthy sip of wine. "You're right. It took me three, almost four months to dump Jonathan." Jude was aware of her slightly slurred speech.

"And one thing I learned is that even though it's as easy to fall out of love as it is to fall into the quagmire, it takes the longest to end it. You have to rip the Band-Aid off quickly. Even if it hurts like hell, a great relief will come all the faster. Lesson learned from Love's Twilight Zone."

"I don't know if that would have helped Sergio," Jude said as Cantaloupe jumped down from his lap and disappeared.

"Probably not." Francine sank into the couch. Why are we conditioned to need another person? Why can't we be like the humpback whales, content swimming through life alone?"

Jude had no answer. They finished their wine in silence in memoriam to Sergio.

"Well, it's been a rough end to the day. I suppose we should get to bed." Francine stood, a little wobbly.

"If I could get a pillow and a blanket, I'll crash on the couch," Jude said.

"Don't be silly. This couch is lumpy and too short for your long legs." It was true. The square back sofa wasn't much longer than a love seat. "You can sleep in my bed."

Jude resisted the idea, but Francine insisted. They walked from the living room through the long hallway. She turned on the overhead light in the bathroom, just off the kitchen.

"There's an extra toothbrush in the medicine cabinet," she said, heading for the bedroom off the kitchen.

Jude shouted to Francine, "Hey, do you have any moisturizer?"

"Help yourself," she mumbled-shouted.

Jude pulled the chain, igniting the bulb in a frosted tulip-shaped sconce above the mirrored medicine cabinet. The bright light caused a garish glow bouncing off the white-tiled walls. Jude squinted. He washed his face with the bar of Dove soap, then squeezed some Close-Up onto the bristles and brushed with the cinnamon-flavored toothpaste. After rinsing, Jude opened the medicine cabinet and looked for moisturizer. He saw generic aspirin, a box of Midol, causing a momentary blush, and a prescription bottle. Curiosity got the best of Jude, and he gingerly turned the bottle to see what it was. *Prozac.* Jude fumbled the amber container and returned it to its original position. Tweezers, eyelash curler. *Where was the moisturizer?* Turning around in the cramped bathroom, he saw a tall, narrow armoire. He opened it to see an assortment of towels, linens, and blankets. The top shelf harbored assorted makeup and toiletries, a box of Tampons (causing further embarrassment), and finally, the elusive Oil of Olay. Jude applied a coating to his face, checked himself in the mirror, and headed for the bedroom.

Francine was in an oversized SUNYA sweatshirt and plaid boxer shorts—her sleeping attire—and her hair was in a ponytail.

"I'm going to get ready now. Make yourself at home," she said and went to the bathroom.

As Jude undressed, he felt awkward being semi-naked and sharing a bed with Francine. After folding his jeans and sweater, he placed them on a chair and climbed into bed wearing just his white briefs.

Francine returned a little off balance and clumsily fell into bed. "Thanks for staying with me," she said, kissing Jude on the cheek. "I still can't believe Sergio is dead. Murdered! It's nice to know you're here for comfort." Francine moved in closer, placing her arm over Jude's chest, continuing to inch nearer. Then, her leg lay on top of his. She uttered a soft sigh, climbed on top of Jude, and attempted to kiss him on the mouth.

Jude resisted. "Whoa. Are you coming on to me?"

"What do you think, dummy? You're here in bed with me and—" She slurred her words.

"Yeah, well, just because I'm in Macy's doesn't mean I'm there to buy," Jude said, struggling to sit up. "I think you need to know I'm gay. I'm *gay!*"

Francine sat up, pouting. She pounded the bed with her fists before falling back on her pillow with a big sigh.

"I'm sorry, but that's who I am."

"It figures." Her hand limply smacked Jude. "Sergio—" she muttered.

"Try not to think about him."

"He insisted you were gay. He was right. I swore you were straight, maybe bi. Wishful thinking only to have the wish blown to smithereens."

"How did he know I was gay? Am I that obvious?"

"Scotch. Lime. Gym."

Jude laughed. "Well, it must have been the scotch and lime that gave me away because I can tell you, the world is plenty full of narcissistic straight guys who go to gyms, too."

"Why are all the good ones gay, married, or complete assholes," Francine lamented.

"Think of it as Mother Nature's idea of natural birth control."

"Fuck her. Fuck Mother fucking Nature." Inebriation got the best of Francine. "Too much alcohol," she mumbled under her breath. Then louder, "Fuck her." She moaned and rolled on her side.

"Good night, Francine."

"Good night, gay boy!" Jude smiled and lay down. Moments later, he heard Francine breathing heavily.

***

The early morning sun assaulted the room with blinding brilliance, forcing Jude to squint against the intense light. He could hear Francine rustling around in the kitchen. After putting on his jeans, he pulled his sweater over his torso entering the kitchen.

"Good morning."

"Morning," her voice was clipped.

"You're up early. After all you drank last night, I expected you to sleep till noon."

"I couldn't sleep. Besides, I had to feed Cantaloupe," Francine continued to speak in a flat tone as she busied herself with making coffee.

"Something wrong? You're acting kind of strange."

Francine stopped spooning the coffee grounds into the filter. "Well, frankly, I'm a little embarrassed about last night—mortified is more accurate. I shouldn't have—"

"There's no need to be embarrassed—"

"*Mortified,*" she stressed, turning towards Jude before returning her attention to the coffee.

"Okay, mortified about last night. You had a little too much to drink, and you were acting on, well, you did what you thought was a natural progression—after all, I am irresistible," Jude added to lighten the mood.

"Now who's the narcissist?" There was a pause before she continued. "I like being with you. I don't want what happened last night to affect our friendship."

"I promise it won't."

She turned to face Jude. "Just don't expect me to hang out at gay bars with you. It'd be like fishing in a barren lake."

"I promise." Jude hugged Francine and reassured her their friendship would be fine.

After coffee, Jude announced that he had to get to the gym.
"Oh yes, the gym. Gay Mecca."

Chapter Five
Pandora's Out of the Box

November 1983

A week later, Francine's mother, Mary Duffy, called with exciting news. Francine's sister, Janis, was going to be featured in an article in the upcoming issue of *Ms. Magazine*.

"The magazine should be out when you're down here for your father's 75th birthday party. We're so excited for Janis and to see you, dear."

"Is Janis going to be there?"

"No, she said she had some business to tie up with a group of nuns in Switzerland. I'm not sure what that's all about, but I'm sure we'll find out. We'll see you on the first. Good-bye, dear."

The day after Francine arrived in Florida, her father, Frank, was up early and went to Andy's Newsstand to buy *Ms. Magazine*, hot off the press.

In the Duffy kitchen, drenched with Florida sunshine, the high-pitched whistle from the kettle reached its crescendo in piercing irritation.

"Did Janis say what the article is about?" Francine asked, leaning against the counter. She took a bite from a lemon bar Mary made the day before.

"No, she just mentioned she was going to be among a group of upcoming women to watch." Mary plunged the tea bags into two steaming cups of water and brought them out to the screened-in lanai, setting them on the table. Francine followed carrying the plate of lemon bars.

The Florida air was already thick and heavy.

"Feels like it's going to be a hot one today." Mary blew a long puff across her teacup before gently slurping in a trickle of tea.

Inside, a door slammed. "Mary! Fran! I got the magazines," Frank bellowed.

Francine and Mary eagerly got up, abandoning their tea. Fran grabbed a lemon bar.

"I bought ten copies." Frank plopped them on the wicker coffee table. "Andy wanted to know if I was becoming a feminist." He chortled. "The wise ass."

They each picked up a copy and riffled through the pages. On page thirty-nine, they read the caption in bold letters under her photo: *Janis Duffy: Lesbian theologian.*

Neither Frank nor Mary bothered to read further. They did not read that Janice and Dina Dow (also a lesbian theologian), co-founded the women's organization, *F.L.U.S.H.—Feminists and Lesbians United for Symbiotic Humanitarianism.*

Mary clutched her chest and crumbled into a chair like a marionette whose strings were severed.

Frank threw the magazine against pink, floral sofa cushions. "What the hell is wrong with her? Outing herself to the world!" Frank shouted in his ex-Marine voice. He paced back and forth like a duck in a shooting gallery. "I lived through the Depression, a World War, polio, Republican presidents, and now this!" He raked his fingers through his thinning grey hair.

Mary sat, dazed, pressing her fists into the magazine as if to keep the contents of their Pandora's box from escaping. "And to think I told *everybody.*"

"Mary, get me a drink!" Frank's voice boomed.

"Dad, it's nine-thirty in the morning."

"Even Father Flanagan." Mary's voice was strained and fragile.

Frank turned with military precision. "What?"

"Father Flanagan. I told Father Flanagan."

"Jesus Christ! The son-of-a-bitch will probably have us excommunicated." Frank resumed pacing. "Mary! My scotch."

Mary got up, the magazine slipping from her lap, and walked to the bar cart in a daze.

"Make us all one," Frank thundered, channeling his inner George Patton.

Knowing it was futile to resist her father's command, Francine washed down the rest of her lemon bar with scotch, realizing that, despite the time of day, it was going to take several more to get her through the rest of her visit to the Sunshine State, now clouded in gloom.

***

Aftershocks roiled after the mega earthquake that shook the Duffy household to its foundation.

Back home, Francine discovered that Janis was planning to visit their parents for Thanksgiving, *accompanied* by Dina. Francine, with the foresight of a seasoned meteorologist, sensed the brewing storm of family dysfunction. She made a firm decision to steer clear of the gathering thunderclouds, finding solace in the safety of upstate New York.

Over dinner at Francine's, she shared her traumatic visit to Jude. She confided in him that she had decided not to return to Florida for Thanksgiving. In a gesture of true friendship, he extended an invitation to spend the holiday with his family, which she gratefully accepted.

After dinner, Francine called her mother. She put the phone on speaker as she cleared dinner dishes. When she told her mother she was not coming for Thanksgiving, Mary, still shell-shocked, said, "What? Thanksgiving? Oh, yes, of course." Her timbre was monotonous, as if hypnotized. "You have a Merry Christmas, too, dear." Mary hung up.

Francine expelled a puff of air and nodded toward the phone. "That's the result when one has a lesbian theologian in the family."

Chapter Six
It's Jilda with a J, Not Gilda with a G

A Week Before Thanksgiving, 1983

Over the past weeks, Francine shared many a *homemade* dinner with Jude and his parents, and Dolores welcomed her into her humble home with gracious hospitality. She treated Francine with the same love and affection as her daughter-in-law, Katie, who was married to Jude's brother, Anthony.

On Saturday nights, Dolores insisted on eating out after preparing dinners all week.

They dined at Cornelli's since Lorenzo Cornelli was a customer of Augie's barbershop. Jude often joined his parents; lately, so did Francine, as was the case on the Saturday before Thanksgiving.

"Augie Doggie," Lorenzo said, shaking Augie's hand and patting his shoulder with the other.

"Lorenzo!" Augie beamed.

"Dee Dee! Bella!" Lorenzo planted a kiss on her cheek. Then, pinching Jude's, he said, "Handsome as ever. And who is this?" He turned to Francine.

"Jude's girlfriend," Dolores interjected with what Jude detected as pride—and not the gay kind.

"Actually, we're just friends," Jude clarified.

"Well, she's a girl and your friend, right?" Lorenzo pinched Jude's other cheek as he chuckled.

Francine leaned in and whispered to Jude, "I see Italians use the same rationale."

Lorenzo took everyone's drink order before Augie spotted a customer and went over to talk to him.

"He thinks he's the mayor," Dolores said to Francine. "Oh, look, Frannie," Dolores spoke with hushed urgency. "That's Lorenzo's wife." She tilted her head in Gilda's direction. "She's got an attitude because she's married to a restaurant owner. I went to school with her, and I know her name is *Jilda* with a J. But she started calling herself *Gilda* with a G after that Rita Hayworth movie." Dolores' steely eyes narrowed with Jilda/Gilda in the crosshairs.

Sitting atop Gilda's petite frame was a mass of curly, red hair shellacked with enough Aqua Net to make it look like it could have been a wig from Marie Antoinette's closet. The pink satin ribbon threaded through the nest of curls matched her flouncy chiffon dress with sheer, puffy sleeves. On her feet, she wore translucent Lucite sling-back pumps. Her toes looked like Vienna sausages tightly bound together by Saran Wrap.

"Now I know what feet look like in shoes," Francine said.

Halfway through dinner, Gilda stopped by, placing a hand on Augie's and Dolores' shoulders. "How are your dinners?"

"Hello, Dolly," Augie chirped. "Delicious as always."

"Again, with the Broadway musical," Jude whispered in Francine's ear.

"It's his thing," she responded with a shrug.

Dolores just offered up a fake smile.

Lorenzo motioned for Gilda to give the *announcement*.

Attracting a high-end crowd of physicians, lawyers, and business owners, Cornelli's was the *it* place to be, especially on weekends, which made parking an issue, and cars often obstructed others. When that happened, Gilda had to make the *announcement*.

Gilda picked up a microphone and announced, "License plate F-L-A-4-0-5-5, you're blocking.' 4-0-5-5," you're blocking."

A squat man with curly black hair and wire-rimmed glasses, Schenectady's premiere cardiologist, Dr. Edward Dagostino, rose, tossing a napkin on his chair. "Sorry, Gilda. It won't happen again." He rushed for the door.

"You say that every week, but you keep blocking." Gilda didn't realize she was still speaking into the PA system.

Dolores hmphed. "So, Frannie, are you going to Florida for Thanksgiving?

"No, I decided not to go back."

"Jude, invite your girlfriend to Thanksgiving dinner." Dolores took a bite of her pork chop and cherry peppers.

"I already invited her," Jude said.

"Wonderful." Dolores leaned forward with knife and fork held upright like ski poles. "We'll have a nice old-fashioned, home-cooked

Thanksgiving dinner."

"Well, you will make things *in* the home," Jude quipped.

Francine smiled to keep from laughing at Jude's mockery.

On the ride home, Francine questioned Jude about Dolores' perception of their relationship. "Dolores knows you're gay, right?"

Jude was nonchalant. "I don't know. Maybe she suspects."

"What? You haven't told her?"

"No."

"Why not?"

"I don't see the point. My brother didn't have to tell her he's straight. Why should I have to tell her I'm gay? It's who I am."

"I just think it's a courtesy to your parents. Look how my parents reacted to Janice. They may end up in therapy for life."

"That's different. Your sister came out in a national magazine. They were ambushed, like Pearl Harbor. When I'm in a national magazine, I'll warn my parents of my tagline—*Jude Giacolone: Horny homosexual.*"

Francine rolled her eyes. "You're such an ass."

"Look, I'm not doing anything that says I'm gay, and until I do, I have no reason to announce it."

Francine crossed her arms and settled back in her seat. "Have they ever seen you primp and preen in front of a mirror?

Thanksgiving Day

Once again, Francine shared a meal with the Giacolones, who greeted her with affectionate hugs and kisses.

Augie addressed Francine, "Hi, Dolly." He grinned at Jude, "See? I didn't say *hello, Dolly.*"

Jude shook his head. "Crafty, Aug. Really crafty." Jude began making martinis. After a holiday toast, Dolores returned her attention to the Butterball turkey in the oven.

"Your brother and Katie will be here soon. And you be nice to her." Dolores pointed her turkey baster at Jude. A coating of yellow grease clouded the glass tube. "Don't make her cry like you did last Christmas." She sucked up pan drippings and drizzled the golden-brown bird with its juices.

"I didn't start it." Jude threw up his arms in defense against his headstrong sister-in-law.

"Never mind. You have a tongue like a knife."

"I promise to be on my best behavior. See, Fran? Every family has its dysfunctions."

"Please. Compared to what's probably happening at my parents' house, I feel like I'm in a Norman Rockwell painting."

The doorbell chimed, signaling Anthony and Katie's arrival. Katie handed Dolores roses as red as her wavy hair, and Anthony gave Augie a bottle of wine.

"Where are your glasses, son?" Augie asked.

"I'm wearing contacts." Anthony blinked.

"So that's why you look like you're sending Morse code with your eyes," Jude said, grinning.

At Dolores' Thanksgiving table, everyone took their seats and bowed their heads as she thanked the Lord for "a *cornucopia* of blessings" (she always tried to be relevant with her benedictions).

Cutlery clinked and clanged as Dolores passed bowls and platters around, everyone filling their plates.

"The stuffing is delicious. How do you make yours?" Francine asked.

"I open a couple of boxes of Stovetop Stuffing, break up some fried Italian sausage, and throw it in. It tastes like I slaved all morning," Dolores said, winking.

"And it complements the instant mashed potatoes," Jude cracked, to which Dolores waved the remark off.

"Who wants to peel, boil, mash?" Dolores waved her hand in the air.

"Anthony, Jude tells me you write?" Francine asked.

"Yeah, I just finished a story called *Transplant* about a lonely woman who morphs into an exotic plant because it's the only way she can get people to pay attention to her."

Francine wiped her mouth, trying to hide her *what-the-hell-do-I-say-to-that* look on her face.

It was so sad but fascinating. She was such an interesting character. And what's the new one you're working on?" Jude asked.

"*Queen and Martyr.*"

"That's it."

"It's a philosophical tale about a man who has an internal argument with his feminine alter ego," Anthony summarized.

"Dolores, how did you end up with these two weirdoes?" Katie asked.

Anthony laughed, biting into a Pillsbury crescent roll. "We're eclectic."

"Eccentric is more like it," Katie said.

Dolores ladled her heated canned gravy over a slice of turkey. "My boys are gifted in their own ways. They both have vivid imaginations. Frannie, Anthony…" she pointed her fork at him, "…was put in accelerated classes—"

Laughing, Jude interrupted, "While Dolores and Augie had to have a conference with my kindergarten teacher because every nap time, I got caught crawling military-style trying to kiss all the girls."

Francine choked on her wine.

"Like father like son," Augie guffawed, causing Francine to cough harder. Katie patted her on the back.

"Thank you, I'm fine now," Francine said, then sipped her water.

"Here, I thought I was marrying someone normal." Katie draped her arm around Anthony's neck and gave him a peck on the cheek.

"There's nothing abnormal about reading Russian novels," Anthony said.

"Not when you should have been reading *The Hardy Boys*," Katie retorted. "I love you, anyway."

As dinner progressed, more onion layers peeled away, revealing the Giacolone family's quirky characteristics, enlightening and amusing Francine.

Dolores continued singing the praises of her boys, saying, "When he was in first grade, Anthony's art teacher told us he had a talent for drawing and painting and encouraged us to foster his gift—"

Augie interrupted, adding, "On top of that, we discovered his natural athletic ability."

"And don't forget musically. He took up the guitar and practically taught himself how to play. Anyway, that Christmas, we bought him a bunch of art supplies—" Dolores went on.

"And a baseball glove," Augie chimed in.

"That was the year I got a toy phone—" Jude began.

"So he could call his *imaginary* friends," Dolores said, smiling at him.

"Johnny West and G.I. Joe action figures," Jude added.

"He used to like to take their uniforms off and bring them into the bath with him," Dolores said blithely.

"He gave new meaning to *Three Men in a Tub*," Augie laughed at his humor.

Francine faced Jude with a look of shock/horror. Arched eyebrows crowned Francine's eyes. He just smiled and shrugged.

Dolores and Katie started clearing away the dinner plates.

"I also got a miniature reel-to-reel tape recorder so I could tape my reenactments from the soap operas I watched with Dolores before I started school," Jude added.

"I was hooked on a few, including *Search for Tomorrow* and *The Guiding Light,*" Dolores said, scraping the turkey and stuffing remains in the trash.

"And especially *Another World,*" she added, rinsing the dishes.

"As a kid, watching them made me want to be an actor."

Francine mouthed, *drama queen* at Jude, who sent an air kiss in her direction.

Dolores continued, "I told him he'd have a shelf lined with Oscars whenever he had one of his dramatic tantrums." She turned from the sink to eye Jude before concentrating back on cleaning the dishes.

"Other than their creativity, they're as different as night and day. Anthony was an introvert. He'd spend his days locked in his room with those Russian books and his guitar, while this one…" Dolores pointed the carving knife at Jude, "…went around introducing himself to all the neighbors. I had to go pick him up. That's how I got to know everyone on the block."

Francine struggled to hold in her laughter.

After feasting on a Mrs. Smith's pumpkin pie (topped with Redi Whip) and an apple pie (bought from a bakery), the family sat around the dining room table conversing over grapes, figs, and assorted nuts while Jude and Francine sat on the couch sipping Anisette.

"I'm still in shock that you bathed with two naked plastic dolls. How did your parents *not* know you were gay? Were they lobotomized?"

"If they had any reason to believe they had a gay son, it was Anthony. He had a best friend, Donny, who shared his affinity for baseball…" Jude sipped his Anisette, "…and his fear of girls. These twins, Margaret and Mary Woods, had a crush on them, and whenever the girls saw the two, they'd run after them like apocalyptic zombies spotting fresh meat. Like two frightened rabbits, they'd run into Anthony's bedroom and slam the door closed. Thirteen years old and running from girls while I was the kissing bandit." Jude gave

Francine's hand a smooch.

"Someone must have switched your heads at some point."

When the Thanksgiving festivities ended, everyone said goodbye, sharing hugs and kisses.

"Thanks, Dolores. Everything was delicious," Katie said.

"Bye, mom." Anthony blinked rapidly.

At the door, Dolores spoke her usual mantra when her children were about to get into a car, "Don't speed. Call me when you get home."

"I'm probably going to meet some friends out," Jude said.

"Don't drink and drive," Dolores' other mantra, always directed toward Jude.

"Yes, Dolores," he said, kissing his mother.

"Francine, you're welcome for Christmas Eve and Christmas if you don't go to Florida."

"Thanks, I'll let you know." Francine had to wonder what the day was like at her parents'.

In the car, Jude asked Francine if she was going to call her parents.

"Oh, God, no. If there's nothing on the national news, I'll know everyone is at least still alive."

Chapter Seven
Black is the New Black

October 1995

While preparing a seafood and artichoke sauce over spinach fettuccine with Francine the night before his party, Jude insisted all the decorations be black: black balloons, streamers, paper plates, cups, and plastic utensils.

"What am I throwing you a, birthday party or a funeral?" Francine balked.

"Do it. Or I'll boycott." After a pugnacious staredown, Jude acquiesced. He sighed and his shoulders slumped as if suddenly deflated. "Oh, alright. Throw in some orange. Maybe people will think it's a Halloween party and not my crossing over to the dark side."

They proceeded to prepare Jude's celebratory birthday dinner. Francine suddenly stopped peeling the shrimp.

"Oh my God." She paused to take a sip of her Cabernet. "I just realized. Do you know what today is?"

"I'm-sorry-I'm-throwing-you-a-thirtieth-birthday-party-so-let's-call-the-whole-thing-off day?"

"Forget it. The party's planned. Besides, Chickie is bringing Dakota, the art gallery guy."

"*Dakota?* Jude nearly spit out his wine. "Is he gonna ride in on a wild Mustang?"

"Never mind. I'm being serious. Today's the anniversary of when we found out about Sergio."

"Sergio!" Jude reflected. "Is today the day?"

"Uh-huh. All these years later, it still haunts me."

A moment passed before they raised their glasses and toasted to Sergio. They continued to prepare dinner silently while Cantaloupe gnawed on half a shrimp Francine gave her.

They sat in Francine's kitchen where, just days earlier, it was a battleground against wasps. Now, they sat in the faint candlelight as if mourning in a sacrarium for their departed friend.

Over dinner, Francine announced between mouthfuls of pasta, "I have a special gift that you're going to love. I can't wait to give it to you."

"Give me a hint." Jude's natural curiosity was piqued.

"It didn't cost me a thing, but it could have cost me my freedom," Francine said, followed by a light laugh.

Jude poised his fork at his mouth. "Fran, how generous," he said, then consumed a forkful of pasta and artichoke.

Detecting cynicism, Francine said, "Well, of course I bought you something too, but you're going to like this other gift so much more."

When they finished dinner, they retreated to the couch where two boxes wrapped in gold paper and tied with white ribbon sat on her glass-top coffee table.

"Open this one first," Francine said, giggling.

In it was a bottle of Halston's Z-14, Jude's favorite cologne with its subtle sandalwood undertones.

"Aw, you know me so well." He leaned in, kissing her cheek.

"Okay. Now you're *really* going to love me for this." She handed Jude the second package. She was about to explode with the excitement of a child on Christmas morning.

When Jude unwrapped the box, a hardcover of the novel *Sophie's Choice* was inside.

"Wow. But Fran, you know I already read this."

"I know, silly." She reached over and flipped to the title page. "Look." She poked the page. "It's signed by William Styron!" Francine was champagne-fizzy.

Jude looked at the page with amazement. "Oh my God, Fran. Where did you get this—and for free? And why would it cost you your freedom?" He paused and looked suspiciously at Francine. "You *stole* it?"

"Well, yes, and no." Francine shrugged her shoulders. "I didn't intentionally steal it. I picked it up at the house Chickie, Horny, Ellen, and I rented in the Hamptons last summer. I accidentally left it in my beach bag and didn't discover it until I got home."

"Fran, don't you think the people will miss it? I mean, it's signed."

Francine shrugged it off as no big deal. "It's been months. I doubt they even know it's missing. They had tons of books. Happy birthday!" Francine held out her open arms in anticipation of a *thank you* hug, which Jude obliged, adding a kiss.

"It's the best gift. Thank you. I love it. But if the police come knocking on my door, I'm throwing you under the bus."

Chapter Eight
Hot Chocolate

After leaving Francine's, Jude went home, showered, dressed, and headed to Waterworks for the Friday night festivities.

Waterworks was a bi-level gay establishment, with the downstairs offering a rustic, machismo ambiance with its long, wood-planked bar, dartboard, and pool table lit by an overhead faux Tiffany lamp advertising Michelob beer. Upstairs was a disco.

Sunscreem's "Love U More" grew in volume as Jude ascended the steep, narrow stairs that bridged the two bars. He scanned the crowd as he approached the bar four steps up from the checkered dance floor with a mirrored ball above it.

Suzie, the curly-haired lesbian bartender, came over.

"Hey, sweetie," she yelled over the music. She smiled, creasing her blue eyes, rendering them horizontal incisions above her plump cheeks. "Your usual?" Her smile revealed a swath of gum and stubby teeth that looked like her dentist sawed them in half.

"Absolutely."

"Hey, Suzie!" An older man yelled. "I've been waiting ten minutes to get a drink."

"Siphon my bladder, dick wad. I'll be right there." Suzie went to make Jude's drink. The patron next to Jude left and was unintentionally jostled by another trying to wedge himself in place to order a drink.

"Sorry," the deep voice said.

Jude turned. His conciliatory smile melted into a slack-jawed gaze. His eyes locked on the handsome face of the guy sharing his space.

Suzie rescued Jude from his apparent goggling as she brought over his drink. Jude held out a five.

"It's on the house," Suzie said. "A little birdie told me it's your birthday."

"Not until after midnight. I'm hanging on to my twenties with bloody fingertips. But thanks."

"Hold on, handsome," Suzie said to the man next to Jude. "Let me take care of the ass pipe at the end of the bar." She popped the cap off a Rolling Rock. "Okay, penis breath, here's your beer."

"She's quite the character. Hi. I'm Walter." He stuck out his hand.

"I'm Jude." Walter's handshake was firm.

"I love you, Suzie," the man at the end of the bar yelled.

"And I love you, too. Like the clap."

"Okay, sweet cheeks, what can I get you?"

"Gin and tonic, please." He flashed a Pepsodent smile revealing blazing, bright teeth.

A spotlight hit the twirling disco ball, sending white diamonds of light spinning around the bar. Spangles of light zoomed across Walter's face like a Kinetoscope, highlighting his caramel-colored handsomeness.

If he were a photograph, he'd be accused of being airbrushed. Tempting as it was, Jude resisted the urge to reach out and caress Walter's flawless face.

"Did I hear you correctly, you're thirty? Remembering it might be a sensitive subject, Walter added, "*After* midnight, of course."

"Unfortunately, yes."

When Walter got his G&T, they stepped from the bar and leaned against the brass railing overlooking the dance floor. A little shorter than Jude, Walter stood with perfect posture. He held his head like a golf ball resting on a tee.

Does this dude have any flaws?

"For what it's worth, I thought you were in your early twenties."

"Flattery will get you everywhere." Jude's gaze locked on Walter's eyes like a magnet to metal. A beige ring encircled his otherwise translucent hazel irises.

Jude broke his cardinal rule when he came face to face with a gorgeous-looking guy and blurted out, "Christ, you're *really* hot-looking."

A puff escaped past Walter's full, sensual lips that turned into a laugh.

"I'm sorry I embarrassed you." Jude rushed to explain, "I swear I never say that kind of thing to guys. I don't want to inflate their already overblown egos. Not that I think you're an egomaniac…" Jude rushed to say, "…it's more a defense thing. I…I…I need a hole to crawl into." Jude felt heat overtake his face as if standing too close to a fire.

"It's fine. I'm not embarrassed. I'm a Leo. I love being objectified." Walter's smile radiated. "I hear that all the time but, I don't see it."

Jesus, hot and *modest.*

"Let me add that you could be a model. I mean, you have seen yourself in a mirror, haven't you?" Jude said.

Walter's head tipped forward, and he grinned. "Since you mentioned it, I finally got tired of people telling me just that, so I had some photos taken and put together a portfolio. People told me it's best to start with a small agency. Agencies like Ford or Elite are too competitive. I took that advice and was offered a place at Models, Inc., an agency in Brooklyn. They do mostly local stuff around the boroughs. In time, it could lead to a bigger agency. I'm moving at the end of the month."

The Lord giveth, and the Lord taketh away.

"Great. I meet a hot, undeservedly, but thankfully, modest guy, and now you tell me you're moving? Just my luck. But when you hit the big time, and your face is plastered all over Times Square, I can say I knew you when. I guess it's better finding out now before I fell madly in love with you," Jude joked. "Seriously, congratulations." Jude held up his glass.

"It's just that there are a lot of good-looking guys in the world. Take you for example. I noticed you the minute you came up the stairs. Um…" Walter looked down at the ground, then back to Jude. "I have a confession. I intentionally came to stand next to you, hoping to meet you."

"You sure know how to flatter an about-to-turn-thirty-year-old."

With a playful twinkle in his eye, Walter said, "I have a penchant for hot, older men."

"*Older* men? Ooooh! So close to the perfect seduction." Jude cracked a rakish smile.

Walter pointed to the USC Trojans baseball cap Jude was wearing. "You go to college there?"

"I was supposed to, but I ended up with mono. But I like the hat. It's my subliminal message for safe sex."

Walter laughed, thumping his hand against Jude's shirtless chest exposed under his Carhartt jacket. "You are quite adorable, birthday boy."

"And the seduction is back on track."

"How much does it take to seduce you?"

"I'm a Scorpio. I'm a bottomless pit."

"Would a kiss seal the deal?"

An adrenaline rush spiked Jude's blood flow, catapulting his heart into his throat; his lungs felt desperate for air. Jude took a deep breath. His words floated out on his exhale. "It couldn't hurt."

Walter placed his hand at the back of Jude's neck and pulled him in, and with an open mouth (but no tongue) softly, but firmly pressed his lips against Jude's. A reflexive moan from Jude, barely audible over the strains of M People's "One Night in Heaven," escaped through their sealed kiss. Jude opened his eyes when they broke apart and gazed into Walter's.

"And naturally, you have to be a good kisser. You sure you want to be a model instead of my boyfriend?" Jude grinned from ear to ear.

At closing, Walter asked if he could bum a ride. He lived on Willet Street, around the corner from Jude's apartment building.

"So how do you live so close to me, yet I've never seen you out?"

"I worked on weekends, but I was also in a relationship that ended not too long ago."

"Oh, I'm sorry."

"He was too jealous, too insecure. He was always afraid I was going to run off with someone else."

Can you blame him? Look at you.

Stopping in front of his apartment, Walter asked, "Would you like to come in for some coffee or hot chocolate?"

"If by *hot chocolate* you mean you, yes, I'd love some." Walter burst out laughing.

Jude parked his car, and they walked down the steps to Walter's basement apartment. It was a pokey, claustrophobic, one-room space made more confining because Walter boxed most of his things for his move and they took up more of the apartment's space.

Jude absorbed the scant artifacts, trying to figure out the architecture of Walter's life, other than a hot wanna-be model. Walter entered Jude's life through a desultory encounter and, sadly, would exit as fast as a flame consuming the last of its candlewick. There wasn't much to see. The one room functioned as a living room, bedroom, and efficiency kitchen.

Jutting out of an open closet was a wooden futon. Clothing lay strewn about in piles like raked leaves about to be bagged.

So, he isn't the neatest or most organized person, but his hotness makes up for that.

As if Walter read his mind, he said, "Sorry for the mess. I'm trying to get rid of stuff. Less to move."

An understanding smile spread across Jude's face. He asked for the bathroom.

"Over there." Walter pointed to a door next to the closet.

The melismatic sound of Mariah Carey filtered into the bathroom from the main room. Jude checked his breath, swished water around his mouth, and studied his reflection. When Jude returned, he immediately took Walter in his arms and placed an aggressive kiss on his full, sensual lips (now with tongue). Walter moaned. His eyes emitted a submissive, trance-like stare as he melted into Jude's embrace. Jude piloted the sex, and instinct told him Walter preferred it that way. He'd let Jude fly the plane.

Without breaking their kiss, Jude whipped off his Carhartt. They tugged at Walter's cream-color sweater, with Jude getting the upper hand, pulling it over Walter's head. He threw it, and it landed on a table under the apartment's only window, eye level with the sidewalk. They stripped off the rest of their clothes in a sexual frenzy.

Jude turned his baseball cap backward, and they fell on the futon. He was lying on top of Walter's lithe body, his skin as smooth and delicious-looking as milk chocolate and unblemished like his complexion. Walter returned the kisses with the eagerness of a hungry baby bird. The bramble of Jude's goatee raked across Walter's face in their fevered desire for each other. Jude ran his mouth along Walter's ear and neck, causing his body to shiver. His eyes pressed tight against the intensity. Walter rolled on his side. Jude stopped momentarily as Walter's eyes drilled into Jude's.

"What's wrong?" Jude asked. His breathing was heavy.

Walter shook his head and said, "Not a thing."

A slavering smile fanned across Jude's face, and he went in for another taste of Walter's lips.

Walter reached under his futon and groped through a shoebox, spilling its contents. He felt around like a child fumbling through the spilled contents of a piñata. Finally, clutching the prize—a packet with *Trojan* splayed across the foil. He ripped the condom packet open and rolled it down Jude's erection. Walter's eyes widened as he coated it with a minty lubricant. A lustful smile bloomed across his face.

Jude began with Walter on all fours, pulling Walter's arms back as if they were reins. He pressed into Walter, who sucked in a lungful of air before exhaling in pain, which soon turned to pleasure. Jude flipped Walter on his back without pulling out and stared into his acquiescent eyes with a concentrated, singular focus. After some length, Walter jacked himself into a volcanic orgasm. Jude's body tightened shortly after as he pushed deep into Walter and released several animalistic grunts before collapsing onto Walter, their bodies glued by Walter's ejaculate.

During a prolonged period of after-sex kissing, Jude politely declined Walter's offer to sleep over. Jude gave a flimsy excuse about having to get up early. But the truth was he would never be able to sleep in the claustrophobic conditions with Walter's futon half in an overflowing closet. Jude never lived in the closet and he wasn't about to sleep in one. His decision not to sleep over was purely symbolic of his gay pride.

Jude kissed a naked Walter at the door and asked him if he was doing anything tomorrow evening.

"Not really."

"How would you like to help me usher in my thirties?"

"With more sex?" Walter was all smiles.

"I'd love to give an encore performance, but first, we have to attend a party my friend Francine is throwing me."

Walter walked over to write down his number. Jude observed his tight, round ass and shapely legs; his brown skin practically shone like caramelized sugar. Jude resisted the temptation to take Walter again.

"I'll call tomorrow to tell you when I'll pick you up."

After a final juicy kiss, Jude walked to his apartment building, leaving his car where it was.

It was going on 7 a.m. when Jude collapsed onto his bed; the faint glimmer of the new day trickled into his bedroom. His last thought hit him bluntly—he was now officially thirty. Too tired to scream, he mumbled, "Fuck you, Father Time," before burying his face in his pillow and dropping into sleep.

Chapter Nine
Fasten Your Seat Belts. It's Going to Be a Bumpy Night

Jude coordinated his dress for his party with the color scheme, wearing a black mock turtleneck, black jeans, black combat boots, and a black Sox baseball cap—along with Black Walter on his arm.

Francine scanned Jude from head to toe.

Jude noticed and said, "What? I dressed according to the theme."

"Christ, you look like Johnny Cash."

Jude responded to Francine's rejoinder with a cheeky smile before kissing her cheek.

"Walter, meet our hostess with the mostess, Francine." After the salutations, they walked through the living room.

Bleary flames flickered in votive candles, casting a warm glow atop the modern Danish-style coffee table, which mingled with the several antique items Francine collected over the years.

Two clusters of black and orange helium balloons adorned each side of the living room archway. More candles stippled the hallway like tiny, dull spotlights.

In the kitchen, Francine had her table pushed against the wall, under the Charles Greer poster, to make more room. On the table was an enticing array of party foods: a bowl of succulent shrimp on ice, several cheeses adorned with fresh grapes and strawberries, and various savory crackers. At Jude's request, there was a platter of pizza from Peretti's Italian imports that Francine had thoughtfully cut into bite-size squares. On the counter, bottles of liquor and mixers in varying sizes and colors created a three-dimensional still life in the dramatic lighting.

Jude went and poured himself some scotch (of course, Francine had lime wedges). He poured Walter and Francine a glass of Cabernet Sauvignon.

"So, when are Chickie and your future husband arriving?" Jude bit into a shrimp dipped in cocktail sauce.

"They'll be here soon, and don't eat all the shrimp before the other guests arrive."

"You see, Walter, this birthday bash is really an excuse for Francine to meet the man of her dreams. He's an uncircumcised, artsy type who moved up from the city to open a gallery in Hudson, and she thought throwing me a birthday party would be a good excuse to have a close encounter of an intimate kind." Jude reached for another shrimp; Francine smacked his hand.

"What if you're not attracted to him?" Walter chuckled.

"Well…" Francine began defensively, "…that's what this party is for…to find out." She tried to hide her annoyance with Walter's inquisition at the possibility.

"So much for celebrating your dearest gay friend's thirtieth birthday." Jude quickly shoved a shrimp into his mouth before Francine could stop him.

"Oh, you know what I mean. Besides, you didn't even want a party. You only agreed when I told you Dakota had some hot, gay friends he could bring." Jude forced a cough and tilted his head in Walter's direction. "Ix nay."

Francine was in mid-sip when the doorbell rang. She dabbed her mouth with a napkin, quickly fluffed her hair, crimped into soft waves, and answered the door. Moments later, Jude and Walter heard muffled chatter getting louder as the new guests approached the kitchen. Entering was Chickie, followed by a curiously flamboyant, gender-challenging person sporting an oversized silver lamé blouse and baggy black Capri pants. His rouged, chubby cheeks popped like two red apples against his otherwise alabaster skin.

Who the hell is that? Jude's eyes screamed as they darted from Francine to Chickie, who ignored him, trying to remain civil.

The last to enter was the eagerly awaited arrival of Dakota, the man of Francine's dreams. His SoHo sophistication preceded him like the radioactive waves from a nuclear blast sucking the breath out of Francine—and Jude. His aura was almost tangible, as he was dressed in a black sports coat over a white Lycra T-shirt, cashmere scarf, worn noose-like, and jeans with strategically placed rips. Chickie made the introductions.

Jude tried not to stare into Dakota's smoldering dark eyes. His shoulder-length, coal-black hair (so straight and silky, it looked ironed) framed his classically chiseled Native American face.

Feeling Francine's stare, Jude tried to breathe normally. "Hi, I'm Jude."

"Ah, the birthday boy."

"And this is Walter."

"Jude's date," Francine quickly interjected.

"This is for you." Dakota handed Jude a velvet bag tied with an organza ribbon.

Jude undid the bow and took out a bottle of Glenfiddich. "Wow, thank you." Laughing lightly, he said, "You don't know me, yet you know me so well."

"And these are for you." Dakota handed Francine Calla lilies wrapped in silver tissue paper.

"Oh, they're beautiful." Francine glowed as she went to put them in a vase. Passing Jude, she cracked an *in-your-face* smile.

Dakota then introduced the cherubic mystery person whose name was Stephano. He held out his hand as if Jude and Walter were supposed to kiss it, queen-like, which wasn't far from the truth in Stephano's case. His smile scrunched his face reducing his watery blue eyes into mere slits.

"Charmed, I'm sure," Stephano said.

Jude shook his downturned fingers, followed by Walter, who then excused himself to use the bathroom, allowing Jude to grill Chickie.

"Always good to see you, Chickadee." He embraced her petite frame, kissing the top of her head. Her hair smelled like lemons. Through a fake smile, Jude said, "I thought you said he had *hot* gay friends? Instead, I get Belinda Carlisle in her chubby days with the Go-Go's."

Chickie widened her already doe-like eyes in unsuspecting astonishment. "I didn't know he was bringing him, and besides, I never said *hot* gay friends."

"Of course not. That was Fran's clever way of baiting me into agreeing to this party. Who is he? Don't tell me he's Dakota's boyfriend!"

"No, he's an artist Dakota is featuring for his opening. Besides, aren't you with that gorgeous hunk in the bathroom?"

"He's moving to the city to become a model," Jude said mournfully. What's Stephano doing here?"

"He's up from the city for the weekend to discuss the details of his show. He's a character, isn't he?" Chickie said in her thick Long

Island accent.

Cantaloupe sauntered into the kitchen. Stephano gasped. "Oh, look!" He scooped up Cants in his arms. "Hello there, you cute little pussy."

"Now there's a phrase you wouldn't expect to come out of his mouth." Jude's tone was hushed.

She tried to sip her wine but snorted into her glass, sending an airborne spray of Cabernet Sauvignon.

Cantaloupe hissed and clawed at Stephano before jumping out of his arms.

The seemingly demure Cantaloupe apparently had an aggressive side, considering the occasional bruise she came home with. The oddest injury was a tiny hole in the tip of her right ear. One night, after several glasses of wine, Francine got the warped idea to put an earring through the tiny hole.

"It's the right ear. That means Cants is a lesbian," Jude said.

Cantaloupe started violently twitching her ear, so Francine quickly removed the post, but not before Jude snapped a few photos of the adorned kitty.

Stephano screeched like a girl, fluffed his lamé blouse, and acted like nothing happened.

Francine picked up Cantaloupe. "I better put her in the bedroom," she said, closing the door.

"What was all that screeching?" Walter said, returning from the bathroom.

"There was a pussy incident."

"A what?" Walter snorted a confused laugh. Jude waved his question off, draped his arm around Walter's shoulder, and then dropped it when he caught Dakota's stare.

"What's with all the black?" Chickie eyed Jude.

"I'm mourning the passing of my twenties."

Chickie tittered. Walter smiled. Stephano fluffed. Jude stared (at Dakota). Francine leered (at Jude). He replaced his arm around Walter to diffuse Francine's glare and suddenly feared he was living an *All About Eve it's-going-to-be-a-bumpy-night* moment.

Chapter Ten
A Second Helping of Hot Chocolate

By ten o'clock, the party was a flurry of activity. Several of Jude's friends arrived, including his ex but still dear friend, Michael Antonucci.

"Hey, girl," Michael's signature salutation for Jude, pirated from Lucy and Ethel. "Happy birthday." He handed Jude a bottle of wine.

"Do people think I'm a lush? All I'm receiving is alcohol."

"Aren't you?"

"If I am, then you're a whore." Their lips smacked in a friendly kiss. "Thank you."

Shortly after, Dominick Viscusi gusted in, tossing his navy blue overcoat on a chair with reckless abandon, commanding the room immediately. His short bangs made him look like Caesar, but his stature and attitude were Napoleonic.

"Haay!" Dominick's voice boomed. He handed Jude a card. On the front was a muscular, naked man with a cake in front of his privates. On the inside of the card, the man held the cake to his side, exposing his endowment. The card read: *Now you can have your cock and eat it too. Happy Birthday!*

"Very touching. Hallmark would be envious," Jude said. A few inches shorter, Jude kissed Dominick's forehead. The card also contained several lottery tickets, the standard gift from Dominick.

"I got it at Romeo's Gift Emporium. Romeo said to wish you a happy birthday."

"You mean Joey," Jude said.

"No, Romeo."

"Yes, Joey Romeo."

"You mean his first name isn't Romeo?"

"No, it's Joey."

A puffed laugh escaped Dominick. "I kept calling him *Romeo*."

"Outside of Shakespeare, how many people name their child *Romeo?* Come here, you." He thanked Dominick for the tickets," and planted another kiss on his head.

There were more introductions, this time by Jude before he made drinks. Dakota was braided in conversation with Francine but stole several glances at Jude. Each time Jude caught his stare, it made his heart lurch, momentarily stealing his breath. Regaining composure, he nodded. A polite smile crossed his face.

With the time approaching midnight, Stephano was rather inebriated and toppled into Dominick, draping a deadweight arm around his shoulder. Checking out the flowing blouse on Stephano, Dominick declared, "Easy there, Liza." He turned to Michael and Jude. "She's drunkles."

"I'm fine," Stephano slurred, then kissed Dominick's forehead. Dominick's round Italian eyes widened with horror and amusement.

The mellow, eclectic sound of Enya played softly as background music. Stephano leaned into Dominick's face. "I think we need to liven this place up with some real party music, huh, precious?"

On the word "precious," a spray of saliva assaulted Dominick's face, which he aggressively wiped away.

"Hey, Liza, I already showered." He continued to wipe the spittle away.

Stephano tried to focus. "Why d'you keep callin' me Liza? My name is Stephano." He dangled his other arm around Jude, where it hung like a lifeless appendage. "But between us, my name is really Stephen." He raised his finger to his glossed lips. "Shhhh! But it was so common. I changed it to Stephano." He addressed Michael. "It's more European, don' cha think, han'some? Classier." With his face inches from Michael's, he squinted and widened his eyes, trying to focus like a camera lens zooming in and out. "God, you're gorgeous," Stephano slurred. His hefty weight pressed on Jude, who had to balance himself to avoid falling over.

Michael, who accepted a compliment from any source, thanked Stephano with pride tattooed on his face. Knowing he was good-looking, Michael always exuded sexual confidence, and any encouragement led to his inability to, as Jude always said, *keep the horse in the barn,* the cause of their breakup. But their mutual obsession with youth, a penchant for guys, and their affinity for the film *Who's Afraid of Virginia Woolf?* eventually closed Jude's wounds, healed his scars and they remained close friends.

Stephano staggered to Francine's CDs. Rummaging through her

collection, he decided on Cathy Dennis. Stephano began singing and dancing around the room as "C'mon and Get My Love" blasted through the apartment. He bent over, grasped the back of the sofa, and bounced his ample behind, sending earthquake tremors through the apartment.

"Go, Liza!" Dominick encouraged.

"I'm Shaniqua!" Stephano yelled.

Francine, Chickie, and Dakota, who had migrated to the kitchen, rushed into the living room.

"What the hell is going on in here?" Francine did not disguise her anger.

"Shaniqua is entertaining us," Jude said over the music.

Francine went to turn down the music. "Okay, *Shaniqua,* that's enough before you give new meaning to *bringing down the house.*"

Stephano pouted and fell into the antique rocking chair. "I jus' wanted to entertain the troops—like Marilyn Monroe." He crossed his arms and rocked himself into a slumber.

"I better go check to see that everything is in place. My grandmother's good china survived a boat trip from England, and in one night, *Shaniqua* could have reduced it to shards." Francine rushed off to the kitchen. Chickie followed, leaving Dakota with the guys.

"Well, I haven't spent time talking to you gentlemen." Dakota directed his words exclusively to Jude. "You'll have to forgive Stephano. He's a bit eccentric but a truly gifted artist. I'm featuring him in my gallery opening. Hopefully, you can be there." His eyes, still focused on Jude, were like red-hot branding irons.

"When is the opening?" Jude asked.

Dakota's gaze short-circuited Jude's brain, sending nervous energy surging through his body.

"Possibly, in a few weeks. And bring your friends." For the first time, Dakota acknowledged the others. He handed Jude a business card. "Here's the address of my gallery," he said, adding, "my number as well. Don't be afraid to use it." A suggestive smile curled his lips.

Walter was savvy about Dakota's seductive charms. "I think I'll freshen my drink," he said and excused himself.

"I hope I didn't offend your boyfriend—"

"Oh, he's not my boyfriend," Jude said reassuringly—unwittingly—no longer lamenting Walter's upcoming departure. "He's moving away to become a model." He held on to Dakota's stare like a treasured heirloom.

Dakota's lips curled into a puckish smile.

Jude felt his face, as well as other body parts, prickle. *What message was Dakota sending?* He was here to meet Francine, but his eyes connecting with Jude's sent mixed messages.

By 3 a.m., the party broke up. The only people left were Dakota, a passed-out Stephano, and Chickie. As she and Jude gathered cups and plates in the living room, Dakota helped Francine in the kitchen.

"Thank you for a fantastic time. It was a pleasure to meet you. You must come to see my gallery."

"I'd love to. When is the opening?" Francine asked.

"I was thinking of giving you a private tour, let's say next Saturday. And after, I could take you to this fantastic restaurant a little further down from Hudson, where we could have dinner."

Francine's electrified heart thumped as if shocked with a thousand volts from a defibrillator.

"I'd love that."

He handed her a business card. "Call me during the week, and we'll make plans. Oh, and let's keep this between us for now. I don't want to look like I'm playing favorites."

Francine wrinkled her brow, but she agreed.

As Jude and Chickie entered the kitchen, she stuffed Dakota's card in her pocket.

They all returned to the living room, Dakota roused a sleeping Stephano, who flailed like one of those air tube balloons in front of car dealerships. Jude helped Dakota walk Stephano to the door.

"Thank you, Francine." Dakota leaned in, kissing each cheek. "Jude, happy birthday, and I hope I see you both at my opening." Dakota tottered under Stephano's weight as he extended his hand to Jude, whose shake lasted a split second longer than necessary.

"Call me." Chickie hugged Francine.

"C'mon there, sleepy head." Dakota labored, trying to hold Stephano up.

As they headed down the walk, Stephano waved limply. "Bye-bye," he said in a falsetto whisper, then slumped against Dakota.

Walking back to the kitchen, Jude asked, "What did you think of Dakota? Is he husband material?"

She played innocent. "Oh, I don't know. He's certainly handsome."

"I think he's gay," Walter blurted out, eyeing Jude and smiling.

The words jarred Francine, causing a bowl to slip from her hands, spilling onion dip onto the counter.

"Oh, he is not," Jude protested but couldn't stop thinking about the looks Dakota shot at him like sexual darts all night, even though he spent most of the evening talking to Francine.

She began to mop up the splattered dip. "He probably *is* gay. Who cares? Gay. Straight. Bi. All these labels." Francine went to the sink to rinse the rag used to clean up the onion dip. "Why is the world so complicated? Nowadays, women not only have to contend with other women, we have to worry about you gays. I mean, we have to practically grow a penis to compete."

"Well, it may not be a *Leave It to Beaver* world, but I'm sure, if you give it time, things will develop between you and Dakota. He was obviously interested in you." Jude's mind replayed his interaction with Dakota, whose eyes—like two hot coals—seared Jude like a marinated steak hitting the grill. *What was his modus operandi?* Dakota was a sexual mystery that needed Hercule Poirot or Miss Marple to solve, perhaps with a little help from Masters and Johnson.

Fran smiled, slicing a glance at Jude. She was a bubble ready to burst. She wanted to tell Jude about her upcoming plans with Dakota. After all, they always shared the intimate details about guys they met and the sex they had with them. But she had to keep her clandestine meeting with Dakota secret. It was what he asked for.

At the door, Jude thanked Francine for the party with a hug and a kiss. Walter followed with a friendly peck on her cheek. "Great to meet you, Fran."

Remembering Walter's assessment of Dakota's sexuality, she said, "Too bad you're moving. You and Jude make a great-looking couple." Though she spoke the truth, Jude knew it was wishful thinking on her part to alleviate the threat of him hooking up with Dakota.

***

When Jude pulled up to Walter's apartment, he turned to him and said, "I could go for some *hot chocolate.*"

"You just want birthday sex." Walter's phosphorescent smile triggered a rascally grin to spread on Jude's face and jumpstarted the hard-on in his pants.

Inside Walter's apartment, their lips met in a lustful mash. They were naked in minutes. The friction of their conjoined bodies created a bonfire of sexual desire. Walter's gaze was one of utter surrender, and it wasn't long before a condom was on, and Jude was thrusting in and out of him. Knowing it would be the last time he had sex with Walter, Jude's eyes penetrated him like spears, yet all he saw was Dakota's face.

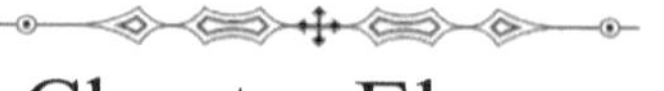

Chapter Eleven
Hallo-Teeny-Weenie

The following Saturday, Jude picked up Dominick, dressed in a pinstriped suit and fedora and carrying a toy machine gun, and went to his cousin's Halloween party. Jude didn't like dressing up. He preferred dressing in his usual provocative style when going out to the gay bars on Halloween weekend. But all week, Dominick, who had a persuasive way with Jude, convinced him to dress up. So, to compromise, he wore an unbuttoned baseball jersey his brother gave him with a *wife beater* underneath and topped it off with his trademark baseball cap, which fit perfectly with his "costume." He rubbed a little charcoal under each eye to complete the look.

When they arrived, Dominick's cousin, Liz, answered the door wearing a bustier, leather shorts, fishnet stockings, and stilettos. She held a riding crop in one hand and a leash attached to a collar around her boyfriend's neck in the other. He was shirtless, while his bottom half was clad in assless leather pants exposing his drool-worthy tight, alabaster buttocks.

They walked to the living room, where a television played porn.

"Is this a sex party or a Halloween party?" Jude whispered in Dominick's ear.

Dominick laughed. "Let's get a drink."

According to Dominick, his cousin and boyfriend were very open sexually, which was apparent by their mode of dress (or undress) and by the mix of gay and straight partygoers.

On the way to the kitchen, they passed a guy costumed as a zombie, a gay couple dressed as baby Jane and Blanche Hudson (complete with wheelchair), and a straight couple who channeled 60s Sonny and Cher. Glen, a friend of Dominick's, was Las Vegas Elvis, which wasn't much of a stretch since Dominick told Jude he was obsessed with *the King* and dressed like him all the time, anyway. And then there was the guy decked out as Carol Channing, wearing a white, sleeveless evening gown and a blond pageboy wig with bangs that disappeared below large, round glasses.

"Well, hello, fellas," he said.

"Haaay, Carol," Dominick said, squeezing one of his fake boobs. "Carol" lightly slapped Dominick on the head with a hand, white-gloved to the elbow.

"What do you think of Liz's boyfriend? He's hot, isn't he?" Dominick asked as they made drinks.

"He's definitely got a nice chest—and ass."

"I gave him a blow job once," Dominick confessed.

"You gave your cousin's boyfriend a blow job?"

"They weren't going out, technically," he added. "But he's got a small dick." Grimacing, Dominick finger-snapped, waving his hand as if banishing the boyfriend to small dick purgatory.

Where Jude was not fond of the uncircumcised penis, Dominick did not like them small. He was your classic size queen, known to grab the crotch of a passerby in a bar and, more often than not, declare, "Pants!" indicating he did not feel much of a dick, just *pants.*

Back in the living room, Liz and her boyfriend were putting on a show to Madonna's "Erotica." The boyfriend was down on all fours; his ass stood out like two muscled orbs, white as light bulbs against his black leather chaps. Liz choreographed her moves to the rhythm of the song, occasionally smacking her boyfriend's buttocks with the riding crop. She seductively gyrated her crotch in her boyfriend's face as the partygoers cheered her on.

Somewhere, a glass shattered. "Carol Channing" shouted, "Did Shammy Davish's glassh eye fall out?"

Around midnight, Jude and Dominick hit Waterworks. With most of the crowd dressed in outlandish costumes and makeup, it was hard to determine who was hot and who was not. After an hour, Dominick suggested going to Roxy's Diner for breakfast, declaring the bar "*bor-bors.*"

Chapter Twelve
Smooth Operator

arlier in the evening, Francine, all tingly and giddy, drove down to meet Dakota. Several days prior, Jude asked her if she wanted to go to the Halloween party Dominick's cousin was throwing, but Francine told Jude she was having a girl's night with her college cronies, Chickie, Ellen, and Horny. Once again, culpability plagued her about deceiving Jude. Guilt stitched together with fear and burrowed into her conscience like a rabid animal. She was not a good liar, and she hoped she was convincing enough not to rouse Jude's suspicion, knowing she was as easy to read as a *Dick and Jane* book.

But when Jude said, "Have fun and say *hi* to the girls for me," her fear evaporated. However, the guilt stuck to her Catholic soul like a leech. When she was able, she'd tell Jude about Dakota with all the enthusiasm of a town crier and free her mind from this self-imposed mental prison.

Francine convinced herself as she drove down Route 9 to relax and enjoy her evening. Though she lost the battle seducing Jude, she took a little delight in knowing she scored with Dakota. At least she hoped to *score* with him.

Francine cruised slowly down Warren Street, past antique shops, high-end stores, and trendy restaurants run by those who left the scourge and competition of the Big Apple years ago but still wanted to show off their New York City sass and style in Mid-Hudson.

She found a spot half a block from Dakota's gallery. Emerging from her car, a gust of autumn air winnowed through her hair, rustled leaves, and sent a plastic bag aloft in a dreamy, slow-motion dance. Francine clasped her coat around her neck as she crossed the street. When she came upon the white cast iron building, with its Greek-style columns and large windows flanking the entrance, she rang the bell to the upstairs apartment. She puffed into her palm, checking her breath, and smoothed her wind-tossed hair as Dakota opened the door. At that moment, all her ease of mind fluttered away like leaves tumbling haphazardly by a sudden gale, leaving her wracked with jangling nerves. *Stay calm,* she told herself. *He's just a man. Who am I kidding? He's husband material.*

"Welcome," Dakota said with an effervescent smile. His thick, black hair was pulled back in a ponytail, showcasing his sculpted features and lash-fringed, coffee-colored eyes. He leaned in and gave Francine a sandalwood-scented hug. *Shit. One of Jude's favorite scents.* She dismissed the troubling association from her mind as if swiping chalk from a blackboard.

"Hello. I hope I'm not too early," Francine said. Dakota was barefoot, wearing jeans and a T-shirt but just as sexy as his Bohemian chic look the night they met.

"No, I'm running behind."

They headed up the narrow, dimly lit staircase.

"I was doing some work in the gallery and lost track of the time. Make yourself at home," Dakota said upon entering his apartment. "I promise I'll change for dinner," acknowledging his casual look.

Honey, you'd be sexy in a potato sack.

Francine scanned the minimalistic décor in the huge loft. She felt like a raft adrift in the open waters, and when Dakota announced he was getting them wine, his voice echoed. She turned in his direction and saw him at a stainless-steel island. A fancy modern faucet rose from the center, curved like a swan's neck. He pulled glasses from cabinets matching the chrome island.

Though it was evening and dimly lit, the stark-white walls lent an iridescent glow to the spacious loft. Francine's eyes were drawn to the platform bed jutting out from a far corner of the room. Her heart thumped at the sight, imagining herself in it with Dakota.

He was at her side with goblets of Cabernet Sauvignon. He handed her one. "You look so pretty tonight."

Heat flooded Francine's face, complementing her blush-colored Angora sweater. They clinked glasses. A harmonic note resonated briefly.

"Cheers," he said. "What do you think of the place?"

"It's beautiful. So bright and spacious."

"I'm not one for clutter. I like a few simple objects for accent. Less is more, I always say. An architect designed the place, so I didn't have to do much. I gave it a fresh coat of paint, the silver leaf on the molding, and added a few personal touches here and there."

Francine tasted her wine. "Jude would be jealous."

"Would he!"

The ugly green monster in Francine reared its head, and she regretted mentioning Jude's name. She quickly changed the subject. "Um, who did the paintings?" Over Dakota's shoulder, she noticed three abstracts hanging on the exposed brick wall stretching the length of the apartment.

"I did." Dakota's modesty was uncharacteristic. They migrated to the paintings to observe them closer.

"You seem embarrassed."

"I don't consider myself an artist."

"But they're lovely. I'm not an art expert, but they appeal to me."

Under the track lighting zeroing in on them, Francine got a closer look.

"I prefer to think of myself as a connoisseur of art. I like to seek out new talent, which is why I'm opening a gallery. I love bringing talent to the art-loving public."

"Why did you leave New York then?"

"New York is too money-driven. The art scene is more interested in discovering the next Warhol or Haring. A lot of gifted artists go unnoticed because they don't get the backing of rich patrons who think they're experts but only know how to suck up to museum curators and benefactors of the arts. I find the Hudson area not as chaotic and money-hungry, yet there is an appreciation for art."

"Is there a meaning or theme to your work?" Francine hoisted her glass towards the paintings.

"Actually, yes. There is a theme. This painting…" Dakota said, pointing to the one on the far left, "…is called 'Nativity.' In these two larger masses, the pale blue represents Mary, and the brown and tans symbolize Joseph. They watch over the smaller circular shades of white, depicting Jesus."

"I see. Your technique makes the infant Jesus seem glowing."

"Very astute. That was my intent." He placed an arm on her shoulder, guiding Francine to the other paintings. A tingling shiver traveled down her spine.

"The middle painting is called 'Crucifixion.' The last painting, I call 'Resurrection.' The blurry funnel of white in the center represents Jesus' ascension."

"Fascinating," Francine said. "You're a religious person?"

He laughed. "No. These paintings were an artistic idea that came to me from…um…Divine inspiration." Dakota flashed his glowing teeth. "Come. Let me show you my art gallery. Then, I'll take you to Café Tamayo, a fantastic little restaurant in Saugerties. You'll love it."

Dakota led Francine down a back stairwell.

"There's still work to do, but it's getting there."

Upon entering the gallery, Dakota switched on the lights, flooding the space with blinding irradiance. Halogen lights glowed like tiny Klieg lights strategically placed around the gallery. The sudden change from dark to glaring brightness assaulted Francine's eyes.

"Lighting is key in a gallery, affording patrons to see and fully appreciate the art on display."

"And every pore and blemish on one's face," Francine said.

Wires dangled above them like hanging snakes.

"I have an artist, Libby Larsson, who will showcase her sculptures on these." Dakota referred to the intermittent tall, cube-like pedestals scattered throughout the gallery. "Wait till you see them. They are geometric works of wonder. She drew her inspiration from the Icelandic sculptor Asmundur Sveinsson. They combine Art Deco with the spirit of cubism like Sveinsson, but she brings her distinct style and attitude achieving differentism," Dakota said.

Francine listened and nodded to his intellectual art-speak as if she knew what he was talking about. She stumbled over the edge of a drop cloth that blanketed the floor, nearly knocking over a covered can of paint. Dakota reached out, grabbed Francine, and pulled her to his body. She looked up into his face and practically passed out from the delirium of their closeness.

"Sorry for the mess." Dakota helped Francine regain her balance. "Are you okay?"

Reluctantly, she pulled away, rebounding from the embarrassment of her graceless bumble.

"Yes, perfectly fine. Well, it appears that it will be quite the gallery," Francine said.

"Are you hungry?"

Though famished, Francine did not want to appear eager to eat. She said, "Oh, I could nibble on something."

They headed back upstairs.

"I've showered, so I just have to change." Dakota pulled off his T-shirt as he walked to his armoire. Francine inhaled as if taking a hit from a bong upon catching a glimpse of his lithe torso. His chest was as smooth and sculpted as his cheekbones; his waist, Scarlett O'Hara-enviable.

Dakota put on a crisp, white shirt with a Mandarin collar, leaving a few buttons undone and a black blazer. He slipped into a pair of Gucci loafers while checking himself out in a full-length mirror, leaning against the wall. He removed the elastic band from his ponytail. His hair fell to his shoulders, poker straight and lustrous. He combed his fingers through its silky blackness and announced he was ready to go.

In awe of Dakota's effortless, stylish transformation, Francine asked if she could use the bathroom to freshen up. Dakota directed her to a room off the spacious kitchen. When Francine entered the bathroom, it took her breath away. Like the apartment, it was a vision of luxury. Opposite her was an oval bathtub, like a large-scale porcelain rice bowl. Francine imagined she and Dakota in it, with votive candles lit in the rectangular recess above the tub, giving off a romantic glow as they sipped wine and exchanged saturated kisses, the air redolent with sandalwood oil.

Looking into the mirror above the sink, she opened her purse, took out a tube of mascara, flicked a coating on her already long lashes, and delicately applied more lipstick. She pinched her cheeks and fluffed her hair.

"Showtime," she said softly. Francine's high heels tapped out a clacking echo as she walked across the Italian marble floor.

She exited the bathroom. "Ready."

They drove the half-hour distance to Café Tamayo, a tiny, intimate restaurant south of Hudson. They sat at a cozy corner table. A fresh-cut rose stood in a silver vase on a white linen tablecloth. Stippling the black ceiling like stars were dozens of clear bulbs hanging in varying lengths.

"What do you think of the place?" Dakota asked.

Romantic. "It's charming."

Dakota ordered a bottle of Cabernet Sauvignon from the Chateau Montelena vineyards in Napa Valley.

When dinner arrived, Dakota devoured his filet mignon topped with melted Saint Agur bleu cheese; Francine sparingly picked at her asparagus risotto, not letting her usual voracious appetite on display, instead eating like a devout anorexic.

*****

Back in Dakota's apartment, Francine settled onto the grey leather sofa between the two floor-to-ceiling windows overlooking Warren Street. She tried to relax while looking sexy. She rested her arm on an orange chintz throw pillow, but it sank so low she nearly toppled over. Far off in the kitchen, Dakota opened a bottle of wine; his tall stature seemed minuscule in the scale of the apartment.

Dakota dimmed the lights and undid a few more buttons on his shirt, exposing the cleft between his chest muscles.

With a wine bottle in one hand and glasses in the other, he ambled to the sofa as if he was starring in a Calvin Klein commercial. He placed the wine and glasses on the Baughman patchwork coffee table and sat inches from Francine. After pouring their wine, they bumped glasses, setting off a pitch-perfect ring, a sign of his expensive taste in glassware—in everything.

"Thank you. Tell me about your family." Taking a sip, Francine tried to look nonchalant.

He leaned back, tasting his wine. "I'm originally from New Mexico. My father is Native American, my mother was an anthropology student, and she met my father while researching the Puye cliff dwellings in New Mexico. They married, and I grew up in Espanola until I moved to New York to attend NYU as an art major." He moved in closer to Francine. "I worked in the art community in the city for several years and decided to come to Hudson to open a gallery so I might showcase artists that might never get the attention they deserve. That's the condensed version." Dakota proffered a sexy smile.

"That's very admirable. I'm excited for your opening."

Dakota began to pour more wine.

"I really shouldn't. I have to drive back to Albany." Francine didn't want to assume she was staying but hoped Dakota would take a cue from *The Godfather* and make her an offer she couldn't refuse.

"Nonsense. It's getting late. Stay the night—if you want," Dakota added.

A shimmer passed through Francine like light through a prism, creating an explosive refraction of color in her head. "I don't want to impose." She hoped her false politeness was not apparent.

His arm came to rest on the back of the sofa, inches from Francine.

His hand slid from the couch to the fuzzy sweater and caressed her shoulder as the sultry sound of Sade's "Smooth Operator" oozed from the sound system. He moved in closer. "I wouldn't have offered if I didn't want you to." A dreamy smile morphed across his face. His breath blew soft against her cheek. Her eyes begged him to kiss her, and it was as if by osmosis, her innermost desire seeped into his brain as he lifted her chin, delicately pressing his lips to hers. Francine moaned and acquiesced to his advances.

Dakota's tongue became more fervid, prodding past her parted lips, exploring the cave of her mouth.

Francine felt a sudden rumbling in her stomach. She pulled away and faked a loud cough to silence the gurgling, now reaching a crescendo.

"Sorry. I had a tickle in my throat."

Dakota leaned in for a lingering kiss, his lips supple but determined. His tongue circled and swept in and around her mouth with the skill of a painter using his brush to create a work of art.

Like a distant storm, Francine felt another gastrointestinal thunder percolating. Pulling away, she forged another cough to camouflage the gurgles. "Oh, I *am* sorry. I can't seem to shake this annoying cough."

"Are you okay?" Dakota asked.

"Yes. Fine. Will you excuse me for a moment?" Despite the momentary calm in her stomach, she produced another phony cough to make her performance Meryl Streep-like. She got up, grabbed her purse, and fake-coughed her way to the bathroom.

Inside the pristine bathroom, Francine fumbled for the granola bar she remembered having in her purse. She tore the wrapper with the resoluteness to end a starvation diet and took a bite. In her haste to devour the granola bar, she inhaled an oat and actually choked, giving her performance method-acting realism.

When she finished, she rinsed her mouth and checked herself in the mirror to make sure there was no evidence of the honey and oat bar she consumed. Before exiting, she turned to the bathtub. "Hopefully, see you later."

"Is everything alright, Fran?" Dakota's voice resonated through the length of the apartment.

"Oh, yes. Fine." Francine walked back to the couch. "Now, where were we?" She sat down.

"I believe I was in the process of seducing you," Dakota said like a *smooth operator.* He took Francine in his arms, pressed his body to hers, and covered her with hot-blooded kisses. She melted under his embrace like a Popsicle left in the sun while she felt his *Popsicle* grow rigid.

"Shall we take this to the bed?" There was a hormonal growl in his voice. He helped Francine off the couch.

As Sade ended, the next in his 5-disc CD player was the ethereal sound of Madonna's "Bedtime Stories." The first song in the shuffle was the bewitching "Inside of Me." *Can't wait.* Francine's burning desires sparked her self-immolation.

Dakota led Francine by the hand to the platform bed. He removed her clothes slowly, methodically, with teasing deliberateness—the Angora sweater. A kiss. The jean skirt. Another kiss. Bra. Each breast received a suck from his mouth. Dakota squatted, pulling down her panties; his tongue flicked at her abdomen. His hands roamed over her now naked body before removing his clothes. He lowered Francine to the bed. Dakota reached down and pulled out a condom. As he knelt over Francine, he ripped open the foil wrapper with his teeth, rolled it down his erection, and crawled between her legs. Francine eagerly obliged, lifting her legs with gravity-defying swiftness as if hot air balloons were attached to each ankle. Dakota entered slowly before his jackhammering progressed; Francine clung to Dakota, her legs flapped in the air like the wings of a baby bird trying to take flight. His long, silky hair bounced around Francine's face.

As "Take a Bow" echoed through the apartment, Dakota's body tensed, signaling the end of the ride. Like a child's first time on a roller coaster, Francine thought it was over too soon. He rolled off her onto his back, brushing his hair away from his face.

Dakota caught his breath. "Was that good for you?"

Though she felt he was not quite worthy of the song's title, she said, "Like the fourth of July," hoping she didn't sound too cynical. She propped herself against the headboard.

Dakota gave Francine a quick kiss, and pulling off his condom, he walked to the bathroom. He passed through a swath of moonlight streaking through the windows, spotlighting his backside. His buttocks glowed briefly like two full moons.

When he returned, Francine excused herself to freshen up, but not wanting the moonlight highlighting her buttocks, she wrapped an Egyptian cotton sheet around her. She passed through the same patch of moon glow, looking like a wandering specter.

Inside the bathroom, her eyes were drawn to the giant bathtub again. *No romantic candlelit bathing tonight.* "Next time, for sure," she mumbled.

Returning to the bed, Dakota was fast asleep. "And no post-coital making out, either," she whispered. Disappointed, Fran slipped into the bed and waited for sleep to come.

Chapter Thirteen
A Cross to Wear

Around noon the day after the Halloween party, Jude called Dominick and suggested they go to Quintessence for brunch. The 1930s Silver Diner was one of Albany's most popular restaurants and always had a good mix of gay and straight clientele. While the exterior retained its original Art Deco design, the owner refurbished the interior with a contemporary decor. Tall chrome stools with red leather lined the mahogany bar, and high-back booths covered in red tuck and roll leather flanked the opposite, window-lined wall.

Jude and Dominick preferred to sit in the back, where a dozen tables crammed the tiny space with a checkered floor. "Better to see and be seen," Jude rationalized in case there were any hotties in view. Though a bit claustrophobic, especially when crowded, as on this Sunday, Quintessence had a cozy charm and atmosphere, which lent to its popularity.

While they waited for a table, they stood at the bar and indulged in a Bloody Mary.

Bibi, one of the servers, approached Jude and Dominick. She was a cheerful girl with a wild flock of blond curls and large blue eyes, with one that ever so slightly crossed.

"Hey, fellas," she said in her deep, gravelly voice. "I'll have your table ready in a few minutes. It's crazy in here today. It must be the warm weather."

Halfway through their Bloody Marys, Bibi returned. "Boys, your table is ready. I'll bring you over another round on me," Bibi rasped.

She sat them next to two other gay guys Jude knew casually through a mutual friend. One was Connor McCracken, a good-looking, dirty blonde with foamy sea-green eyes and a relatively quiet, soft-spoken personality who hung with a very preppy crowd. Connor still possessed one of Jude's crosses, which he frequently wore around his neck. It ended up in his possession when Connor's former boyfriend,

Adam Blanchard, left for San Francisco. Adam, also a preppy gang member, looked like he could have descended from occupants on the Mayflower with his sandy-colored hair, crystalline blue eyes, and pale complexion. Though the antithesis of what Jude typically was attracted to, he found the "preppy poster boy" pleasing to the eye. And Jude, with his unorthodox, provocative style of biker jackets, denim, and baseball caps, never thought Adam would be attracted to him until last Memorial Day evening.

Six months earlier

Through the meager crowd at Waterworks, Jude saw Adam approach. Standing beside him, Jude thought nothing of it and offered a clenched smile.

"What's with all the crosses?" Adam asked. Jude was wearing a quilted zipper vest, opened enough to expose a phalanx of silver crosses against his shirtless chest.

Thinking he was being critical, offending Adam's buttoned-up, Ralph Lauren style, Jude replied, "I'm going through a Madonna phase."

Adam chuckled. "I like them. It looks hot."

When Adam asked if he could wear one, suspicion furrowed Jude's brow.

"Just for the night," Adam said. "I promise."

"I don't know. What if I lose track of you through the night?"

"It'd be hard to lose me in this crowd." A lurid smile etched Adam's face. "Besides, I was hoping you would come home with me."

"Aren't you the presumptuous one? What gives? I'm not exactly your type. As you can see, I don't look like I stepped out of a Brooks Brothers catalog."

"And how do you know what my type is? Who's being presumptuous now?" Jude suspected that if Adam had feathers, he just ruffled them.

After Adam's shaming riposte and being drawn into his charms and sexual advances, Jude acquiesced and let him pick a cross to wear. He chose the silver cross from the rosary Jude received when he made his first communion and salvaged it after he inadvertently destroyed the beads in a freak radiator-melting accident.

"Good choice, but it has sentimental value, so guard it with your life," Jude advised.

"Promise. Does this mean you accepted my offer to come home with me?"

"What happened to your boyfriend, Connor?"

Adam detailed how they drifted apart and broke up.

Jude's heart fluttered as if he held a captive bird inside his chest. "Why this sudden invitation?"

"Can I confess something?"

Jude jiggled his crosses. "I'm practically ordained my son."

After a laugh, Adam admitted being attracted to Jude for quite a while. "I always thought you were one of the nicest-looking guys around. You carry yourself so well, so confident, but without the ego. You stand out in a crowd."

Jude was stunned by this revelation. "Be careful, or you'll be responsible for *giving* me an ego." He offered to buy a round of drinks. "I'm shocked. I didn't think I was your type."

"I don't have a type. I know what I like, and I think we would have made an enviable couple. I just wish I told you sooner."

"Sooner?"

"I just got a promotion to manage one of our Abercrombie and Fitch stores in San Francisco. I'm moving in a few weeks."

Jude's rippling heart flatlined. *Another Walter. Just my luck.* "You tell me how great we'd be, and then tell me you're moving across the country? Well done, sadist."

"I'm sorry. But to paraphrase one of my favorite films, we'll always have Albany." Adam grinned and gave Jude a quick peck on the lips.

"And you like films? Now you're going for Marquis de Sade status."

***

Back in Adam's flat, he aggressively began making out with, Jude and they fell to the overstuffed couch. Amid the heated kissing, Jude heard a door open and footsteps approaching.

"Don't mind me. I'm just getting some water." It was Connor McCracken.

Jude's insides jolted with a rush of adrenaline and broke the vise-like embrace with Adam. They acknowledged Connor and watched him return to his room and close the door. Adam drew Jude in his clutches and went in for another kiss.

"Wait. I thought you said you two broke up?" Jude said.

"We did. But it was easier to remain living together."

"I feel weird now, like I'm in the middle of some Norma Desmond-Max von Mayerling scenario to reference one of *my* favorite films."

"Believe me, it's okay. We both have moved on." Adam started unzipping Jude's vest. Sloughing it off his torso, he went for Jude's jeans with a vengeance, then his clothes. The room was a furnace of sexual heat. They were naked in minutes; their limbs braided and tangled like rope plies. They thrashed and flopped around like two fish thrown on the deck of a boat. A leg knocked a TV remote and a few magazines off the square coffee table as their mouths explored torsos. The friction their compressed bodies created soon led to the constriction of Adam's muscles and multiple loud grunts—that Jude was confident Connor could hear, despite his closed door—signaling his orgasm. Jude slithered in the slippery warmth of Adam's ejaculate, reaching his own volcanic climax, the breathless weight of his body pressing down on Adam.

They cleaned up and returned to the couch, where Adam drifted off to sleep, his arm resting across Jude's chest. Jude lay awake on the narrow strip of cushions, unable to find the sleep he craved.

Around seven a.m., Jude had to go home and get ready for work. He fought every temptation to lie down, fearing he'd oversleep. As Jude showered, the night's events kept playing, over and over, in his mind, and it smacked his memory that Adam still had his cross. But he had to admit, what started out as a mundane Memorial Day turned out to be quite *memorable*.

***

Sitting with Connor at Quintessence was Lawrence Gillespie, a pompous, affected homosexual that Jude dubbed *Mr. Howell* because he frequently wore a navy blue, double-breasted sports coat with gold buttons and white pants. Though he dressed like Mr. Howell, he was portly and plump, like the Skipper. Jude found him unfriendly and arrogant. Today was no different, except he wore a nondescript grey suit while the rest of the Sunday brunch crowd dressed casually.

Connor turned and smiled. "Hey, Jude."

"Hi, Connor."

Lawrence acted as if Jude was invisible and said nothing to him.

"Nice suit," Dominick chimed in with false admiration. "Where'd you get it?" he asked, baiting Lawrence.

"Manhattan." Lawrence's nose went up.

"No, I mean like Men's Warehouse or J.C. Penney." Dominick's sarcasm vexed Lawrence, whose rosy cheeks crimsoned deeper with indignance, the tint bleeding down to his fleshy neck spilling over his collar.

"I got it at Barney's in New York!" Lawrence fired back, dragon-like. Jude practically saw the puffs of smoke coming out of his nostrils.

"Oh, because I swear, I saw one just like it in Sears." Dominick's words flew off his tongue like acidic droplets.

Thankfully, Bibi arrived with their Bloody Marys. "You boys know what you want?"

"I'll have a spinach and Swiss cheese omelet with rye toast," Jude said.

"And for you, sweetie?"

"Belgian waffles." Dominick took a long sip of the fresh Bloody Mary.

Still exasperated by Dominick's remarks, Lawrence said to Connor, "Let's go. We'll pay at the bar." Lawrence had to maneuver his chubby body through the tiny space between tables, jostling a woman about to sip her coffee. She shot Lawrence an irritated look.

"Going to Tea Dance later?" Connor asked Jude.

"It wouldn't be Sunday if I didn't."

"I hope to see you there." Connor's stare lingered.

"Yes, and can you remember to bring my cross?" Jude shouted as Lawrence whisked Connor away. Jude feared the din of the brunch crowd overpowered his words.

"Please! If he got that nasty suit in Manhattan, it was probably at one of those discount clothing stores on 42nd Street." Dominick grimaced and gnawed off a piece of celery from his Bloody Mary.

"It was boring no matter where he got it," Jude added. "He's so full of himself. Why does Connor hang out with him and the rest of that pretentious group?"

"Do you like Connor? He's hot," Dominick added.

"I barely know him even though I've been trying to get my cross back from him since May."

"Maybe he likes you." Though Jude dismissed Connor despite his good looks, the idea that Connor was interested in him didn't cross his mind—until now. *Thanks, Dominick!* Shaking off the fact as improbable, Jude replied, "Please. He hangs out with all those preening, pretentious types. I'm too Bohemian for his taste."

"I don't know. I saw how Connor kept looking at you." For all his flightiness, Dominick *was* very perceptive. His words continued to nibble at the back of Jude's mind like a locust on a wheat stalk.

Bibi returned with their dishes. "I put a rush on your orders cuz, you know, I love you guys." Bibi waddled away on her blocky waitress shoes.

Bibi treated Jude and his gay posse with extra care ever since a few summers ago when Jude helped a drunken Bibi call for a cab.

Bibi tottered into Oh Bar that summer night wearing a linen sundress—the kind with elastic puckered under the bosom—and a big floppy hat. She wobbled to the pay phone but kept dropping her money. Jude witnessed the impaired Bibi and assisted her by inserting the coin and proceeded to dial the cab company for her. He guided her back and helped her onto a barstool while she waited for her ride.

Bibi indecipherably muttered while she sat, but it became apparent she was angry with some guy slurring, "He can suck my left tit," even though she grabbed her right one.

When the cab came, Jude helped Bibi in the back. Jude asked her where she was going, and she mumbled out her address. She clutched Jude's arm and stammered out a *thank you, honey*. Her lids drooped, and her one eye looked more crossed than usual, but Jude conceded it was because she was drunk. The cab sped away. He watched for a second, grateful he would not be her head in the morning.

Ever since that night—though she never brought it up—Bibi was particularly attentive to Jude and company.

Bibi returned with their dishes. "Enjoy, fellas."

"I want to tell you about this new service to meet guys." Dominick sawed off a piece of his Belgian waffle. "It's called the Confidential Connection Hotline. It's a hook-up line where you record a personal ad, and guys can respond if they like what they hear. I created one," Dominick said as if he had done something dirty. He stabbed his waffle, hacking off another mouthful.

"I can imagine what yours says."

"I gave my description and said, 'Looking for hot guys with big dicks. No fats or fems, please.'" Dominick sipped his Bloody Mary.

"You're too much." A string of Swiss cheese dangled from Jude's fork before ingesting it.

"I'll call you later and give you the number. Try it out." Dominick stuffed a forkful of his Belgian waffle into his mouth. Jude was skeptical, but it roused the horny Scorpio in him.

Chapter Fourteen
The Hotline Goes Cold

When Dominick returned home, he called to give Jude the Confidential Connection Hotline number. Jude acted indifferent, yet deep down, was eager to listen to the personals. He called the number and listened to a few of the ads.

The first guy had a deep Brooklyn accent, which Jude found sexy, so he called. His name was Nick.

Nick asked Jude to describe himself.

"Sounds good. So, you wanna be my bitch?"

"Um, let me get back to you." *Yeah, like I'm going to fly into that spider web.*

The second recording sounded promising but soon deteriorated when the guy said he was looking for a Daddy who would spank him for being a bad boy.

"One more strike, and you're out Confidential Connection Hotline."

The third recording said his name was Chuck and claimed he was a well-built Italian who people said looked like Burt Reynolds.

"Let's hope you mean young *Playgirl* Burt and not present-day Burt," Jude said to himself. Chuck's voice was deep and sexy. After mustering enough nerve, Jude left a message and then laid down to take what Dominick referred to as a *disco nap*. Jude had just fallen asleep when his ringing telephone jolted him out of his slumber.

"Yes, Dominick," Jude answered.

It was Chuck from the hotline. They talked briefly before Jude agreed to meet at Chuck's house around 4 p.m. Hanging up, Connor's eager desire for him to be at Tea Dance scratched his conscience. Determining nothing would come of hanging out with Connor, Jude put his money on *Burt Reynolds.*

Jude surveyed his closet with the precision of Anna Wintour and contemplated an outfit—something alluring but not slutty. He settled on a tight T-shirt, worn jeans, and a red Yankees baseball cap. The night was muggy, but he tied a plaid shirt around his waist in case a chill crept in later.

Apprehension snuck up and gripped Jude as he drove, but it was too late to turn back.

When he arrived at Chuck's, he sat in his car for several minutes, palms sweaty, his heart throbbing. Walking to the door, he felt like a contestant on *Let's Make a Deal.* Jude gambled, passing up a sure thing—Connor —for what was behind his curtain of choice. He would either win a blazing red sports car or the gag prize. With finger shaking, he pressed the luminous doorbell. His heart felt like a sledgehammer banging against his chest. The door opened. Jude's heart pounded out of his chest and fell to the ground. Standing in the doorway was a year's supply of Rice a Roni. Chuck's only connection to Burt Reynolds was his resemblance to Burt's best pal, Dom DeLuise.

A short, cropped beard outlined his moon face while he was balding on top. His message said he weighed 190 pounds—*on Pluto!*

Chuck's face burst into a beatific smile, obviously pleased with Jude's look, while Jude forced a hellish, quivering grin to snake across his face.

"Hello. You must be Jude." Chuck's eyes did an entire body scan as he held out his hand. He escorted Jude in. The house was small and cluttered, filled with clunky wood furniture and knick-knacks everywhere. Dust covered the clutter like magnetic shavings. Jude noticed a stale odor permeating the house as if he had just entered a crypt.

Chuck told Jude to sit. Jude eyed the sofa with its worn plaid cushions. A hole on one exposed the corner of murky-colored foam rubber. Jude lowered himself onto the couch as if he was about to sit on eggs.

"Can I get you a beer?" Chuck asked.

Jude accepted. His mind revved, plotting a way to end the encounter.

When Chuck returned, he sat next to Jude, even though there could have been plenty of space between them. Jude's lips twitched as he accepted his beer. Remembering his flannel shirt, Jude attempted to put it on.

"Don't put that on. I like you without it." Chuck grabbed at Jude's shirt.

"I must. I feel chilled. I have thin blood," Jude said as he pulled the flannel shirt around him.

"Oh," Chuck said, disheartened. "Well, you're hotter than I expected." Chuck broke out with all lustful smiles. Jude nervously sipped his beer as he rested his left ankle on his right knee. He saw Chuck staring at his work boot.

"Wow, you certainly know how to dress to turn me on." Chuck caressed Jude's weather-beaten footwear.

Jude swallowed hard. "What? These old things?"

"Would you like a foot massage?" Chuck asked. If there was one thing Jude did not find sexy, it was feet.

"NO! No, thanks." Jude laughed nervously. "I'm not into the foot thing." He placed his foot back on the floor, fearing Chuck would start drooling.

"Oh, okay. Would you like a body massage?"

"Oh, no…thanks. The beer is fine," Jude said, covering his crotch with the hand holding the beer and keeping his flannel shirt closed with the other, like a prudish old maid.

They had an awkward conversation for a while, and then the subject turned into interests. Chuck asked Jude what he liked to do. Jude told him he liked films, reading, and writing. Chuck clapped. "We're a match made in heaven." *He had the nuptial papers signed.* "I like to write, too."

What were the fucking chances? Jude wished he could take back his words.

Chuck abruptly got up and asked, "Would you like to hear some of my work?" Without waiting for an answer, Chuck went to a cluttered desk overflowing with papers and mail. He rummaged through a drawer and pulled out a file.

Jude didn't really want to listen to his stories, which were—no doubt—going to be terrible, but he thought it would be a good distraction from his work boots *and* himself, so he feigned interest in his writings.

Chuck returned to the couch. "I call this one *Hidden Infection.*"

Oh God. Jude prayed for mercy.

Chuck wrapped up his story, "…stabbing his mother over and over until he was drenched in her wicked, evil blood. He had rid the house of the hidden infection. The End. Whaddya think?"

"I…have no words." Despite the beer, Jude's throat was dry, his voice raspy. Now Jude wondered if the odor in the house wasn't from dead bodies rotting in his cellar.

Claustrophobia entombed Jude. Trapped in the house's maw, he felt Chuck's eyes stripping him naked. He had to act fast.

"Oh. Look at the time." Jude eyed his Swiss Army watch, feigning shock at the lateness of the day, even though it was only approaching five o'clock. There was time to salvage most of Tea Dance if he hurried. Meeting Connor was back on track since *Burt* struck out. He gave Chuck a flimsy excuse about meeting friends and stood up to go. Chuck suggested getting together again. "I'll give you that foot massage." He raised his eyebrows, Groucho Marx-style.

Not in this lifetime. Jude forced another smile. "I have your number. I'll…I'll call." Giving the quintessential kiss-off made Jude feel sorry for Chuck, rationalizing that sometimes people had to hide their unintended cruelty through fake kindness to spare the feelings of others.

At his car, Jude extended his hand, but tenacious Chuck leaned in for a kiss. Jude felt he owed Chuck at least that much and allowed a friendly kiss, but when Chuck thrust his tongue into the hollow of Jude's mouth, he pulled back.

"Whoa, there. Easy, big boy," Jude said.

"Sorry, I got carried away."

Jude thanked Chuck for the beer and story time and sped away from the suffocating pall of Chuck's house and his lusty leers. Jude did not feel good about himself. He hated how he treated Chuck. He was a decent person, and he deserved better. The encounter brought out the worst of his Italian-Catholic guilt, but Jude had to be honest with himself: Confidentially, there was no connection with Chuck.

Chapter Fifteen
Connor: Round One

Stopping home, Jude took a quick shower (he felt tainted by the lustful leers and oppression of Chuck's home) and changed into a thermal undershirt, loose-fitting Khakis, and red Converse sneakers. While dressing, Francine called, asking how the Halloween party was. In turn, Jude inquired about her "girl's night out."

"Great. Always a good time." She kept it brief. The less said, the better to protect her cover.

Jude quickly filled her in on his strange encounter with Chuck.

"What are you doing on one of those dating services?"

"I don't know. Dominick told me about it at brunch today. Curiosity got the best of me."

"More like horniness. You don't need to resort to that shit. Those dating things are for desperate people." Francine paused. "Is there a Confidential Connection Hotline for straights?"

Before heading out the door, Jude grabbed a flannel shirt and tied it around his waist now that the evening air was chilly.

He found a spot on Central Avenue, close to Waterworks. He stopped parking in the lot since some anti-gay hoodlums vandalized several cars, breaking windows and slashing tires last summer.

Shortly after six-thirty, Jude entered Waterworks. With the Tea Dance underway, the bar smelled of beer and cigarettes.

"Hey, Luther." Jude held out a ten-dollar bill, handing it to the doorman—whose skin was as dark and creased as a raisin—for the cover charge. Luther lifted his wool-capped head to get a better look through his wire-framed glasses resting halfway down his nose.

"Oh, hey, baby." His withered hand came out from under his Navajo print poncho, took the ten, and gave Jude a five back. "Enjoy yourself, honey." Luther's smile exposed a few of his missing teeth.

Halfway through the bar, a few of Jude's friends—well on their way to inebriation—cornered him. Eager to seek out Connor in hopes he hadn't given up on him, Jude made a hasty getaway and headed upstairs to the dance bar where "Another Night" throbbed from the speakers.

"Hey, hot stuff," Suzie greeted Jude with her nubby smile. "The usual?"

"Naturally."

"Say, whatever happened to that hot guy you met a few weeks ago?" Suzie began pouring Jude's scotch on the rocks.

"You mean Walter? He moved to the city to become a hot shot model."

"Really? Good for him. He definitely was model material."

"Tell me about it."

An impatient, middle-aged redhead at the end of the bar shouted, "Hey Suzie, a vodka and tonic."

"Hold on, dick wad. Can't ya see I'm busy?" Suzie handed Jude his drink. "Looks like you got another one on the hook." Suzie nodded in the direction of the stairs. "He was asking about you earlier." She gave Jude a wink.

Jude handed Suzie a dollar tip and turned to see Connor McCracken heading towards him; his body tingled with anticipation. The redhead called out to Suzie again.

"I'm coming, jerk off," Suzie shouted.

"Hey, Jude," Connor said. "I didn't think you were coming."

"Oh, something came up, or rather, didn't." He sipped his drink. "You like saying that, don't you, *hey Jude*. That your favorite Beatles song?"

Connor smirked. "No, it's just your name. Did your parents name you after the song?"

"No, I was born a little before that. My mom named me after the saint."

Connor's face was a blank canvas.

Jude cleared his throat. "Where's your entourage?"

"My entourage?"

"Yeah, you know, Lawrence, or as I call him, Mr. Howell, and the rest of your gang, the professor, and Mary Ann?"

Connor burst out laughing. "Why don't you like my friends?"

"Maybe it's because they act like a bunch of snooty Upper East Side socialites. My question is, why do *you* like them?"

"They're nice guys. You just have to get to know them," Connor reasoned.

"Well, they don't make it easy. And what would they think of you talking to me?" Jude's brow furrowed. "They consider me a different species." Jude pushed up the sleeves of his thermal shirt. Jude noticed Connor's eyes zeroing in on his chest, which strained against the waffled patterned undershirt. "Can I get you a drink?"

"Thanks. Bud Lite. But that's what I like about you. You're not afraid to be different. You're a non-conformist."

Jude held out a five-dollar bill to get Suzie's attention. "I just do what I like, dress the way I want. If that's being a non-conformist—"

Suzie came over and took Jude's order.

"Keep the change." Jude turned his attention back to Connor. "You know I always thought you didn't like me because of…" Jude hesitated, wondering if he should bring up Adam.

"Because of what?"

"Well, you know. The night I went home with Adam, I honestly thought you guys broke up. I mean, that's what Adam told me. I didn't expect you to be there, wandering around like the ghost of boyfriend's past."

"We *were* broken up."

Just then, one of the preppy boys approached. It was Donald Grogan, the one Jude called *Elephant Man* because he had such a high forehead. It did not compliment his round, pasty face. Donald gave Jude a frosty glare, but Jude remained poker-faced.

"Where's Lawrence? I thought you were coming out together?" Donald inquired.

"Change of plans. I decided to come out early, so I rode with Reid." His eyes concentrated on Jude.

"Where is Reid?" Donald looked around.

"I think he left."

"Oh. Well, I'll be around. I'm waiting for Lawrence to show up. Stop by if you can tear yourself away." Donald's eyes lasered Jude in half. He walked away, but his indignance hung in the air like a foul odor.

"You should put some powder on that forehead. The disco ball is reflecting off it." Jude shouted, but Zhané's "Groove Thang" muted his words.

Connor spent the rest of the evening talking with Jude, though Jude did most of the conversing. Talking to Connor was like trying to crack open a safe, but his hot looks were the impetus for Jude to keep the conversation going. The occasional glance by Donald and Lawrence revealed impatience and frustration with Connor.

At the end of Tea Dance, Jude impulsively asked Connor if he needed a ride. Connor—luxuriating in a mild buzz—answered in the affirmative and walked out with Jude. They passed Donald and Lawrence.

"I'll see you guys." Connor gave both a quick peck on the cheek. Realizing he was leaving with Jude, their faces contorted into veils of disgust, like two spinster aunts walking in on their favorite nephew masturbating. Jude could not help but flash an arrogant smile and wave.

They drove along city avenues lined with street lamps. Peripherally, Jude saw Connor vacillate between shadow and light. Connor's gaze on Jude remained constant. At a red light on Lark Street, Jude turned to him. "What? Why are you staring at me?"

Like a rock from a slingshot, Connor hurled himself at Jude, grabbing him by the face, and planted a prolonged kiss, welding their lips together and lasting through the red and subsequent green light. A car pulled up behind. The driver honked the horn.

"Get a fuckin' room!" an anonymous voice bellowed as the car drove past.

The light turned red again.

"Wow! Where did that come from?"

Connor's impassioned eyes drilled into Jude's. His face was just inches away. "I just wanted to do that." Connor sat back in his seat.

When the light turned green, Jude finally drove off. "Why now? Is it because you're buzzed?"

"No. I always wanted—you're intimidating."

"What?" Shocked by Connor's words, Jude swerved to avoid sideswiping a car parked on Delaware Avenue. "How am I intimidating? I'm very approachable."

"I found it…you…" His voice disintegrated into zero decibels.

Knowing where Connor lived from the night he went home with Adam, Jude turned onto Magnolia Terrace.

"It's the white house with the green trim," Connor informed Jude.

"Yeah, I remember."

"Oh, right. You were here before."

In front of his flat, Connor asked Jude if he wanted to come inside.

"You don't have any ex-boyfriends skulking around, do you?"

Connor laughed. "No."

Inside, they moved as one entity to Connor's bedroom. The bed's cherry wood posts, with large knobs flanking the headboard, reminded Jude of the one from his childhood.

Connor aggressively tore at Jude's clothes, then his own. They fell onto the bed and tumbled around as erotically charged kisses electrified the room. They explored each other's naked bodies with hands, mouths, and tongues. Connor had Jude on his stomach, and what happened next was a blur to Jude. Connor, performing some Houdini-like feat, had a condom unwrapped, placed upon his eager hard-on, and plunged into Jude in a matter of seconds. Jude didn't have time to prepare for the impalement. It was like a technician who drew blood: With no warning, the upper arm had a tourniquet wrapped around it; the arm swabbed with an alcohol wipe, and the vein pierced in a matter of seconds.

After the initial painful shock, Jude eased into the onslaught. Connor picked up his pace going at Jude with the ferocity of a sewing machine needle at full throttle, his dick throbbing up and down, stitching Jude to the mattress.

In minutes, still face down, he heard Connor gasping for air like a winded asthmatic and collapsed.

Jude rolled over, propped himself on his elbows, and looked at Connor. "Aren't you the sexual titan? You, Simba. Me, raw meat."

Connor emitted an embarrassed laugh. The reserved Connor was back.

"I may need to walk with crutches for a few days."

Connor smiled, leaned over, and kissed Jude. When Jude returned from the bathroom, Connor was already asleep. No cuddling like lesbians, a sarcastic phrase Dominick used for any post-coital affection.

Jude was not sure why Dominick was so cynical about love and affection, especially since it contradicts the time when Matthew Zyskowski broke his heart and reduced him to a puddle of romantic mush in Jude's car one night a few years back. So, it didn't quite make sense that Dominick would think lesbians were more affectionate than gays. But then, figuring out how Dominick's mind worked was not easy.

Jude crept into bed and waited for sleep to come.

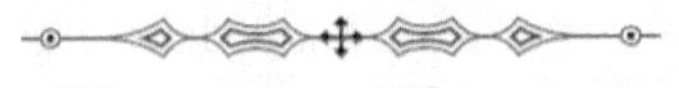

Chapter Sixteen
Connor: Round Two

Around 6 am, Jude woke up. "Where am I?" he mumbled. The throaty rattling on his left brought him out of the mental fog, realizing he was in Connor's bed. Remembering the unexpected turn of events from last night, Jude was still in disbelief that he had sex with Connor, part of the snobby crowd who acted like the upper-level residents of *Upstairs, Downstairs.*

"I had a great time last night," Jude said.

Connor stood silent at the door in his briefs and smiled, his dirty blond hair a mass of disheveled tufts. He exuded a sexiness that made Jude wish he had the day off.

Jude wasn't sure if Connor expected him to say something like, *call me,* or *let's get together again.* Connor didn't offer the suggestions either, so Jude left it at, "Well, I guess I'll see you around."

"Okay."

That's all you have? Jude left perplexed and likened Connor to a William Faulkner novel: hard to read.

***

Jude next encountered Connor the following Friday in early November when he and Dominick went to Oh Bar. Entering, they found a plethora of lesbians. Dominick grimaced at the lack of guys. Atop one of the tables in front of the leather bench lining the wall was a centerpiece consisting of several helium balloons. Gifts, wrapped in an array of rainbow colors, covered the rest of the surface.

Adrift among the sea of women was Connor and Daryl, another of the preppy posse Dominick dubbed *'Reds'* because of his rosacea-like complexion. They were talking to a petite, pretty lesbian with spiked hair and a face delicately painted with makeup. Jude admired her attire. She wore distressed jeans, a white button-down shirt, and a tie designed with van Gogh's *Starry Night.*

If she were a guy, I'd be into him.

Connor caught Jude's eye but did not come over immediately, causing Jude's nerves to wind as tight as a ball of rubber bands. He wondered if Connor had decided that sleeping together was an error in judgment.

"C'mon," he said to Dominick. "Let's get a drink."

"We're staying? There's no dick."

"Connor's here. I need to see what's going to happen with him." Jude pushed Dominick towards the bar.

"I knew you liked him," Dominick said.

A cue-stick-carrying lesbian passed by with two Heinekens, their bottlenecks clamped between her fingers.

"Fierce party, k.d." Dominick snapped his fingers.

First looking perplexed, but then getting the caustic innuendo, she sneered at Dominick. "Fuck you, shrimp."

Dominick laughed at his humor while Jude scolded him. "Don't mess with the lesbians. You want to get us beat up?"

As they stood at the bar, a voice barely audible over the percussive, synthesized sound of "100% Pure Love" whispered like a salutation from another dimension.

"Hey Jude."

Jude turned around; his breath caught in his throat. "Connor." The luster of indigo neon tinted his fair skin and custard-colored hair. His eyes looked glassy. Still, his good looks were on full display.

"What's going on here? Did Melissa Ethridge play the Palace or something?"

"It's my friend Tracey's birthday."

"Oh, the lipstick lesbian you were talking to?"

Connor chuckled. "I didn't know if I'd see you."

Like a switch flicked on, Jude felt a sizzling current of electricity flow between them.

"Gay Albany is not that expansive. You'd see me at some point."

"I meant…you know."

"You mean to have sex again?"

"No. Yes. I mean…" Connor's eyes fluttered in frustration.

"You two lovebirds have fun. I'm going to Waterworks this place is *bor-bors*. Call me." Dominick gave Jude a peck on the cheek.

A lesbian with an ice-white crew cut, wearing a T-shirt that said *Lesbionic Woman,* rushed over and grabbed Connor's arm, announcing they were about to do shots of Patrón, and whisked him away.

"Hang on. I'll be back."

When Connor returned, he proffered a shot glass of tequila and a wedge of lime to Jude. He held up a fisted hand with a clump of salt plateaued between his index finger and thumb. As usual, Connor didn't speak, but he communicated with a drunken twinkle in his eyes.

Jude's fingers hooked around Connor's wrist, and without breaking their gaze, lapped up the dime-size carpet of salt with a seductive lick, threw back the tequila, and sucked on the lime segment. They ordered a round, then another round, yet another, and still, another round, and ended up at Jude's apartment.

Inside the *'Rosemary's Baby'* elevator, Connor latched on to Jude, forcing him against one wall before ping-ponging onto the other side of the elevator in a Technicolor kiss that would have made Elizabeth Taylor and Montgomery Clift jealous.

Inside Jude's bedroom, Connor, with his sleight-of-hand magician skills, disappeared into Jude with his condom-covered dick (thanks to the stash next to Jude's bed) in mere seconds. Jude hung on for dear life as Connor jackhammered him as if he were breaking up concrete. Then, in scant minutes, it was over.

After the sexual storm, Jude returned from the bathroom to find Connor steeped in the bluish tint of a full moon seeping through the window, deep in a dream like the first time they had sex. Turning his attention to the window, Jude studied the luminous orb's pockmarked surface until he drifted off into a dream state.

Chapter Seventeen
Sorry, Wrong Number

Sun replaced the moon. Jude jolted awake to find Connor staring at him—his head propped up in his hand.

"How long have you been awake?" Jude's voice was groggy.

"A little while. I was watching you sleep."

"Really? Why?"

"Couldn't sleep anymore." He kissed Jude. "Have you ever been in love?"

Jude was taken aback and unprepared for such a deep conversation first thing in the morning, especially since Connor barely eked out a complete sentence.

Jude stretched and rubbed his head, contemplating the question. "I don't think so. I had strong feelings for some guys. I thought I loved one once, but it was more infatuation."

"You'd know it if it was love."

"Sounds like you were in love."

Connor stared at Jude. After a long pause, he said, "Yeah."

Jude concealed a grin, thinking Connor was referring to him. He didn't want to risk humiliation if that wasn't the case; after all, Connor didn't know him well enough. *Did he?*

Connor rolled over onto his stomach and supported himself on his elbows. "I remember the first time I saw you. It was in the downstairs bar at Waterworks," he recalled. "You wore overalls with a wife-beater T-shirt and had an LA Dodgers baseball cap on backward. You looked really cute, and sexy at the same time."

"And?"

Connor shrugged.

"Why didn't you come and talk to me?"

"I don't know. Shy, I guess."

"You sure weren't shy in my car a week ago." Jude sat up cross-legged and pulled a pillow over his lap. "Or in bed. You're like a Chinese box. The more mysteries you reveal about yourself, the more enigmatic you are to me. By the way, you still have my cross that Adam left with you?"

"Yes. It's in safe keeping." Connor glanced at his watch and quickly changed the subject as if he didn't want to discuss it. "I have to get going. I have some computer issues I have to tend to at work." Connor crawled past Jude and dressed.

"Ah, you're an IT guy?"

"Yup." Connor pulled his T-shirt over his torso.

"Hmm. Another piece of the Connor McCracken puzzle revealed." Connor grinned.

When Connor finished dressing, Jude suggested exchanging numbers. "It would be nice to do something outside the bars and bed."

They swapped numbers. Connor absentmindedly stuck the paper in his pocket. "Call me."

"Or you call *me.*" Jude forced a retaliatory smile.

Connor went in for a quick kiss. Jude leaned his brief-clad body against the doorjamb, crossing his arms and ankles. Inside the *'Rosemary's Baby'* elevator, Connor waved.

"Next time, maybe you can return my cross," Jude called out as the sliding door closed.

A few days later, Jude decided to call Connor, but he got his answering machine. Jude was somewhat relieved because he had nothing to say and hung up. Conversing with Connor face to face was enough of a struggle (at least he could fill the void looking at him), so it would be even more of a struggle over the telephone.

Several days passed, still without a call from Connor, and with the sun ablaze, adding to the explosion of endorphins in him, Jude decided to give Connor another call. If he got his answering machine this time, he would leave a message asking him out to dinner, putting the proverbial ball in Connor's court. He'd have to respond—or not—but Jude had to find a solution—for better or worse—to Connor McCracken.

When he dialed, he got a strange busy signal. He checked the slip of paper and punched in the numbers and again got a rapid busy signal. On a third attempt, and getting the same result, a nervous jolt ran through Jude's body, the kind of jarring kinesis you experience running into your ex for the first time after the breakup and seeing him with a new boyfriend.

Jude's body, first shaking from rattled nerves, soon switched to indignance. What the hell kind of game was Connor playing? And why was he allowing Connor to torture him?

Chapter Eighteen
The End of the Beginning

Jude and Dominick enjoyed a good laugh critiquing the early Saturday night crowd upstairs at Waterworks. Worthy of particular criticism was the lanky guy with a bowl cut, wearing just a pair of nylon running shorts and knee-high white socks.

"Why, Tina, why?" Dominick said, quoting *Mommie Dearest* as he often did.

"That's not appropriate summer attire, let alone for mid-November." Jude's eyes were transfixed, but beyond the tall figure scantily clad in nylon, something else caught Jude's eye: Connor McCracken at the top of the stairs, followed by Tracey, the lesbian he wished was a guy and Lawrence Gillespie. Jude's pulse raced with both anticipation and apprehension.

"Oh shit." Jude turned his back to Connor, twisting Dominick with him. "There's Connor." The onslaught of his presence unleashed an adrenalin rush, causing Jude's heart to beat like a percussive war cry. With no call from Connor since they exchanged numbers, Jude didn't know what to expect. He dragged Dominick to the far wall with a long shelf strewn with plastic cups and empty beer bottles.

"I thought you liked him?"

"I don't. I do. I don't know," Jude said in frustration. "Connor's hard to figure out. I get the feeling he likes me, but he doesn't come out and say so. He's like a journal with no key—I can't read his innermost thoughts. I get the feeling he only talks to me when he's buzzed and wants sex."

"Why don't you tell him how you feel?"

"*What?* Are you crazy?"

Dominick said, "You better think of something." His eyes shifted over Jude's shoulders and flashed a puckish smile at Connor.

"Hey, Jude." Connor's eyes appeared glassed over again. A peek of white undershirt was visible under the Tartan plaid button down.

"Hey, yourself."

Dominick informed Jude he was going to get a drink.

"I thought I might have heard from you since we exchanged numbers. You forget how to dial a phone?" Jude tried to sound light and comical but still make his point.

"Did you forget how to leave a message? I saw that you called." His voice drawled from a fermented mix of alcohol and chewing gum.

Damn caller ID. That never crossed Jude's mind.

"I tried calling again to ask you to dinner but kept getting a busy signal. What gives?"

"I moved. My phone wasn't connected."

Jude felt a sense of relief like the first time you see your ex, and the guy he's with is not a new boyfriend but a gay cousin from out of town. "You didn't think to tell me you were moving?"

He paused. "You could have left a message the first time." Connor's eyes drooped.

"You could have called me back," Jude touchéd in the verbal sparring match. Without warning—like the night at the red light—Connor lunged at Jude and kissed him. Jude attempted to resist the kiss, chalking it up to the alcohol, but the wrecking ball force of Connor's lips broke through his defenses and allowed the kiss to linger. Connor backed Jude up against the wall, their lips never parting. When Jude opened his eyes, the dots of light from the mirrored ball spun in rapid succession, lending a hypnotizing sexiness to Connor's face. Jude felt like his head was in a sex fog, probably from the scotch *he* drank. Connor pressed his hand on Jude's chest and went in for another aggressive kiss. Connor's pheromones mingled with the intoxicating scent of scotch and spearmint. It was Kryptonite to Jude, rendering him helpless against Connor's assertive advances.

In a weakened state, Jude asked, "You want to come home with me?"

Connor looked over to Tracey and Lawrence. "Okay," he absentmindedly responded as if he was asked to go get coffee.

A nocturnal glow saturated the bedroom. Connor was silhouetted against the window, sitting atop Jude. With the speed of a magician's trick, Connor rolled Jude on his stomach, had a condom on, and was thrusting into Jude like he was on fast forward. The scotch Jude drank helped dull the pain, but his senses let him know this, unlike the previous sexual sessions with Connor, was not particularly enjoyable.

Tonight, it felt like Connor was drilling his way to China. Jude didn't know if Connor's aggression was a matter of heightened sexual energy or if he was releasing some pent-up hostility on Jude's sphincter. All he knew was Connor was fucking like a man just released from solitary confinement. And just like that, as usual, it was over.

When Jude returned from the bathroom, Connor was, yet again, fast asleep, as evidenced by the rumbles escaping through his lips. The pattern was now apparent to Jude.

An exasperated Jude got into bed. He decided this was another negative checkmark in the plus/minus columns he mentally kept about Connor. Jude had overwhelming doubts about a future with him. He stared at the shadows on the ceiling, listening to the pops of breath passing through Connor's lips. Jude turned on his side, not knowing what to make of Connor McCracken, before letting a sleepy tide wash over him.

Chapter Nineteen
The Hotline Goes Cold Again!

Despite the fiasco of meeting Chuck and things not working out with Connor, Jude's curiosity and hormones got the best of him, and he answered another ad. His name was Steve. His voice was smooth and sensual. They arranged to meet later at Barnes and Noble.

Jude arrived first and got a bitter-tasting coffee from the café. When Steve arrived, it was apparent he did not live up to his description either, except in his myopic vision, given the thick glasses that magnified his eyes. He looked like the subject in a Margaret Keane painting. The slouch of his shoulders on his frail frame indicated he wasn't exactly truthful about working out. Steve confessed he was married and had kids.

"Why are you on the Confidential Connection Hotline?"

"I was from a generation where you buried your desires for the same sex and got married and raised a family. Now my kids are grown. I've been curious about men my whole life, and now I want to scratch that itch."

Being married allowed Jude to gently let Steve down.

"Well, I'm sorry, but I really don't feel comfortable being the *"other man,"* which was not true. Jude had been with several married men, engaged men, and men with girlfriends; it didn't matter. If they were looking for a hookup and Jude was interested, he gave them his incontrovertible attention, but with Steve, the hotline delivered another disconnect.

"I understand," Steve said.

"Have you ever been to a gay bar?"

"Oh no. But now I'd like to go."

Jude gave him the names of the gay bars around town. "Does your wife know about your desires?"

"Oh, she may suspect." Steve pushed up his glasses, animating his eyes.

"There's no shame in being gay. It would help if you were honest with your wife. You owe it to both of you."

Steve continued to quiz Jude about gay life as they finished their coffees.

At the end of their encounter, Jude wished Steve well. Jude felt he should have charged Steve fifty dollars for the hour-long session but was happy to give him the advice for free.

Steve thanked Jude for taking the time to meet with him. They shook hands and parted ways. Again, Jude felt a crushing guilt for rejecting someone based on looks alone. Jude hoped for personality *and* a physical attraction from the Confidential Connection Hotline. But the Hotline short-circuited his connections. *That's it. No more chance meetings with people without knowing what they looked like.* The image their sexy-sounding voices created was a powerful aphrodisiac; the reality of meeting in person was a dose of saltpeter.

On the other hand, Dominick had a different experience with the Hotline, which could have been disastrous.

Chapter Twenty
He Ain't Heavy, He's My Sister

Dominick called Jude a few days later and said he had to talk to him. He asked if he could come over to his apartment.

Jude returned from the kitchen with another round of gimlets. He sat next to Dominick, placing their drinks down.

"So, what did you need to talk to me about?"

"Don't judge me. I did something foolish." Dominick's usually cheerful face was shrouded in despair. He sat on the edge of the couch, his legs jogging from nerves as he stared at Jude with sad, gibbous eyes, trying to free the words vaulted in his throat.

"And?" Jude threw up his hands in suspense.

"I had unprotected sex with someone from the Hotline." It wasn't like Dominick to be so reckless, but Jude knew that even with the threat of AIDS, people still were careless sexually, so he would help his friend deal with it.

Typical of Dominick's often politically incorrect humor, he made flip remarks about AIDS, referring to HIV as *hi-five,* or on Sundays, before Tea Dance, he announced he had to take an AIDS (replacing *disco*) nap.

"If we didn't laugh, we'd cry," Dominick responded when Jude asked how he could constantly make jokes yet be so consumed by the subject.

Jude inhaled and looked out his tenth-floor window. Twilight was settling over the city.

"Who was the guy?" Jude asked.

"His name is Ben. I went to his place, not expecting much, but he was really nice and nice-looking. So, we talked and started doing shots of tequila. He assured me he was negative—"

"You never believe horny guys."

"I know. I know. I was stupid drunk, and I let Ben fuck me."

Jude saw Dominick was visibly shaken and didn't want to make him feel worse.

"I fear getting AIDS and dying before my parents. I don't want to be the cause of that kind of grief for them again."

"Again? What do you mean again?" Jude wasn't sure if it was the gimlets or if Dominick wanted to unburden himself from some tormenting secret, but he opened up like a lotus flower.

"I had a younger sister, Gabrielle. We called her Gabby. She was killed by a drunk driver when she was twelve."

The approaching buzz Jude was already feeling from the vodka vanished like lit flash paper.

"Her death devastated my parents. My father and mother cried for weeks. It wasn't a good time for my family." His voice was weak and distant, as if speaking from another dimension. As anesthetized by Dominick's serious, never-before-seen side, Jude was equally sorry to hear about Gabby.

"We were very close and would have grown up even closer. I would have been able to tell Gabby anything, especially that I was gay, unlike anyone else in my family. So, you see, if I ever contracted AIDS, I wouldn't know how to tell my parents."

"AIDS isn't a death sentence anymore," Jude assured Dominick.

"It would be to my parents. It would break their hearts. I couldn't put them through that pain again."

Jude realized all Dominick's joking about the subject was a sheath, a way to entomb the dread within him about the disease, and looked at his friend with bitter irony. His heart plummeted to a dark place, imagining one of his best friends might have contracted HIV.

"Okay. So tomorrow, you make an appointment to get tested."

Dominick sat like an anxious leopard, waiting to pounce. "Will you come with me?" His voice was pleading, vulnerable.

Jude was reminded of when he and Dominick bonded, the night the seed of their friendship—or sisterhood, as Dominick called it—germinated. Jude first met Dominick when Matthew Zyskowski brought him around, though he didn't hang out with Dominick until Matthew broke Dominick's heart.

Like most guys caught in the gravitational pull of Matthew's orbit, Dominick fell for him. They met at Waterworks. Newly out and naïve and set in motion by Matthew's charismatic spell, Dominick's head swirled in an emotional twister of embryonic gay love. That was until the night he saw Matthew out with Winn Galarneau. The sight cut a swath through Dominick's heart. It was his Molly Ringwald moment from *Pretty in Pink* after Blane broke his prom date with her.

Jude spotted Dominick outside Waterworks on that chilly January night. They settled into Jude's Altima, and as Dominick poured out his heart about his love for Matthew, the car transformed into a confessional minus an imposed penance—just some sound advice Jude gave him about guys and love in the gay world. Like a warm blanket, Jude's words enveloped Dominick. It was that poignant moment when he took Dominick under his wing.

"Of course, I'll come with you."

"You're a good sister." A half smile cracked the veneer of Dominick's stoic face.

"When you call me *sister,* doesn't it make you feel bad about Gabrielle?"

"No, it comforts me because you're like her in a lot of ways."

Jude was so touched he wanted to cry but didn't want to make a melancholy scene sadder.

"Yeah? That's nice. I'm glad." Jude hugged Dominick. "Just don't ask me to braid your hair."

Chapter Twenty-One
High Anxiety

The next day, after work, Jude drove Dominick to his doctor. The lengthy wait in the sterile examination room gave way to a brief encounter with the physician assistant, who took his vitals before drawing Dominick's blood.

"We'll have your results in three days."

"Three days!" Dominick bellowed as the PA left the room.

The woman behind the counter reviewed his paperwork. Her dark complexion was the antithesis of the color drained from Dominick's face. She looked at him over her half-glasses with sympathetic eyes. "You'll be fine, honey." As she accepted his co-pay, an encouraging smile bowed her lips.

"Thanks." Dominick returned to Jude in the waiting room, white-faced. "I have to wait three days before I get my results."

They walked through the parking lot in silence. In Jude's car, Dominick exploded. "Three days!" he shouted. "How am I going to survive? The anxiety will kill me. It's enough to turn me celibate."

"Now, don't go putting the chastity belt on yet. Look, you made a careless mistake. Learn from it. You're probably fine. Think positive."

Dominick scrunched his round eyes into slits and glared at Jude.

"Sorry. I mean *optimistically*." They broke out in laughter. "Seriously, Dominick, I'm sure your test will come back negative."

Jude's tender ministrations for Dominick made him feel like a big brother—or sister, as Dominick would insist—instead of a close friend. For all his crude humor, Dominick was a vulnerable softie at heart.

For the next three days, Jude was like a human Prozac tablet, constantly calming Dominick, who called him at work no less than a dozen times a day.

"Go have a couple shots of vodka," Jude suggested.

"It's only ten in the morning."

"Mix it with orange juice. I have to go now. Duty calls. We'll do something tonight after work."

Later that evening, they went to Quintessence for dinner—Italian night.

Dominick took his fork and knife and cut into his chicken Parmesan with a vengeance.

Jude acknowledged Dominick's violent attack on the cutlet. "Any harder, and you're gonna cut through your plate."

Ignoring Jude as he swallowed, he declared, "Nasty. You can't get good Italian food outside a real Italian restaurant."

"I'm happy to see your anxiety hasn't killed your cynicism."

Dominick jittered as if he was sitting in a vibrating chair. "This waiting is killing me."

Jude motioned for Arliss, another member of the iconic Quintessence staff, who hobbled her way over. Arliss always walked with a stagger, and for the longest time Jude and company thought she drank on the job, but learned from Bibi that she had one hip higher than the other. Because of the preconceived notion that she drank, Dominick, long ago, dubbed her *Drunks*.

"Bring him another Long Island iced tea and a martini for me, please."

"I'm buzzing from the one I had."

"I'm trying to sedate you."

On day two, the calls continued. By mid-afternoon and the eighth call from Dominick, Jude tamped down his annoyance. He imagined the situation reversed. How would he react if he had to wait for an AIDS test result?

"Just one more day. Let's go bowling tonight. I haven't bowled since my days in the gay bowling league. It'll be cathartic for you. You can take your anxiety out on the pins," Jude said.

On Friday, day three, Jude anxiously called Dominick. "Call me the minute you hear."

At four p.m., as Jude entered his cubicle, his phone rang. He pounced on it like a cat chasing a mouse. Jude didn't even get a chance to say hello. Dominick's booming, singsong voice resonated through the receiver.

"I'm negative!" Jude pulled the phone away from his head, saving his eardrum from bursting like an over-inflated balloon. He imagined Dominick doing his notorious can-can kick whenever something good happened.

That night, they celebrated. First, they hit Oh Bar and then Waterworks. At the end of the evening, an inebriated Dominick asked if he could crash at Jude's. Naturally, Jude obliged. Stripping down to their briefs, they fell into bed.

"Thanks for bein' there for me," Dominick said sluggishly. "I really dodged a bullet."

"Yes, you did, and may I suggest you stay away from loaded guns going forward?"

After two sleepless nights, Dominick's snicker turned into snorts of a well-deserved, deep sleep.

Chapter Twenty-Two
Pre-Pube-Essence

"**D**akota's opening is this Saturday." Chickie's voice vibrated over the phone's speaker. "He figures more people will be around because of the holiday."

"Really? That soon?" Francine handed Jude a glass of Riesling.

He took a sip and returned to cracking open a crab leg for the quiche they were having for dinner.

"Will you be able to go, or are you going to Florida for Thanksgiving?" Chickie's voice buzzed.

Francine shivered at the thought. "No. I'm spending it with Jude's family." She opened a package of Swiss cheese and began to grate it. "Um…if you want to drive with me..." Francine stopped grating the Swiss cheese. Jude detected hesitancy in Francine's voice.

"Thanks, but I'm not planning on staying too long at the opening. I'm going to my sister Joan's in Middletown from Hudson. It's my nephew's first birthday party the next day."

"Oh, that's right. I forgot about that." Francine returned to shredding cheese.

"Okay then, I'll see you at the gallery."

"Bye, Chickie. Love you."

Jude fractured a crustacean claw, extricating the meat as Francine disconnected the call.

"The Saturday after Thanksgiving? He thinks like us gays."

Fran bristled. "Here we go with the gay thing again."

Jude chuckled. "No, I mean that's the same reason we homos like going out on Thanksgiving weekend, lots of fresh meat in town for the holiday."

"I love it when you talk like a barbarian," Francine said, opening a pack of Gruyere cheese.

Jude chopped the crabmeat into chunks. "I think I'll drive down to the gallery myself just in case it's boring and I want to leave. After all, the bars will be hopping."

"Good idea," Fran's voice sounded too eager and quickly added, "I know you can't live without your nights at the bars."

***

On Saturday, Jude got ready for Dakota's gallery opening. Though his body was smooth, he trimmed below the belt, his usual grooming habit every two weeks. Jude liked cropping down south. He felt wild, unruly pubes appeared like someone had Phil Spector's head in a leg lock. Jude got in the habit of giving himself a crotch crew cut a few years ago after he hooked up with a guy he went to grade school with.

James Natel and Jude became best friends in sixth grade. They hung out after school every day. James went over to Jude's house and flexed his biceps, which had developed enviable peaks for a sixth grader. Watching James flex sent undecipherable jolts through Jude's maturing groin. James told Jude he could build his biceps by lifting the side of his bed ten times every day. As he demonstrated, Jude's eyes were receptors of James' athletic aesthetics, sending tingling sensations throughout his body. The feelings were foreign, but he soon learned he was experiencing his first male crush.

It devastated Jude when James moved and the two lost touch, so when he walked into the State Street Pub a few years back, a seductively dark bar with a plethora of wood and window on the corner of State and Lark, the two had an amorous reunion.

"I'll be damned! Jude Giacolone!" James broke out in a sugary smile.

Jude examined him in his tank top. "Still lifting your bed every night, I see," he said as he felt James' biceps (they appeared to have tripled in size since sixth grade). Even in the dimly lit pub, Jude saw he still had that all-American, clean-cut good looks about him. Now, post-puberty, his baby face matured into strong angles still visible through the five o'clock shadow, his dark brown eyes veined with gold.

James laughed. "I progressed to real weights. And look at you. You must have followed my bed-lifting advice." James examined Jude.

"I did. Now I go to a real gym, too."

"Well, it shows."

"Back in sixth grade, I lifted my bed every night, like you showed me, hoping to impress you. After all, you were my first crush," Jude confessed.

"Really? I was your first crush? You knew back in grade school you were gay?"

"Well, I didn't know about being gay or straight. I just liked what I saw staring at you."

After several drinks during their mutual admiration reunion, Jude was sitting in James' hunter-green BMW. *Someone has money.* Jude learned that James had inherited the family plumbing business after his father died over a year ago.

Inside James' plush apartment, he offered Jude some cocaine.

"Oh, no thanks, I turn into a slobbering fool with coke. I prefer alcohol." Jude remembered the first and only time he tried cocaine. His throat was so numb he thought he was going to drown in his saliva. Instead, he just drooled in front of his friends like a senile old man.

James proceeded to do several lines of coke. He also made some very potent White Russians with vodka he bought during a recent trip to Moscow. They ended up on James' king-size bed. When Jude pulled down James' boxers, he was taken aback by the stubbly patch surrounding his enormous erection, standing like a mighty oak in a field of freshly mowed grass. He had never seen such neat pubes. The gay in Jude found it incredibly sexy; the neat freak in him, hygienically tidy.

The next day, Jude took scissors and an electric razor to his *field* and *mowed* it down to a nice, short swath worthy of a golf course green. Jude has continued the practice ever since.

Jude hoped for a lasting relationship with James, but over time, Jude realized James was too heavily into drugs, and within the year, he learned James had died from an overdose. Though Jude came to realize James was not boyfriend material, it saddened him to hear of a childhood friend dying before his time, needlessly, because of drug abuse.

Chapter Twenty-Three
You Can Take Manhattanites Out of New York…

After primping and preening, Jude put on a grey Lycra T-shirt. Over it, he wore a blazer with a tiny checkered pattern he bought from the Gap, especially for the occasion. Jude completed his look with faded jeans, black combat boots, and his trademark baseball cap. He chose a Boston Red Sox hat to piss off any obnoxious New Yorkers up from the city.

His look was appropriate for an opening: casually sophisticated yet sexy enough in case there were any hot prospects among the crowd. *Dakota?* Recalling his failed Confidential Connection Hotline encounters, he'd see the goods this time before deciding to purchase. The CCH meetings were all returns based on false advertising.

When Jude arrived at the gallery, he saw a modest crowd, though he did not see Francine among them. There was definitely a New York City vibe, and Jude suspected several Manhattanites were among the crowd. As Jude passed by clusters of mostly black-clad guests, he heard snippets of their phony intellectual babble.

"Have you seen the Lucian Freud exhibit at the Met? His work borders on the brilliant and the grotesque. I presume his grandfather would have had a field day psychoanalyzing his work," a pretentious older gentleman with grey, straw-like hair said, cackling at his humor. His skin was crazed, like an aged painting. "You must check it out," he added.

An elegant, dark-skinned woman in a purple pleated turban and a paisley pantsuit was gesturing with the dramatic flair of a silent film star to a group of other women. Her large gold disc earrings were flailing to the point Jude expected them to fly off like metallic Frisbees.

Another matronly woman with grey, braided hair that hung— snakelike—to the middle of her back was munching a cheese-covered cracker as she examined the artwork. Standing directly in the ray of a glaring halogen bulb, Jude saw her rumpled face caked with makeup, filling in the wrinkles like spackling, concealing the cracks in a fractured wall. Though he delighted in her character, Jude sensed a sadness about her that wiped away his cheeky grin.

Jude enjoyed observing the people more than he did Stephano's paintings, which were nothing but still lifes and landscapes done in a style too pedestrian for his taste and certainly not worthy of a gallery opening.

Jude made his way towards the back of the gallery for some wine. He passed the cube-like pedestals topped with sculptures of squat, abstract human forms.

Through the crowd, Jude spotted Dakota talking to a young woman with a bad posture. *If she keeps that up, she'll be ringing bells at Notre Dame.* Compared to the rest of the chic crowd, she seemed out of place in her boring navy blue cardigan over a white button-down shirt. The thin strip of her fish-white knees separated her dull, grey skirt from the dark, knee-high socks. Jude watched as she fixed the barrette, holding one side of her lusterless, stringy hair away from her face. She looked ready for class at Catholic school instead of an artsy affair.

As for Dakota, he exuded the chic style of an art gallery owner in cuffed jeans, a starched white shirt, and a black blazer. He folded his shirt's cuffs over his jacket's sleeves and pushed them midway up his sinewy forearms. He wore his enviable blue-black hair pulled back in a ponytail.

Dakota's eyes beamed like fireballs spotting Jude. Excusing himself from the mousey thing, he greeted Jude. "Hello, there." He gave Jude a hard squeeze. "I'm so glad you could make it to my opening." Jude inhaled a whiff of sandalwood, activating hormonal awakenings. His heart bounced as if on a trampoline.

"I wouldn't miss it." Jude looked around. "Have you seen Fran?"

"No, but I'm sure she'll be here soon. Perhaps she's coming with Chickie. Come, let me introduce you to the artist of these splendid sculptures." Dakota placed his hand on Jude's shoulder and led him to the drab-looking, cardigan-clad waif. "Jude, this is Libby Larsson. Libby, this is Jude, a new-found friend of mine." Dakota now wrapped his arm around Jude's shoulder, pulling him close, turning his groin into the epicenter of sexual tremors resonating through his body.

Libby spoke in such a whispery tone Jude barely heard what she said. Her handshake was as limp as her hair.

"I was admiring your sculptures. They're very distinct. They have an Art Deco yet abstract look to them," Jude said. "It's a unique combination."

Libby giggled, shrugged, and mumbled something inaudible. Her cheeks turned red as apples as if he had commented on her virtually non-existent bosom.

Applause broke out, and there, in the doorway, was Stephano, the featured artist. He made a grand entrance in a flowing black cape. His blond, gelled pompadour poked out of the beret he wore like a sculpted piece of art. He walked through the gallery as if a newly crowned Miss America, throwing kisses to some people along the way as he continued through the gallery. It was an entrance fit for a queen, and Stephano fit the bill to a T.

"Well, hello again, handsome," he said, air-kissing Jude on both sides of his face. "Darlin'," he addressed Dakota. More air kisses. "I can tell it's going to be a spectacular night. I'm thrilled to see so many people here, especially the New York crowd."

Dakota introduced Stephano to the sculptress.

"You're the artist of these sculptures?" Stephano scrutinized Libby with incredulity. "Well, you certainly can't judge the gift by the wrapping paper, can you?" A high-pitched laugh escaped his throat.

Libby's sotto voce words went unnoticed.

Stephano waved his hand in the air. "I'm in desperate need of some wine," he said and sashayed over to the bar, his cape unfurling like a flag in the wind.

Chapter Twenty-Four
Things That Go Bump in the Night

As Francine was packing an overnight bag (she was planning to stay overnight at Dakota's), her telephone rang. It was Chickie.

"Hi, Chickie. What's up?"

"I'm afraid I'm not going to be able to go to the gallery opening."

Disappointment filled Francine's voice. "Oh no. Why not?"

"My sister is frantic trying to prepare everything for Jason's first birthday party. She asked if I could come down earlier than planned and decorate for the party while she went and did some last-minute shopping for party goods, so I'm heading down to Middletown now." In the background, she heard rustling. "What's all that noise I hear?

"Sorry. I'm packing an overnight bag," Francine said.

"An overnight bag? Why do you need that?"

Francine hesitated, then blurted out like a guilty Catholic in the confessional. "I slept with Dakota."

"What? When?"

"A week after Jude's birthday party."

"How did *that* happen? And I'm just finding out about it *now?*"

"He invited me down to see his gallery and then took me out to dinner. We went back to his apartment and slept together, but I couldn't tell you because he made me keep it a secret. He didn't want to look like he was playing favorites, showing me his gallery first," Francine confessed.

"Was he uncircumcised like he said?" Chickie's curiosity was piqued.

"Now, why would he lie about that?"

"Did you see it up close?"

"It was dark, and he had a condom on before I could see anything," Francine added.

"So, how was the sex?" Chickie was like a virgin asking the school slut about doing the varsity football team.

"It was…brief."

"Brief?"

"It was about as long as a Madonna song. I'm hoping for a longer encore, so I'm going prepared."

"Well, let me know how it goes this time."

"I will. Stay tuned. Have fun at the party tomorrow. Bye, Chickie."

***

Around 8 pm, Francine headed down to Hudson. For the occasion, she wore a black silk blouse with a few buttons undone for a hint of cleavage—not that Dakota needed a hint since he already saw the goods—and designer jeans with a high-heeled boot. She went bold with a cherry red lipstick and even highlighted her hair earlier in the day.

She hit a bump at some obscure, non-descript point on Route 9. At first, she thought she had run over some nocturnal creature, but the continuous thudding forced her to pull into a deserted parking lot. Upon examination, she found her front tire spread flat as if suctioned to the ground like a snail.

"Fuck! Fuck! Fuck!" she shouted. "Of all the nights…" Panicking at first, she looked around, and thankfully, she saw a pay phone. Gravel crunching under her feet sounded louder than usual, given the silence of the desolate area. She dug in her purse for her Triple A card and some change. She took out a quarter and dialed the number for roadside assistance.

"And what is your location?" the dispatcher asked robotically.

"My location?" She had no clue. "East Jesus, New York. How do I know?" Her sarcasm went unnoticed.

"You'll have to be more specific than East Jesus, New York, ma'am. I'm not familiar with that town." The voice was flat, like her tire.

Flustered, Francine looked around and saw the business of the parking lot she was in. "I'm in the parking lot of the Everything Old Antique Shop."

"Located where, ma'am?"

"Oh my God! What am I, a road map? I'm on Route 9, heading into Hudson and in the parking lot of the Everything Old Antique shop. That's all I know."

"Okay, take it easy, lady. Our truck will be on the way. Do you have a flare that you can light?"

"A flare? Yeah, I keep one in my purse next to my tampon."

Again, sarcasm not acknowledged. "Okay. If you can light it, that will help our man spot your car.

Francine shook her head and hung up.

***

The throb of Annie Lenox's version of "Downtown Lights" was piped in over the sound system Dakota installed. Dakota led Jude to the bar.

"Let's get a drink. I have something I think you'll like." He pulled out a bottle of Glenfiddich. "Just for you, hoping you'd be here." He poured two glasses. "Cheers." The knocking of their plastic glasses made a dull clunk. Dakota never broke eye contact with Jude, who was aware of the stare.

"C'est bien?" Dakota asked.

"Mmm. Very."

Reassured, Dakota pulled Jude a little closer, causing more below-the-belt tremors. He led Jude along the wall with Stephano's paintings.

"What do you think of Stephano's work?" Dakota asked.

"It's very good." Jude fibbed—no, lied. "Better than his showgirl performance at my party," which was not a lie.

Dakota laughed. "Agreed."

Jude looked toward the front entrance. "I wonder where Francine is. I thought she would be here by now."

"I'm sure she will be here soon. Perhaps she is coming with Chickie."

"In the meantime, would you like to see some of my paintings? I can show you my apartment as well," Dakota suggested, remembering Francine's proclamation that Jude would be impressed.

"I suppose." Jude glanced towards the front of the gallery again. "Perhaps we can tell Libby to be on the lookout for Fran and let her know we're upstairs."

"Good idea." Dakota and Jude stopped to give Libby Francine's name and a description of her.

"Let her know where we are, and we'll be down shortly," Jude instructed.

Libby mumbled something incoherent.

Dakota freshened their drinks in their faux crystal-looking plastic glasses. Taking the bottle with him, they headed towards the stairs. Weak beams struggled to light the narrow hallway.

Inside his apartment, Dakota flicked the light switches. Daylight intensity flooded the apartment. Jude squinted with the sudden assault of brightness. When his eyes adjusted, he looked around, absorbing the expanse and falling in love with its character.

"Wow! What an amazing space. I'm jealous."

Dakota approached, placing his arm around Jude's neck as they strolled the apartment. "The former owner, an architect, designed it. I did some cosmetic things and gave it my personal touch."

"We share similar tastes."

"I'll bet we have more in common than you think." He gave Jude a quick jostle as a burgeoning smile unfurled his lips. "Come let me show you my paintings." Dakota guided Jude to the abstracts and explained their meaning.

"Wow, I totally love the symbolism," Jude said.

"Do you?"

"Yes, and the color schemes are so evocative."

Dakota beamed, staring at Jude. He replenished their glasses and suggested they sit on the sofa. He dimmed the lights and played Julia Fordham's "Falling Forward" CD, then removed his sports jacket and tossed it on the arm of the couch.

"Good choice," Jude said.

"Oh, you like Julia Fordham? Make yourself comfortable."

"Very much. She has a distinct voice and writes great lyrics, very poetic." Jude took off his jacket and tossed it over the back of the sofa, leaving him in his short-sleeved Lycra T-shirt.

"Someone works out," Dakota had a little lust in his tone.

Jude was a little embarrassed. "I do what I can."

"Whatever you're doing, it shows." Dakota settled into his spot and draped his arm on the back of the sofa, his hand inches from Jude. "So, tell me about Jude," his fingers tapped Jude's shoulder. "We didn't get to talk much at your party."

"What do you want to know? That's a broad question."

"Tell me about your family."

"I'm Italian—Giacolone—can't get any more Italian than that. My parents are characters. My mom is very religious *and* superstitious. She'll rub the fur off a rabbit's foot with one hand and the sheen off her rosaries with the other."

Dakota laughed as he grabbed Jude's shoulder, squeezing it.

"She's the nervous type. My dad owns a barbershop and is the antithesis of nervous. He goes through life like he's under mild sedation, always smiling and laughing. He's a cross between Chauncey Gardiner and a hyena."

Again, Dakota laughed. "That's quite a description. You're very amusing."

"I have one brother. He's a musician and an artist—"

"An artist? Really? What kind of work does he do?"

"He mostly does oil paintings. He'd love your trilogy. He does these really cool pastel paintings of these odd-shaped vessels, some still lifes, some abstracts. He's very talented. And he's colorblind."

"What! And he paints? That's amazing. I need to take a look at his work. Perhaps I could show his work in my gallery."

"He'd love that. He does a lot of art shows, especially the annual Stockade Art Show in Schenectady. He won best in show last year."

"He sounds gifted."

"Yeah, he's the gifted one, alright," Jude smiled.

"Oh, you must have some gifts of your own." Dakota moved closer toward Jude as he removed the elastic band from his ponytail. His long hair fell like silk curtains around his face.

Jude felt his heart jitterbugging. "I do like to write. But then again, my brother also writes. He's got a way with words. It's enviable."

"I'll bet you're good at it, too."

"I have a different style. I hope to write a novel someday, the great American gay novel."

"I'll be the first to buy a copy. I bet you're gifted in *other* areas as well."

Inquisition painted Jude's face.

Dakota's eyes were strobe lights, hypnotizing Jude. He turned Jude's baseball cap around and went in for a seductive kiss.

After the initial shock, Jude's mind spun like detritus in a cyclonic spiral. He surrendered, body and soul, to Dakota's soft, pliable lips. Jude's mouth followed in the sensual dance of their prolonged kiss.

"Now, there is something you're gifted at," Dakota said, staring into Jude's transfixed eyes.

"What's that?" Jude said as if in a dream.

"Kissing." Dakota leaned in for another kiss, which intensified. His tongue swabbed around Jude's mouth and lips. He pressed Jude down into the leather sofa. After some time on the couch, Dakota broke away. "Why don't we take this to my bed?" He stood, pulling Jude off the couch. With arms entwined and hands grasping their clothing, they lumbered to the platform bed, their lips super-glued together the entire way. They fell upon the bed, their garments jettisoned like cloth shrapnel. When Jude removed his baseball cap, Dakota said, "No. Keep it on. And put your combat boots back on, untied."

"But your sheets. They look expensive."

"They're just sheets."

Jude obliged and pulled on his cap and boots. Dakota pulled Jude down, wrapping his arms and legs around his body like octopus tentacles snaring its prey.

Things continued to heat up until a conflagration of sexual lust consumed the bed. Dakota pulled a condom from under his pillow, ripped it open with his teeth, and rolled it down Jude's erection.

"Definitely Italian," Dakota said, getting on all fours. From behind, Jude grabbed his long hair, pulled it like the reins on a horse, and pushed into Dakota.

"Oh God! Most *definitely* Italian."

Fueled by Herculean stamina, they morphed through several positions, ending with Dakota straddling Jude, a lubricious smile plastered on his face. Taking Jude deeper, Dakota bounced like a cowboy on a bucking bronco until reaching his climax, his semen jettisoned on Jude like an oil spill, triggering Jude's explosive orgasm. They lay among the smoke and ash of their extinguished carnal firestorm.

"I may never walk normally again." Dakota was breathless.

As he regained composure, Jude faced a dilemma. *How will I tell Fran Dakota is gay?*

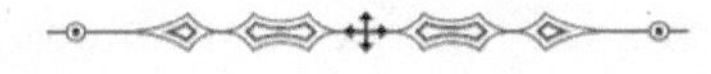

Chapter Twenty-Five
What Goes Up, Must Come Down

As the cigar-chomping mechanic from Triple-A finished bolting the spare tire to Francine's car, she signed a form and thanked him before getting into her car and continuing down Route 9 to see if she could salvage anything from the evening.

"Hopefully, there will still be people at the gallery," she muttered, turning on the radio. She blithely sang along to Alanis Morissette's "You Ought to Know."

Around 11:30, Francine parked her car on Warren Street, a few doors from Dakota's gallery. As she approached, she could see several people through the large windows. Inside, her eyes searched for Dakota. Everyone stood clustered like berries except Libby Larsson, who was alone, pulling a piece of lint off her sweater as Francine approached.

"Excuse me. Do you know Dakota?"

Libby nodded, giving a barely audible, "Yes, I know him. Are you Francine?"

Barely catching her name, she said, "Yes, I'm Francine. Is Dakota around?"

Libby uttered something that only a dog could hear.

"I'm sorry, I didn't hear you." Libby strained Francine's patience.

Libby repeated herself, though not much louder, but Francine could make out the word *upstairs.*

"Thank you." Rolling her eyes, she left Libby, who returned to scrutinizing her sweater for pilings.

Francine fumbled up the stairs in the dark, hearing the faint strains of music. Francine knocked on the door and waited. She knocked harder. After no response, she turned the doorknob and entered.

"Dakota?" she called out, but k.d. Lang's "Sexuality" blared from the speakers. Francine headed towards the platform bed, where clothes in the faint light lay randomly scattered as if a dryer had exploded. She tiptoed through the kitchen. A flickering, yellowish glow from the bathroom reflected off the stainless-steel cabinets.

In the bathroom doorway, Francine saw Dakota and another person kissing in the oversized bathtub.

"That should be me," Francine mumbled softly, disheartened before anger took over. "Well, isn't this a cozy sight!" Her voice rose above the music.

A startled Dakota and the now recognizable Jude faced Francine.

"Fran!" They shouted in unison.

"What are you doing here?" Dakota asked, stunned. "You…you should have knocked."

"Well, I did." She approached the bathtub. "But apparently, you were too wrapped up in each other's arms to hear. YOU!" She pointed at Jude. "Sneaking behind my back!"

A stunned Jude asked, "What? What are you talking about?"

"Maybe you should change your name to *Judas*…or *Brutus* or some other back-stabbing son of a bitch!" Her voice cracked. She was on the verge of tears. "I come down here and find *you* in the bathtub I hoped to be in. Traitors! Both of you!"

Jude saw rage envelop Francine's face through the candle's glow, turning it scarlet.

"Oh, and maybe you boys have been in the water long enough. Looks like you're both a little *shriveled*." Francine's eyes darted below the deep, clear pool in the tub. "Better yet, stay there. I hope you both drown." She stormed out.

Jude was frantic and reached for one of the bath towels. In the process, he almost knocked over the lit candles. He wrapped the towel around him and ran after Francine, leaving a liquid trail behind him.

He followed her down the narrow stairway, almost tripping. When Jude reached the gallery entrance, Francine was slamming the front door. The people still there looked towards the door in bewilderment.

"Oh, look! A male stripper!" Stephano shouted with glee, catching sight of the towel-clad Jude, dripping wet. Stephano applauded, walking towards Jude to get a better look. He pulled out a five out, ready to stuff it into Jude's toweled waist.

When Libby turned to see what Stephano was referring to, her eyes widened. "Well, hello there!" she shouted, clear as a bell.

***

Jude returned to Dakota's apartment and gathered his clothes. "What the hell just happened? Why is she so pissed?" Jude stopped short of pulling his T-shirt over his head and approached Dakota, wrapped in another towel. "Did you sleep with Fran, too?" His eyes registered disbelief.

"Yes, I did." He spoke as if it was common knowledge that he slept with her.

Jude tugged his T-shirt down. "Oh my God! What the hell were you thinking having sex with both of us?" Jude yanked up his jeans.

"I was just being friendly," Dakota rationalized.

"*Friendly!* Friendly is making your neighbor a Bundt cake or brownies, not passing your dick around like free Jell-O shots at happy hour."

"I don't know why you're making such a fuss. Chickie said Fran was hoping to make a connection."

Jude was beginning to really hate the word *connection*.

"I gave her what she wanted," Dakota rationalized.

"Knowing Fran, she was probably planning her wedding while you fucked her." Jude searched for his boots.

"Oh, I'm not the marrying kind."

"Obviously."

"Why don't you get undressed and come back to bed." Dakota dropped his towel. "See? I'm all hard again." Dakota went in for a hug, but Jude broke the embrace.

"Didn't we all get what we wanted?" Dakota said. "Fran's a big girl. She'll get over it."

"You egotistical son of a bitch," Jude shouted as he pulled on each boot, leaving them untied. "You know nothing about friendships, and given Stephano's work, not much about art, either." Grabbing his baseball cap, Jude exited Dakota's apartment, leaving him alone with his now deflating erection.

Chapter Twenty-Six
Sunday, Bloody Mary, Sunday

"Fran, talk to me," Jude pleaded into his phone. It was the zillionth time he called throughout the morning. "I had no idea you slept with Dakota. I only found out when he admitted it after you stormed out of his apartment. I didn't know you were hoping to see him again." Jude paced. "You should have told me. We don't keep secrets as big as that. We tell each other everything." He paused, hoping his explanation would register and she'd pick up. "Fran?" After no response, Jude shouted, "Fuck you. I didn't know." He disconnected the call and slammed the phone down.

Moments later, Jude's phone rang. He eagerly picked it up. "Fran?"

"The whore is finally home." It was Dominick.

"Oh, it's you."

"Don't act so thrilled."

"I'm sorry. I thought you were Fran."

"I left a message earlier thinking you were still at your trick's house."

"I was going to call you back. I need several Bloody Marys. Let's go to Quintessence."

"What's wrong?"

"I'll tell you over brunch."

Half an hour later, Jude met Dominick, who was already at the bar. Arliss, the off-kilter server, took them to a table in the back.

"Drunks," Dominick whispered. Jude elbowed him in the ribs.

"Can I start you off with a drink?" Arliss asked.

"Yes!" Desperate for alcohol, Jude ordered a Bloody Mary.

Dominick ordered the same. Arliss wobbled to the bar to put their order in.

"How was it out last night?" Dominick asked.

"I went to Dakota's art opening, remember?"

"That was last night?"

"Hello? What have I been telling you all week?

"How was it, bor-bors?"

"I ended up having sex with Dakota."

"Small dick?" The foremost question asked by Dominick whenever Jude slept with a guy. "Is that why you're upset?"

"It was a perfectly fine penis, though you probably would have disapproved."

"Get out! Nasty." Dominick dismissed Dakota's penis, sight unseen, with a snap.

"But then Fran burst in and found us."

"She walked in on you having sex?"

"No, we were in his tub after the sex."

"Did you cuddle like lesbians, too?"

Arliss tottered over, causing tiny back-and-forth tsunamis in the beverages on her tray.

"Don't spill any, honey." The cacophony from the brunch crowd drowned out Dominick's words. "Why is Fran so upset about you having sex with Dakota?"

"Because unbeknownst to me, she slept with him and was hoping to see him again. I tried calling her a dozen times, but she doesn't answer, or return my calls, so fuck her. She should have told me she slept with Dakota…"

There was a pause in their conversation as Arliss placed the drinks on the table and took their orders before tottering away.

"I've done all I can. It's up to Fran." Jude took a hefty sip from the first of four Sunday brunch Bloody Marys.

Chapter Twenty-Seven
Connor: Round Three, TKO'd

After dismissing Dakota as a potential boyfriend, Jude tried calling Connor in early December for one last chance at redemption. This time Connor failed to keep dinner plans—plumbing issues—Jude decided he couldn't waste any more energy on him. With only a few enjoyable sexual interludes, sleeping with Connor became mundane and, most recently, painful. Things with him came to a dead stop. Jude concluded Connor fucked like a Midwestern farmer merely doing his husbandly duties. It was hard to muster emotion for something that never fully started, like a car that wouldn't turn over. His adorable, good looks weren't enough to fuel the empty gas tank any longer.

There still was the matter of his cross.

Jude was surprised when Connor answered his phone. "Hey, do me a favor. Next time you're out, bring my cross with you." Jude's message was curt.

"I don't always think to wear it."

"You don't have to wear it. There are things on your pants called pockets. Put it in one." Jude hung up. Agitation caused his heart to pump as if he had run a marathon.

On Saturday night, Jude showed up at Waterworks. His eyes were like searchlights seeking out Connor. He didn't have to look far. Connor was at the bar.

"Do you have my cross?"

Connor turned, startled. "Oh, hey. Why are you so angry with me? I thought we had a good thing going."

"What?" Jude's face was a contortion of incredulity. "What are you talking about? We had a trio of sexual encounters, each about as memorable as Madonna's acting career, well, except for *Evita* and *A League of Their Own.* You didn't even care if I got off. The only time we see each other is in the bars or bed. Getting to know how you feel is like, like—"

Connor went in for one of his lethal kisses. Jude pushed back. "No! Not this time, Connor. You're not going to seduce me with your kisses. You're too much work. I can't figure you out."

"I'm an open book."

"Written in Russian!" Jude's voice reached a crescendo. "Do you have my cross?" Jude's tone was thoroughly aggrieved.

"No."

Fire ignited Jude's eyes.

Speaking with controlled rage, Jude said, "Why not?"

"I forgot it." The defensive plea sent the cadence of Connor's voice an octave higher.

"I. Want. My. Cross. *Back!*"

"Okay. Okay. I'm going to brunch tomorrow. Quintessence. If you go, I'll bring it then."

"I'll be there. One o'clock." Jude stabbed his finger into Connor's chest. A sad, puppy-dog look spread across Connor's face. Jude wondered if he was too harsh. *No,* he had enough. He tamped down his anger, which would explode like a solar flare-up if left to its own devices. The glare on Jude's face sent Connor slinking off downstairs.

Chapter Twenty-Eight
Sip. Swallow. Stare

Despite Dominick's late night with a guy he met through the Confidential Connection Hotline, Jude coerced him into going to brunch. Jude said he'd pick him up.

After letting Jude in, he watched Dominick return to the bathroom, where he worked a dollop of gel into his hair with the precision of a sculptor.

Approaching one o'clock, Arliss, the human *Leaning Tower of Pisa,* tottered through the dense Quintessence brunch crowd, leading Jude and Dominick to their table as Jude scanned the sea of faces for Connor. Arliss sat them at a table in the back. She took their Bloody Mary orders and made her way to the bar.

"He better show up."

"Are you sad things didn't work out with Connor?"

"No. He frustrated me to a breaking point. He was like that one clam that, no matter how long it steams, won't open." Jude fluffed his napkin and placed it on his lap. "So, tell me about your hot date."

"Big dick."

"And?" Jude said with ennui.

A sinister smile snaked across Dominick's face. "I let him fuck me," he said in a hushed tone.

"*What!* I hope you used protection this time. I don't want to nurse you through that waiting game again."

"Yes, we were safe. I learned my lesson. But I really like him, too. We're going out again."

Arliss's tilted body looked like a walking gyroscope as she leveled a beverage tray in her hands. She placed the Bloody Marys down and took their orders before tottering away.

"You're turning into a big ol' bottom, you know that?" Jude swizzled his celery stalk in his Bloody Mary.

"No, I'm not." Dominick laughed defensively.

"What? How can you say that? At the rate you're going, you'll be begging to stay awake during your colonoscopy," Jude said a little too loudly.

Dominick spluttered Bloody Mary through his nose.

The proximity of tables in the claustrophobic dining space made it impossible not to hear Jude's crass remark. A woman at the next table with straw-like hair pulled back in a messy bun put down her forkful of omelet. Like two rifle barrels, her eyes shot a scornful, spinster look at Jude. But another frightening sight approaching grabbed his attention.

Lawrence Gillespie loomed over Dominick and Jude, his bloated bulk stuffed into a navy blue suit, like the grey one he wore the last time they saw him at brunch in October. A fleshy double chin spilled over the collar of his shirt.

Jude's eyes narrowed in microscopic scrutiny. He picked up his Bloody Mary.

"Why Lawrence. I thought I smelled Paco Rabanne and polyester."

Lawrence bristled. His dark blue eyes squinted in a dueling staredown. They seemed sunken in his chubby face like two blueberries squished into a pound of dough. With nothing but stubble for hair, it dawned on Jude that Lawrence resembled one of those cherubic-faced, rubber baby dolls from the 60s, minus the cutesy smile.

"What do you want?" Jude asked. Sip. Swallow. Stare.

Lawrence dangled a chain as if someone dipped it in arsenic. "I believe this thing is yours."

Lawrence dropped it in Jude's palm, rubbing his fingertips together as if to flake off the contamination.

"My cross." Jude shook his head. "And why couldn't Connor give it to me?"

"He wasn't feeling well. He asked me to deliver it." His tone was odious.

"Oh, suffering from a bad case of the chicken shits, is he?"

Jude heard the woman next to him slam down her fork.

Lawrence threw his nose in the air with such a trajectory Jude thought he might have snapped his neck. *Wishful thinking.* He turned to walk away.

"Nice suit. Two-for-one sale from Men's Warehouse?" Dominick's voice dripped with sarcasm. Lawrence flipped Dominick the finger without looking back.

"Being friends with that pompous ass is reason enough to end things with Connor." Jude caught the woman with the animated face of a Disney villainess staring at him again.

"Oh, did you catch all that? Better than watching *Days of Our Lives* with an all-gay cast, isn't it?"

The harpy harrumphed with embarrassment and returned to her omelet and home fries.

Keeping his eyes fixed on her, Jude picked up his Bloody Mary. Sip. Swallow. Stare.

***

The following Sunday, as Jude walked through Washington Park, Dunkin' Donuts coffee in hand, the familiar warble of *hey, Jude* bellowed in the distance. Despite the radiant sun melting a powdered sugar coating of snow and the baby-toothed bite in the December air, the words caught Jude off guard, freezing his blood. *Connor.* Over the past week, Jude's anger, once burning supernova bright, flickered out, leaving a ghostly trail of disintegrated indifference. After all, his cross was back from hostage hell, so he decided to be civil. He turned as Connor pedaled his mountain bike up to meet him.

"Hey, Connor. I see you recovered from your illness." *Okay, there's a bit of residual resentment.*

"Did you get your cross back?"

"Yes, thanks. Hand-delivered by Thurston Howell III." The remark caused Connor's lips to bend slightly upward.

"Do you still hate me?

"I don't hate you. I mean I did for about five minutes, but nothing Prozac and a vodka chaser couldn't cure. As the Edith Piaf song goes, *no regrets.* But take some advice from another songstress and learn to express yourself, will ya? You're like a bionic coconut. You're hard to crack open."

That got a more significant laugh. "Okay, I promise. So, uh, remember our conversation—"

"We had a conversation?" *Snide but funny.*

"The one about being in love? I hope someday you know what it's like. I was there once, and it felt really nice, but it didn't work out. Probably my fault—"

"Mmm. Probably." *Be nice.*

"Edith Piaf was wrong. It's my regret, but life goes on, and maybe

I'll find love again, but whoever it is will always be second place to the one that got away."

Jude swallowed hard as if he ingested a pit that lodged in his throat. *Is he referring to me? Adam? He didn't know me well enough to say he loved me. Did he?* Nevertheless, a blush clotted Jude's face.

"Well, I better get going." Connor wheeled his bike closer to Jude, leaned over, and placed a light kiss on Jude's mouth. "See ya."

Jude was stunned—tasered by Connor's words. He watched him ride away, getting smaller and smaller until Connor turned around a bend in the road. He was gone as if Jude had witnessed a mirage.

Chapter Twenty-Nine
Merry F'ing Christmas

After his breakup with Connor (though to Jude, it wasn't much of a breakup when there was not even a foundation to build upon), Jude once again put up a gate around his heart. He indulged in a couple of one-night stands. One, named Barry Young, was, in Jude's estimation, a real cutie, but at twenty-one, was *berry young.* Enamored with Jude, he left his telephone number and encouraged Jude to call. Jude threw it out after Barry exited.

Jude informed the other, Trevone, a hot Black man (but not as hot as Walter), also on the rebound from a disastrous split from a year-long relationship, that he was just looking for sex, to which Trevone said, "Good, we're on the same page."

After their torrid, lengthy bout of sex, they shook hands like business associates sealing the deal, and Trevone left.

A few days later, Jude's co-worker, Rosalie, stopped by his cubicle at work.

"I just had a bizarre call." Her elfin face was a portrait of consternation. "Someone from Telecommunications phoned. He thought he was calling the office in White Plains. I told him it was the Albany office, and he said he thought our phones were to be disconnected as of today. When I asked why, he hung up."

"Shit. That's not a good sign." Jude called Verna and Wilma into his cubicle.

Jude and the three women worked together for the last two years of his eight years with the company on a New York State pilot project marketing an Empire Blue Cross low-income HMO. Recently, the project reached its target ahead of schedule.

"I think today's the day we're going to be axed, girls. We're on the Titanic, and there's no room in the lifeboats."

"It's Christmas time. Are they heartless?" Verna asked.

"Yes, Verna. HR is the Grinch before he got one," Jude said.

Wilma smoothed her pixie cut, a reflexive habit when she was nervous.

"Corporate sycophants." Rosalie couldn't hide her disdain. "Sycophants!"

At 11:30, Jude's telephone rang.

"Hello, Jude. This is Donna Meyers from Human Resources. Can you come to my office, please?" Her tone was cheery and bright. Jude did not respond; he just hung up.

"This is it girls. I got called down to HR. The bitch sounded like she was inviting me for Christmas cookies and eggnog."

In her office, Donna offered Jude a seat. She sat down with professional stiffness, her hands folded in front of her. Her beady eyes were the antithesis of the painted-on twinkle in the ceramic Santa's eyes behind her.

"Well, this is never easy." Donna let out a dramatic sigh.

"Oh, you HR types," Jude joshed with false modesty. He cleared his throat and sat upright, leaning forward. "Let me make it easy for you. You're sorry, but you're terminating me. Having such a valued employee here at Empire Blue Cross has been a pleasure, but blah, blah, blah."

The beady eyes bulged. Donna retracted her non-existent chin into her neck, wrapped in a Christmas scarf. Her face hardened as she took a pen from a Santa boot pencil holder, a termination letter, and a release form and shoved them at Jude. "Sign by the 'X,' please," Donna spoke with clipped words.

"What am I signing?"

"A statement that you accept Empire's termination policy and won't take legal action against the company. If you don't sign, you forfeit your severance package, which is your bi-weekly salary, for the next four months, plus your three weeks' vacation pay, which will carry you through the end of May." Donna's smile dripped with vengeful glee.

Jude spotted Rosalie and Verna walking past Donna's office with two other HR representatives. Rosalie flashed him a mischievous smile. Jude signed the release form, nearly cutting through the paper, and whipped it at Donna. *His* smile oozed antagonism.

"Fine. Now, if you will hand over your security badge, I'll have someone escort you to your car."

"My things are upstairs."

"You can make arrangements to pick them up."

"You're kidding?"

Donna stood up and arched her back. "I assure you I am in earnest."

"My coat is at my desk. The keys to my car *and* apartment are in my coat. I can assure *you* in earnest, I'm not leaving without them." Jude felt heat rise in his chest and singe his face to a Christmas red.

"Well, this goes against protocol. You'll have to be escorted." Donna went to the door. "Arlene!"

Arlene, the stout, apple-cheeked Administrative Assistant, approached.

"See that Jude gets his things and exits the premises *immediately.*"

"Do you want a box for your things?" Arlene asked flatly, obviously having been in this position before.

"Thank you. That would be nice." Jude looked at Donna. At least someone in HR has compassion. Arlene and Jude began walking down the corridor.

Donna took umbrage at the remark. "Ten minutes, Arlene!" Donna barked in frustration, clutching her Christmas-scarfed neck.

In the elevator, Jude asked, "Why are people in Human Resources so phony? Present company excluded."

"They're nothing more than corporate shills. Management pulls the strings, and they react like obedient puppets. It's a thankless job."

Back at his desk, as he was gathering his things, Wilma entered his cubicle.

"Are you safe?" Jude asked, nearly done putting his possessions into the box Arlene gave him.

"Yes, and I feel so guilty."

"Don't." He finished boxing the last of his things. "I'd feel terrible if they let you go after all the years—twenty years—you've been with the company." He hugged Wilma and put on his coat.

"Good luck, Jude."

"Merry Christmas, Wilma." Jude picked up his box and exited his cubicle for the last time.

Wilma smoothed her hair.

***

Francine would have been the first person Jude called to say he lost his job, but they still weren't speaking, so Jude called the auto repair shop where Dominick worked.

"Meet me at Oh Bar after work. I could use a little *happy* in my happy hour.”

At five o'clock, Jude put on his Carhartt jacket and took the *'Rosemary's Baby'* elevator to the lobby. Walking to Oh Bar, a thick December snow began to fall, dotting the landscape like an impressionistic painting. Though the snow and the white lights coiled around the lampposts on Lark Street gave off a Christmassy vibe, Jude did not feel in the holiday spirit at all.

Entering Oh Bar, Jude saw a sparse crowd. He immediately saw Mickey Flynn, the hot, handsome bartender with whom he had a brief May-to-July relationship.

Shortly after, Dominick blew in with the wind and a flurry of snow and quickly found Jude at the bar. Flakes, like crystalized dandruff, soon melted on the shoulders of his navy blue overcoat.

“What's up, Judith? You sounded so stressed.”

“Corporate office Pearl Harbored me and the girls I work—worked with. We lost our jobs.”

“They laid you off at Christmas?”

“They have no heart.”

“What are you gonna do?” Dominick asked.

“I don't know. I didn't see this coming, so it wasn't something I planned on happening.”

“You'll get another job.”

Mickey approached wearing a leather vest, exposing the divide between his meaty pectorals and the crevices scoring his abdominals. A lustful flash traveled from Jude's brain to his groin, like a lightning bolt slashing the sky, knowing his hands, mouth, and tongue once traveled the delicious topography of Mickey's body. The leather armband around the expanse of his bicep looked like it would burst apart with one inadvertent flex.

“Hey, sexy.” Mickey's eyes, fixed on Jude, gleamed.

“Hey, yourself.” Jude gave Mickey a wry smile.

“Haven't seen you in a while. Still single?”

“What's it to you?” Jude's smile was ironic.

“Just asking. You shouldn't be.”

“You're right. I shouldn't be.” Jude stared unapologetically. Mickey's face revealed a hint of shame, telling Jude he had inadvertently opened an old wound.

“I'm kidding, Mick. It's all good. Blood under the bridge.”

Mickey shook his head with a half-hearted laugh. “What'll you guys have?"

Dominick ordered a Corona.

"Scotch with lime."

"Some things never change." The corner of Mickey's lips curled into a semi-smile.

"And some things change over time." Jude noticed a thinning patch in Mickey's sandy blond hair in the mirror behind the bar before he went to get their drinks. Jude kept his eyes glued on Mickey. *Still handsome. Still sexy.*

"He's so hot." Dominick practically drooled. "Too bad you guys broke up."

"Don't remind me."

Jude's mind wandered back to when their mutual passion exploded like a firework.

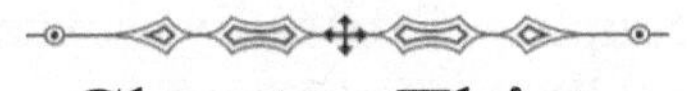

Chapter Thirty
Oh Mickey, NOT So Fine
May – July 1990

At six feet one, with a build to induce uncontrollable drooling, his rugged face, and aquamarine eyes, Jude couldn't deny Mickey's Irish good looks.

Jude sensed an attraction on Mickey's part as well. They often chatted at length in the bars. Jude always made him laugh with caustic humor, poking fun at people in the crowd.

A few years ago, on a humid Saturday night at Waterworks, Jude was talking with Mickey, wearing a tank top that looked spray painted on his body, showcasing his muscled torso. Jude tried not to stare at the rounded contour of his deltoids, the thick veins running through his biceps, or his mountainous pectorals crowned with nipples poking at the fabric of his clinging shirt.

"Vogue" blasted through the airwaves. Jude searched for a distraction to take his eyes off Mickey's body.

"See them, Voguing?" Jude pointed to a few guys and a girl he dubbed *Cafrankles* because she looked like an 80s version of Connie Francis with her black, teased-to-Jesus hair and her virtually non-existent ankles.

"Look at them, trying to be so cool, but they really look like they're spastically swatting at flies," Jude said.

Mickey burst into spontaneous laughter and leaned into Jude, who felt his rock-hard body.

Indeed, someone as hot as Mickey would never consider going out with him, so Jude buried his feelings for Mickey, fearing his fragile inclination toward rejection. So, he was coy about his attraction. Sometimes, Jude felt Mickey was doing the same, but it wasn't a risk he was willing to take, so there was this cat-and-mouse playfulness between them.

Then, on that hot night, it changed. Mickey said it was too warm in the bar and told Jude he had to leave, bidding him good night, and he left. From behind, Jude felt someone jostle the brim of his backward baseball cap. He turned to see Joey *"Buffalo"* Santiago, a Hispanic hottie Jude had a couple of friendly sexual flings with. Jude nicknamed him *Buffalo* because the first time they engaged in sex, Joey backed up to the foot of the bed when he was about to orgasm.

"Where're you going, *Buffalo?*" a bewildered Jude asked.

"You'll see."

When Joey climaxed, his semen jettisoned the length of the bed, past the headboard, hitting the wall with an audible *splat.*

An astonished Jude propped himself on his elbow and said, "If there's ever an Olympic event for orgasms, you'll be a gold medalist."

Tonight, Joey was playing Dolly Levi for Jude and Mickey. "Why aren't you leaving with him?" he asked. "It's obvious you guys like each other. One of you has to make the first move."

"I didn't want to be presumptuous."

"Go after him." Joey encouraged. "Be bold." He nudged Jude. "Go!"

After hesitating, Jude cut through the Saturday night crowd, hoping to catch Mickey. Working his way down the narrow stairway, he felt like a salmon swimming upstream against the current influx of people heading in the opposite direction. Halfway through the downstairs bar, Jude saw Mickey exit.

Outside, the night was sultry. The air was heavy with moisture, reaching an explosive saturation point. Mickey was spotlighted under a streetlamp, engulfed in a hazy white aura, compliments of the misty humidity, his Irish skin, and his white tank top. He glowed like a sexy, gay angel without the feathered wings.

Jude caught up with him. "Hey, Mick."

A combustible smile exploded on Mickey's face. A gleam in his eyes flickered to life.

"I was, um…wondering…if, um, you'd…if you'd…"

"Go home with you? Yes, I would. I've only been waiting six months for you to ask me."

Astonished, Jude said, "What? Why didn't you ask *me?*"

"Fear of rejection."

Look at that. We already have something in common.

"There's just one thing you should know. I'm HIV positive."

"Oh." Jude was nonplussed. "I appreciate your telling me. I respect your honesty, but it doesn't change my mind. I still want you to come home with me. I'm sure you're not the first person I slept with who has AIDS." *Here's hoping you'll be the last.*

"A little birdie told me once when your name came up in conversation that I would never meet a nicer guy than you."

"And they were right," Jude smirked.

Mickey gave Jude a playful nudge with his elbow.

As they headed down Henry Johnson Boulevard, the clouds released their pent-up fury in a furious downpour. The rain's force hit Jude and Mickey like liquid pellets. By the time they reached Jude's building half a block away, they were drenched. They laughed down the corridor, leaving watery trails from the deluge on the speckled marble floor.

Inside Jude's apartment, they took their soggy clothes off and hung them over the shower rod. Jude swallowed hard, watching Mickey undress. Jude swooned with Mickey-mania, drinking in his emerging nakedness. *Am I going to wake up and realize this is just a dream?* They dried themselves off, and the sudden touch of Mickey's big arms, trapping him in an embrace, smacked Jude back to reality. Despite the cool dampness of their skin, Jude felt the fevered heat in Mickey's body, igniting his sexual firestorm.

Tangled in each other's arms, they shambled to Jude's room and tumbled onto his bed. They writhed and shifted in fevered kinesis, exploring each other's bodies with heightened sensual delirium.

"Have you got a condom?" Mickey's question was urgent.

Jude reached over to a silver box and grabbed one from the variety he acquired over time from all the gay bars that doled out free prophylactics like straight bars offered bowls of peanuts and pretzels.

"Aren't you obliging?" Mickey's mouth curled in a delightfully wicked smile at the speed at which Jude produced one.

"I'm like a Boy Scout. I'm always prepared." Jude ripped the foil with his teeth, Neanderthal-style. He lowered himself onto Mickey, whose strong arms squeezed him in an aggressive grip, but his translucent eyes held Jude's gaze with submissive surrender. With cobra-like intensity, Mickey wrapped his tree trunk thighs around Jude. He pushed into Mickey, slow at first, but became more aggressive as Mickey's pleasure with the increased vigor was apparent.

The lengthy, rigorous sexual workout eventually brought Mickey to a climax, followed shortly by Jude's eruption. He collapsed onto

Mickey, panting.

Lying in bed after cleaning up, Mickey held Jude in his arms. "Could you see yourself going out with someone with HIV?"

"Of course."

"Could that someone be me?"

"If we were in high school, I'd swear you're asking me to go steady." Jude slid his hand up the back of Mickey's arm, where Mickey's tricep was too big for Jude's palm.

Mickey laughed, throwing his head back on the pillow.

"But if you *are* asking, the answer is yes." Jude leaned over Mickey and placed a kiss on his lips to seal the deal. "It's official. We're going steady."

"Do I get a ring?"

"I have a cock ring, does that count?"

Mickey let out a guttural laugh and wrapped Jude in his arms, compressing Jude until he thought his eyes would pop out.

With Mickey in his bed and his fluttering stomach, Jude felt as if a grenade with the pin pulled out exploded within him, sending feelings of newfound love coursing through his veins.

Jude rolled over on his back. "For some reason," he said, "I feel like a Connie Francis song should be playing in the background."

***

The following morning, after minimal hours of sleep and a quick bout of morning sex, Jude and Mickey went to brunch at Quintessence, where a haggard-looking Bibi walked with a deliberate pace as if she would shatter like Baccarat crystal if she moved too fast.

"I could use a few of these myself." She placed two Bloody Marys down. "I should know better than to get shit-faced when I have to work the next day. I'll put your orders in, fellas." She tottered away in slow motion, rubbing her temples.

"That was quite a workout you gave me last night. It's been a while since I had such intense sex." Mickey sipped his drink and stared at Jude with lamplight eyes.

"It's the Italian Scorpio in me." Jude hesitated, toying with the celery stalk in his drink. "If you don't mind me asking, how long have you been HIV positive?"

"It's going on two years."

"Two years? Well, you look great."

"I'm really happy last night finally happened" Mickey admitted. "Here's to new beginnings." They raised and clinked their Bloody Marys.

"Me too."

***

Several weeks into their relationship, while nestled on Jude's couch, Mickey informed him he accepted the managing position at Oh Bar. Mickey thought it was cause for celebration and suggested dinner at Justin's. For Jude, it was time to call Hospice. *Prognosis: relationship with Mickey terminal.*

"Great." Jude's sentiment was unconvincing.

"What's wrong? You don't seem happy for me," Mickey said.

"No, really, it's great. Congratulations."

Wearing Jude down, he opened up like the prosecution's star witness. He broke from the security of Mickey's embrace.

"I know how bartenders operate. They're like celebrities. Everybody wants to *do* them. I know. I've done a few."

"Is that what you think? I'm going to be having sex with all these guys?"

"Well, look at you. You'll be like Jesus in the desert surrounded by all these temptations coming on to you, and no offense, I don't think you have Jesus' willpower."

"Don't you trust me?"

Jude stared into those sparkling green pools of Mickey's and wanted to say *yes* and mean it, but the words one bartender told Jude after the boyfriend walked in on them rang in Jude's mind like a death knell: *He knows it's a perk of the job.*

"Yes, I trust you," Jude said, trying to convince himself. "It's those devils in the desert I don't trust. Guys are going to flirt with you and it will take just one to bring down your defenses faster than the walls of Jericho."

Mickey offered up a lighthearted laugh and folded his arms around Jude. He could see the disconsolate look in Jude's eyes. He kissed his forehead. "You're the best thing to happen to me. Why would I mess it up? Trust me. I'm yours."

Jude's facial muscles pulled his lips into a forced smile. But the threat nagged at Jude like a constantly poking finger at his subconscious. Out there was a Hitler, and Jude's heart had *Poland* written all over it.

"Tomorrow, we'll go to Justin's and have that pecan-encrusted rack of lamb you're always talking about."

The following night over dinner, Jude wasn't sure if it was the two martinis, or if he was merely acquiescing to trusting his hot boyfriend working as a bartender, or both, but a calm settled his jangled nerves as if he were in the eye of a hurricane. But with all hurricanes, that momentary tranquility didn't last long, and the storm surged again in the remaining dog days of summer.

***

On a Sunday at the end of July, when Jude returned home after seeing *Wild at Heart* at the Spectrum Theatre, Mickey was sitting in the kitchen wearing only his briefs. He didn't care for films. *Jaws* was the last film he saw. Jude swallowed hard upon hearing that. "That was nineteen seventy-five." A skeptical look wandered onto his face. "Thank God you're pretty." So, Jude went to the Spectrum alone while Mickey slept.

"Hey, sleeping beauty."

"How was the film?" Mickey's voice was hollow.

"My least favorite David Lynch film." Jude kissed the top of Mickey's head. He tensed.

"What's wrong? You look like you accidentally killed someone."

Mickey cupped his head in his hands and then blurted it out. "I…I had sex with someone Thursday night." His lamplight eyes went dark.

It took a moment for those words to sink in. When they did, it was like rattlesnake fangs puncturing Jude's soul. He felt nausea rise within him and explode in a fiery rash across his face.

"You *what?* You said I could trust you." Jude's voice sounded injured. He inhaled. He didn't want to play the victim, so his words were strong and vitriolic this time. "You Fuck! You said I could trust you!"

Mickey stood. His near-naked Greek physique would not blindside Jude, frozen in his spot.

"I'm so sorry. I fucked up." Mickey's face twisted in grief. "You're the last person I wanted to hurt."

After absorbing the initial blow, Jude trembled with rage. "Don't flatter yourself. I'm not hurt. I'm angry." Jude threw a fist into Mickey's bicep. It felt like punching a brick wall. Jude bit his lip to hide the painful impact.

Mickey's eyes begged for understanding. "It didn't mean anything."

"You sound like the Old Faithful of cheating clichés, spouting one every few seconds. Sorry, but we are officially *un*-going steady. You're dead to me."

Mickey's heavy brows arched, his face contorted in bewilderment. "You don't mean that."

"Well, unless I'm into necrophilia, I most certainly do."

"I'll make it up to you. Trust me. Please give me another chance. Don't give up on us."

"Another eruption," Jude said. "Get this through your head." Jude approached and rapped his knuckles on Mickey's skull. "Oh, I'm sorry. Apparently, that's not the head you think with." Jude drove his fist into Mickey's Calvin Klein-covered crotch, forcing him to double over. "I'll never trust you again, and without trust, there can be no *us*." Jude took a deep breath. "Go get dressed and get out," Jude demanded, knowing it would be the last time he saw that gorgeous, two-timing body.

Mickey, hunched over from the blow to his groin, his face scrunched in pain, hobbled to the bedroom.

After dressing, he stood at the door. "I hope you'll be able to forgive me in time, and we can at least be friends again.

"I probably will. But I'm like an elephant. I never forget. I'll always see your cheating ass…well, face."

"You're a special guy, and I'm very sorry I ruined this."

"Yeah, you did. But then, you don't like films, so who knows how long I would have tolerated that." A hint of a bitter smile bent Jude's lips.

Mickey blinked. A watery lens clouded his otherwise bright eyes before he exited Jude's apartment—and life.

After Mickey left, Jude leaned against the door and sighed. "Fucking men. I should have been born a lesbian."

With Francine and Dominick out of town, Jude was left alone in a jungle of emotions. He didn't want to give Mickey the benefit of tears, but he felt a good cry would be cathartic. As a Scorpio, Jude ranked loyalty a paramount trait among friends and boyfriends, and like *The*

Godfather, he demanded it. Mickey's betrayal felt like a secret the whole world was in on, except Jude. He hated that feeling, and it only fueled his anger. But for now, he needed a quickie cry.

He rummaged through his CDs to find the perfect one, the mud to draw out the sting of Mickey's infidelity.

Billie Holiday. "I want to cry, not kill myself." He settled on Sinéad O'Connor. As "Nothing Compares 2 U" bled from the speakers, a transfusion of the painful breakup reflected in the song coursed through Jude. The urge to cry crept up on him like contractions before vomiting.

Halfway through the song, the purge set in, and the tears flowed, slow at first, then like a steady rain, making tracks to Jude's ears. His relationship with Mickey mirrored the lifespan of that beautiful firework, setting off their relationship. After its moment of glory, it fizzled out into oblivion.

By the song's end, Jude declared, "That's all the tears you deserve, Mickey Flynn." Jude sailed off on a ship of emotional sleep as the CD continued.

***

A few days after his breakup with Mickey, Francine returned from her annual vacation with her college friends in the Hamptons, and she and Jude went to Quintessence for dinner—Asian night. Over his crispy Japanese chicken, he lamented about his breakup with Mickey.

"Of course, I try to tell myself it wouldn't have lasted anyway. I mean, he hasn't seen a film for almost two decades." He swizzled his martini with the speared olives.

"Sweetie, you don't have to try to rationalize the breakup. He cheated on you. That's enough." Francine sipped her wine. "You've— we've all been through it before. It will pass, and you'll be stronger for it."

"Stronger? I should be Hercules by now." Jude swallowed a bite of chicken with a dollop of wasabi, instantly burning his sinuses, bringing tears to his eyes. "Wasabi tears, not Mickey tears." He dabbed his eyes with his napkin.

"He was so fucking sexy," Jude whined.

"Honey, relationships aren't built on *sexy* alone. Sexy alone is like one of those hollow chocolate Easter bunnies, pleasing on the outside but empty inside. There has to be something more like love, devotion…a three-dimensional personality. Remember handsome, sexy Renaldo I went out with?

"How could I forget? Your therapist upped your Prozac, and I had to talk you down from the cliff."

"He was everything—intelligent, European good looks, good in bed, and *critical.* 'Oh, Fran, you're so pretty. Why do you have to wear so much makeup?' 'Oh Fran, you have such great hair. Why do you have to wear it in such an unflattering style?' 'Fran, you could use some new clothes.' I put up with it because he was all muscly and handsome, and I was proud to have him on my arm, yet all the while, he made me feel like shit. And then the son-of-a-bitch beat me to breaking up. He told me he needed someone more his style. What a shallow, empty bastard." She bit through a stir-fry shrimp with a vengeance. Jude imagined Fran envisioning it to be Renaldo's head.

"But at least you don't have to run into him. Mickey's still orbiting around in my universe. How can I go to Oh Bar and face him?"

"You go and hold your head up high, preferably with a hottie at your side."

"Well, conjure me up one, oh mighty sorceress."

"You'll meet someone, honey. You always do."

They finished their meals, and after dropping Francine off, Jude went home. He decided to go out and cast his line into the sea of men. He needed to catch a whopper to restore his wounded ego. He picked himself up by the proverbial jockstrap, dressed in an alluring outfit— a cotton sweater vest, sans shirt, with a hint of white boxers poking above his jeans—and went to Waterworks to forget about his heartburn over Mickey. He wasn't heartache-worthy.

Chapter Thirty-One
Coffee Grounds Zero

December 1995

A few days after losing his job and completing some last-minute Christmas shopping, Jude stopped at The Coffee Clutch Café, where he spotted Francine and Chickie.

"Hello, Fran. Chickie."

"Hi, Jude," Chickie said. "Nice to see you. Merry Christmas."

"Merry Christmas, Chick."

"Hello." Francine avoided direct eye contact.

"I think I'll go to the ladies' room." Chickie got up and excused herself.

"Why haven't you returned any of my calls? For weeks?"

Francine didn't budge.

"Well?"

Now, she shrugged.

"That's it? A shrug? Aren't you going to say something, or are you going to continue to sit there like a lump of meat?"

"Oh, what is that, one of your gay expressions?"

Jude slid into Chickie's seat opposite Francine. The backgammon-designed tabletop became their battlefield, shooting verbal barbs across at each other.

"You know, I think you resent the fact that I'm gay. You're always making derogatory remarks to me. I tried to tell myself it was just your caustic humor, but I really believe you hate that I'm gay. Is it because I couldn't be the boyfriend you were hoping for?"

"Well, aren't you the egotistical one?" Francine fired back.

"You came on to me, sweetie." There was a snide upturn at the corner of Jude's mouth.

"Oh, go to hell. I hate that you slept with Dakota. You knew I liked him."

Jude leaned in closer; his voice pitched an octave. "I did *not!*" He checked to see if he roused the curiosity of nearby patrons. He brought his voice down to a whisper. "How could I have known? You didn't tell me *you* slept with him. You're like the Mata Hari of sexual affairs. We used to tell each other that stuff. Dakota is the enemy here, not me."

Francine sat in silence. Jude knew he was right. She threw her nose in the air and shrugged off the remark. "You have to have everything you want, even if it belongs to someone else."

Jude's arms crossed over his chest. He sat back. "Well, obviously, Dakota didn't belong to you."

By the exasperated look on Francine's face, he could tell his pointed words stung like a swarm of hornets.

Francine stared at him. "You always brag about how spoiled you are like it's a badge of honor."

"Yeah, I admit my parents spoiled me, but not when taking things away from friends. You act like I took something from you that wasn't yours to begin with. I came over here to patch things up, but apparently, you're too stubborn to mend our friendship." Jude stood up. "Well, I want to thank you for helping me decide. Since I lost my job—"

Francine's face registered shock.

"That's right. Had we been talking, you would have been the first person I told. But this conversation has convinced me nothing is keeping me here. I've been thinking about what to do, so thanks to you, I've decided right here and now that I'm going to San Francisco and may stay out there. For good. So, thank you, *friend,* for helping me make that decision."

Francine's face morphed from shock to dismay.

Jude started to leave, then stopped. "I thought our friendship was stronger than your petty jealousy. I guess I was wrong. How do you expect to sustain a relationship if you can't get over a rough patch in a friendship? No wonder you can't hang on to a guy. Have a nice life."

Jude walked away. He left Francine sitting frozen like a block of ice. At the door, he turned and saw Francine watching him. He wondered if their heated exchange would melt her glacial veneer. It didn't matter. He made up his mind, he was San Francisco-bound. The bell above the door jangled as Jude let it close on another chapter of his life and apparently on his friendship with Francine.

Several minutes later, Chickie returned. "How did it go with Jude?"

Francine sat motionless, her face dispirited.

"I can tell not good."

"He's leaving for San Francisco and may stay out there." Francine's welled-up eyes reflected the light.

"Excuse me," Sarah, whose tongue piercing had healed, addressed Chickie. "It's been reported that you have been loitering around the ladies' room, which has made one of our customers uneasy."

"Oh, I was just giving my friend some space—" Chickie began but was interrupted.

"Please keep your kinky inclinations to yourself and out of the Coffee Clutch Café. A warning from the management." Sarah turned in a huff and bounced/walked away.

"Oh my God! Get me out of here." Attempting to distance herself from her ignominious accusation, Chickie hid her face as she bolted for the exit, leaving Francine to gather up her things and follow.

***

Later that night, Dominick expected Jude for their Monday night ritual of ordering Chinese food and watching *Melrose Place.*

Dominick opened the door seconds after Jude rang the bell. "Judith," Dominick said.

"Jesus. Were you standing by the door?" Jude entered, kissing Dominick on the forehead.

"I saw you parking."

They walked to the living room. Dominick lived in an old apartment complex converted from a brewery. His living room had a large, drafty window with vertical blinds, and on top of the building's shitty heating system, Jude knew to wear a heavy sweater and keep his scarf wrapped around his neck the entire time.

As they munched on Sesame Chicken, they watched *Melrose Place.* It was a rerun, which Jude had missed, but Dominick saw and forewarned Jude of the episode highlights.

"Watch what Sydney does to Jane." Dominick was giddy with anticipation for Jude to witness what he already knew. "Can you believe Sidney drugs her own sister's drink?" As Dominick chuckled at Sydney's antics, Jude zoned out, recapping his run-in with Francine and how he would break the news to Dominick about going to San Francisco with the option to stay permanently.

When the show was over, Dominick made another round of gimlets. "Have you decided what you're going to do about work?" He squeezed fresh limes into the ice-filled cocktail shaker.

"Funny, you should bring that up. I have. I'm going to visit Matthew."

Dominick stopped pouring vodka into the shaker and looked at Jude. "Zyskowski? In San Francisco?"

"No, Matthew from biblical times."

Dominick laughed as he resumed pouring in the vodka. One of the endearing traits Jude always loved about Dominick was his ability to laugh at sarcasm directed at him.

"If I like it, I'm thinking of staying there now that she-whose-name-shall-not-be-mentioned isn't talking to me, and my relationship with Connor was stillborn. I might as well see what San Francisco has to offer."

Dominick walked around the half wall separating his kitchen from the living room and handed Jude his gimlet.

"But San Francisco is so far. What will I do without you? Who will I watch *Melrose* with?" Dominick fake cried.

Jude took a sip of his drink, a mischievous glint in his eye. "Come out with me. It'll be like the old days, you, Zyskowski and me. The Three Muske-*queers* reunited," He raised his glass and tapped it against Dominick's with a playful smirk.

After Dominick's heartache over Matthew healed, Jude was the link between the three who nurtured their friendship. Another trait that Jude admired in Dominick was his forgiving heart, and he came to realize that he and Matthew were better off as friends, and the three shared adventures in which they were all for one and one for all.

Chapter Thirty-Two
We'll Take Manhattan

June 1990

The adventure that started their camaraderie was the first time they spent a weekend together in New York City.

"How would you like to spend some weekends in the city with me? We'll invite Dominick." Matthew's voice was excited.

"I never turn down an opportunity to hit the Big Apple!" Jude was equally thrilled. "What's going on?"

"My friend Holly, from B. Forman, has a cousin with an apartment in the West Village, and he wants me to do some design work in it."

Matthew was employed at B. Forman's as the store's designer, where he put up displays and dressed the windows.

"You're Rhoda, but without the headscarf," Jude joked when Matthew got the job.

Matthew hoped to move to the city to attend Parson's School of Design and working on Carlton's apartment would help build his portfolio.

"Carlton will stay in his uptown apartment, so we'll have the place to ourselves."

"Jesus, two places in the city? What's he do?"

"He's a psychiatrist. He also has a place in the Hamptons."

"He single?"

"He's not your type, very Scandinavian. Very blonde, very blue-eyed."

"I could be colorblind."

The three crowded into Matthew's Dodge pick-up that Friday after work and headed down the thruway to New York City.

After parking on Charles Street, they crammed into the Memphis building's elevator, which took them to the 18th floor. Carlton's apartment was not big but offered a breezy charm with its large windows and modern design, though it did need some jazzing up.

Dominick stepped onto the small balcony overlooking midtown. Jude followed when Dominick burst into a chorus of "Don't Cry for Me, Argentina."

"Cool it there, Patty LuPone," Matthew began after recovering from a laughing fit. "You'll get us kicked out."

"Hey, look. Queens," Dominick shouted.

"You can't see Queens from here," Jude balked.

"Not the borough, *Judith.* Drag queens." Dominick pointed over Jude's shoulder.

Two balconies over were three guys dressed in sequins, lamé, and chiffon and sporting bouffant wigs and exaggerated makeup.

"Hey, girls!" Dominick waved.

"Hello, boys!" said one wearing a flaming red beehive.

Seeing Matthew, who joined Dominick and Jude, another in a wig with bangs and a shoulder-length flip, yelled, "Hi, Sugar."

"What's shakin' ladies?" Dominick encouraged the conversation.

The third had cocoa-colored skin and wore a spikey champagne-tinted wig and eyelashes that crowned her large doe eyes. She was like a hybrid between Tina Turner and Liza Minelli.

"We're kicking off Gay Pride month with a big drag show at the Duplex. Come see us," the Tina/Liza look-alike said. The voice was deep but sweetened with a feminine cadence. He pirouetted, lifting his arm above his head like a Dreamgirl.

"What time is the show?" Matthew asked.

"Ten sharp, honey," the one with the *That Girl* coif replied.

"We'll be there." Dominick blew them a kiss.

"I hope so, sweetheart," said the drag queen in the beehive wig.

As "Rhythm Is a Dancer" blared from inside, they sashayed back into their apartment.

***

The boys stopped at the Monster for a drink before going to the Duplex just across the street from the iconic gay bar. The Monster was packed with remnants of the after-work happy hour crowd and new arrivals ushering in the weekend.

Dominick cut through the gay denizens. "Excuse me! Coming through!" he said with an occasional "Hello, hottie!" Jude and Matthew followed as Dominick parted the clientele like a gay Moses.

At the end of the bar, a group of older gays clustered around a Grand piano and belted out show tunes. The chorus was currently singing "Can't Help Loving Dat Man." Listening to these older generational gays performing classic standards was an endearing attraction and one of the bar's more entertaining appeals.

The Monster represented a bridge between the new generation (there was a dance bar downstairs) and the pioneers of the gay movement. Many of these older gentlemen lived through the era leading up to—and including—the Stonewall riots, perhaps even participated in them. The Monster became a symbol that, for many, represented home, family, and a place to express themselves openly, freely, and as gaily as they wanted. The young generation owed a great debt to these show-tune-singing bastions, veterans who fought for gay rights, who paved the way for the freedoms and pride they now celebrate every June. Their homosexuality formed a camaraderie that united the generations. It's what made the Monster a landmark and a popular bar in the New York City gay scene.

Of course, there was always a character or two from both sides of the generational aisle who added to the festive fun and hilarity. Tonight was no different.

A short, stout man dressed in white, including a white fedora with a black band, eyed Jude and company and sauntered over while he sang.

"Don't look now, but I think we're about to be serenaded by Truman Capote," Jude said through a fake smile.

Sure enough, the man approached the trio and stared them in the eyes, singing as he walked by each of them, forced smiles frozen on their faces.

"...loving that man of mine," he sang as he caressed Dominick's cheek before sashaying back to the piano.

Helium balloons always adorned The Monster, and in honor of Gay Pride, the ceiling was stippled with dozens of latex orbs in rainbow colors. Tonight, they were under assault.

As the air current propelled them in a dainty, slow-motion crawl along the ceiling, Jude noticed a young man with crazed, bugged-out eyes who nonchalantly grabbed their ribbons when they floated in proximity and yanked them from flight, systematically untying their knots and deflating them from their bloated state, and shoved them into his pockets.

Jude, Matthew, and Dominick watched in amazement as the man

(who looked like someone who dismembered a body) took one after another out of commission and stuffed it into obscurity.

"It's a balloon Holocaust," Jude said.

"What's he going to do with them?" Matthew questioned.

"Hey, Balloon Man—" Dominick started before Jude yanked him to silence.

"Don't poke the sleeping bear. Besides, we should be going to the Duplex. It's almost show time."

As the three headed for the exit, the crooners bellowed, "Some Enchanted Evening." Passing a distinguished, grey-haired gentleman, Dominick boldly asked, "Why aren't you over there singing, honey?"

The man stared back, perplexed; a vacant smile crossed his lips.

"Forgive him, father. He knows not what he says." Jude offered an apologetic grin. From behind, he shoved Dominick. "Move it."

They walked to the corner of Christopher Street and 7th Avenue, where the Duplex stood like a beacon in the heart of Greenwich Village. Its name, emblazoned in white bulbs, was worthy of a Broadway marquee.

The trio jostled their way through the dense crowd as CeCe Penniston's "We Got a Love Thang" overwhelmed the bar clatter.

After a ten-minute wait for a drink from the well-built, shirtless bartender, they worked their way with inchworm determination to a spot close to the stage.

A drag queen strutted onto the platform in a full-length Ostrich feather coat. A roar from the crowd erupted. Plumes on her coat wavered back and forth like thousands of tentacles on a sea anemone.

"Hello, homos!" she bellowed. "Welcome to the Duplex. I'm your hostess with the mostess—" pushing up on her fake bosom, she continued, "—Irma La Douche." As she pranced across the stage, the crowd roared with thunderous acclamation. Irma attempted to blow off a stray feather that adhered to her ruby-red lips and eventually had to pluck it off with her lacquered press-on before introducing the first performer.

Anna Rexic took to the stage as she rolled out a cart. The spotlight hit her silver mini-dress bristling with sequins, which gave off spark-like flashes. It was the Tina Turner look-alike from the Memphis. She performed to Donna Summer's "McArthur Park." She took ingredients for making a cake from under the cart and began mixing them as she sang. The mob exploded into uproarious laughter and cheers.

After her solo performance, Fay Dingaway and Ida Dunham, the other drag queens from the Memphis balcony, joined Anna. In unison, they expanded their rainbow-striped umbrellas and performed "It's Raining Men."

Around midnight, the show ended. The boys decided to call it a night since Matthew wanted to get an early start in the morning on his design work for Carlton's apartment.

They walked down Christopher Street on their way back to the Memphis building. A muscular man with a cropped beard and an open shirt approached them, exposing his well-manicured chest.

"Haay, hottie," Dominick said.

The man shot Dominick a lethal dose of his New York attitude.

"Love you, too, bitch," Dominick yelled, passing by the Lucille Lortel Theatre.

Jude's elbowed Dominick in his side. "You want to get us killed?"

On the corner of Christopher and Hudson, Dominick stopped. "Let's have a group kiss."

Matthew protested.

"C'mon. It was such a fun night. Let's top it off with a kiss." Dominick pulled Matthew and Jude close and reluctantly leaned in for a group kiss. Dominick did his infamous can-can kick. Then, they continued their walk home.

***

Inside the apartment, they readied themselves for sleep. They piled into the king-size bed that practically took up the entire bedroom.

"It's like sleeping in a shoe box." Dominick sprawled out on the bed.

"Never mind, it's a free place to stay," Matthew said, shoving him over as Jude climbed in, flanking Dominick's other side.

Matthew gave a brief itinerary of his day. "I'll hook up with you guys around five at the Monster for happy hour. Then we'll have the whole night. I want to check out this new bar called the Lure down in the Village."

"Our New York adventure continues." Dominick did another kick, lifting the bedding.

"Enough with the can-can kicks. You think you're at the Moulin Rouge?" Jude nudged Dominick.

"We're like the Three Musketeers," Dominick said.

"More like the Three Muske-*queers,*" Matthew added.

"More like the Three Stooges," Jude corrected. *Moe and Larry's* snoring lulled Jude into sleep in minutes.

***

The following day, Jude was the last to get up. Slivers of sun striped the bedroom through the vertical blinds. He slipped on his jeans and joined Dominick and Matthew in the living room.

"Coffee?" Matthew began to pour Jude a cup.

Jude scratched his head. "Did I hear a scream earlier, or was I dreaming?"

"That was me," Matthew said. "The water pressure in the shower is like getting a *Silkwood* scrub down."

"I was going to say you look sunburned." Jude gulped some coffee.

After they finished breakfast, Matthew began to prepare the living room wall, which he was going to paint in broad, alternating beige and Robin's egg blue stripes.

Jude and Dominick headed out into the abundant sunshine to hit the stores on Christopher Street. Dominick was checking out T-shirts with a Dr. Seuss theme in one store, ironically named Tops and Bottoms. He examined one with *The Cat in the Hat* emblazoned on it.

He folded it haphazardly and tossed it back on the pile.

"Hey, there." It was a sales associate behind the counter. "Hey! I'm talking to you," he yelled in a thick Jamaican accent. His long hair was sectioned off in cornrows, each with a different color bead securing the ends.

"Who? Me?" Dominick's face was puzzled.

"Yes, *YOU!*" the sales associate shouted as he walked towards Dominick. "Don't throw the merchandise around like that." He pointed to the untidy T-shirt and began to fold it professionally.

"I didn't *throw* it."

"Next time, show a little respect for our inventory." He placed it back to its proper position. Then he put his hand on his hip, his head tilted to the side, setting off a clacking of beads, his eyes bulging with scorn.

"Don't worry, Mary. There won't be a next time. You just lost a customer." Dominick headed for the door. Jude shrugged at the incensed clerk.

"Big fucking deal. To paraphrase Gloria Gaynor, we will survive, bitch." He snapped his fingers as Dominick slammed the door so hard the rattling bell above rivaled Big Ben's chimes.

Dominick burst out laughing.

Jude couldn't control himself and joined in. "Oh my God! It was like Bette Davis and Joan Crawford on the set of *Baby Jane*."

Their laughter propelled them down Christopher Street to the intersection at 7th Avenue, where Jude stopped in a store and bought the first of his trademark baseball caps. His choice was a dark blue L.A. Dodgers hat. Jude put the cap on. "Whaddya think?"

"So butch," Dominick drolly remarked.

After spending the afternoon hitting SoHo and some trendy stores like Urban Outfitters, they took a cab back to The Monster to meet Matthew. Bored by the slow-moving traffic, Dominick announced, "Rehearsals were exhausting today."

Jude looked perplexed.

Dominick's audacious grin caused Jude to roll his eyes. Dominick checked the cabbie in the rearview mirror for a reaction, but he was concentrating on the crawling West Houston Street traffic and oblivious to Dominick. Dominick persisted: "I'm tired of being in *Cats*. I hope a show called *Dogs* comes along and chases it off Broadway. Rehearsals would have gone better if you remembered the lines to your song, Judith."

Jude shook his head and looked skyward.

Alberto—according to the cabbie's identification—never took Dominick's bait.

"Which side of Hudson yous guys want to get off on?" Alberto said in a thick Brooklyn accent.

"The right," Jude told Alberto.

After battling the heavy traffic, Alberto finally pulled to the curb at Hudson and Christopher Street with a jarring lurch. Jude handed him a twenty. "Keep the change."

As Dominick exited the cab, he leaned towards Alberto's open window. "Come see us in *Cats*."

Alberto didn't acknowledge Dominick and sped away, tires screeching.

"You really are embarrassing," Jude said.

"But you love me." Dominick gave Jude a friendly peck on the cheek.

***

Jude put on a grey tank top with red trim and his L.A. Dodgers baseball cap, which he had purchased earlier in the day. The Three Muske-*queers* stepped out in the balmy night and headed to the new bar, Lure.

Outside Lure stood a burly Black man. His bearded face was the antithesis of his smooth, shaved head. He pointed to Jude and Matthew. "Five-dollar cover," he announced, his imposing frame nearly blotting out the entrance. He took their money and turned to Dominick. "No entry for you." His voice was gruff and authoritative.

"Why?" Dominick was indignant.

"No sneakers allowed." He pointed a thick finger at Dominick's feet.

"They're Nike's, for Christ's sake."

"I don't care if *Christ* himself made them. No sneakers."

"But I'm with them. What am I supposed to do?"

"We have boot rentals. Five dollars."

"I'm not sticking my feet into boots some gross fat ass wore."

"No entry then." The bouncer folded his vascular forearms across his chest, and a stony look crossed his face.

"C'mon, Dom," Matthew pleaded. "They're sanitized, right?"

The bouncer nodded once, looking like a genie granting a wish.

"I don't care. I'm not sticking my feet into some nasty boots."

"You've gone bowling," Jude began. "And you wore shoes that other people wore. What's the difference?"

Several minutes passed before Dominick acquiesced and reluctantly rented a pair of well-worn biker boots two sizes too big.

Inside, as Matthew and Jude threaded their way through the denim and leather-clad crowd, Dominick shuffled behind as if his ankles were shackled. He snorted, "Waterworks." His way of saying *bor-bors.* Jude knew he was disgruntled about having to wear communal boots.

The bar was spacious and dimly lit, with patches of neon casting a multi-colored glow. Chain-link fencing divided sections of the bar. Posters of Tom of Finland and other male erotica adorned the brick walls. Felix's "Don't You Want Me?" thumped as they inched their way to one of the three bars.

Matthew went to check Rawhide, an in-house leather goods store.

After getting a drink, Jude and Dominick settled near a chain link partition. A drink later, Matthew, who bought a bottle of poppers, joined them. "It's a one-stop shop for all your leather and sex accouterment needs."

"I know someone who would like a twelve-inch dildo." Jude smiled at Dominick, who was not amused.

After his fourth Rolling Rock, Dominick was loosening up. As a distinguished man with salt and pepper hair wearing jeans and a leather vest walked by, Dominick stuck out his hand and grabbed the man's crotch. "Squeeze," he said in a high-pitched voice. Looking at Jude, he uttered, "Pants." A bewildered look formed on the man's face.

Seconds later, a hand the size of a Ping Pong paddle seized Dominick and spun him around. "Did I see you grab my partner's crotch, punk?" A leather-clad Goliath bearing brawn and biceps dwarfed him. For once, Dominick was speechless.

"He didn't mean anything—" Jude interjected.

"I'm talking to this little weasel." His voice meant business.

"Sorry, I didn't know he was your boyfriend," Dominick squeaked apologetically.

"So, you just go around grabbing men's dicks?" The man's eyes narrowed.

"Actually, he does," Jude tried to sound jovial. "But he's harmless—"

The man turned to Jude, shooting him a deadly look. Jude retreated like a cuckoo into its clock. The angered Hulk turned back to Dominick. "Well, runt?" He picked Dominick up by the throat. His bulging eyes aligned with the jealous boyfriend's fire and brimstone face. Dominick's legs flailed; his oversized boots slipped to the floor. Matthew and Jude tried to intervene. Even the man's partner came to Dominick's rescue, as did a nearby bouncer with a handlebar mustache. He grabbed the man by the shoulder dropping Dominick, who almost lost his balance. As the bouncer continued to calm the enraged man down, Jude and Matthew grabbed Dominick and bulldozed through the crowd, getting as far away from the trouble as possible.

"The boots," Dominick shouted over Technotronics, "Get Up."

"Never mind. They're not yours, anyway."

They continued to push and bump patrons on their way to the exit, causing drinks to splash and spill.

"Watch it, asshole," one angered muscle-bound patron yelled.

Running away from Lure, Dominick stopped and shouted, "My sneakers!"

Jude stopped. "Buy new ones."

"They're the only pair I have with me."

"Who's going back to get them? Trouble here can't," Jude said to Matthew.

After a lengthy staredown, Matthew gave in and went back to retrieve Dominick's sneakers. Matthew returned ten minutes and as many dollars later with Dominick's Nikes.

Back in the safety of the apartment, Jude scolded Dominick. "You're in the city for less than two days, and you cause controversy wherever you go. Keep it up, and we'll never be able to show our faces anywhere in New York."

"It's all good. I got my sneakers back." Dominick went to the balcony and burst into a few bars of "Everything's Coming Up Roses."

Jude and Matthew laughed, but Jude yanked Dominick into the apartment. "Get in here before you get us arrested. You're a frustrated drag queen."

Dominick did a can-can kick with his sneakered foot.

Later, they piled into bed, exhausted from the night's events.

"Back to Smallbany tomorrow," Dominick said.

"New York is probably glad to see you go," Jude yawned.

"All's well that ends well. Chalk it up to the adventures of the Three Muske-*queers*." His voice went high-pitched and squeaky on *'queers.'* It was the last thing Jude heard before sleep overcame him.

Chapter Thirty-Three
San Francisco, Open Your Golden Gate

December 1995

It was six p.m. on the day before Christmas Eve when Jude telephoned Matthew in San Francisco.

"How would you like a visitor," Jude asked.

As much as he loved New York, Matthew decided that going to San Francisco would be less competitive and stressful, so in the summer of '93, Matthew loaded up his truck and drove across the country to the *"City by the Bay."*

"Are you kidding? We'd love it." The *we* being his partner, George LaFontaine.

"Oh, yes, the new beau. How are things going with Boy George?"

"It's going great."

"Where'd you meet him again?"

"At an art gallery."

Hearing the words, *art gallery* sent a heart-stopping tremor through Jude, reminding him of the breakup with Francine resulting from the disaster over Dakota. Matthew's art gallery story had a happier ending.

"How long are you staying?"

"Until I find a place of my own. I lost my job. Fran, my supposed best female friend, isn't speaking to me. I'll fill you in on that story, so I think this is a good time for a change. If I like it, I'll stay. Permanently."

"Oh my God! You're going to love it out here."

Jude practically felt Matthew's high-voltage excitement through the phone.

"I'll break the news to Dolores over Christmas dinner and let you know when I plan to come. Stay tuned."

***

"Merry Christmas." Jude kissed Dolores. "What's with the candle?"

he asked, spotting a fat, red candle sitting in a holly wreath on the Formica counter.

"It's for good luck in the New Year."

"Isn't the votive candle in front of the Virgin Mary good enough?"

"You can never have enough protection," Dolores said, grabbing a box of instant mashed potatoes she was preparing for the Christmas dinner the Giacolones were sharing with the Zyskowskis.

"And, so says the condom industry."

"Don't be crude, it's Christmas."

"Love the gift." Jude held up his wrist with a thick Cuban link silver bracelet. "Thanks!"

"You're welcome, you bastard. It's a good thing I don't give you my credit card whenever you want something."

"Sorry. You said to pick out something for Christmas, so I did." He bit into a jumbo shrimp. "I didn't notice the price."

"You never look at price. I always said you have champagne taste with beer pockets, unlike your brother who—"

"Would squeeze the buffalo off the nickel. I know," Jude said, finishing the oft-repeated rejoinder.

"What a shame Frannie can't join us for Christmas," Dolores said, tending to her roast.

"Yeah, she felt she should spend it with her family." Jude lied, not knowing where Francine was spending Christmas.

"Hey, son!" Augie bellowed as he came in the back door. "Merry Christmas."

"Merry Christmas. How was church?"

"Nice. Big crowd."

"Yeah, all those good Catholics who think going to church on Christmas and Easter makes up for skipping the rest of the year," Jude said.

"Martini time, son," Augie declared. "Want to do the honors?"

The doorbell rang, signaling the arrival of the Zyskowskis.

"Hello! Merry Christmas," Teresa said upon entering the kitchen. "Oh, Dee Dee, everything smells so delicious!"

Jude made drinks for everyone.

"God bless us in the New Year," Teresa said, raising their cocktails.

While they sipped their martinis, the families exchanged gifts.

After dinner, Jude broke the news. "I have good news and bad news," he began. "The bad news is I lost my job—"

"Oh, Jesus!" Dolores stopped making the coffee and made the sign of the cross.

"It's okay. My severance will pay me through most of May, but the good news is I've decided I'm going to visit Matthew in San Francisco to see if I like it enough to stay and start a new beginning. You know, find myself."

"And where is the *good* news?" Dolores balked.

"Matthew will love having you out there," Teresa said.

"All the way out there? You have to go to California to find yourself? I can see you. You're right here. Now you're found," Dolores snarled, returning to the coffee. "Now I've lost count of how many scoops I put in here." Dolores pressed her fingertips to her brow.

"My life is a blank canvas. Maybe I'll get my Master's in writing. There's a program at San Francisco State University."

Teresa attempted to comfort Dolores. "I was devastated when Matthew left for California, Dee Dee. Sometimes we have to let go of our kids," Teresa reasoned and hugged Dolores to comfort her.

"It's like my mother used to say, 'When your children are young, they step on your toes. When they're grown, they step on your heart,'" Dolores lamented.

A gust of air caused the flame of the "good luck" candle to waver and blow out. Dolores looked over to the candle. "A fanabla to you!" She brushed her fingers from under her chin toward the extinguished good luck candle.

"It's just a trial, Dolores. I may not like it."

"You'll love it," Augie said. "Me and my buddies went to San Francisco before the army sent us to Hawaii during the war and—"

"You're encouraging!" Dolores said in a singsong voice and shot Augie a scowl.

"I'm just saying," Augie gave a throaty laugh.

"He'll be fine," Zig added. "We talk to Matthew every week. It's like he's in the same room."

"A room six hours away," Dolores countered as she served a Mrs. Smith's pumpkin pie and coffee. "Go. Go find yourself," she said begrudgingly. "I only want what's best for you." She kissed Jude on the head.

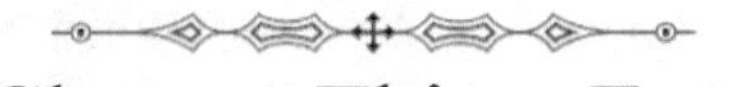

Chapter Thirty-Four
Push It. Push It Real Good

Matthew was like a live wire when Jude called with his flight information.

"We have a fun night planned when you arrive. They're having a sing-along to *The Sound of Music* at the Castro Theatre."

Jude feigned excitement but had no desire to see *The Sound of Music*. As much as he was into films, especially classics, he presumed the beloved musical to be overly sentimental, a cinematic Hallmark card. Still, he could hardly refuse to go and disappoint Matthew, whose excitement was palpable.

Jude was on a 6:40 a.m. flight to San Francisco the Friday after New Year's Day. Besides a handsome, middle-aged, blue-eyed flight attendant, Jude kept ogling, the plane ride was uneventful. It was a bonus when the sexy flight attendant worked the aisle where Jude was sitting.

On the second round of snacks and beverages, Conrad— according to his nametag—approached and stepped on the cart break. "Well, hello again. Something to drink?"

Jude smiled and ordered a scotch with lime on the rocks.

"Now that's a coincidence," Conrad said with an affected tone as he scooped ice into the plastic cup.

"What is?"

"I have a gay friend who also drinks his scotch with lime." Conrad gave Jude a knowing smile. He placed a tiny bottle of Johnny Walker Red on Jude's tray.

Jude grimaced. "Is it really *that* gay to put lime in scotch?"

Conrad plucked a wedge of lime with a pair of tongs and deliberately let it plop in Jude's cup. "Oh no. It's..um..adorable, like your outfit." Jude wore denim overalls, a white shirt, a paisley tie, and his Dodgers baseball cap.

After serving the other passengers in Jude's row, Conrad gave Jude a flirtatious wink. "Push your call button if you desire anything else, handsome."

"Oh, I'll push it. I'll push it real good," Jude said to the attractive flight attendant with the salt and pepper hair. Smiling seductively, Conrad unlocked the brake and shoved the beverage cart down to the next row.

***

Spotting Jude at the baggage claim, Matthew ran up to him, and the two squeezed each other with blood pressure cuff compression. "Welcome to San Francisco. I'm so happy to see you. You look great. You'll be a big hit with the San Francisco crowd."

"Let's hope so. I could use a little ego boost." Jude grabbed his suitcase from the baggage claim conveyor belt.

"Why? What's going on?" They pinballed their way through the hoard of travelers en route to the parking lot.

"In addition to losing my job, I aborted a potential relationship with this guy named Connor."

"What was wrong with him?"

"Let's just say he was a delicious-looking truffle with not a lot to offer inside."

"Well, the truffles in San Francisco have a bountiful variety of delicious fillings."

On the half-hour ride to where Matthew and George lived, they discussed the most recent events in their lives.

"So, what happened with Fran? Why isn't she talking to you?"

"Because I slept with a guy she was interested in, but I swear I didn't know. She didn't tell me *she* slept with him, too. I thought because he slept with me, he was gay."

"It's the 90s. Sex is no longer black or white, or should I say, gay or straight." Matthew's view of the world and life was always pragmatic and philosophical.

"It gets more complicated every day," Jude lamented.

As they drove along US-101, Jude observed the hilly terrain with clusters of neatly rowed houses in pastel colors. Peppered throughout were the multitude of billboards and businesses also dotting the landscape. It looked so different from the East. He couldn't wait to see San Francisco, especially the Golden Gate Bridge. Jude was bursting with the anticipation of a game show contestant waiting to hear what he won.

"George can't wait to meet you."

"And I can't wait to meet my new in-law. You think George is the one for keeps?"

"I hope so."

"Don't you worry about the temptation of being in Gay Mecca?"

"There's temptation anywhere you go. Look what happened with Mickey Flynn in Albany."

"True, but San Francisco must be like a big Piñata; hit it, and the gays fall out everywhere."

Matthew laughed it off. "Well, there is a lot more selection on the menu here, that's for sure. In fact, I have a few guys I'd like you to meet."

"Bring 'em on."

As they neared Webster Street, Jude looked up through the windshield. "Is that the building where you live?" It was a tall cylindrical cement and glass structure.

"Yup, Webster Tower."

"You live in a high rise? In San Francisco?" They pulled into the parking garage.

Matthew laughed. "It's not a high rise. It's only twelve floors."

"Yeah, twelve floors that can pancake in an earthquake."

"I felt more earthquakes in New York than I have living in San Fran." Matthew found a spot close to the elevator. "We live on the eighth floor."

"Wonderful." Jude's voice was deliberately sarcastic. "And can you not call it San *Fran?*" Jude pulled his suitcase from the back of Matthew's truck. Matthew laughed and threw an arm around Jude.

The hallway to Matthew's apartment looked more like a hotel with its large floral print rug, striped wallpaper, and the occasional print dotting the walls. Matthew unlocked the door to 810.

"George will be home after his classes. He's studying computer programming at The Computer Learning Center. I asked for the night off from my job at Daddy's, so we could go to *The Sound of Music* sing-along."

"I thought you worked for Trickey Design Studio?"

"I do, but this place is fifteen hundred dollars a month! And with George in school full-time right now, I had to take a second job as a bartender at Daddy's."

Jude looked around the apartment. It was clean and bright but not spacious. He placed his suitcase next to a nook with a long dining table. Matthew did his interior design magic to the apartment, building the dining room table and the bench along the wall. The cushions lifted for storage—something needed, as there wasn't a lot of space to put things.

A narrow distance opposite was a compact kitchen separated from the living space by a laminate-topped half-wall.

"You're kidding! This place is fifteen hundred dollars a month? My apartment is twice as big and half the price."

"It's San Francisco. It's very expensive to live here."

"How do people do it?"

"They live with other people and work multiple jobs." Matthew showed Jude the bedroom. It was a large room, but considering it also served as their television room, it contained a small sofa and side table, rendering it claustrophobic to Jude.

"Doesn't leave much room for a slumber party," Jude quipped.

"Doesn't leave much room for George and me."

There was a huge closet where George had his computer set up among their hanging clothes and storage shelves crammed with a variety of miscellaneous items.

Back in the living room, Matthew pointed to where Jude would sleep.

"I built this trifold screen, and behind it is a mattress. I hope you'll be comfortable enough."

The mattress was next to sliding glass doors that led to a cement deck.

"That's fine. I just hope I'm not inconveniencing you."

"No, not at all. We're so glad you're here."

"I'm excited to be here." Jude hugged Matthew.

A million questions raced through Jude's mind. How would he afford a place? Jude was very particular and did not relish living with other people. So far, San Francisco had a major strike against it.

Chapter Thirty-Five
Sing-Alongs, Porn Stars, and Human Chia Pets

Around 4:30, George came home, tossing his distressed leather backpack on the dining room table.

George smiled. His wispy beard scratched Jude when he gave him a gregarious, it's-so-good-to-meet-you hug. "I've heard a lot about you. It's nice to finally meet."

"Likewise."

"It's Happy Hour. Gimlet time." George pulled out a bottle of Grey Goose and fresh limes.

"Grey Goose? No wonder Matthew needs two jobs," Jude joked.

"You need good vodka since that is pretty much what's in a gimlet."

In minutes, the three were toasting to Jude's arrival and hopefully permanent stay in San Francisco.

That evening, the three ventured out for dinner to a cozy little place called Casha's. Matthew parked just up the street from the corner of Market and Castro. They walked through the enormous intersection with trolley tracks below their feet, above a tangled network of electric cables that crisscrossed the busy intersection.

A giant rainbow flag to their right flapped and wavered. The brisk wind carried a patch of fog, partially obscuring the banner before it fully emerged again in all its colorful, gay reverie.

Crossing the street, they passed Twin Peaks, a gay bar on the corner. Its prominent rectangular sign jutted out from above the entrance, its name ablaze in orange neon against a green mountain-shaped background. Huge windows encased the interior.

"The younger gays call this the *Glass Coffin* because it has an older clientele," George said jocularly. As Jude peered in, a collection of older men with varying degrees of balding grey hair sat beneath several Tiffany lamps. A man with a white beard and glasses seated by the window smiled and waved as the threesome walked by. Jude instinctively waved back.

"They deliberately made the windows big so people could see in. It was symbolic that homosexuality was no longer something to hide," George said, like a tour guide of gay history.

Inside Casha's, they were seated and served by a petite waitress wearing an oversized blazer and a Gatsby cap.

They started the meal off with a round of gimlets before ordering.

"I don't know your plans for tomorrow, but I have the day off, and it's supposed to be a freakishly mild day. I thought you might want to go for a bike ride," George offered.

"Oh, are you willing to give up your time on the computer?" Matthew goaded. "George is addicted to video games."

"I thought I'd show Jude around San Francisco, give us a chance to bond."

"Yeah. I'd like that. I'll get to see the city. Where can I get a bike?" Jude crunched a piece of crispy calamari.

"You can use mine," Matthew offered.

"We got bikes to take rides through the city, and he never uses his," George said, scowling at Matthew.

"San Francisco is too hilly," Matthew complained.

"Uh, hello? That's why we bought ten speeds." George rolled his eyes.

After dinner, the threesome headed down the street to the historic Castro Theatre for *The Sound of Music* sing-along. As they passed a group heading in the opposite direction, one of the guys said, "Look at the chest on that one." The guy stared at Jude's torso, straining against the thermal undershirt he wore.

"Your first compliment. You'll do well here," Matthew said, wrapping his arm around Jude's shoulder.

The iconic vertical sign proclaiming its name and the marquee were ablaze with an abundance of colorful Art Deco-style neon as they approached the theatre.

People in themed costumes stood in clusters on the sidewalk and around the box office in the middle of the tiled foyer. There was one person dressed as the Baroness, another as Frauline Schweiger, and another cleverly costumed as a half nun and half bride, the two sides of Maria von Trapp.

Though Jude was not thrilled about seeing *The Sound of Music,* he enjoyed the event's pomp and circumstance. He was awed by the theatre's majestic detail with its Italian-Spanish-influenced design and the energy generated by the enthusiastic crowd.

When the lights dimmed, the red velvet drapes parted. Silence fell over the capacity crowd, but when Julie Andrews did her iconic twirl, the audience burst into uproarious applause, singing along with Julie—*the hills are alive with the sound of music*. Such was the crescendo from the crowd; no doubt the hills of San Francisco must have come alive as well.

Jude sat enthralled, lost in the unexpected thrill of sight and sound displayed on the giant screen. By the end of the film, Jude was a convert, falling in love with the classic movie. To be part of such a vibrant, exciting city, *maybe I could live here after all*. San Francisco made Jude feel gay, very, very gay, in the happy, as well as the homosexual sense of the word.

After the film, they went to Daddy's, where two rainbow flags atop each end of the blue awning above the entrance flapped in the steady breeze. Jude did not expect to pass through the weighted, heavy leather curtain at the doorway. It felt like the apron dentists use when taking X-rays.

"Are San Franciscan gays afraid of radiation or something?" Jude asked; Matthew just chuckled.

The bar was long and narrow and had atmospheric, low lighting. They worked their way through the crowd. Shirtless bartenders busied themselves tending to the customers. Opposite the oak bar, in a dark, recessed area, men of various ages stood conversing at small pedestal tables. Matthew slipped into an opening at the bar beside a handsome young man.

"Hey, Matty. Can't stay away, even on your night off," the bartender said.

"Hi, Corey. I'm showing my friend, Jude, our bar. He's from out of town. This is Corey."

Shaking hands, Corey introduced Jude to the man next to Matthew. "And this is my boyfriend, Aiden." He was quite handsome. His face, a flawless landscape of smooth skin, was adorned with penetrating blue-grey eyes.

"Hello. A pleasure to meet you." Aiden spoke in a refined British accent. He held out his hand. His sleeveless flannel shirt exposed a rose tattoo on the side of a delicious-looking slab of his bicep.

"Likewise." Jude glanced at Matthew with a suspicious flicker in his eyes. There was something familiar about Aiden.

"Are you enjoying your visit, Jude?"

"I just got in town today but loving it so far."

"I see. There's a lot to love in San Francisco. And you're from New York?"

Surprised, Jude answered in the affirmative.

"I could tell. Your accent."

Befuddled, Jude smiled and said, "I don't believe I'm the one with the accent."

A patronizing grin crossed Aiden's face. "Of course you're not."

Jude wondered if Aiden's words were playful or condescending.

"I'll see you at home." Aiden addressed Corey and leaned over the bar for a kiss. "Nice to have met you, *boy from New York.*" Aiden walked away.

As Corey excused himself to tend to a customer, Jude turned to Matthew. "Was that Aiden Shaw, the porn star?" His eyes filled with the same awe as when he entered the Castro Theatre.

"The one and only."

"I just shook hands with a porn star!" His voice shot up with porn star-mania. "Knowing where that hand has been, I'll never wash this again." He examined his fingers as if he just touched the Holy Grail of gay erotica.

"You'll probably meet a lot of porn stars. They're always in the bars," George added. "We know a few. We'll introduce you."

Halfway through their drinks, a man in a leather cap, vest, and pants approached. His broad shoulders balanced on his telephone pole body. His shoulders and exposed chest had a dense carpet of hair as thick as his handlebar mustache.

"Hello, Matt." He kissed Matthew and George. "Enjoying your night off? It's busy tonight. Good for tips. And who is your friend?"

"This is Jude. He just got into town, so I wanted to show him our bar. Jude, this is Ari, better known as Daddy."

To Jude's surprise, *Daddy* leaned in and kissed Jude. The coarse hair of his mustache felt like a horse's tale against his face.

"You must be from New York."

"Uncanny guess."

"What borough?"

"Um, where else but Queens."

"Ah, yes. No place like New York, except San Francisco." Daddy turned and addressed Matthew. "Our new barback starts tomorrow. You'll be here?"

"Yeah, I'm on tomorrow."

"Good. I'll see you then. Well, I've got some work to do in the back. I hope you enjoy your stay, Jude."

Out of earshot, Jude said, "I don't think I've ever seen a hairier guy. He's like a human Chia pet."

Matthew raised his glass to sip but stopped abruptly. "Oh damn. I never thought. I should have recommended you for the barback position. Damn. Daddy would have hired you in a minute."

"But I don't know anything about barbacking," Jude said.

"There's nothing to know. You'd be fine."

At two o'clock, the bouncer at Daddy's began ordering the clientele to leave. It didn't matter if they had a fresh drink in their hand, the bouncer whisked them out the door.

"What's going on? Is the bar *closing?*" Jude was perplexed.

"Yeah, it's two o'clock," Matthew said.

"I know. That's my point. It's *only* two o'clock." Jude was used to New York bar time, where they didn't close till 4 am.

"It's a California law. The bars close at two, and they mean business," Matthew added.

A check in the negative column for San Francisco.

Chapter Thirty-Six
The San Francisco Treats

Jude woke feeling like he was in a greenhouse with the sun's rays streaming through the glass doors to the terrace. He stepped out from behind the trifold screen and dressed in a pair of jeans and a T-shirt just as Matthew emerged from the shower in a towel and buzzed between the kitchen and the bathroom like an aimless fly. As long as Jude knew Matthew, he was a bundle of energy, constantly in motion.

"Good morning. I made some coffee. Help yourself," Matthew said. "Did you sleep well?"

"Yes, I did, seeing I'm still on New York time."

"Don't expect George up anytime soon. But feel free to watch TV, you won't disturb him. Or do whatever you feel like doing." Inertia stopped Matthew long enough to pour a cup of coffee before he resumed flight. He brought the San Francisco Chronicle to Jude.

"Check out the want ads. There should be lots of job opportunities," Matthew said. He downed half his coffee before flitting to his bedroom to dress.

Jude was skeptical. He was very particular about his jobs, unlike Matthew, who was more practical and would do anything to earn money to keep his dream of having an interior design business in San Francisco alive. Jude was not about to sacrifice his security for any job to live in San Francisco. He loved his apartment in Albany and rationalized that he could fulfill his dream of writing the great American gay novel anywhere. If things didn't work out in *Fog City,* his apartment was his safety net.

Jude poured a cup of coffee and went to sit at the dining room table Matthew designed in faux Terrazzo Formica. Matthew was right. There were several pages of job opportunities. Jude began to scan through the categories specific to his experience.

Matthew emerged, dressed for work in jeans and a white button-down shirt; he chugged the last of his coffee. "Any job prospects?"

"Well, I could apply for a Marketing Manager position at Top Dawg Studios," Jude joked.

"Gay porn is very lucrative," Matthew said, stuffing a few things in his backpack.

"Dolores and Augie would be so proud."

"Seriously. You should apply. We know a few people in porn who could help you get a job." He flung his bag over his shoulder. "I'll see you tonight and take you to more bars." He kissed Jude on the head and then rushed out the door. Jude contemplated applying. He imagined encounters like the one last night with Aiden Shaw daily! *Talk about your job perks.*

The apartment was tomb-silent with George still sleeping. Jude took out a copy of his résumé. "Needs some work," Jude whispered. He could redo it on either Matthew's or George's computer.

Around 11:00, George rose from the dead and shuffled into the room. "Good morning. I desperately need caffeine. Are you still up for that bike ride? It looks like a gorgeous day for biking around the city," George announced as he microwaved a cup of coffee.

"Absolutely."

"I'll show you some great sights."

After George had coffee and showered, they went to the basement to get the bikes.

Despite the occasional patch of fog, the day was bright and in the low 60s. As they rode down Fillmore Street, Jude wondered what Fran would say about the mild temperature. Even though it was not the northeast, Jude knew it was not typical for a January day in San Francisco. He'd be hard-pressed to dissuade her about global warming.

They rode for several blocks, turning onto Steiner.

"We'll rest on top of Alamo Square Park. I'll show you a magnificent San Francisco sight," George said.

They walked their bikes along an asphalt path to the top of the hill, where they took in a spectacular view that comprised the historic Painted Ladies, a row of seven Victorian-style houses known for their ornate facades and palette of bright colors. Their steep roofs, detailed gables, and decorative latticework made them stand out among the other Victorian homes on the block. The modern, geometric shapes that formed the city's skyline just above the ornate houses juxtaposed their distinct, intricate style. The Painted Ladies were an iconic San

Francisco landmark second only to the Golden Gate Bridge.

"It's one of the best views in San Francisco," George claimed.

After the Painted Ladies, George led Jude up Steiner Street to Pacific Heights.

"Since Matthew told me how much you like film, I thought you'd be interested in seeing the house used in *Mrs. Doubtfire*," George shouted back to Jude.

Jude was touched by George's thoughtfulness, considering his interests, so Jude did not want to tell him that, at best, *Mrs. Doubtfire* was merely a guilty pleasure good for a few laughs. But still, when they arrived at the corner of Steiner and Broadway, the stately character of the house impressed Jude. Plus, he always found it thrilling to see locations used in films.

Next, they rode to a neighborhood known as Sea Cliff. Looking around at the estate-like homes with their meticulously landscaped lawns, Jude almost ran into George, who stopped in front of a sprawling Mediterranean-style house with a washed-out, blotchy pink exterior.

"This is where Robin Williams lives," George announced. "Can you imagine waking up to that view of San Francisco Bay every day?"

"Must be nice to be rich."

They looked at other houses in the affluent neighborhood before George asked, "Are you ready for the ultimate San Francisco treat?"

"Rice a Roni?"

George laughed. "Better. Let's go."

They rode to Golden Gate Overlook, which provided a spectacular view of the Golden Gate Bridge. After, they followed Merchant Road until they approached Pacific Coast Highway and the foot of the bridge. Up close, Jude drank in the magnificence of the intimidating structure.

"Pictures don't do it justice," Jude said, amazed. "It's funny how it's called the *Golden Gate* Bridge when it's more of an orange color."

"Orange Vermillion, it's called. But I guess back then, they thought San Francisco was a golden opportunity, so they named it the Golden Gate Bridge." George readied his foot to the pedal. "It gets windy on the bridge, so hang on to your baseball cap," George warned.

The two began their bike trek over the iconic bridge. George stopped under the first of the two Art Deco-influenced towers. Seeing it up close, Jude examined the huge rivets that held it together and marveled at the vertical suspension metal ropes and the two main cables, thick as telephone poles. He looked up. The towers' dizzying height sucked the breath out of him.

"Almost a dozen men died constructing the bridge," George shouted against the continual traffic stretching across the span like a never-ending locomotive and the wind's constant roar.

Jude shouted to George, "You should be a San Francisco tour guide!"

At the end of the bridge, they crossed Highway 101 to take in the view from the opposite side. Midway, they stopped to check out the skyline of downtown San Francisco. Seeing the cluster of buildings from a distance was an amazing sight. Prominent among the view was the triangular structure of the Transamerica Pyramid.

"It's a great view, but despite the warm day, it gets very cold standing in the wind," George said. "C'mon. I think we deserve a treat."

"More treats? The only thing that could top riding over the Golden Gate Bridge would be sex with Aiden Shaw."

Chapter Thirty-Seven
Scenes From a Friendship

They rode some distance to a Safeway market outside Golden Gate Park. Jude stayed with the bikes while George shopped. When he emerged, they rode into the park and settled on a patch of perfectly manicured grass outlined with shrubbery and speckled with other people absorbing the sun's warmth. The road surrounding the grass was as active as an ant colony, with dozens of other bikers, joggers, skateboarders, rollerbladers, and people walking their dogs.

George took out a bunch of green grapes and a bottle of Merlot from his backpack.

"Where did you get wine?" Jude asked.

"In Safeway. In California, you can buy any liquor in a market."

"Really! California, here I come. Put another check in the plus column for San Francisco."

George went to wash off the grapes in a nearby water fountain. When he returned, he took two paper cups and a corkscrew out of his backpack, opened the wine, poured some into a cup, and handed it to Jude.

"Is this an everyday occurrence," Jude pointed to the human activity on the road.

"Only on weekends when they close the roads in the park."

A shirtless guy in his twenties with reddish-brown dreadlocks down to his waist performed his fancy footwork on rollerblades while an elderly grey-haired man with tanned, weathered skin stiffly rolled by on old-fashioned skates. He was in direct contrast to the rollerblading Rastafarian.

"It's like a before and after photo came to life." Jude watched, amazed by the old man.

"He's always around. Rumor has it he was an Olympic figure skating hopeful in 1944, but because of World War Two, the games were canceled, and he missed his golden opportunity to participate in the Olympics," George said, plucking a grape from the bunch.

The elderly skater was spinning and jumping with cautious awkwardness, but he certainly looked to Jude as if he was enjoying life to the fullest.

A euphoric wave washed over Jude as he observed the young and the old making the most of the day, drinking wine from paper cups, and hearing the Go-Go's "Our Lips Are Sealed" blasting from a boom box in the distance.

"You know, George, this is what I think of as a *cinematic moment.* Like this scene belongs in a film." Jude reminisced about another movie magic moment that popped into mind. "One Fourth of July, Matthew and a few of our friends were heading to watch the fireworks display at the Empire Plaza in Albany. We were drinking margaritas as we walked single file through a grassy field. There was an orange glow from the setting sun. I told everyone we looked like we were in a scene from a Fellini film. I called it our fabulous Fellini Fourth."

George laughed as he tossed a grape in his mouth and washed it down with wine. "I love how your mind sees things in terms of film. How come you don't have a boyfriend? You should have them lining up."

"The ones I had ended in disaster, cheaters mostly. Liars. Gays, like all men, lie. Gays have their own set of deceits, however." Jude bit into a succulent grape.

"Yeah, like 'I'm really straight, I'm just bi-curious,'" George added.

"Or, 'I'm a top. Then you get the guy in bed, and he kicks his legs up faster and higher than a Rockette." Jude pointed his cup to George. "How many times has that happened?"

"Too many, especially if you're a bottom," George confessed. They howled in unison before taking a sip of Merlot.

"How about, 'I haven't been with many men,' then in bed they act like a porn star."

Their laughter was growing so boisterous they were attracting attention from others on the grassy patch.

"Oh, and I love 'I have nine inches' only to find out you need a magnifying glass to find his dick," George laughed so hard he spilled some of his wine. "Well, don't give up, Jude. Look at me and Matthew."

"You think Matthew is the one?"

"Yeah, we have to function as if we're right for each other. There's no guarantee when it comes to love or anything in life, but we can't be afraid to take the chance. Right now, I feel Matthew is the right one. If you don't take chances, the right one could be in front of you, and you'd never know it."

"You make sense, but it's easier said than done for me. Life and experience have made me cynical. After the last boyfriend failure, I put up a wall around my heart," Jude confessed.

"You're a great catch. If the guy you're with turns out to be a jerk, consider yourself lucky to be rid of him. You dodged a bullet."

"Lately, I feel like target practice at a shooting range."

"I have a friend you'd be perfect for. His name is Grady Savage. He's hot and smart and teaches Women in American Literature at San Francisco State University. I think you'd like him."

Jude was suspicious. "Well, put him on trial. I'll be judge and jury." He downed his wine.

After they polished off the bottle of wine and finished the grapes, George said he had one last treat to show Jude before they went home.

They rode a short distance to the Conservatory, where the Spreckels Temple of Music was located. Dotting the foreground, among the green slat benches, was a copse of English sycamores with thick, gnarly branches and knobby, bulbous ends. The multitude of unusual-shaped trees had a dichotomous appearance, looking both eerie and like something out of Dr. Seuss's imagination. As they pedaled along the wide walkway with the rows of strange trees, Jude exclaimed, "Oh my God! This is where the end of Philip Kaufman's *Invasion of the Body Snatchers* took place!" They stopped to take in the sight. Jude was like a kid with a new toy.

"I figured you'd want to see this."

"This is amazing. It happens to be one of my favorite films. It's as good as the original fifties version. Thank you for doing this and for the day. I had a great time." He paused. "I have a good feeling about you and Matthew."

"Me too," George said, looking at his watch. "It's almost gimlet time. Let's head home. I'll give Grady a call. Maybe he'll be the wrecking ball to break down that wall around your heart." George winked and gave Jude a sly smile as they began the trek back home. After a picture-perfect *cinematic* day, a euphoric blast went off in Jude's mind. Riding the emotional high, Jude decided to send his résumé to Top Dawg Studios for the Marketing Manager position.

Chapter Thirty-Eight
Hunter

"**G**rady is going to meet us tomorrow night at Daddy's," George said. "He's looking forward to meeting you." He mixed gimlets in a cocktail shaker and poured them into rock glasses filled with ice.

Matthew sipped his gimlet between getting ready to work his shift at Daddy's. The fly was back in flight. He emerged from his bedroom dressed in a black, long-sleeve pullover, tan painter jeans, and a Daddy's baseball cap. Downing the last of his gimlet, he kissed George and headed for the door. "See you guys later."

After a light dinner at Fuzio's, Jude and George entered Daddy's as the thumping sound of "Be My Lover" boomed through the bar.

It was a meager crowd since it was just after 9 p.m. Weak beams lit the bar.

"Hi, babe." George leaned over the bar to give Matthew a quick kiss. "Make us a couple of gimlets, please."

Jude removed his flannel shirt and tied it around his waist, leaving him wearing a quilted zipper vest. He attracted the attention of the guy next to him.

"It's a little hot in here." Jude felt the need to explain.

"I'd say it just got a little hotter." He eyed Jude. "Nice arms." He held out his hand. "Hunter." His smile beamed, lighting up the otherwise dark interior.

"Is that your pastime or your name?" Jude shook his hand and flashed him a shameless grin.

Hunter laughed, putting a glint in his bright eyes. "Just my name. I don't kill things."

"So said Jeffrey Dahmer," Jude said and followed with a beaming smile to let Hunter know he wasn't calling him a serial killer.

Matthew delivered the gimlets.

"I can tell you're not from San Francisco. My guess is you're from New York," Hunter observed.

"Are people from San Francisco psychic? You're the millionth person who asked if I'm from New York."

This time, Hunter smiled. "It's obvious—your style, your accent. Are you visiting, or do you live here?"

Jude didn't bother to address his *non-existent accent.* "I'm visiting, but with the option to move here. I lost my job and thought I would consider moving here."

"Let me tell you, don't believe what you hear about San Francisco."

"Like what? It's a beautiful city. Everyone is so friendly."

"They may be friendly, but they're phony. You'll feel welcome, but in time, they'll resent you. San Francisco is overcrowded with gays who don't want to befriend you, especially if you're good-looking. In their eyes, you're just more competition. Everyone here is out for himself." The gleam in his eyes was snuffed out and became steely and cold.

"That doesn't seem like what I've experienced so far."

"People are deceitful. They make you think they're your friend, but they're not."

Somebody burned this guy with a blowtorch. "Well, everybody can't be like that."

"Have you tried to get an apartment? You must submit a credit report and three references, show a driver's license and at least one credit card, and provide a utility bill. It's impossible to get an apartment without roommates. And try to get a job. You're competing with virtually the entire state of California."

So much for not killing things. You just murdered my mood. Jude forced a smile. He excused himself to use the bathroom. Further talk with him and Jude would be on the next flight back East.

"Who was the hottie you were talking to?" George asked when Jude returned.

"Just some cynical jerk. He was like a handful of barbiturates followed by a vodka chaser."

"Oooh. One of the haters?" Matthew grimaced.

"Let me put it this way—if San Francisco falls into the ocean, it won't be because of an earthquake." Jude spotted Hunter, who was nearby. "He keeps staring at us," Jude said through a clenched smile.

"C'mon, we'll go to Detour, another fun bar. We'll see you at home." George leaned and kissed Matthew goodbye.

With that, George and Jude left Daddy's, crossed Castro, headed towards Market Street, and entered the chrome and neon-glow interior of Detour for a few final drinks before the bewitching 2 o'clock hour.

Chapter Thirty-Nine
Madame Fortuna

The following morning, Jude roused in his makeshift "greenhouse" to the ringing telephone. The call went to the answering machine. It was for George, something about a bonfire.

Later that day, Matthew, George, and Jude went to Sunday Beer Blast at the Lone Star, a bar filled with mostly burly man-types.

After getting a drink, they migrated to the outside patio to take advantage of the late afternoon warmth. It was a maze of round tables and slatted benches. Tiny white lights studded the top of the tall wooden fence encasing the large outdoor space.

The crowd was thick with men dressed in varying degrees of leather and denim, displaying their hairy bodies.

At a table was an attractive transvestite doing Tarot card readings.

"Let's get a reading," George suggested.

"You go. I want the future to surprise me," Matthew said cynically. "C'mon, Jude, let's do it."

Jude acquiesced and got a reading after George.

Her name was Madame Fortuna.

"Hello, sweetie." Her deep voice was inflected with an articulate femininity. She gestured to Jude to take the chair opposite her.

A paisley headband kept her long black hair out of her beautifully made-up face. Her teeth and full, ruby lips stood against her caramel skin that shimmered like satin.

"What brings you to Madam Fortuna?"

"Him." Jude pointed to George a few feet away.

"You have to be open to the power of the tarot card, honey, or you'll be wasting your time and money." Her thick, mascaraed lashes fluttered like tiny furry fans.

"Sorry," Jude said, like a disobedient child. Madame Fortuna took her readings seriously. Jude arched his back, sat up straight, and inhaled. "Okay, I'm open." Her scent of patchouli mixed with beer, sweat, and cigar smoke.

She shuffled the deck. Her hands were elegant. Red, lacquered nails crowned long fingers that moved with the grace of tiny octopus tentacles moving through the ocean as she flipped the first card. "The Chariot." She paused. "You're traveling a weary road. You had some upheaval in your routine, and you're trying to reassess things. You're anxious to get off that troubled road and seek a different route to new-found happiness."

His job loss and a possible move to San Francisco ricocheted off the walls in Jude's mind.

She flipped another card. "The Sun. Reversed," she said, tapping the card with her fake nail. "You're trying to overcome doubt, but safety and security keep you on that same well-worn path."

It's like she knows me.

Madam Fortuna revealed the Moon card next. "You're having emotional and mental struggles, but you must let go of the doubts." She turned over the Star card. "Have faith in yourself. Madame Fortuna senses you're level-headed and have common sense. This card is telling you to trust your instincts."

Jude secretly smiled at how fortunetellers seem to always refer to themselves in the third person.

"The perfect follow-up to the Sun," she said, revealing the World card. "It reinforces the confidence you need to follow your heart's desire. Otherwise, you may have trouble reaching what you truly deserve.

"Ah! The Lovers card. Although it may not have lasted, you've had great success finding love—"

And she lost me.

"—and you will find love again, but you must be willing to give people and relationships a chance. If you do, great rewards will be yours. There will be opportunities you must take advantage of in romance and all things that come your way."

When she turned the next card, she hesitated. "Judgment," she said solemnly. "There's a health issue somewhere, not necessarily yours, but your insecurity and fear about such matters will make you skeptical to take that new road. Don't give in to your fears. Have faith. Follow that new path."

The last card. The Ace of Swords. "Life is not fully lived without taking risks. But in the end, destiny will lead you to the path you are to follow." She leaned back and extended her hand, palm up, and smiled. "Twenty-five dollars, honey."

"*Twenty-five?*" Jude's eyes widened.

Madame Fortuna nodded, "Twenty-five. And I'm not bashful about tips." She gave Jude a knowing glare and a wide, sassy smile.

Jude hesitantly took out thirty dollars and handed it to Madame Fortuna, who stuffed it into her bosom.

"Come see me again, honey."

Standing up, Jude responded, "Yeah, sure. Any chance you see a windfall in my future?"

Madame Fortuna gave a throaty laugh. "You're cute." Jude thanked her and returned to Matthew and George.

Chapter Forty
The Silver Fox

Around 8:00, the three went to meet Grady.

Outside Daddy's was a barrel-chested man with skin as dark as the night, dressed in all leather. He sported a thick, close-trimmed beard and forearms resembling inflatable arm-floating devices that he crossed over the expanse of his chest. The burly man was sitting on a barstool with one black-booted foot planted firmly on the ground, the other hooked on the stool's lower rung.

"Hey, baby," he said in a voice that defied his body mass. The sound was comparable to a pterodactyl tweeting like a canary. He wrapped his massive arms around Matthew and kissed him. When he unfurled his folded arms, the sound of his leather biker jacket squeaked like two balloons rubbed together.

"Hi, Bluto. Meet my best friend, Jude. He's here visiting. Jude, Herman, but we call him 'Bluto'."

Jude eyed Matthew with a repressed laugh, his face lit with acknowledgment of the separated-at-birth similarity to the Popeye nemesis. Bluto held out a hand the size of a catcher's mitt, wrapping his sausage fingers around Jude's hand, dainty in comparison. Further enhancing the similarity to the cartoon character, Bluto flashed a toothy smile that monopolized his face. "You visiting from New York?"

Jude acquiesced to another prognostication of his origins with exhaustive acceptance.

"Hope San Francisco is good to you, Jude. Well, enjoy your night, guys." Bluto sat down. The friction of leather on leather groaned as Bluto shifted on his barstool.

Inside the bar, Ari (aka Daddy) strolled through the crowd in his usual leather man attire. It took Jude a moment to realize that Ari's pants were ass-less chaps and that his buttocks were covered in a carpet of hair so dense it blended in with the leather.

"I swear the man has some chimpanzee in his gene pool," Jude said.

Looking around, George said he didn't see Grady.

"Just as well. I hate blind set-ups." Jude recalled his encounters with the men from the Confidential Connection Hotline yet still showed minor disappointment.

"Don't worry. He'll be here," George assured.

They stood at the moderately crowded bar and ordered drinks.

Ray, a shirtless bartender, leaned over with his hairless torso (a rarity) and kissed Matthew, who then introduced him to Jude.

"Nice to meet you and yes, I'm from New York."

Ray narrowed his close-set eyes. "Okay?" he said more as a question. Confusion clotted his eyes.

"I'll have a vodka Martini," Jude said.

"What kind of vodka, handsome?"

"Surprise me," Jude said playfully.

As Ray made drinks, a good-looking guy of average height sauntered over. It was Grady.

"Hey guys." He gave George and Matthew a hug and a friendly kiss and stared at Jude, who was not expecting much, but his eyes were like sponges, soaking up the vision before him. Grady's hair was a lustrous silver—not gray—that glistened under a direct beam of light, and the cut buzzed short and slightly longer on top, making him look too young to be a college professor. The sterling hoop piercing through his left eyebrow added to his funky style while complimenting his hair and piercing eyes.

He's a silver fox. This professor was hotter than a fantasy.

"Grady, this is our friend, Jude," George said.

Jude extended his hand, expecting a handshake. Instead, Grady leaned in and hugged him. Jude gladly hugged back. *I can tell he works out.*

"Great to meet you. Are you enjoying San Francisco?"

I like it a lot more now. "Yes, I am. I'm still deciding if I want to stay. It depends on getting a job and a place to live. So far, I'm hearing it's tough to get both," Jude confessed. He told Grady about some job opportunities he saw, including the one at Top Dawg, the porn production company, and another at Blue Shield of California. "I need to punch up my résumé before I apply."

"I'll be glad to help you. I'm pretty good at knowing what employers look for in a résumé."

"Yeah? I'd appreciate that." He caught himself staring, trance-like, into Grady's eyes while registering the entirety of his hotness. From the thick stubble, he guessed that Grady was the kind of guy who had a five o'clock shadow twenty-four hours a day.

"I'm free tomorrow afternoon if you want to get together," Grady said. Then he asked Ray for a piece of paper and a pen and jotted down his telephone number. "Don't be afraid to use it." Grady flashed an intoxicating smile equal to several shots of tequila. Jude stayed close to the bar in case he had to grab hold of it to keep from swooning.

Jude pointed to the silver hoop through Grady's eyebrow. "Did that hurt?"

"Nah, probably no more than your ears. But then, I have a high tolerance for pain."

"I like it. It looks good on you." *You'd look good with a bone through your nose.*

"I think you'd look hot with one, too." The glacier blues were glued to Jude as he sipped his drink.

"I'm afraid the ears are the only thing getting pierced on me. Unlike you, I don't have a high tolerance for pain." Jude thought he detected a slight pout on Grady's face.

After several Stoli martinis (Ray's choice to surprise Jude), Grady said he had an early class and had to leave. "I enjoyed talking to you, Jude. Please call me about getting together tomorrow."

"I definitely will."

"I'm looking forward to it already." Another smile melted Jude. Grady surprised him with a quick kiss goodbye.

When Grady exited, George and Matthew approached.

"Isn't he hot?" George asked.

"If he were any hotter, I'd be molten lava."

"Did he tell you about his fetish?" Matthew asked.

"Fetish? Oh God, don't destroy my fantasy."

"He likes to tie his sex partners up," George said, amused.

"Really? Is that all? I kind of find that intriguing," Jude mused with a twinkle in his eye as he downed the last of his Stoli martini.

Chapter Forty-One
In Frisco, They Kiss on Main Street

Whenever Jude exchanged numbers with a guy, he didn't like calling first. He thought it made him look eager and desperate, but Jude did want Grady's advice for his résumé, so he dialed his number. They made plans to meet at Starbucks on the corner of Castro and 18th Street. Jude wanted to make sure he looked good, so he put on a form-fitting red thermal undershirt, a jean jacket, and his favorite Abercrombie and Fitch jeans that everyone always said fit him so well. He topped it off with his blue L.A. Dodgers baseball cap.

He took the bus down to Market Street and walked past the "Glass Coffin" and the Castro Theatre to Starbucks. Grady was sitting at a table wearing an oatmeal-colored sweater with orange trim. When Jude approached the table, Grady got up, greeted him with a kiss, and offered to get him a coffee. Jude didn't have the heart to tell him he didn't like Starbucks' coffee, but he'd drink mud for Grady.

"Cream and sugar." Jude reached for his wallet, but Grady said, "It's on me."

Can I put me *on you?*

When Grady returned, Jude pulled out a copy of his résumé. Grady looked it over and wrote some notes. By the end of their coffee, Grady's ideas completely streamlined the look of Jude's résumé.

"Even though you have an impressive résumé, San Francisco is competitive. I think these changes will help you stand out." Grady downed the last of his coffee and said, "C'mon," he gathered up his things. "I'll take you to a stationary store, and we'll pick out résumé paper."

"Wow. You'd do that for me?"

"Of course, I would." Grady stood, grabbed Jude by his hand, and headed for the exit. "I can tell from your experience and talking to you that you're an intelligent, great guy. And if I may be blunt, sexy."

Jude practically got a hard-on. Grady's hand was a conduit

carrying heat up Jude's arm, fanning across his face, chest, and down to his groin.

Outside, the air felt good, washing over his inflamed body.

When they finished choosing the résumé paper, it was going on four o'clock.

"I say we earned a drink," Grady suggested going to the Castro Station, where he said he worked part-time. *Even a college professor had to work a second job to live in San Francisco?*

The Castro Station was another in a series of bars on the infamous Castro strip. It was a spacious bar, and since the day was temperate, the large French doors were open, affording a broad view of the street and allowing a cooling breeze to circulate the bar.

The bartender approached wearing a tight black T-shirt accentuating his buff body.

"Hey, Grady," Danny said, leaning over and kissing him on the cheek. "You working tonight?"

"No, I'm on tomorrow evening. Danny, meet Jude. He's thinking of moving out here."

Danny stopped wiping a glass to shake Jude's hand. "Oh, where are you from?"

"You mean you don't know?"

Danny looked perplexed. "Should I know?"

"Whenever my friends introduced me, people immediately think I'm from New York."

Danny laughed. "Now that you mention it. I hear the accent now."

Secretly, Jude groaned.

"What'll you have?"

"I'll have a Grey Goose martini."

"The same," Grady said.

Danny left to make the drinks.

"I can't thank you enough for all you did to help me with my résumé."

"It was my pleasure. I think you're a cool guy and would love to see you get a job so you can move here."

During their conversation, Jude was hit by the proverbial thunderbolt. He sat transfixed, lost in a sexual fog. *It would be great if this "thunderbolt" ended up like it did for Michael Corleone and Apollonia, except without Grady getting blown up.*

Jude sensed that beyond the kinetic sexual charge Grady sent through him, he was one of the rare ones who also had a great personality, generous spirit, and intelligence. Perhaps George was right. Grady could be *the someone* who freed his protected heart.

"If you're free one night this week, I'd love to take you to dinner," Jude suggested. "To show my appreciation for helping me with my résumé."

"I would like that, even though it's not necessary. Does Friday work for you?"

"Yes, Friday is perfect."

After three martinis, Jude thought he should be getting back home. Grady walked Jude to the bus stop.

"I'm a little impulsive, so I hope you don't mind this." Grady grabbed Jude and gave him a lingering kiss (complete with tongue). Jude acquiesced and returned the kiss (complete with tongue). Jude felt at ease kissing Grady on the street and did not care who saw; after all, this was San Francisco. It felt freeing—and liberating. *Bonus points for gay Mecca.*

Grady saw his bus on the opposite side of the Castro. He gave Jude another quick kiss, excused himself, and dashed off before the bus left. From the window, he gestured for Jude to call him. Then his bus took off.

Jude rode home, exhilarated by the time spent with Grady, especially his impulse to kiss him. He closed his eyes as his bus traveled up Market Street. Based on his kiss, Jude imagined what sex would be like with Grady. He even thought of being his boyfriend. Then, the thought of calling Francine to tell her about Grady interrupted his dream. He was the kind of guy Jude would gush over, sparing no detail for her. His eyes opened, and reality set in. Francine was MIA. But his feud with her couldn't deflate the high uplifting him. He rode home on a cloud, thanks to Grady Savage.

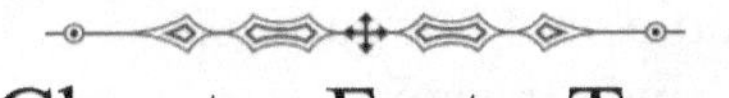

Chapter Forty-Two
Sly As a Silver Fox

Jude spent the next day typing up his résumé on Matthew's computer and printing it. There was a post office on Geary Boulevard, a few blocks from Matthew's apartment building. He felt accomplished and excited about the possibility of getting a job in San Francisco. He dropped his résumés in the cream-colored envelopes Grady picked out in the mail slot.

Back in the apartment, he called Grady to finalize plans for dinner on Friday. When he called, a voice answered that was not Grady's. Jude's heart thrummed in panic. He swallowed hard. "Hello, is Grady there?"

"Not at the moment. This is his roommate. Is there a message for him?"

Jude sighed with relief. The pendulum of pros versus cons seesawed in Jude's mind. *A second job AND a roommate?* "Just tell him Jude called, and I will try him later."

Grady returned his call shortly after. They made plans to meet at the Castro Station at 6 o'clock on Friday.

***

Friday came, and Jude felt like he was going to his prom with the hottest guy in school. He spent time choosing what to wear before deciding on jeans, a flannel shirt buttoned halfway over a white ribbed tank top, and to show local camaraderie, he borrowed a San Francisco Giants baseball cap from George. At the last minute, he added a chain with a pair of mini handcuffs around his neck, which he bought at a boutique on Castro Street.

Over a martini at the Castro Station, Grady suggested going to Agave Maria on Market Steet, an upscale Mexican restaurant with an interior brightly decorated with deep navy blue and dazzling yellow tiles.

Maria, the attractive middle-aged owner with a mantilla-style hair comb made of silver, pearls, and rhinestones, greeted them before they were seated at a cozy table with a lit candle. Maria came back with tortilla chips, guacamole, and margaritas.

"Dinner is on me," Jude insisted.

"Here's to your success." Grady raised his margarita. Jude followed, and they tapped glasses. The quivering candle flame created a scintillating shine on Grady's silver hoop and hair.

"Tell me, what drove you to become a professor of women's literature?" Jude inquired.

"I was a voracious reader. I loved dissecting books and delving into their meaning. There's nothing better than a great metaphor. How words are put together and take on new meaning fascinates me," Grady explained.

Jude's eyes lit up. "I was the same way. The first book I read was *Charlotte's Web*, which changed me or tapped into something in me. I think I was born with a creative gene. In college, studying film taught me how tedious it is, so now my dream is to write."

"I would love to read your work," Grady confessed.

"Who are some of your favorite authors?" Jude savored a sip of his margarita.

"Oh, there are so many—Virginia Woolf, Mary Shelley, Harriet Beecher-Stowe, Flannery O'Connor, The Bronte sisters, Eudora Welty."

"Why women authors?" Jude was genuinely curious.

"I just felt I wanted to stress women writers because they get overshadowed by men." Grady's eyes shifted to the mini handcuffs hanging between Jude's open shirt.

"Are you into bondage?" A glint of a sinful smile pulled at Grady's tempting lips.

Jude blushed. "Well, I've never really done anything heavy."

"What do you think about being tied up during sex?"

Forewarned of his fetish, Jude replied, "I'm open to a lot sexually. If done with consent and within boundaries, it could be exciting. I mean, sex has as much to do with mental stimulation as it does the physical."

The sinful smile expanded. "Can I tell you again how great you are and how much I enjoy talking to you?"

"Yes, you can tell me as often as you like." Jude cracked an unholy smile.

Towards the end of dinner, Grady downed the last of his margarita and said, "I'm going to be impulsive again and suggest you come home with me."

Jude knew Grady had much to drink between the Grey Goose martinis and the several margaritas over dinner, but his heart leaped into his throat. "There's nothing impulsive about that. I was hoping that you'd want me to."

Jude paid the bill, and they walked back down Castro to catch the bus to Grady's apartment.

"We just missed the bus we need to take. Shall we get a drink?" Grady suggested.

"Sure."

They went to Daddy's, where Corey made them another margarita. Jude and Grady spent their time in a darkened corner in such proximity Jude could smell the tequila on Grady's breath. Eventually, he wrapped his arms around Jude's waist.

"I hope you stay in San Francisco," Grady said in a slight drunken slur and pulled Jude close to him, gently touching his lips to Jude's.

Jude acquiesced. "You're helping the odds in favor of it happening." He lightly grazed his fingertips over Grady's exposed forearm. Grady closed his eyes and inhaled at Jude's touch. When he opened them, he stared at Jude. Their eyes were conductors of sexual currents that sparked and crackled in the short distance between them. Grady went in for a more passionate kiss. Jude's head spun in carnal vertigo.

Upon finishing their drinks, Grady suggested they leave. He grabbed Jude's hand, and they left.

They strolled hand in hand down the Castro to the bus stop, and in minutes, one arrived. On the bus, Grady put his arm around Jude's shoulder. Jude took advantage of San Francisco's openness and kissed Grady. A middle-aged woman with veins of grey streaking through her Afro looked on. She scoffed. "Mm-hmm! Somebody's getting laid tonight!"

Chapter Forty-Three
Tie Him Up, Tie Him Down

When they arrived at Grady's apartment, it was modestly furnished with a plaid couch and matching chair A few empty beer cans and magazines cluttered the coffee table. A large aquarium was on a half wall between the entrance and the living room. *It was not the best of taste or the neatest, but who cares?*

"Wait here," Grady said. "I have to do a quick straightening up in my room." He disappeared and closed his bedroom door.

After what seemed like hours, the door opened, and Grady ushered Jude into his bedroom. Looking around, Jude wondered what Grady *straightened up.* An unmade, four-poster bed overpowered the small room. Grady messily yanked up the sheets and bedspread to mask the disarray. Bookshelves sagged under the weight of their contents. A wooden dresser with brass handles further diminished the space in the room. Atop the dresser was a ceramic figurine of a gladiator, some loose change, and grooming artifacts. A wicker hamper with the arm of a shirt hanging out stood in a corner.

No sooner did Jude assess the room when Grady pounced, aggressively pulling Jude to him and kissing him hard. Grady's hands pulled roughly, tugging at Jude's clothes. He practically popped the buttons off Jude's flannel shirt and almost ripped his tank top as he pulled it over Jude's head. Grady partially unlaced Jude's work boots before yanking them off. Grady ripped the last of Jude's clothes off and started talking in a daddy/son role-play, surprising Jude. Though Jude was open sexually, he always thought that role-play was silly. *Let's just get down and dirty!* But being slightly buzzed and with Grady, the *silver fox,* he found it rather humorous and played along.

"Now Daddy is going to get undressed." Grady ripped at his clothes, throwing his jeans across the room.

In his mind, Jude's eyes rolled in his head. *If you were my Daddy, you would have had me when you were eight or nine years old, but whatever, your body is smoking hot.* Jude went in for a lusty embrace and kiss.

Grady tottered as he pushed him back. He uttered a scolding sound. "Daddy will tell you when you can touch him. From now on, you address me as *sir* and answer everything with *sir*. Got it?"

"Yes," Jude replied, trying not to laugh.

"*YES,* what?" Grady tried to sound tough, but his drunken slur killed the effect.

"Yes, *sir.*" Jude saluted.

"Don't salute me," Grady said with disgust. "I'm not a drill sergeant." His voice suddenly affectionate, "I'm your Daddy." Grady took Jude in his arms. The scent of alcohol billowed from him and hung like a gaseous cloud between their faces. Then the palm of Grady's hand slapped against Jude's buttock, shocking Jude, yet he struggled to hold back a smile from bursting on his face.

"Understand?" Grady asked, toughening up again.

"Yes...*sir,*" Jude added in haste before Grady delivered another hand-to-buttock smack.

They fell onto the large, messy bed. Jude was ready for action, but Grady was not. Jude toyed with his soft yet still enticing dick, but it remained flaccid. With the drinks they had before, during, and after dinner, Grady was too buzzed to do anything but told Jude he would get a good whipping in the morning, especially if he didn't answer with *yes, sir* to everything.

Whipping?!

They crawled under the crumpled bedding as Grady told Jude, "I like my feet rubbed," and moved them next to Jude's, sending a dreaded chill through him.

A foot fetish? Oh shit!

Grady was a sexual onion with some new kink revealed under each layer. Jude, not being into the foot thing, moved his feet away. Grady reprimanded Jude, warning him of the whipping he would get if he disobeyed *Daddy,* and reluctantly returned his feet to Grady's. Jude grimaced as if swallowing distasteful medicine. He closed his eyes as Grady made foot-to-foot contact.

Sleep came fast for both.

In the morning, Grady woke and put an arm around Jude, who stirred at his touch. Grady kissed his shoulder. "Are you ready to please Daddy?"

"Can't I sleep a little longer?" Jude yawned.

Grady's hand slapped against Jude's bare buttock. "What did I say about answering me?"

"Can't I sleep a little longer? *Please, sir?*"

"Don't you want to make Daddy happy?" Grady's foot caressed Jude's foot, ankle, calf. Jude cringed as he felt Grady's clenching toes grasp at the flesh of his leg.

"Yes, *sir,*" Jude said, squeezing his eyes shut. The once flaccid penis from last night was now a rock-solid monolith pressed up against Jude. He, like Adam, was tempted by the forbidden fruit, in this case, a Congo plantain instead of an apple, and answered a series of Grady's questions with an obliging *yes, sir, no, sir,* or *please, sir.*

After some intense kissing and groping of bodies, Grady got up and grabbed a riding crop hanging from the wall. The view from behind was another fruit lover's delight. His buttocks were as hard and round as coconuts.

Grady hopped back into bed and rolled Jude on his stomach, running the riding crop along the small of his back, intermittently slapping the leather pad on Jude's ass with gentle smacks. He propped himself up on his knees and made circular motions along Jude's flesh.

"Daddy wants a foot massage."

"Must I, sir?" Jude said, rolling his eyes.

The riding crop came down with a little more force.

"You don't want to make Daddy angry, do you?" Grady spoke with a cajoling cadence as he made sequential taps down Jude's spine before one hard smack landed on Jude's behind.

"Ow! That hurt."

"Daddy will make it better." Grady kissed Jude where the leather pad made contact. Then he gently rubbed Jude's other buttock before smacking it.

Jesus, it's like sex with Jekyll and Hyde.

"Now give Daddy a foot rub."

Hesitating but seeing Grady poise the riding crop in the air, Jude reluctantly moved to the end of the bed. Now, on his back, Grady raised his feet deliberately for Jude to rub.

Jude analyzed Grady's feet, then looked away as he pressed his thumbs into the soles of his feet.

"Now, kiss and lick Daddy's feet," Grady said dreamily but with authority.

"Um, I'm really not into feet...*sir,* I don't think I can do that."

Grady leaned forward and swung his riding crop, making contact with Jude's ass again.

"Ow! That hurt—*again.*"

"Then kiss and lick Daddy's feet."

With riding crop ready to strike again, Jude reluctantly had to put his foot-loathing aside. He grimaced as his lips made contact with the soles of Grady's feet. Shortly into his mouth-to-foot connection, Jude suffered a dry heave.

"Now lick. Give 'em a good bathing."

Jude stuck his tongue out, but millimeters away, he cracked and had another violent heave. He let go of Grady's foot. "Okay, beat me. Whip me. Tar and feather me. I can't lick your feet. I'm so…" Jude heaved. "…sorry."

"Come to Daddy," Grady spoke soothingly, invitingly.

Sticking straight up from his groin was a very alluring erection.

Grady beckoned Jude to his side and asked, "So, you said you found being tied up exciting and sexually stimulating?"

Jude was suspicious. "What have you got in mind…*sir?*"

Grady reached into a nightstand drawer. "Just a little light bondage."

"What's your definition of *light?*" But as Jude was asking, Grady rolled him over and, like some rodeo champeen, had his hands tied behind his back in mere seconds. Grady took more rope and wrapped it around Jude's genitalia, and bending his legs at the knees, tied the other end around his ankles. Then Grady got a cat-o-nine tail from a hook on his wall.

Oh shit.

With Jude on his stomach, Grady dragged the leather straps over his back and buttocks in a back-and-forth motion as if he were mopping a floor. He bounced the tips off Jude before letting go with a succession of whips. *Thwack! Thwack! Thwack!* Surprisingly, the impact stung more than it hurt, like downing shots of tequila. After a series of whippings, Grady took the riding crop, ran it across the bottom of Jude's feet, and began lightly tapping his soles. The sensation caused Jude to flex his ankles, which tugged at his tied-up genitals.

"Jesus! Did you study at the College of Marquis de Sade?"

Ignoring Jude, Grady did the most sadistic thing Jude could imagine: He tickled his feet, triggering further wrenching of his tied-up testicles. If there was one thing he hated (other than feet), it was getting tickled, especially when Grady tied his balls to where he tickled Jude. The more Jude writhed and shouted, the more turned-on Grady seemed to get. *Where was the sensitive kisser? The considerate, thoughtful, coffee-buying résumé spin doctor?* Having his balls shackled to his ankles was not the erotic fantasy of being tied up Jude had in mind. The tickling became unbearable. He thought he saw drool on Grady's chin. Jude was about to yell the proverbial *uncle* as opposed to *Daddy* or *sir* when Grady stopped. Jude looked behind him. Grady grabbed Jude's feet and was thrusting his engorged penis between them. In mere seconds, Grady's body quaked, and he went off with Mount Vesuvius ferocity, dousing Jude's backside.

After catching his breath, Grady untied Jude and wiped him down. Jude rubbed his wrists, which had slight rope burns.

"Daddy's ready to jack you off."

"No, that's quite alright…*sir.*" Jude rose from the bed and, in a cross-reflection of a wall and freestanding floor mirror, noticed several welts on his back from the whippings he received. He began to gather his clothes and dress. Jude looked down and saw the chain that had once been around his neck. When he picked it up, the mini handcuffs fell to the floor.

"Oh, I'm so sorry." Grady's apologized sincerely. "Let me give you money for breaking your chain." Exorcized from the demon within, gentle Grady was back.

"It's fine. I can get another chain."

After Jude dressed, Grady walked him to the door and told him where to get the streetcar back to the Castro. He pulled Jude in and kissed him, while Jude kissed his dream life in San Francisco as the boyfriend of the silver fox goodbye.

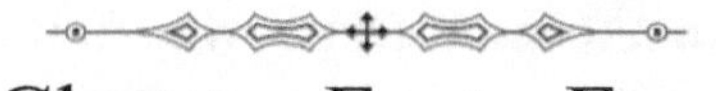

Chapter Forty-Four
Eudora Weltys

As the number 52 streetcar headed down the hilly roads, Jude recapped his night with Grady. An ironic smile crossed his lips. Grady may not have turned out to be his soul mate, but it was one hell of an encounter, a tale to tell friends. *Francine.* Jude stared forlornly out the window and watched a patch of fog burn off in the late morning sun. Naturally, Francine was the first person he thought of. She would have scolded Jude for allowing himself to be used as a *whipping boy* no matter how sexy Grady was, but she would have appreciated the hilarity of the Grady Savage story. But like the vaporized fog, Jude's friendship was a faded memory. She felt burned and betrayed by Jude. It was his heart, not his ass, that now felt the stinging lashes from a lost friendship. There had to be a way to get her back. Taking a cue from Scarlett O'Hara, he'd think about that tomorrow. Right now, he had to tell the second person he thought of about Grady's *house of torture:* Matthew.

He was working his noon to seven shift at Daddy's, a name that would now forever conjure up images of the Women in American Literature professor with a riding crop in his hand and a foot fetish.

When Jude got off the bus on Castro Street, he went straight to the Daddy's. Being in a bar long before happy hour officially began was strange, but this was San Francisco, another plus for the city.

Seeing Matthew, Jude said, "I'm still alive, though slightly bruised from my time with Grady and his depraved predilections."

"I can tell you have a juicy story to tell. Let me make you a Bloody Mary."

Jude settled onto the leather barstool. "The hot, deceitfully mild-mannered professor may be sexy as hell, but he is a freak! It was like spending the night with a sadist."

Jude continued to recount his night with Grady, which brought Matthew to hysterics. In retrospect, it even seemed funny to Jude.

"There was role-playing with more *yes, sirs, no, sirs,* and *please, sirs* than a gay porn production of *Oliver!*"

"Did he tie you up?"

"Oh yes, but not in the hot, erotic way I imagined. He tied my testicles to my ankles—"

Matthew doubled over with laughter.

"And George failed to tell me the professor of women's literature likes to play with whips and riding crops."

"Whips! Seriously?"

"Oh yes. Instead of being fellated, I was flagellated. I have the Eudora *Weltys* to prove it." Jude stood and lifted his shirt. Matthew was stunned but couldn't control his laughter as Jude layered his encounter with Grady like lasagna with detail after saucy detail.

"He was like the opening of *Blue Velvet*—*the* gorgeous white house with a picket fence lined with roses on the outside, but beneath the surface, there's sinister, bug-crawling aggression."

A man in his mid-forties a few barstools away couldn't help but hear Jude's recollections and chortled with each embellishment. Jude hadn't noticed him until now.

"I'm sorry for subjecting you to my sordid sex life."

"No, no," the bespectacled man offered. "I don't mean to laugh at your…um…tortuous plight, but hearing you tell it is quite amusing. Let me buy your next drink."

"Thank you. There's more." Jude raised his glass to the man. He turned his attention back to Matthew, who was making another Bloody Mary.

"Did you know he has a foot fetish? I had to massage the balls of his feet—not exactly the balls I was hoping to massage." Jude finished off his first Bloody Mary.

"Then, he wanted me to slobber all over his feet. But I told him he could torture me to death before I gave one lick to his feet. It was bad enough I had to touch them." Jude grimaced.

Matthew shook so hard he spilled some vodka.

As Jude recalled the events with Grady, he could not believe he allowed him to do what he did. "Chalk it up to one hilarious sexual adventure. Why do all the apparent good ones turn out to be cheaters or freaks?"

"That's San Francisco," Matthew said, bringing the Bloody Mary to Jude.

Jude took a hefty sip of his freshly made cocktail. Jude sighed.

"Better line up those Bloody Marys for me, Matt. It's going to take a lot of vodka to wash away the shame of allowing the deceptive charming, but pervy silver fox to seduce me.

Chapter Forty-Five
Jude Swallows His Pride

"This is Riley St. Regis from Top Dawg Studio calling for Jude G-i-a-c-a-l-o-n-e. I'm calling to set up an interview with Harvey Wetlock, CEO of the studio. Give us a buzz back to schedule a time…" The message came a week after Jude sent several revised résumés, including one to Blue Shield of California for their marketing positions. *Figures I hear from the porn company.* Jude reluctantly jotted down the number.

A few hours later, Jude dialed the studio.

"Hello, this is Jude Giacolone returning your call, Mr. Saint Regis."

"Jude, who?"

"Giacolone. G-i-a-c…You called earlier about an interview." Jude heard some shuffling of papers.

"Oh, yeah, I have your résumé in front of me. Hey, Harvey wants you to come in for an interview to see how you'd fit in with the Top Dawg team. What's a good time?"

"Well, seeing I'm unemployed, anytime."

"Ah yeah, hungry. Harvey likes his *dawgs* hungry. Means they're eager."

"Yes, as you can see from my résumé, I have a degree in Communications and lots of marketing experience."

"Yeah, sure. And hungry, right?"

"Right, hungry," Jude placated Riley, making a *what-the-fuck* face.

"How 'bout Thursday, noon? Right now, Harv's in Las Vegas for the Pubies's. He's up for a few categories."

"Pubies's?"

"Yeah, the gay adult video awards ceremony. Harvey's up for Best Threesome, Best Blow Job, and Best Production for *Swallow My Pride.* Pretty exciting, huh?"

Jude held his head in his hand. "Yeah, thrilling." Jude rolled his eyes.

"Okay, then Thursday at noon. Oh, and come dressed casually, jeans, T-shirt, whatever. Harvey's not formal, doesn't like to interview guys all bound up, at least not in suits and ties," Riley emitted a dirty laugh.

Jude hung up the phone. "Jesus, what am I getting myself into?"

***

Jude dressed in jeans, work boots, and a white thermal undershirt per Riley St. Regis' request for the interview. After walking a few blocks from the bus stop, he was in front of the Top Dawg office, its name written in nondescript lettering on nondescript doors on a nondescript building on Mission Street.

Jude swallowed *his pride* and entered with no expectations. Passing through the tinted glass doors, he entered the lobby. Expecting a seedy-looking interior, he was surprised to see the lobby's sleek, modern décor, including a red and grey leather sofa. On his right was a glass showcase filled with awards and plaques the studio won.

The recent copies of Forbes and Fortune 500 magazines seemed adrift in the sea of gay porn magazines on a glass table. Other than the Plexiglas logo on the wall of an aggressive-looking bulldog wearing a spiked collar humping a surprised, floppy-eared canine, it looked more like the lobby for a law firm than a gay porn production company.

Jude approached the white Lucite desk and cleared his throat.

"Can I help you?" asked the girl behind the desk. Her face remained in her *Entertainment Weekly* magazine, affording Jude a glimpse of her flaming red puff of hair.

"I'm here to see Riley St. Regis for an interview." Jude could not help but notice the ample cleavage, probably wasted on the clientele who passed through the lobby.

"Name?" She flipped a page in her magazine.

"Jude Giacolone."

"Asia. Pleasure." The boredom in her voice told Jude it was anything but.

"Excuse me?"

"Asia. My name, like the continent, honey," she said, stabbing three numbers on her push-button phone with the tip of a long, bright orange press-on.

Jude mouthed a silent *Oh*, whose apparent affront irked her.

"There's a Jude…what's your last name?" Finally, making eye

contact.

"Giacolone. He'll probably know me better by just Jude." He forced a smile, suddenly aware of his sweaty palms.

"Jude, just Jude, is here for an interview." Hanging up, she said, "Follow me." She rose, exposing her black-and-white striped mini skirt and orange, opaque stockings.

She led Jude through a windowed door and down a long hallway. She even walked with boredom, shuffling along the Parquet floor in her platform shoes as if wearing cement blocks.

Jude eyed the movie posters and framed photos of shirtless men with great bodies (*imagine seeing them all day)* and a large white-haired man puffing a cigar that lined the corridor's walls. Jude recognized Chi Chi LaRue with the stogie-chomping, heavyset man in one photo.

Asia stopped in a doorway and announced, "Riley St.Regis." She extended her arm; her hand flopped with apparent boredom.

Jude stepped into the office. Riley was wearing an open leather vest and no shirt. His face was lined and weathered, and he sported a thick handlebar mustache, looking like a refugee from the 70s—or the Civil War.

"Well, well, well. Look at you!" Regis clapped once. His eyes did a full body scan. Jude detected a little lust in his voice. Riley stood, extending his hand bedecked with gaudy gold rings on most of his fingers and several bracelets, not to be outdone by the Olympic medal-size medallion that hung in a dense patch of chest hair.

"Come in. Have a seat." Riley fell into his high-backed chair and clasped his hands behind his head, exposing his bushy armpits. As meticulously minimalist as the lobby was, sitting among the clutter in Regis's office squeezed the breath out of Jude's lungs.

"So, you ever work in porn before?"

"Well, there aren't a lot of porn opportunities where I'm from."

"Where'd you grow up? Idaho?" Riley said, followed by snorted laughter. "Say, can I get you something to drink?"

"Perhaps some water."

"Scotch? Gin? Vodka?" Regis asked, ignoring Jude's request.

This is the weirdest interview I've ever been on. But a scotch right about now would take the edge off.

"Since you're offering, I'll take scotch. Please."

"Great. Harvey should be here in a few minutes. He's got a noon massage scheduled, so we'll just chew the fat over a scotch or two."

"Oh, I thought my interview was at noon?"

"It is." Riley took out a bottle and two glasses from a minibar. "He'll interview you during his massage. He's a very busy man. He's got three films going into production." Riley handed Jude his scotch in an ostentatious crystal glass that felt like it weighed about ten pounds.

"Jameson, Bow Street. Aged 18 years. One hundred eighty dollars a bottle. Nothing but the best for Harv. Cheers." He clicked glasses with Jude. "Here's to your future at Top Dawg."

Riley sat on the edge of his desk, dangling a denim-clad leg. He began a lengthy recital about the history of Top Dawg Productions.

"Harvey came along and saved the company after AIDS almost decimated the gay porn industry. He was one of the first producers to insist the actors have regular AIDS tests and use glass slippers—"

"Glass slippers?" Jude asked.

"Yeah, rubbers, condoms. Earned Harv the nickname *Cinderella* in the biz." Riley guffawed. "Returned gay porn to the guilt-free fuck fest it used to be back in the 70s."

Now, there's a term you don't hear every day in an interview.

Jude's facial muscles pulled his lips into a clenched smile.

"Where was I? Oh, yeah. So, he's got three films going into production. *Bottoms Up* and *Heavy Load.* And he's casting one now called *All That Jizz.* Speaking of bottoms up..." Riley downed his scotch. Jude mimicked the action.

Riley waved for Jude to extend his glass. "Can you see yourself working here at Top Dawg, the biggest production company in the gay porn industry?"

"I have a lot of experience and talent I can bring to the position."

"A lot of experience and talent, huh? I bet. Good-looking guy like you probably have guys knocking down your door." Riley choked out a laugh. "I can tell you got confidence. You'd be a natural in front of the camera."

Jude cracked a quizzical smile, the innuendo lost in the beginning of a scotch fog.

Riley reached out to pour Jude more scotch.

"I think I've had enough. I don't want to be drunk when I meet with Mr. Wetlock."

"Oh, don't call him *Mr. Wetlock*," Riley said in a hushed voice as if Jude uttered some hundred-year-old secret code. "He insists upon being called Harvey or Harv. We're very relaxed around here, not stiff at all unless the fluffer gets to us." Riley exploded into a bawdy laugh. "Hell no, we don't get formal about interviews. We want to see the *natural* you, so drink up. Eighteen years aged!"

The phone rang.

"Riley St. Regis." There was a pause. "Okay." Regis eyed Jude with a lusty stare. "I think you'll to want to reconsider him for something else instead of an office job. He's got real potential." There was a pause. "Okay, see you soon." He hung up. "Harvey's running a little behind." The scotch went down easy and smooth. Jude was oblivious to Regis's conversation as heat spread across Jude's face.

Halfway through the eighteen-year-old scotch, the phone rang again. Regis picked up. "Okay." Hanging up, he addressed Jude. "It's show time."

Going down easy as it did, Jude didn't feel the effect of the scotch until he stood up. He grabbed the chair for support.

They walked down the hall side by side. Regis' heavily ringed hand smacked against Jude's clavicle, causing him to wince.

"So kid, you like to top? Bottom?"

"You could say I'm versatile," Jude said absent-mindedly, his brain in an eighteen-year-old scotch stupor.

"Ahh!" Regis clapped. "Harvey likes versatile. Gets more use out of a performer. You're gonna like Harvey. He may be CEO, but he considers himself an equal."

Riley herded Jude inside a blinding white massage room. Harp music played softly, and an athletic, handsome man in a white T-shirt and shorts squeezed the back of Harvey's flabby thigh.

"Boss, this is Jude…how do you say your last name again?" Riley inquired.

"Giacolone."

A terrycloth towel covered Harvey's massive ass, but Jude recognized his face as the cigar-chewing man from the photos in the hallway.

Harvey raised his head. "Jack alone? That your last name or your hobby?" He bellowed, which turned into a wheezing, coughing jag. Resting on an elbow, he removed a soggy cigar with one hand and extended the other to Jude. Coughing now composed, he addressed Jude. "How ya doin', kid?" Jude pumped the stout, moist hand, then discreetly wiped his palm on his jeans.

"Hope you don't mind me getting massaged, but I got a tight schedule."

As the room spun, Jude thanked Harvey for meeting him, especially with such a busy day.

"Let me get a good look at you, kid." Harvey reached for his glasses. "Stop!" he ordered the well-built masseuse, who, with military precision, straightened up and clasped his hands behind his back. Harvey grabbed the towel and brought it around to cover himself as he sat on the edge of the massage table. Grey hair long enough to wrap around beer cans covered his chest.

Why are men in San Francisco so hairy? Jude wondered through the scotch-laden haze shrouding his brain.

Harvey's beach ball-sized belly hung over the towel. "You were right, Riley. The kid's got real potential. What's he packing?"

Riley looked at Jude.

"What? What's he wanna know?" Jude slurred.

"How big's your dick?" Riley asked.

"Doesn't matter. He must be well-hung, judging from the package in his jeans. Besides, he's got a good physical appearance. I think he'd be perfect in *All That Jizz*. I see him in a scene with Axel Rod. Whaddya think?"

"I thought the same thing," Riley concurred.

Harvey dialed the phone next to him. "Tell Axel to come to the massage room pronto." With great effort, he grunted as he got off the table and fumbled with his towel, struggling to secure it around the thick circumference of his waist. The sound of his bare feet slapped like fleshy paddles on the tile floor as he walked. His body jiggled with a Jell-O-like consistency.

"Take your shirt off, kid."

"*What?*" Jude was incredulous.

Before he knew it, Riley lifted Jude's thermal shirt above his head.

"Nice. Good definition." Harvey slapped a palm against Jude's pectoral, then walked around Jude, grabbing his buttocks, appraising him as if he were a farm animal at a county fair.

"Good package, nice ass. He'll be a hit on camera. Might even win a Pubie for Best Newcomer," Harvey surmised.

"I think there is a misunderstanding here. I applied for the Marketing Manager position."

"Kid, with your looks and body, I say you could pull in two thou your first year, depending on how many scenes you want to do," Harvey said with authority.

"Really?" Jude had a moment of sobriety.

"Two thousand? *Dollars?*" Then Jude's parents flashed before his inebriated eyes. "No, no, no. I didn't come—"

The door opened. Jude turned. His eyes saw the naked, buff blonde with a classically handsome face and chiseled body of an Adonis. His focus shifted to the large appendage that swung like a pendulum as Axel Rod approached.

"What's up, boss?" I'm about to do a scene."

"Axel, baby. I want to introduce you to Jude *Jack alone*." Harvey blurted out a singular mucousy cough. "I wanted to see what you think. I say he's perfect to do a scene with you in *All That Jizz*."

Without warning, Axel's eyes sized up Jude, lifting him off the floor in a bear hug that nearly forced the eighteen-year-old scotch out of him, jounced him up and down, and grabbed his ass before putting him back down. "Yeah, I like it." Lust oozed from Axel's voice.

"Wait a minute," Jude said, suddenly sober. "First of all, I'm not an *it*. And secondly, I didn't come here for an *audition*. I thought this interview was for a Marketing Manager."

"Asia can handle that shit for the time being. After looking at you, I'm offering you a chance to be in porn, kid."

Nearly half a year into his thirtieth birthday, Jude secretly relished Harvey's continued reference to him as *kid*.

"You'd be a hit," Harvey shouted, waving his arms. Gravity pulled on the pendulous flab of his arm as it flapped. His towel fell under the strain against his hula hoop-size waist, exposing his stubby penis. Through the dense pubic patch, it looked like the top of a shiitake mushroom poking through the black soil.

"Thanks, but no thanks." Jude grabbed his shirt from Riley's hands. He stopped in front of Axel. "Nice to meet you." Jude gave Axel's semi-hard-on a tug and a squeeze instead of the traditional handshake, then headed for the door. Harvey waddled after him, feet smacking the floor like the flippers of an excited seal, his gelatinous body waggling in all directions.

"You could have been in porn. We could have all made money. You ungrateful son of a bitch!"

Jude tugged on his shirt as he continued down the hallway and shouted, "I have my pride. My *gay* pride."

***

Shortly after Jude's interview, Matthew met him at a small café for lunch on Market Street. Though the weather had cooled a bit, it was sunny and comfortable enough to sit on the patio encased by vine-covered trellises.

"How'd your interview go?" Matthew took a seat opposite Jude, who was waiting for him.

As Jude explained, he watched a patch of fog drift over the distant hills and then roll away. It reminded him of Carl Sandburg's poem: *The fog comes on little cat feet,* unlike Harvey Wetlock, who shambled on his wide, flat appendages with ungraceful smacks.

An adorable waiter in jeans and a tie-dyed tank top placed glasses of water on the table and took their orders.

"Who is Riley St. Regis?" Matthew asked.

Jude stopped to think. "I don't know who he was. Probably a leftover from nineteen seventies porn."

Halfway through Jude's recitation recounting his interview, the cute waiter brought their lunches. Listening to another outlandish adventure of Jude's, Matthew nearly choked on his California burger from laughter.

"I've been in San Francisco for over two years and never had any experiences like yours, and you've only been here two months," Matthew said.

"I know. I feel like I'm at a sexual Disneyland."

Matthew crunched on a crisp French fry before saying, "Axel Rod, huh? He's hot. He's been in Daddy's a few times."

"Can you see me telling Dolores and Augie I got a job as a porn star? Proud of me, folks? College sure paid off."

"Oh, I almost forgot to tell you. Some woman from Blue Shield called and left a message. Maybe it's about an interview."

"They better serve eighteen-year-old scotch, or I'm not going."

"Hopefully, it's more promising than Top Dawg."

Jude picked up his deli-style pickle. "It can't be any worse than my short-lived career in gay porn." He simulated giving his pickle a blowjob before biting down on it with a vengeance.

Chapter Forty-Six
You Can't Fight Fate

The following morning, Jude returned the call from Blue Shield of California with optimism rushing through his veins.

"Hello, Jude. My name is Doris Zemaitis, and I am the Human Resource Director at Blue Shield of California. I'm calling regarding your résumé you submitted for the Marketing Supervisor position…"

Jude's heart fluttered with the tenacity of a baby bird's desire to fly.

"…and unfortunately, we had to offer the position to one of our internal candidates."

The wings were clipped, and his heart fell to the ground.

Ms. Zemaitis went on, "But I wanted to speak to you personally to tell you how very impressed I was with your résumé, and I am truly sorry I can't offer you an interview at this time."

Jude tried to sound cheery and thanked her for the personal call, but his mood was DOA.

"I certainly will keep your résumé on file should another position that meets your qualifications open up."

"At this point, I may have to return to Albany."

"Albany, New York?"

"Yes," Jude said, dejected.

"Hmm. I see." Her voice was mysterious. "Well then, you have a good day, Jude," Ms. Zemaitis said.

Jude hung up. Even though it was only 9:30 a.m., he wished he had some of that eighteen-year-old scotch. Instead, he settled for a Bloody Mary.

Despite the several résumés Jude sent, he either didn't hear from the company or the positions were already filled. Jude's hopes of starting a new life in San Francisco dissipated faster than a patch of fog. The last thread of hope was severed when Dolores called towards the end of April.

"How are things going, honey?"

"Not so good. I'm striking out trying to get a job here, and my severance package runs out in a few weeks. So, I think it's time I return home."

Over the phone, Jude heard the unmistakable tinkling of Dolores' crystal rosary beads. He imagined her making the sign of the cross and giving thanks to God for his decision.

"Perhaps it's for the best because I have some bad news. Your father has been diagnosed with cancer."

Jude was silent for a long time before speaking.

"Jude, honey? You there?"

"Yeah, I'm here," his voice quivered. "I'm just stunned. Aug is so full of life. How did he take the news?"

"Oh, you know your father. He was devastated, but he took it in stride. He went out and bowled that night after hearing the news."

"Why am I not surprised? If Augie had a theme song, it'd be "That's Life." Jude laughed weakly.

"He does love Frank Sinatra."

"It's treatable, though. I mean, there's chemo, right?" Jude forced optimism.

"According to the doctor, the cancer is growing *in* the liver, not on it, so chemo and radiation aren't options, but your father wouldn't subject himself to that anyway. He says the cure is worse than the disease. Doctor Buff is going to schedule an appointment at Sloan Kettering to see what his options are. He'll be glad to have you back home."

The news still shook Jude. "Cancer. Augie! I can't believe it." He took a deep breath. "I'll make arrangements to be home as soon as I can. I'm so sorry, Dolores."

"I know, honey. And your father wouldn't want you to sacrifice coming back home if things were working out for you in San Francisco, you know that."

"Of course I do, but I decided to come home anyway. I guess I belong on the East Coast. I'll let you know when I'm coming back."

"I'll pay for your flight. Here's my credit card information."

"Dolores, you don't have to—"

"Yes, I do. Get a pen."

Jude knew there was no sense resisting Dolores when it came to helping her children. Jude jotted down the card number.

"Thanks, Dolores. Give my love to Augie."

"I will. Goodbye, honey. And don't worry about money if you don't get a job right away. Your father and I will help you."

"I love you both."

"We love you, too."

After Jude hung up, he sat, feeling the blood pounding at his temples and a throbbing sensation on every inch of his flesh. He made another Bloody Mary and researched flights on Matthew's computer.

The following day, Jude purchased his ticket back home. It was May 1st, almost four months to the day after arriving in San Francisco, excited to start a new life. Jude suddenly felt very foolish. He felt foolish for wasting his time chasing that new life in San Francisco, foolish for allowing himself to be subjected to the humiliating fetishes of Grady, and for going on the interview at Top Dawg. But most of all, Jude felt foolish for letting things get so out of hand with Francine. So much time passed between them—lost time, never able to be retrieved.

Hearing the news about Augie, Jude realized how precious time was. Every second since that stupid fight over Dakota was time wasted, gone forever. He wanted to call to tell her about Augie. She certainly would want to know. It might just generate the heat to melt the glacier that had formed between them.

When he called Fran's number, he got a recording saying the number was disconnected. *Disconnected?* Jude sat perplexed. It was just another rock in his pocket weighing him down into the depths of despair.

Chapter Forty-Seven
Land of the Midnight Sun

Later that night, while Matthew was working at Daddy's and George immersed himself in a video game, Jude decided to head down to Midnight Sun, the video gay bar that showed *Melrose Place* on Monday nights, which Jude was addicted to, thanks to Dominick.

Jude approached the Midnight Sun's windowless façade just off Castro Street, pushed through the heavy leather curtain, and saw a good-sized crowd. Guys filled the red bench along the wall and crowded around the pedestal tables, ready to be entertained by the campy fun of the nighttime soap opera.

Currently, the two giant screens at opposite ends of the bar played Belinda Carlisle's video, "I Get Weak."

Jude worked his way through the crowd to the bar and ordered a Johnny Walker Red with lime. After he finally ordered, Belinda Carlisle's video morphed into a montage of Beatrice Arthur's best sarcastic moments as Dorothy on *The Golden Girls*. Jude was caught up in the acerbic clips when he felt someone nudge him.

"Who let you in here?" the mystery person said.

Jude turned and was surprised to see Adam Blanchard. "Adam!" They embraced, sharing a friendly kiss. "I wondered if I would run into you while out here. How are you?"

"I'm well. What are you doing in San Francisco?"

"Visiting my friend, Matthew Zyskowski."

"And what do you think of Gay Town, USA?"

"Love it. I think. I had some stranger-than-fiction adventures, but the city itself is great."

"It's hard not to have some stranger-than-fiction things happen to you in San Francisco. When did you get into town?"

Jude sighed. "I lost my job in December, so I thought I'd visit my friend, Matthew, to see if I liked San Francisco enough to move here."

"You'd be very popular here." Adam gave Jude a poke in the ribs and a smile that would charm the snake out of the wicker basket.

"Unfortunately, I haven't been able to find work. I sent out dozens of résumés over the last few months—"

"Give it time," Adam encouraged.

"But I also found out my dad has cancer, so I'm heading back East next Monday."

"Oh, no. I'm so sorry about your dad *and* that you're leaving San Francisco, too. We could have picked up where we left off," Adam said. A sexual twinkle flickered in his eye. "How is Connor these days?"

"Same as the old days. We attempted to start something, but…"

"Still the elusive butterfly? Oh, by the way, did you ever get your cross back from him?"

"I got it back, but not from him. That pretentious Lawrence gave it to me. I never understood why he disliked me so much."

"He never liked me, either. It should be obvious."

"But you were part of that preppy posse, no offense."

"Only because of Connor. Lawrence didn't like me for the same reason he didn't like you. He was jealous because Connor liked us, not him. He's crazy in love with Connor, and Connor was so oblivious he told Lawrence every detail of his love and sex life."

"I'm surprised Lawrence didn't try to sabotage things knowing all he did."

Adam laughed. "Lawrence is a big pussy. He wasn't conniving like…" he turned his attention to the giant monitor. "…Amanda," Adam said, pointing behind Jude, referencing the cunning, devious Heather Locklear character in *Melrose Place,* which now filled both screens. "No, Lawrence just stewed and loved Connor from a distance, hoping Connor would fall for him one day."

"Fat chance." Jude caught himself. "Oops. Pun intended."

"Sorry things didn't work out between you and Connor."

Jude recited how things started hot and heavy, beginning with the evening Connor attacked him in his car while at a red light. "Up till that moment, he seemed so quiet and reserved, but when it came to sex, he acted as if he was in solitary confinement for ten years."

Adam laughed. "Yeah, he was aggressive."

"Whenever I tried to do something with him outside the bedroom, I got nowhere. He was offering me just enough attention to keep me on the line. We'd end up having sex, and then he retreated into his shell. Finally, I had enough."

"I know exactly how you feel. It's the reason we broke up. Connor was like Jekyll and Hyde."

"I tried for months to get my cross back from him. Why did he make it so difficult?"

"It was his passive-aggressive way to hang on to you. He kept his connection to you alive as long as he had your cross. He has intimacy problems."

It was like Adam flicked a switch, and a light went on in Jude's head. It all made sense now. He was grateful for the chance encounter with Adam, who filled in the missing piece of the puzzling Connor McCracken. Adam's talk reassured Jude that he was not the issue, but he still felt morose. He liked Connor in his good moments and had hoped things worked out. Given Adam's revelation, Jude hoped that deep in the recesses of Connor's vaulted heart, there was a stamp that said, *Jude was here.*

In a moment, all the other flawed relationships, from Michael Antonucci to Mickey Flynn to the latest stop along love's highway, Grady Savage, ricocheted around Jude's mind and wondered why we were prone to pursue love. But Jude knew he'd swim again in the universal pond, eventually taking the bait and getting hooked on someone else's line. *That's life.*

Jude decided to catch a ride with Matthew, whose shift ended soon. He thanked Adam for the cathartic chat, hugged and kissed him goodbye, and left the Midnight Sun as Janet Jackson's "Runaway" video flashed across the giant screens.

Chapter Forty-Eight
The Bonfire of the Virgins.

The Saturday before Jude flew back home, George, some of his classmates, and their friends finally organized a bonfire on a stretch of Ocean Beach.

In preparation, Jude emerged from the shower, wearing only a towel. Mindy, a petite, adorable girl who went to school with George, was at the apartment. She had her pink hair in two little ponytails that barely stuck out of the back of her head. They complimented the round pink frames that magnified her blue eyes.

"Oh, hello. Sorry for the mode of undress," Jude said, clutching the towel around his waist.

"That's okay. I'm a lesbian. It doesn't do anything for me," Mindy said.

Though she was a lesbian, it still wounded Jude's pride. "Oh, good to know."

He disappeared behind the trifold to dress. He put on a heavy sweater, jeans, and his work boots. When he emerged, he borrowed a Buffalo plaid jacket and woolen scarf from Matthew since George suggested wearing something warm. "It gets chilly down by the ocean, especially at night," he warned.

After stopping for some beer and wine, they drove across the city and parked in a lot near the ocean. They walked a stone path to a cliff and down a steep wooden staircase leading to the beach, where the bonfire was ablaze. The heat generated from the flames created a bubble of warmth within the chilly evening air.

About twenty people dressed as if it were winter in upstate New York. They drank, standing around the roaring fire, its flames spiraling towards the sky from the deep pit.

It was a perfect night for a bonfire. A million stars freckled the clear sky and showcased the moon, a mere sliver of itself. The ocean was invisible in the void of light, yet the soundtrack of the waves crashing on shore made its presence known.

After opening a beer, George mingled with a group of friends.

"Wow! My first ever authentic ocean bonfire," Jude said, amazed.

"It's mine, too," Matthew added.

"Mine as well," Mindy echoed.

"I guess that makes us all bonfire virgins." Jude cracked a cheery smile.

"So, how do you and Matthew know each other? George said you're both from Schenectady," Mindy asked, addressing Matthew.

"Our mothers grew up together, so we became one big family." Matthew put his arm around Jude's shoulder.

"Plus, we discovered we were both gay," Jude added, placing his hand around his friend's shoulder. It sank into the soft material of Matthew's down vest.

"We also liked the same kind of music. Outside of Jude, I don't know anyone who appreciates Joni Mitchell like I do."

"Well, you exposed me to her. As a wanna-be writer, I was amazed by her gift for words. She's a true poet." Jude excused himself and went to get some wine. He poured some into a plastic cup and walked down to the ocean's edge. Hearing, not seeing the ocean, was daunting. He felt infinitesimal and helpless standing on its shore. The constant roar and its ominous expanse were intimidating. Alone with his thoughts, he also felt helpless for Augie. Would he be around for his next birthday? Christmas? Would *he* ever get to see the ocean again? There were so many questions only time would answer.

Jude was there for quite a while before a familiar voice came from behind him.

"I thought you might need some more wine." Matthew was at Jude's side.

"Ah! You read my mind."

"You doing okay?" Matthew poured wine into Jude's cup.

"Yeah. I'm just amazed at how life can change so quickly. I mean, you wake up full of optimism and high hopes, and one by one, they're shot down like ducks in a shooting gallery. Then you find out your parent has cancer." Jude sipped the freshly poured wine.

"I know. I'm so sorry about Augie."

"But we must be resilient. Life goes on as unpredictable as it can be. I'd go through a lifetime of Grady's house of torture if I could buy Augie more time." They both laughed while recalling Jude's hook-up with the whip-wielding professor.

"I considered a Customer Service Supervisor position for yet another gay porn company, but I couldn't bring myself to apply. Why would a film company that produces porn need a customer service department? Do the actors complain about bad sex?"

Matthew laughed. Jude joined in.

"God, we needed that," Jude said.

"These moments of laughter make me wish you were staying."

"I know. You're like the Ethel to my Lucy. The Shirley to my Laverne," Jude rationalized, adding, "the Edina to my Patsy" for good measure. "You'll always be that to me." Jude looked out at the ocean. The whitecaps emitted an eerie, faint glow like sea-faring specters hovering over the dark waters.

"It's funny, but that tarot card reader, Madame Fortuna, told me destiny would lead me to the path I am to follow. Destiny has spoken."

"I'll miss you."

Jude turned to Matthew. "Now you know how I felt when you left for San Francisco. It was hard enough when Dominick and I took you to Quintessence for a farewell dinner, but that first day I came home from work to that empty flat, I just poured myself a drink and cried."

"I cried when I read your card."

Jude bought Matthew a blank card. On the front was a small photo of the ruby slippers from *The Wizard of Oz*. Inside the card, Jude wrote three times: *There's no place like 'Frisco*. Under that, *I hope San Francisco is your Emerald City*. Then, he went on to describe the immeasurable sense of loss he'd feel with Matthew gone. He was family.

"I literally could not explain the feeling of not having you around. It was like having a limb amputated," Jude admitted. "We did so much together, all those trips to New York City. It's the same way I feel not having Fran around. It's worse losing a close friend than a boyfriend." Jude thought about Augie. "Or a parent."

For a second time, Matthew put an arm around Jude's shoulder, and his arm instinctively rested on Matthew's. They stayed that way for several minutes, listening to the waves crash and recede into oblivion. Eventually, the continual gusts coming off the ocean forced them back to the warmth of the bonfire.

Chapter Forty-Nine
Sex With the Devil, Himself

On Jude's last night in San Francisco, he and Matthew went to Daddy's, but when Matthew said he was tired and was going home, Jude said he needed another drink and ventured to Nightshift, a seedy bar across the street. M People's remake of "Itchycoo Park" tore through the airwaves. He sat on the edge of a pool table not in use and observed the array of men. After a second drink, he noticed a hot-looking guy in a red tank top that displayed his amply muscled form. His lapis lazuli-colored eyes stared as he passed by and remained focused on Jude from a distance. The man stood in the back of the bar, where Jude noticed some clandestine sexual activities taking place. Jude strolled back to the man, gave him his most seductive smile, and introduced himself. The guy's name was Jerome. His eyes sucked in Jude's shirtless torso under his leather biker jacket. Jerome's thick, rough hands roamed over his flesh, causing Jude's nerves to buzz and sizzle. Their mouths pressed together with erotic force, their tongues exploring newly discovered territory.

Jerome squatted and undid Jude's jeans and pulled down the jockstrap he was wearing, then swallowed Jude and worked him until he reached a mind-blowing orgasm. When they finished, Jude looked and realized they had an audience with one guy giving him a great-show-pat-on-the-back. Jude forced an embarrassed smile.

Jude offered to buy Jerome coffee at Orphan Andy's, an all-night diner with red leather swivel chairs lining the long Formica counter. They walked the short distance to the diner around the corner from the Castro.

After coffee, Jerome gave Jude his first-ever ride on a motorcycle. Jerome gave him pointers on how to lean when going around curves. Jude wrapped his arms around Jerome's tight waist and found it exhilarating riding through the hilly San Franciscan streets, the wind whipping through him, the brisk night redolent with patchy fog and salty air. It was like being on a roller coaster built for two.

Outside Webster Towers, Jerome gave Jude a deep, open-mouthed kiss, thanked him for the sex and coffee, and sped off on his BMW motorcycle. Jude's San Francisco adventure ended with a climax (literally) and a *cinematic* ride through the night.

*****

After landing at La Guardia Airport, Jude took a taxi to Penn Station, then a late afternoon train to Albany-Rensselaer Train Station. Another taxi finally brought him back to the comforts of his roomy, less-than-half-the-rent-in-San Francisco apartment. Travel weary, he called Augie to say he was going to come to visit tomorrow.

Halfway through his third day visiting Augie, Jude went to use the bathroom and noticed a yellowish-green discharge in his briefs. The burning sensation as he peed confirmed his worst fear: an STD! He cut his visit short and immediately went home to call his physician.

"Hi, this is Jude Giacolone. I need to schedule an appointment."

"Reason for the appointment?" the bored-sounding scheduler asked.

Jude was not prepared for the question and hesitated.

"*Reason* for the visit," she repeated with impatience.

"I…I think I have an STD." His voice was a whisper, even though he was alone in his apartment.

"You'll have to speak up." Annoyance resonated in her voice.

Jude blurted out his reason.

"Symptoms?" came the monotone question.

"I have a burning sensation while piss…urinating, and there is a greenish discharge—" He didn't have to finish.

"Yup, that's an STD, Jude," the scheduler interrupted.

Jude winced, hoping no one was in earshot of hearing his name attached to the mortifying diagnosis.

"Four o'clock, and don't forget your insurance card, Jude."

Upon use of his name again, Jude squeezed his eyes shut and hung up.

He sat in an anxiety-produced cold sweat on the crinkly tissue paper that striped the center of the vinyl examination table. The flimsy smock he wore reeked of bleach.

After a grueling twenty-minute wait in which he heard about a woman's hemorrhoids through the walls in one adjoining room and a man's prostate issues in another, Dr. Adelson blew in like a human cyclone. "Jude! My favorite patient." He plopped down on his swivel stool with his legs spread so wide Jude thought he'd get a hard-on if Dr. Adelson were the least bit attractive. "So, an STD, huh? Bummer." Dr. Adelson's voice boomed.

Given the apparent paper-thin walls, Jude cringed. *Why don't you people just hold a press conference?*

Dr. Adelson wheeled over to a counter with an assortment of medical supplies and pulled a long cotton swab from a glass container. Rolling back, he said, "Okay, sport, stand up and drop your briefs."

Under the anxiety, knowing where Dr. Adelson was going to put that swab, and the ultimate humiliation of why, Jude's penis retreated like a turtle into its shell. Dr. Adelson inserted the tip and twisted it like he was drilling for oil, or in this case, Gonorrhea. Jude breathed heavily, trying not to pass out.

After the penis torture, Dr. Adelson spread the tip of the swab on a microscope slide and said he'd be right back. Another apprehensive twenty minutes passed before he gusted back into the room.

"Definitely Gonorrhea. What did you do, have sex with the devil himself? Never seen such an active case of the big G," Dr. Adelson exclaimed as he wrote out a prescription for a heavy-duty antibiotic. "This should knock it out of you." He handed Jude a slip of paper with illegible handwriting. "Call me if things persist."

Jude may not have left his heart in San Francisco, but he took back the worst case of the clap his doctor ever saw.

Chapter Fifty
The Two Faces of Swami Ramgoolan

"Can you drive us to New York on Monday? Your father has an appointment at Sloan Kettering. You know your brother won't drive," Dolores scoffed as if Anthony was the only one who didn't like driving. He only got a driver's license because Katie insisted he get one when they got engaged. But Dolores shared her dislike of driving as much as Anthony. Not only did she balk at driving, but she also hated being a passenger. She was the ultimate backseat driver, telling whoever was at the wheel to *watch out, slow down, you're tailgating.* As long as Jude lived in Albany, Dolores never saw his apartment. To her, driving the twenty minutes down the thruway from Schenectady to Albany was like driving to California.

Dolores' nerves were coiled tight on a good day, but they became hot-wired whenever she got into a car. It was her mission to act as co-pilot. *There's a stop sign. Red light. You're speeding.* Then there was her imaginary brake. Approaching a stop, she'd stomp her foot repeatedly as if she could slow the car down.

So, given her history as a passenger, Jude didn't relish driving her all the way to New York City and then through city traffic. But he could not deny the request.

"Of course, I'll drive. But you best take Dramamine, lots of it. I'll do *my* best to make the drive smooth, but I can't speak for the New York cabbies," Jude warned.

Bright and early on Monday, after taking his antibiotic, Jude left to pick up his parents and head down to the city.

"I made sure we got an appointment for any weekday but Friday," Dolores said, getting in the front seat while Augie stretched out in the back.

"What is it about you and Fridays?" Jude said, adjusting his seat and rearview mirror before starting the car.

As Dolores fastened her seat belt and then tugged at her bunched-up blouse, she enlightened Jude. "It's the day of the crucifixion. It's not a good day to do things. It's bad luck."

Jude shook his head. "I swear, Dolores. You could start a whole new dogma. You'd put Scientology to shame." Jude looked in the rearview mirror. "You good back there, Aug?"

"Yup. I'm good." Augie went on to embellish. "Your mother was afraid you and your brother would be born on Fridays. Your brother's due date was the thirteenth. You should have seen the look on your mother's face when she realized it was a Friday. She went ashen." Augie howled.

"And what would you have done if he was born on Friday, the thirteenth? Shove him back in your womb till the next day?" Jude joked.

"Don't be crude. I knew Anthony wouldn't be born on that day," Dolores said confidently. "I prayed to Saint Philomena." Sure enough, Saint Phil blessed Dolores and Augie with a strapping 8-pound baby on the twelfth.

"What's her magic power?" Jude asked.

"She's the patron saint of infants," Dolores said as if that was common knowledge.

"I don't know if I should admire that you know that or have you committed," Jude said, laughing at his humor.

"Never mind. Pay attention to the road." Dolores popped a Dramamine and washed it down with the coffee she brought for the ride.

The mid-May morning was cool and bright. Jude did his best to drive within the speed limit. He could see Dolores' eyes dart over to the speedometer if she felt the slightest acceleration.

Fortunately, the trip down was uneventful; the traffic was light, and Dolores gave the illusion of staying calm. Jude knew of a cheap parking garage on 42nd Street, just off the West Highway. It avoided the stop-and-go morning rush hour commute, which definitely would have triggered Dolores' carsickness and ignited her nerves.

After parking, they hailed a cab to Sloan Kettering for Augie's ten o'clock appointment. Jude held his breath, hoping for a smooth ride.

The cab headed to 8th Avenue, up Central Park West, through the park, across 65th Street, and finally to York Avenue, arriving at Sloan Kettering. As luck would have it, the cab ride *was* uncharacteristically uneventful due to the steadily moving traffic.

At first glance, Sloan Kettering looked like any other large hospital. A plethora of patients, visitors, doctors, clergy, and staff scurried about like an army of ants around a sugar cube. The middle-aged woman behind the glass partition at the welcome desk craned her neck to look through her half-glasses attached to a gold chain around her neck. She greeted the Giacolones, then handed Augie several forms attached to a clipboard.

"Please fill these out and return them to me when you've finished." She spoke with routine mundaneness in a Hispanic accent.

They sat in the expansive lobby with rows of leather and chrome chairs and an occasional table loaded with assorted magazines. Jude hated hospitals, especially after his Aunt Esther got him a job at Ellis Hospital as an orderly one summer in high school. After having every possible bodily fluid projected on him, prepping bodies for the morgue, and having to rub moisturizer on several elderly patient's dry, scaly skin, Jude decided he was not, nor would he ever be, Florence Nightingale material and declared to his parents, "Never again," when it was time to go back to school.

The lobby seemed whitewashed by the harsh glare of the fluorescent lighting but did little to erase Jude's perception that a pall of gloom hung over the room with quiet menace. Grim reminders it was a hospital for cancer patients were written on the pale, gaunt faces.

Mr. Atkinson, a music teacher in high school, was the first person Jude ever saw who had cancer. His emaciated, bleached face was in direct contrast to the slate-grey chalkboard he walked past. His skeletal frame seemed to drown in the suit that once fit a healthy body. His rawboned appearance made Jude queasy.

Now, dozens of Mr. Atkinsons surrounded Jude, and that bilious feeling struck Jude in his stomach with cannonball ferocity. The assortment of hats and turbans worn to camouflage the effects of chemotherapy and radiation were feeble attempts to hide their affliction.

Then, the new patients, like Augie, clutched their large manila envelopes containing X-rays and biopsy reports. For some, it might as well be their death certificate. A few fortunate ones would fare better. Many looked stoic; others sat frozen, a mix of fear and a glimmer of hope in their transfixed eyes. Jude squirmed in his chair as Dolores and Augie returned with coffees after dropping his forms back at the welcome desk.

"Three sugars and cream, not milk, the way you like it," Dolores said, handing Jude the cup.

"Thanks." Jude placed his cup on the table next to a copy of *Time*.

"This is quite a place." Augie was his usual self, trying to make good of the situation. "I'm in good hands." He smiled, but Jude detected a bit of reticence in his usual sunshiny smile.

Patients of all ages paraded through the lobby in wheelchairs or hospital beds. A child of no more than six was wheeled to the elevators in a hospital bed with an IV attached. The child sat upright, looking around. Jude could not distinguish whether it was a boy or a girl as a knitted cap covered the head, and the face was devoid of eyebrows. The child put on a brave front, smiling slightly. It was more than Jude could stand. He wanted to get up and escape from the suffocating surroundings that entombed him.

"Augustine Giacolone?" a voice rang out. Augie raised his hand. An attractive woman with a wide smile approached. "Mr. Giacolone? Hello. I'm Roz Hannah, Dr. Katz's assistant." Her skin was the color of lightly creamed coffee; her dark hair pulled tight into a tidy bun. She extended her hand, shaking Augie's first, then Dolores', and finally Jude's. Though her warm greeting was genuine, it must have evolved from years of turning the multitude of somber faces into blank masks so she could be congenial amidst the sorrow.

"If you follow me, I'll take you to Dr. Katz's office. This way, please." She spoke in a soothing, soft-spoken voice worthy of a yoga instructor. Probably hospital protocol to sound as calming as possible despite the depressing, *un*calming circumstances, Jude speculated.

Inside the cramped office, Roz asked several questions from her opened folder before announcing, "Dr. Katz will be in momentarily. Is there anything I can get anyone?"

"Yeah, double scotch?" Jude cracked.

"Jude." Dolores' voice was flat. She gave Roz an apologetic nod.

Roz smiled knowingly and left the room.

Augie announced that he had to use the bathroom. Dolores said she also had to go, leaving Jude alone in Dr. Katz's office. Moments later, the door swung open, and Dr. Katz entered like a sudden blast of wind, startling Jude. *What was it with doctors entering rooms like a storm front moving through?*

"Well, hello there. I'm Dr. Katz."

"Jude Giacolone." He shook Dr. Katz's hand. "My dad just stepped out to use the bathroom for like the zillionth time since we've been here. My mom went, too."

"It happens to a lot of people when they're here. Mostly nerves," Dr. Katz rationalized.

"Yeah, real cheery place you got here."

"Well, while your parents are out, it will allow me to review your dad's case."

Dr. Katz put on a pair of bifocals. His brow furrowed, causing his leathery skin to wrinkle more. He pulled absentmindedly on his chin.

Jude eyed Dr. Katz. *Seems old—not too old where he can't perform surgery. Must have plenty of experience.*

Dr. Katz ran his fingers through his grey hair. Jude wished his parents would return soon.

Thankfully, they returned moments later. Dr. Katz stood up and introduced himself. "I've been going over your record, Mr. *Gio*-co-lone."

"*Gia*-colone," Augie corrected Dr. Katz.

"Oh, pardon me. I'm good at treating cancer but terrible at names." He smiled confidently. He asked Augie a series of questions, making notes as he did.

"Now, because you aren't a candidate for any chemo or radiation therapy—"

"Yeah, I wouldn't go through any of that anyway," Augie interrupted.

"Understood. What we can do is perform what's called an embolization. It's a surgery where we cut into your thigh, implant a catheter, and send tiny pellets into the main artery that feeds the liver, thus cutting off the blood supply to the cancerous section of the organ. In essence, starving the tumor. It's not a cure, but it will prolong your life. The quality of that life depends on your attitude and how your body responds to the surgery. In your case, there are no other options."

"I'll do it, doc, if that's the alternative to chemo." A Mona Lisa smile crept onto Augie's lips.

"Good." Dr. Katz smacked his thighs with his hands. "I want to get an ultrasound, and then we'll draw some blood, and after that, we'll schedule you for your surgery. Then you're free to go."

Dolores and Jude found themselves back in the lobby. Jude felt like cancer, and all its far-reaching tentacles ensnared him, squeezing the life out of him. He couldn't breathe and needed air. He wanted to bolt, take a subway to the village, go to the Monster and drink away the cloak of doom.

***

After a couple of hours, they were in a cab heading back to the parking garage, which was not as smooth and pleasant a ride as the previous one.

The day turned hot, and the front windows of the taxi were open. The driver, Swami Ramgoolan, the name under his photo on the meter, was very friendly, or so it seemed.

"What a beautiful day," he said in a thick Indian accent. "The flowers are blooming and smell so good," he began with a lilting, pleasant tone. Then, beeping his horn, he yelled to a biker who veered a little too close to his lane, "Get the hell out of the way, you fucking idiot."

While stopped at a traffic light in Central Park pleasant Swami was back.

"Ah, the park air is so fresh," he began. The green light replaced the red. The car ahead didn't move fast enough for Swami, shouting, "Move, you stupid son of a bitch." He laid on his horn. The driver stuck his hand out, flipping Swami the finger, and sped off.

"Parwah nahi, to you. Crazy people." Swami's smile glinted in the rearview mirror as he hit the gas, causing the Giacolone's heads to snap back. Dolores closed her eyes and hiccupped.

"Yes, I love this time of year. It is not too hot, like where I come from in India. So hot you feel like your skin is melting," he spoke as if he were reciting Shakespeare. Then: "I'll run you over, you stupid fuck," Swami shouted with a vengeance out the window to a jogger dashing across the road. The cab swerved, causing the Giacolones to collide with each other.

"Oh, sweet Jesus." Dolores made the sign of the cross.

"It's like driving with Jekyll and Hyde," Jude whispered as he handed his mother water to wash down a Dramamine she pulled out of her purse.

When they arrived at the parking garage, Jude handed Swami a twenty and told him to keep the change.

"Oh, thank you. So grateful. Enjoy the sunshine," Swami said with a singsong lilt, gesturing to the sky. Pulling into traffic, Swami

219

screamed to a pedestrian walking in front of his cab, "Watch out, you idiot bastard!" His tires screeched; he blew his horn.

Back in Jude's car, an ashen Dolores hung her head out the window while an exhausted Augie dozed.

As they drove up the West Highway, a multitude of billboards and placards plastered on buildings advertised everything from morning television and radio shows to perfumes and various liquors assaulted their view. Jude took a double look at one billboard in particular. In a pair of white Calvin Klein briefs, was handsome Walter, Jude's birthday fling. Internally, Jude screamed, *"Dolores! Augie! See that hottie up there in his briefs? I fucked him!"* Externally, the sight of Walter on a giant billboard curled Jude's mouth in a mirthful smile.

A few days later, Dolores phoned Jude to tell him Dr. Katz called, and the news was not good for Augie.

"Your father's cancer has spread. The embolization surgery that could prolong his life is not a possibility now."

Jude's head fell, chin to chest. "How did Augie take the news?"

"He went to Walt's to watch the Yankees."

Then Jude asked the dreaded question: "How long does he have?"

"Dr. Katz said three, maybe four months."

Jude felt the color in his face drain as if a levee in his neck collapsed.

"Call him tomorrow, honey. He's pretending to be stronger than he is."

Jude hung up. He wished he could call Francine. In times like this, Jude reached out to her for comfort and support. She was his Rock of Gibraltar, and he was hers until Dakota, like a nine-point-nine magnitude earthquake, brought their solidarity crashing down, leaving it in rubble.

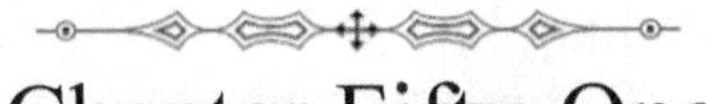

Chapter Fifty-One
The Black Velvet Cure

When Jude moved back from San Francisco, he not only returned to his old apartment building but was also able to upgrade shortly after to one of two suites on the top floor with a terrace overlooking Washington Park and the Empire State Plaza. On a late spring afternoon, Jude sat on his patio with a scotch and lime, listening to Vanessa Daou waft from his stereo. He tried to clear his thoughts of Augie, his failed San Francisco trip, and Francine, who was still absent from his life.

As the sun faded from an azure sky, it cast a tangerine tint to the sporadic white clouds. It was his favorite time of day when an amber glow bathed the landscape. Filmmakers called it the *golden hour,* but now the setting sun reminded him of how the sun was setting on Augie.

When the last of the bright orange ball dipped below the horizon, Jude went in and found a message from Dominick. "It's karaoke night at Oh Bar. Let's go. Call me!"

After considering this, Jude thought Dominick's company and karaoke, which were always good for a laugh, would be the perfect antidote to sitting around and wallowing in depressing thoughts.

Dominick showed up, and the two headed down Lark Street. He told Jude he met someone he liked and clicked with on the Confidential Connection Line.

"Are you still calling that thing?"

"This guy is super nice and sane—"

"And don't tell me. He has a big dick."

"We haven't had sex yet."

"Losing your touch, whore?"

"No, *Judith,* I really like him."

"You? Mr. Unromantic? I thought after your meltdown over Zyskowski, you were like Humpty Dumpty—All the gay horses and all the gay men couldn't put your broken heart back together again."

Jude nudged Dominick, who offered up a reminiscent laugh.

"I'm full of surprises."

"You're full of something."

Approaching Oh Bar's familiar striped awning and the aura of its neon sign was a warm, inviting sight. Yet it struck a dichotomous chord in Jude's heart. Nostalgia braided with failure. It was good to be home, but Jude faced the fact that things didn't turn out as he hoped in San Francisco. Madame Fortuna's words echoed in his ears: *Destiny will lead you to the path you are to follow.*

Naturally, Mickey Flynn was bartending. Jude was over Mickey, but still seeing a cheating ex-boyfriend caused an allergic itch to flare up on his ego. Alcohol would be his salve.

"Nasty," came Dominick's assessment of the crowd.

"Will you stop? You just got here," Jude snapped back.

Thursday night Karaoke always drew a large crowd, and tonight was no exception. Jude and Dominick threaded their way to the bar. Mickey Flynn wore his customary leather vest and armband around his thick bicep. Seeing Jude, he smiled broadly, delivered a drink to a customer, and made his way over to his ex-boyfriend. Jude thought he detected a smoldering ember of love for Jude and a glint of regret in Mickey's eyes.

Mickey leaned over the bar and gave Jude a friendly kiss. "Hey, sexy. Welcome back!"

"How did you know I was gone?"

Mickey looked to Dominick and tipped his head. "Your sidekick. Plus, I haven't seen you around. You didn't say goodbye. Why didn't you tell me you were going?"

"Oh, I'm sorry. I thought I had a mother. I didn't know I had to tell *you* as well."

Mickey chuckled. "Always the wise guy." He reached out and tapped the brim of Jude's baseball cap. "Things didn't work out?" Mickey said with sincerity.

"It wasn't a matter of things not working out. California wasn't the place for me." Jude tried not to sound defensive.

"Well, I'm glad you're back. The usual?"

"Sure," Jude said.

"And for you, sidekick?"

"Corona," Dominick bristled. "And my name's not *Piglet,*" Dominick shouted as Mickey went to get their drinks.

"Well, you are short and can be a pig," Jude grinned.

Dominick scoffed.

Karaoke was underway. The rumors of voice lessons an egg-shaped bald man took to improve his singing didn't appear to help as he belted out "(Sitting On) The Dock on The Bay." It wasn't his voice, but the lyric—*headed for the Frisco Bay*—that struck a discordant note in Jude. The thought of his unsuccessful venture to the west caused a backdraft in Jude's chest, sucking the air from his lungs.

"Fierce, girl," Dominick yelled when the man finished.

Taking the stage next was an androgynous-looking African American woman who went by the name *Black Velvet,* whose voice was anything but. She started singing "New York, New York" in her normal raspy voice, segueing into a Louie Armstrong baritone, eventually morphing into the five-and-a-half octave cadence of Minnie Ripperton, but without the melodic tone of the coloratura soprano. Though the song brought thoughts of Augie's Sloane Kettering trip, Jude wouldn't let it interfere with Black Velvet's performance. She was the comical medicine he needed tonight. Popular among the Karaoke crew, the crowd cheered with great enthusiasm at the end of her performance as if they just heard Maria Callas sing O Mio Babbino Caro.

Walking home, Dominick asked, "Can I stay over? I'm a little buzzed."

"Of course," Jude began, slipping an arm around Dominick's shoulder. "You know, you're the one person I sleep without having sex."

"That's because we're sisters." Dominick wrapped his arm around Jude's waist.

"Hey, let's go to the grand opening of Eight Balls, the new gay bar, next Wednesday," Jude said to Dominick as they readied for bed.

"I can't. We're throwing my grandmother a ninetieth surprise birthday party."

"You're going to have a roomful of people yell *surprise* to a ninety-year-old*?* Are you going to have the EMT squad on standby?" Jude, down to his briefs, slipped into bed.

"I'm in the will." Dominick planted a *sisterly* kiss on Jude's lips and nestled in for sleep to overtake him.

Chapter Fifty-Two
Jude Is Struck by Another Thunderbolt

Jude wore faded jeans, a clinging black tank top, and his white NYU baseball cap for the opening of Eight Balls and headed out the door into the temperate spring night.

Located in a white, flat-roofed building on Central Avenue, a rainbow-colored dome-shaped awning umbrellaed Eight Balls entrance. A grand opening banner was affixed above a large window, illuminating the bar's name with red neon.

Outside, a heavyset man with shoulder-length white-blond hair sat at the entrance.

"Hi, sweetheart. Welcome to Eight Balls. Here's a ticket for one free drink." He spoke with a lilting, soft-spoken voice. Jude thought his blue eyes twinkled with a little too much lust.

"What's your name, handsome?"

"Jude." He accepted the ticket.

"I'm Clarence," he responded with a saucy smile. "Enjoy yourself, honey."

Inside, multi-colored lights flashed and blinked in a paroxysm of visual intensity. Jude worked his way through the crowd to the bar.

"Hey, sweetie," Suzie shouted over the thumping beat of Kristine W's "One More Try." She leaned over to kiss Jude.

"Suzie! Did you abandon Waterworks?"

"These guys offered me more money and better benefits. I couldn't refuse. Whaddya think of the place?"

"Nice. The dance floor looks like something out of a David Lynch production. Good crowd."

"Opening night and all. Want your usual?"

"But of course."

As Suzie went to get a scotch and lime, Jude leaned against the dark wood bar and scanned the crowd.

Rainbow-colored helium balloons stood against the red velvet backdrop at the far corners of the black and white checkered dance floor. The balloons stretched on their long ribbons, wavered and bobbed as if dancing along with the gyrating crowd.

Suzie returned with Jude's drink. "You get a free drink ticket, hon?" she asked, then turned to the guy a few patrons down from Jude. "Waving your money in the air isn't going to make me move any faster, numb nuts."

Jude handed Suzie his ticket and slapped a few dollars on the bar for her.

"Thanks, hon. Enjoy yourself." She headed toward the guy with his money in the air. "Okay, ass pipe. Whaddya want?"

Jude meandered through the crowd and spotted the on-again-off-again couple, Kelvin and Darryl. Kelvin was a densely muscled African American. Darryl was rangy and fair and had a sexy English accent. Their volatile relationship was due to Kelvin's flirtations, usually ending up with Darryl begrudgingly acquiescing to a threesome initiated by Kelvin. Though both were good-looking, it was Kelvin's mesomorphic body Jude would jump in a flash. Yet, a year ago, when a drunk Kelvin cornered Jude in a make-out session, he saw the disheartened look on Darryl's face, and Jude politely declined the offer for a ménage à trois. Darryl still held a particular animosity toward Jude— though he didn't know why; it's not like Jude accepted Kelvin's offer for a threesome—so his icy behavior was a mystery.

Darryl grunted a barely audible *hello*.

"Hey, sexy." Kelvin snared Jude in a bear hug and a kiss. "So, I hear you were out in San Francisco. Oh, honey, the men! I bet you had a field day out there."

"Yeah, it's something. It's like gay pride on steroids."

"I like this song. I want to dance!" Darryl dragged Kelvin towards the dance floor.

"Why do you have to be so fucking rude? I was talking…"

Kelvin's words disappeared over the blare of Sunscreem's "Broken English."

Alone with his drink, Jude was absorbed in the music's pounding, techno beat. His peripheral vision caught a guy wiping down the table next to him. Jude glanced over. The guy's mouth spread into a tight-lipped smile while his eyes lingered.

Jude found himself staring back at the guy's breath-stealing hotness. *If this were a film, a choir of angels would sing out in exaltation.*

Not wanting to be obvious, Jude forced his eyes back to the dance floor.

When the rag-wielding guy came to Jude's table, his smile cracked open like a hammered coconut.

Jude acknowledged his sudden presence. "Oh, sorry," he said, lifting his glass. This time, Jude couldn't help but ogle the hottie before him. The perma-grin staring Jude in the face was like a flamethrower, and he was a six-foot lump of wax.

"Hi. Welcome to Eight Balls. Enjoying yourself?"

"Yeah. Loving the music."

Sunscreem morphed into Captain Hollywood Project's "More and More."

"What do you think of the place?" The smiling hottie continued absentmindedly wiping the table.

"It's great, but if you keep wiping this table, you're going to rub it down to a stump," Jude said with a coy smile.

Grinning, the rag man introduced himself. "I'm Chase Allgood, one of the owners." He stuck out his hand. Realizing it held the rag, he promptly switched it to his left, wiping his right one on his jeans, and extended it to Jude.

"I'm Jude. Glad to meet you." Their eyes locked. Chase's moss-green eyes sucked Jude in like the funneling water in a drain. Jude didn't want to presume, but he got the impression those eyes said: *I like what I see.* He wondered if Chase read the same thing in his eyes.

"Interesting name for the bar. How'd you come up with it?"

"Originally, there were four owners, so we thought Eight Balls would be a great tongue-in-cheek name. But two guys moved to Florida, so my partner and I bought them out. We decided to keep the name." He noticed Jude's glass. "I see your glass is empty. Let me get you another drink."

"Thanks. Scotch with lime."

"With lime?" Chase cocked his head. His strong jaw and cheekbones lent a chiseled masculinity twined with his smooth wholesomeness. Jude was drunk with desire.

"I know, it's so gay—"

"No," Chase said with a light laugh. I never heard of the combination before. It's unique." Chase picked up the empty glass. "Don't go anywhere. I'll be back."

Jude held out a five-dollar bill.

Chase placed his hand on Jude's exposed bicep, sending tingles up and down his spine. "It's on me."

Jude observed Chase as he headed for the bar. *Nice ass.*

When Chase returned with Jude's drink, he said, "I have to take care of some business. If I don't see you tonight, I hope you'll come back."

"Sure. I'll be around," Jude assured. "It's a great bar."

Chase started to walk away, then turned. "Hey, do you like 80's music?"

"Yeah, I was raised on it."

"Tomorrow night, we're having an 80s night. It's also 'Drinkin' with Lincoln,' five dollars, all you can drink from nine till midnight. I hope I see you then." Chase performed a full body scan of Jude before he walked away.

Aware of his physical attraction to Chase, he remembered the last time the thunderbolt struck him. He ended up with tied-up testicles, whipped and tickled into submission. However, Chase didn't seem like the sadistic type and rekindled the optimist and eternal romantic in Jude. It was like Chase flipped a switch, igniting Jude's nerve endings like thousands of optic fibers. Jude felt like he was glowing.

When Jude left Eight Balls, he could have flown home on the energy bursting inside him. The thought of Francine sent an arctic chill through Jude. Chase was the kind of guy he would pontificate to her about. He still had not seen or spoken to her since their argument at the Coffee Clutch Café before leaving for San Francisco. She still didn't know about Augie. Given his condition, she would never know.

In bed, Jude couldn't stop thinking about Chase. He would have to work very hard not to let emotions overrule his head. But already, he felt his walled-up heart was again porous, and Chase Allgood was the liquid seeping in, flooding him with desire. Jude drifted off, already drowning in thoughts of the hot bar owner.

Chapter Fifty-Three
Out of the Blue Shield

eturning from the gym the following day, Jude saw two messages on his answering machine.

The first one was—out of the blue—from Gwendolyn Murphy at Blue Shield regarding an interview for a position in their PR Department.

"If you're interested, please give me a call at…"

"Interested? I'll start today." He jotted down her number. The second was his daily update from Dolores on Augie's condition.

"Hi, honey. It's your mother."

Like I didn't know.

"Your father's holding his own. He has an appointment later today with Dr. Buff. He's having an allergic reaction to one of his medications. Call me later. Love you."

Jude inhaled and then called Ms. Murphy.

A bored-sounding voice announced, "Human Resources."

"Hello, I'm Jude Giacolone, and I'm returning a call from Gwendolyn Murphy."

There was no response, just the sound of being put on hold, followed by a recording of summer health tips by a voice worthy of a game show host. Eventually, Gwendolyn took over. "Hello, Jude. Thank you for returning my call."

"Thank *you* for calling. How did you—?"

"Oh yes, I should explain. Doris Zemaitis, in our San Francisco office, mentioned you would be returning to the area and faxed me your résumé to see if I had something that fit your skills. It just so happened a PR position suddenly became available that I think you would be perfect for. Would you be interested in interviewing?"

"Yes, of course. Thank you."

"Are you free tomorrow, eleven o'clock?"

"Yes, def…" Jude realized tomorrow was Friday. The echo of Dolores's voice filtered through his brain cells. *It's not a good day to do things. Damn her and her superstitions.*

"Um, I just realized I'm not free tomorrow. Will Monday work, same time?"

"Fine. Please arrive fifteen minutes early, so that you can fill out an application. I'll see you then. Good day."

He called his mother to tell her about his interview.

"I'll say a prayer to Saint Joseph. He's the patron saint of employment," she said as if Jude should know that. "You should say one, too."

With a promising interview and Dolores and Saint Joe on his side, Jude's optimism rose to a level not achieved since his time in San Francisco, while thinking about Chase Allgood made his heart gallop like a thoroughbred.

Riding the prospect of a potential job, he went shopping. Despite his unemployed status, he dropped one hundred and fifty dollars, satisfying his sanguine high like heroin rushing through his veins.

That night, Jude put on the new blue tank top with the yellow trim, one of his purchases from earlier in the day. He checked himself out in the full-length mirror, trying to convince himself he was not dressing to impress Chase, but the bar-owning hottie needled his consciousness like a cactus.

I'm just going out to enjoy 80s music. Yeah. Right!

Jude walked confidently to his car as a warm zephyr stroked his body, and the crest of a drug-free high caressed his brain. He hoped the day's plethora of good would overflow into the evening.

Entering Eight Balls, the syncopated beat of Company B's "Full Circle" delighted Jude's aural senses.

Clarence was sitting inside the door. "Hello, darlin'," he spoke in his quiet, mellifluous voice. "Five dollars, hon. All you can drink till midnight."

"Hello…Clarence, is it?" Jude asked as he handed over his five dollars. Clarence's hand ever so slightly caressed Jude's as he took his money.

"That's right. And your name was?"

"Jude."

"Oh, yes. Like the saint. But I'll bet you have a little bit of the devil in you," Clarence said with an ardent smile. "Jude. I won't forget it again, honey. Enjoy yourself."

Jude found something endearing about Clarence. Despite his prurient manner, Clarence seemed harmless, just a refugee from the pre-Stonewall days trying to relive his youth by flirting with the younger patrons.

Jude scanned the crowd nonchalantly as he weaved his way to the bar. Chase was nowhere in sight. After getting a drink, he wandered along the edge of the dance floor to the back of the bar. He stopped periodically to talk to a friendly acquaintance. In the rear, a familiar but unwanted voice came from behind.

"Well, well, well. Looks who's back in town." When he turned around, he saw Lawrence Gillespie, a shark smile plastered across his pudgy face. Connor was standing next to him.

"Lawrence! What an unpleasant surprise. Connor," Jude said flatly.

"I heard you were back from San Francisco," Connor said a little too eagerly, as if he wanted to engage Jude in conversation. *Connor engage in conversation?*

"News sure travels fast around Smallbany," Jude said.

"It's good to see you." Connor smiled, lighting his face like a lightbulb.

"Thanks." After an awkward pause, Jude excused himself.

Heading back towards the front of the bar, he perused the crowd for Chase as the music morphed into Jody Watley's "Looking for A New Love." The song's irony caused Jude to smile internally when a kaleidoscope of butterflies suddenly assaulted Jude's insides. Looking up, he saw Chase talking to the DJ inside the glass booth. Catching sight of Jude, Chase's eyes lit up like flashbulbs. And then his lips unleashed that flamethrower smile. Jude tried to act cool and gave a quick wave. The smile ignited a dynamite stick of excitement exploding in his stomach. Within moments, Chase was standing before Jude.

"Hey! So glad you could make it. Are you enjoying the music?"

"Yes, of course. I was weaned on eighties music." Jude tried not to stare into those hypnotizing, emerald eyes.

"If it goes well, we'll do another one in the future." Chase took a deep breath, and his eyes scanned Jude. "You look great." He grabbed Jude's left bicep and turned it to get a better look at the tattoo on his deltoid. "Cool. I'm digging your tattoo. It's unusual."

Jude took a colorful Ace of Swords Tarot card to Lark Street Tattoo Palace for his eighteenth birthday.

"I want it here," Jude told the tattoo artist, pointing to his shoulder muscle above his bicep. He wanted to be sure Dolores wouldn't see it when wearing a short-sleeved shirt.

"I'll kill you if you ever get a tattoo," she once remarked when Jude casually mentioned getting one.

Chase took Jude's empty glass. "Let me get you another drink."

"Thanks, scotch with—"

"Lime. I remember." Chase's smile was like a lighthouse beam cutting through the fog.

Jude inhaled. His heartbeat competed with the thumping percussion of "What Have You Done for Me Lately?"

A series of black lights came on around the bar. As Jude casually turned, he spotted Clarence conspicuously glowing under the purple lighting. His longish, blanched hair and white clothing made him look like a gay spirit who could not leave his old haunt.

Moments later, when Chase returned, Clarence nodded and gave Jude a thumbs-up.

"What's up with Clarence?"

Chase turned his head. "That's my uncle." Chase waved; Clarence twiddled his fingers.

Returning his attention to Jude, Chase asked him what he did for work.

Taking a deep breath, Jude responded, "I'm currently unemployed, but I have an interview for a Public Relations manager at Blue Shield."

"Fantastic. I wish you good luck, but I doubt you'll need it. Something tells me you'll get the job." Chase continued to speak, but Jude's mind wandered as thoughts of every Debbie Gibson song flashed through his mind:

"Out Of the Blue"—where did you come from, Chase Allgood?

"Lost In Your Eyes"—those eyes, like emerald vortexes whirling me in.

"Only In My Dreams"—I don't want to wake up.

Dominick would be appalled. He always admonished Jude for liking Debbie Gibson.

"High school girl music," Dominick would scoff.

Jude laughed it off, confessing, "I can't help it. I *am* a high school girl at heart when it comes to love."

As Chase raked his fingers through his soft, wavy locks, Jude imagined what it would be like to kiss his Cupid bow lips.

"Jude?"

"Oh, sorry, I was…uh…What were you asking me?"

"When is your interview?"

"Oh. Yeah. Monday at eleven."

"I'll be thinking of you."

I'll be in his thoughts! There wasn't a Debbie Gibson song for that.

Over the din of the music, Suzie shouted to Chase. She motioned that he had a call.

"I'll be right back." Chase disappeared behind the bar and into the office. When he returned, he said, "Business calls. But I'm glad you came by tonight. If I don't get to see you again tonight, I hope to see you over the weekend. And don't forget Tea Dance, Sunday from four to eight! Good night, Jude."

Towards the end of the night, standing close to the entrance and in proximity to Clarence, Jude bristled as Lawrence and Connor approached on their way out.

"You know, he has a boyfriend," Lawrence said through an artificial smile.

"Who has a boyfriend?"

"Chase." Lawrence's eyes were like poison-tipped daggers.

Jude tried not to let the piercing glare bother him. He wasn't successful.

Lawrence snickered.

"C'mon, Lawrence. Let's go." Connor grabbed Lawrence's arm and dragged him to the exit.

"Don't let that pompous ass get to you." Clarence squeezed Jude's arm. "Between you and me, there's trouble in paradise. That's all I can say." Clarence held up his hand, unable to proffer any further information, and gave Jude a reassuring look.

After what Lawrence said, Jude wanted to go home. He finished his drink.

"I'll see you, Clarence."

"Night, darlin'."

Back home, Jude lay in bed recalling the perfect day that suddenly had a crack in its veneer. *Why was Chase being so attentive if he had a boyfriend? Why did Lawrence still hold a grudge now that Connor was out of the picture? Did Connor still harbor feelings for me? There would never be anything between Connor and me again. It was too late. That ship had sailed and sunk. What was the cryptic meaning behind Clarence's telling me, 'There's trouble in paradise?'*

"Jesus, my life is suddenly like a gay soap opera." He lay there trying to decipher it all before being lulled into a restless sleep.

Chapter Fifty-Four
Prognosis: Six Months

"How was your grandmother's birthday party?" Jude asked Dominick while at Sunday Brunch at Quintessence. "Did she survive the shock of surprise?"

"Still alive and kicking. What's the new bar like? Is it *fierce?*" Dominick's trademark cynicism always aimed at Albany's gay bar scene.

"What difference does my opinion matter? You know you'll find something to hate about it."

"You know I will," Dominick said as he raised his hand and did a z-snap.

"I met one of the owners, and he's hot," Jude confessed.

"Yeah, how hot?"

"Sun surface hot. But that bitch Lawrence told me he has a boyfriend, so I didn't go there last night. I went to Waterworks instead." Jude took a bite of his French toast. "How was the straight bar you went to with your kinky cousin and her hot boyfriend with the small penis?"

"They picked up a girl and had a threesome." Dominick was nonchalant and sipped his Bloody Mary.

"Jesus, Alfred Kinsey could write a book about them," Jude said through a mouthful of French toast. "Hey, let's go to Tea Dance tonight so you can see Chase."

"Okay. Then I can judge how nasty Eight Balls is."

***

"He's not working tonight, darlin'," Clarence informed Jude upon entering Eight Balls. "His partner, Evan, is." He nodded in the direction of the bar. Jude tried not to let his disappointment show.

"Oh, that's okay. I'm just showing my friend the new bar." Jude grabbed Dominick by the arm and headed to get a drink. "C'mon. I have to see what the competition looks like."

"Who's Gramps?" Dominick asked.

"Clarence. The doorman. That must be him." Jude nodded toward Evan Orlock, a tall, lanky guy pouring a draft beer. "What's up with that hair?"

His thick, straight hair cascaded down his neck in shaggy tassels. It feathered over his ears and side-swept across his forehead, hanging over his left eye.

"He looks like a girl," was Dominick's blunt observation.

"I suppose he's good-looking. Nice eyes. Eye, judging from the one I can see. Not my type, though."

"Hey, guys. Welcome to Eight Balls," Evan said. "First time here?"

"No."

"Yes," Dominick said in unison.

"What can I get you guys?"

Dominick ordered a Heineken and Jude, a scotch with lime.

As Dominick handed Evan his money, he said, "I like your hair."

Evan gave Dominick a quizzical look. "Thanks?"

Jude kicked Dominick's ankle. "C'mon." Jude shoved Dominick away from the bar. "*I like your hair,*" Jude mocked Dominick. "You're such an instigator."

Dominick laughed, assessing the bar. "I give it six months."

Chapter Fifty-Five
...And Then He Kissed Me

The next day, after his interview, Jude called Dolores. "They pretty much insinuated I had the job."

"Saint Joseph answered my prayers," Dolores said as if she spoke to him personally.

Later that day, Gwendolyn Murphy called to offer Jude the position of Public Relations Manager. "If you accept, of course," she added.

Accept? I'm already planning how to decorate my office.

"Yes, yes, I accept. I wasn't expecting to hear from you so soon."

"I know it's sudden, but given your impeccable employment record, your qualifications, and the endorsement from Doris Zemaitis, Laverne did not feel it was necessary to waste time interviewing anyone else. She is glad to have you join her Communications team. We were hoping to have you start Monday, June seventeenth."

"Perfect. I will see you then."

***

"Hey, you. Where've you been?" Chase said, rushing up to Jude the following Saturday night at Eight Balls. His face was beaming with that smile, upturned higher on one side, making it all the sexier and more infectious.

"I hope I didn't scare you away."

His sudden appearance took Jude aback, and he didn't know how to respond. He laughed. "Not at all. I just—"

"Whatever the reason, I'm glad you're back. How did your interview go?"

"I got the job."

Much to Jude's surprise, Chase hugged him. *If this was a film, this is where the CGI guys would have liquefied my body.* Jude eagerly hugged back.

Chase broke the hug but kept his hands on Jude's arms. "See? I knew you'd get it. When do you start?"

"Monday, the seventeenth."

"We'll have to celebrate, but right now, work awaits. I'll try to catch up with you later."

Jude watched as Chase stopped to talk to Suzie behind the bar before disappearing through the office door.

"Drinks are on the house," Suzie informed Jude when he went for a drink.

"What?"

"Boss's orders."

Though the bar kept Chase busy, he made brief periodic stops to chat with Jude. Each visit was a teasing morsel of a larger treat dangled in front of Jude, just out of reach. But at the end of the night, Chase offered to walk Jude to his car.

"I'm sorry I didn't get to talk to you as much as I wanted tonight. That's great news about your job. Next time I'll have more time to socialize."

"Yeah, I'd like that, but won't your boyfriend get jealous?"

Chase reddened. "Oh, well…um, it's…complicated." He quickly changed the subject. They stopped at Jude's car.

"Good luck with your job." The light from a streetlamp bounced off Chase's blue-black hair. Jude wanted to comb his fingers through it.

Chase raked his teeth over his lower lip, causing Jude to wilt under the sexy heat the simple act radiated. Then, glancing around, Chase leaned in and gave Jude a seconds-long kiss. "Good night. Drive safely."

Jude's eyes glazed over while his heart marinated in the nectar of what he perceived as flowering love. Caught between the memories of being burned by past boyfriends and voluntarily jumping into the volcano once again, he concluded he didn't have a choice. His heart had a mind of its own, forcing Jude into the roiling abyss like a vestal virgin (except he wasn't a virgin). *What am I thinking? He's got a boyfriend.*

Chapter Fifty-Six
Chase Leaves a Cryptic Message

"This is your office." Laverne Goldman pointed inside the small space with an L-shaped desk and wooden bookcase. A large window took up most of the wall behind the desk, making the room brighter.

Jude unpacked his items, logged on to his computer, and set up his voicemail before heading to orientation.

During his break, he got a coffee and checked his e-mails. The blinking red light on his telephone caught his eye, surprising him. *A message? Already? Probably HR.*

Jude was shocked to learn it was from Chase, releasing the butterflies in his stomach again. His face flushed. Jude played the message again: *I wanted to know if you could meet me at the Olde Bryan Inn tonight, around 7. I need to talk to you about something, so I hope you can make it. Let me know.*

Jude jotted down his number but had no time to return Chase's call.

Back in orientation, his ears were sieves, and everything Gwendolyn said passed through his porous brain. Jude's mind was a raft, aimlessly adrift on an ocean of thoughts about Chase. *What could Chase want to talk about? Did this have something to do with Clarence's cryptic, 'There's trouble in paradise?' The kiss at my car?* He felt like a child on Christmas morning, waiting for everyone else to wake up. Seven o'clock couldn't come fast enough.

***

At five minutes to seven, Jude parked his car on Maple Avenue near the Olde Bryan Inn, a tan Colonial-style building with red trim. Inside, there was no sign of Chase, but moments later, when he arrived, his face burst into a broad smile, spotting Jude.

"Hey! Nice shirt." Chase slid into his seat at the booth.

Jude wore the red short-sleeve Lycra shirt from his recent heady pre-employment purchases. It clung to his physique. He was a lure on a hook trying to snag the *big one.*

"Hi. I was surprised to hear from you. How did you know where to reach me?"

"I called Blue Shield and asked for you."

The last of the sun's rays passed through the red flowers and leafy green vines on the stained-glass windows, spilling their colors onto the wooden table where they sat. The fading sunlight highlighted how good-looking Chase was, transfixing Jude. His smooth face was boyish yet had the structure of masculinity. His coal-black hair was a neatly disheveled flock of soft waves. In the light, Jude saw gold veins networking through the green canvas of his irises. Black, thick lashes that could sweep a floor surrounded his eyes.

"Thanks for meeting me." Chase flashed Jude an irresistible smile.

"You sounded pretty serious."

Chase sat with his hands clasped on the table. "Obviously, you know about my partner, Evan. Clarence said that jerk Lawrence told you."

"I guess I thought you meant *partner* as in business partner. Optimistic thinking."

A waitress came by and took their drink orders.

"He's both. But I asked you here to tell you I'm unhappy in the relationship."

Jude tried to conceal his optimism. "Oh? Why is that?"

"Because everything I have is Evan's. The businesses are his. We also own a construction company. I'm only benefitting because I'm his partner. Everything is in his name. With Evan, I'm just a tag-along. I have no identity to call my own."

"Do you love him?"

Chase stared at Jude, silent, before answering, "I love him, but I don't think I'm *in* love with him anymore."

"What are you going to do?"

"I'm going to leave and move in with my parents."

With his heart jogging in his chest and his stomach doing cartwheels, Jude asked, "Why did you want to tell *me* all this?"

Chase's cheeks matched the red blotches the sun projected on the table. One corner of his mouth escalated into a sheepish smile. Jude thought he saw a flicker of new-found love in the eyes staring at him from across the table and suddenly felt a weakness in his heart, which now belonged to Chase Allgood.

Chase's hand reached out, covering Jude's. "I'm telling you because I like you. I want to get to know you and be with you. I could tell from the moment I saw you that you're different from other guys."

Jude felt a rush of heat flare through his core.

After drinks, they walked through downtown. The unexpected thrill of being with Chase made Jude's insides tingle and fizz like the first sip of champagne. He couldn't believe the turn of events, and as they walked through the moonlit entrance of Congress Park, Jude expressed the thought that burned in his brain since leaving Olde Bryan Inn.

"I don't want to sound premature, but if, you know, being back with your parents seems too weird, you can stay with me." Jude turned to Chase. "If you want. No pressure."

Chase grinned and hooked an arm around Jude, pulling him close and said, "Thanks. I appreciate it, but for now, I'm going to help my dad with his construction business, so it makes sense to stay with them since they're up in Queensbury."

Jude saw the rationale since that would mean a daily commute of forty minutes one way.

"Well, you're welcome to stay whenever you want."

"Oh, I will be taking advantage of that." Chase pulled Jude's face close and kissed his cheek. Chase reached for Jude's hand, his long fingers laced with Jude's. Despite the balmy air that clung to their skin, Jude welcomed Chase's warmth. The sudden intimacy inflated Jude with a buoyant lightheadedness.

They passed by a rectangular pool with two marble Mermen at opposite ends, shooting water at each other through conch shells. Locals affectionately dubbed the fountain "Spit and Spat."

Entering a wooded area, Chase pressed Jude against a tree and kissed him deeply. The urgency triggered a reflexive response in Jude, who grabbed Chase by the back of the head, finally threading his fingers through his wavy hair, soft as cornsilk.

With a handful of Chase's hair, Jude tugged his head back. His tongue was in a duel with Chase's. Pulling on Chase's lower lip with his teeth, Jude felt Chase shiver as he emitted throaty moans. Breaking apart, they locked eyes momentarily before Jude's hands went to the sides of Chase's face, pulling him in and fusing their lips again.

Chase lifted Jude's shirt, and hooked it at the back of Jude's neck. Chase's hands roamed over Jude's torso, sending seismic jolts through him. Then Chase worked his mouth over Jude's chest, kissing and licking, sucking and nipping Jude's nipples, causing Jude to shudder under the intense sexual charge surging through his body.

Chase sank to his knees and urgently pulled Jude's jeans and briefs down. With his fingers threaded through Chase's thick curls, Jude encouraged Chase to take him in his mouth. He looked up at Jude as his lips and tongue feverishly worked Jude over, eventually bringing him to a shattering climax. Jude shivered from the release.

He thought of Connor and how selfish he was with sex, never giving a thought to satisfying him, and here, the first time he was alone with Chase, the opposite was true. Yes, Chase was proving to be different from other guys, too.

Later, they walked back up Broadway, boldly holding hands. Jude didn't care who saw, transported back to the openness of San Francisco. Pride became his aphrodisiac, swelling his heart and his groin (again).

At Jude's car, Chase pressed him against the driver's side. His eyes bore into Jude with a hypnotic gaze.

"Thanks again for meeting me."

Jude placed his hands on Chase's lower back; lips skated across lips.

Finally, Jude broke their connection. "I have to stop. I could kiss you all night."

Chase offered up a light laugh. "Okay. I'll talk to you soon. Good night, Jude." After a final lingering kiss, Chase got into his vintage red Mustang, tooting his horn as he drove off.

When Jude got home, he fell into bed, not remembering the ride down the Northway. It was as if he floated home on a cloud.

Chapter Fifty-Seven
Bang! Bang! Bang! Like the Fourth of July

Jude's limbs intertwined with Chase's like strands of a braided rug. Their moist lips were hot with the friction of fevered kisses. Their conjoined mouths suffocated their moans and groans. Tongues licked; lips sucked. Pressed bodies led to explosive orgasms. It wasn't until Jude rolled off Chase that he saw the meat cleaver in Evan's hand. In that instant, the weapon hit Jude's skull, splitting his head like a Ginsu knife through butter.

Jude's shout woke him from the dream-turned-nightmare. He sat in bed as if imaginary puppet strings yanked him bolt upright. His breath was labored. Despite the humid July night, a cold sweat coated his body. Beams of metallic moonlight through his window gave luster to his skin.

Four thirty.

Wide awake now, Jude stepped onto his terrace overlooking Washington Park. To the left, the four skyscrapers in the Empire Plaza, shorter than the Corning Tower, stood in a row like cement and glass dominoes against a cloudless sky. Wearing just his briefs, he savored the gentle breeze brushing over him, cooling his moist body.

He stared up at the sky, dotted with tiny pinpricks of light. In the privacy of his mind, he was consumed with thoughts of Chase and couldn't wait for him to come over tonight to watch the annual fireworks display over the Plaza.

***

Around six p.m., Jude showered and dressed in a tank top, jeans, and a baseball cap.

Promptly at eight, Chase arrived looking adorable yet sexy in a Red Hot Chili Peppers T-shirt and jeans. Upon seeing Jude, his face glowed.

"Hey, handsome. I brought some Prosecco and these roses..." Chase said, handing Jude the flowers, adding, "...representing us." He kissed Jude.

Jude's eyes widened with surprise. His heart ballooned, then burst with an overabundance of—dare he admit it—love?

"This is the first time I ever received flowers from another guy." Their faces connected in another kiss. "Thank you."

"I'm glad I'm the first."

After Jude put the roses in a vase, he opened the Prosecco, got some glasses, and took Chase to the terrace. Wrought iron fencing with fleur de lis finials topped a brick wall encasing the terrace. Two tall Areca palm plants stood in each corner like vegetative sentries.

"We'll be able to see the fireworks perfectly from here."

"It's a beautiful view."

"I was lucky. This apartment was available shortly after I returned from San Francisco. The manager gave me the first choice. He likes me because I give him a bottle of Johnny Walker Red every Christmas. It's like giving a dog a bone. Give it once, and you're a friend for life." He leaned in, giving Chase a quick kiss.

After setting the champagne flutes and the Prosecco on a small table, they settled down in the Adirondack chairs, one red and one yellow.

"How is your dad doing?"

Jude was touched that Chase asked.

"He's hanging in there," Jude began, pouring the sparkling wine into the flutes. "My brother, sister-in-law, and I take turns helping my mom as best we can. They clicked glasses. "He's a tough bird, but it's getting more difficult for us." Jude tore his eyes away from Chase and stared out at the vastness of the park. "We take each day as it comes and deal with what it brings. Thankfully, my mom also has a good support group with her sisters who help out during the day." He sipped his wine. "So, how are things living back home?" He returned his gaze to Chase.

Chase swallowed some wine. "It's okay. A little weird. They're away on a three-week cruise, so they're glad I'm around to watch their dog, Doxie."

"Have you heard much from Evan?"

"Yeah, he yells and screams and constantly reminds me about what I'm giving up. Naturally, I'm banned from the bar and our construction business. Then, in the next breath, he's all lovey-dovey and wants to know when I'm coming back home."

Jude tried not to worry if Evan would wear Chase down.

"I had a dream about him."

"About Evan?"

"Yeah. You and I had just finished a torrid round of sex, and there was Evan, who took a meat cleaver to my head."

Chase laughed, flashing that Hollywood smile. "That's gruesome—I mean about the axe to your head—not the sex part." His eyes twinkled like flickering green flames.

Jude reached across the table and took Chase's hand.

"I like your bracelet. It's masculine looking." Looks good with your watch," Chase said.

"Thanks." There was a slight pause. "Do you have any plans for what you want to do next?"

"I was thinking about taking some classes, maybe in computer science."

"Yeah, that's a great field. I'll help any way I can." Jude tried to sound encouraging without being patronizing.

After finishing their glass of Prosecco, the first boom sounded, indicating the fireworks were about to begin. They stood at the brick wall. From behind, Jude wrapped his arms around Chase, who ran his hands over Jude's forearms. Despite the warmth of the night, the sensation of Chase's touch was like a refreshing breeze washing over him. Slightly taller than Chase, Jude inhaled the coconut scent clinging to his silky locks. Desire ignited and exploded in Jude, mirroring another firecracker bursting into a sphere of red strands, soon fading into twinkling remains like hundreds of lightning bugs. Others followed in different configurations and overlapping colors as John Phillip Sousa blasted from speakers on the plaza, complimenting the pyrotechnics.

Jude felt his hard-on grow to the point where it could drill through the brick-and-mortar wall. He pressed his face against Chase; his lips nibbled and tugged at his ear. Chase inhaled and turned his head until his mouth sought Jude's. They were locked in an embrace as tight as a vice.

"Let's go inside." Jude's voice was a sexual rasp.

Awkwardly, they walked, conjoined by a kiss. They made their way to Jude's bedroom, where they ripped at each other's clothes like lustful virgin teens.

Jude broke away. "Be right back."

When he returned, he grabbed Chase. "Making sure the door is locked. Don't want any ax-wielding intruders."

They fell onto the bed, laughing. Their bodies became tangled in sexual knots. They were like nomads as their mouths roamed over each other's bodies, discovering ways to emit thrills and groans of pleasure, licking and sucking, tasting their masculine saltiness. Jude propped on his elbows, watched Chase work his way down his torso, stopping at his groin. Chase's hands were splayed over Jude's chest and flat stomach as he swallowed Jude, causing him to fall back on the bed, closing his eyes and inhaling a lung full of air. He raked his fingers through Chase's baby-fine hair, guiding his head. The intensity swept Jude up in a dizzying sexual gyre.

Outside, the Boston Pops was hitting a crescendo with "Stars and Stripes." Inside, Chase lifted his head off Jude. His eyes trumpeted desire.

Understanding, Jude reached over the side of the bed and grabbed a condom from the chrome box.

"Well stocked, I see," Chase said.

"From now on, they all have your name on them."

After rolling it down his erection, Jude climbed on top of Chase, bent his legs back, and pushed into him slowly. Chase gasped and sucked in a stream of oxygen as Jude sank deeper and deeper into Chase. He leaned in close, his eyes laser strong, burned through Chase as he began rocking his hips at a fevered pace. Chase pulled Jude down, their mouths glued in a devouring kiss, stifling his grunts.

The explosions became more frequent, signaling the fireworks extravaganza was reaching its grand finale. Constant flickering hues lit the room as if their sexual energy emitted colorful electrical charges.

With one hand clutching Chase's throat, the other palming his chest, Jude picked up his pace and was nearing *his* grand finale. Chase's fingers traveled over Jude's sweat-glazed body as if reading Braille with fierce determination.

"Fuck!" Chase grunted. *"Oh! FUCK! JUDE!"* He shouted as he reached a hands-free orgasm.

Moments later, Jude's body tightened and juddered. He uttered an uncontrollable primal cry, signaling his climactic conclusion in unison with the final notes of the bombastic "1812 Overture" and the fireworks display.

Jude collapsed on Chase.

Outside went silent. Inside, the only sound was their heavy breathing.

"Now that's what I call celebrating the Fourth of July with a bang," Jude said breathlessly, laughing as he struggled to normalize the intake of air into his lungs.

Chase wrapped his arms around Jude, and his tongue pried open Jude's lips, leading to a lingering kiss.

"You're welcome to stay the night."

"I would, but I have to get home to take care of Doxie."

"Oh, yes. Doxie. I hope I get to meet little Doxie sometime."

"You can. Why don't you come to my parents' house tomorrow night?"

"I would, but tomorrow I'm staying to help my mom with my dad. How about Sunday?"

"Sunday it is. I can't wait."

After Chase left, Jude sat in briefs and ball cap on his terrace, finishing off the last of the Prosecco, swooning in the afterglow of the sexual frenzy with Chase. Their physical chemistry was unlike anything Jude experienced before. It was the Atom bomb of sex. But Jude felt a spiritual and emotional connection with Chase as well. He reflected on the short time he knew Chase, and he rejuvenated his life. Compared to former boyfriends, they now dulled his love life, rendering it as sepia-toned as the beginning of *The Wizard of Oz*. Along came Chase, and like Dorothy, upon opening the door to Munchkin Land, he brought vibrant color back to his world.

Chapter Fifty-Eight
Jude Can't Hide from Those Virgin Eyes

"Thank you, Lorenzo. Jude will be there to pick up the dinners shortly." Dolores disconnected the call. Since Augie could not continue going to Cornelli's—their Saturday night dining ritual—Lorenzo Cornelli offered to deliver dinners to the Giacolones.

Half an hour later, Jude returned with Styrofoam containers of broiled lamb chops, roasted potatoes, broccoli spears, tossed salad, and Italian bread.

Halfway through his meal, Augie got up and went to the bathroom to throw up. Jude's concerned eyes locked with Dolores's.

"How can he go on like that?"

Dolores just shrugged.

Jude couldn't finish his dinner. He felt guilty eating when his father couldn't. His mind fissioned as one half was alive with euphoria over Chase, while the other half grieved for his dying father. The cosmic dichotomy left him tossed in a vast sea of emotions.

"You don't have to make up the couch for me, Dolores. I just need a sheet to put over me."

"Never mind. It's hot. I don't want you sweating all over my couch. Besides, it's no trouble. I want you to be comfortable." After tucking the sheet into the cushions, Dolores kissed Jude goodnight. "If your father rings the bell, I'll get up to answer it."

"Dolores, that's why I'm here, to let *you* sleep."

"I'll be fine. Good night."

Jude entered his father's bedroom, bent down, and kissed his forehead. "Good night, Augie."

Undressing down to his Calvin Klein's, he lay on the sheet-covered sofa and closed his eyes. Jude's mind anchored on images of sex with Chase, causing a spontaneous erection. He slipped his hand beneath his briefs. Several minutes passed when his breathing increased, followed by his orgasmic release and a grunt, a little too loud for comfort, realizing the proximity to the bedroom his mother was in.

As if on cue, Dolores asked from the bedroom, "Are you okay, Jude?"

"Yeah, just a little…um…heartburn."

"There's Tums in the medicine cabinet."

"Thanks," Jude said, squeezing his eyes shut in embarrassment.

Jude snuck off to the bathroom to clean up.

When he returned to the couch, he reminisced about all those horny teenage years when he had the constant urge to masturbate. When no one was around, he boldly jacked off whenever and wherever the desire struck, which was often. The danger of being out in the open was part of the thrill. Even jacking off on the couch under the pious painting of *Jesus in The Garden of Gethsemane* and in sight of the Virgin Mary peering out at him from the dining room didn't deter him from the tidal wave of teenage hormones.

After feeling sinful, his guilt soon evaporated as the next wave of testosterone began to swell.

With those lustful teenage years bridged to current libidinous adulthood, Jude's eyes darted to the dining room. A nightlight cast a shadow of the Virgin Mary three times her size. She was all-seeing, all-knowing, an omniscient voyeur looming over his illicit behavior once again.

"Forgive me, Mary, but I think I'm in love."

Chapter Fifty-Nine
I Feel a Partridge Family Song Coming On

Jude arrived at Chase's parents' home with a Cuban link silver bracelet in his pocket matching the one he wore. When Chase opened the door, Jude's insides lurched like he was on a downward plunge of a rollercoaster. *That smile.* The upturned slant on one side of his mouth revealed blazing teeth. His sparkling eyes and smooth skin that practically glowed, nearly short-circuiting Jude's mind.

It took a few seconds to realize Chase was holding Doxie, a long-haired Dachshund, in one arm and the other wrapped around Jude's neck, reeling him in for a kiss.

"And this cutie must be Doxie." Jude ruffled the dog's head. Doxie responded with several licks to Jude's arm. His tongue felt like fine-grain sandpaper. "I think he likes me."

"How could he not? Come in," Chase said and stepped back to let Jude in.

The Allgood home was spacious. Rich, brown leather furniture surrounding a fireplace complemented the pistachio-colored walls and dark wood trim.

"Wow, this is quite a place." It was evident Chase grew up in the comfort of being financially well off.

"C'mon, I'll show you around." Chase grabbed Jude's hand and gave him a tour. They circled through the downstairs before heading up the mahogany staircase.

"This is my room." They entered a large bay-windowed room trimmed with the same dark wood.

"So, this is where the action took place." Jude hooked his arms around Chase and pulled him close.

"Yeah, with my parents right down the hall."

"Well, your parents aren't here now." He tattooed a firm kiss on Chase, who surrendered to it, melting into Jude's strong embrace, his hands lost in Chase's curls.

"You don't know what you do to me. You're the only guy who can get me hard with your kisses," Chase confessed dreamily.

Jude slipped his hands under the back of Chase's T-shirt, pulling their bodies together.

"Careful, or you could hurt someone with that," Chase said, responding to Jude's pressing hard-on.

"One man's pain is another man's pleasure." Sealed lips muffled Jude's words.

He pulled Chase's shirt off. Jude's hands roamed up his back, over his broad shoulders, settling on each pectoral. Chase was a tight package of lean muscle.

"I say we find out your threshold," Jude said.

Their kisses became more fervid as tongues swabbed lips and mouths; Jude's teeth intermittently tugged on Chase's lower lip, causing throaty groans of approval.

They aggressively shed the rest of their clothes and tossed them helter-skelter. They fell naked on the king-size brass bed.

Jude climbed on Chase, grasping a handful of his lustrous hair, and firmly pressed his mouth against his, continuing their rhythmic dance of lips and tongues. Chase moaned as his hands wandered over Jude's body. They writhed and undulated in the heat of desire. Chase wrapped his legs around Jude, knotting them with his ankles. Lost in their sexual passion, it took a moment for Jude to recognize the familiar feel of that fine-grain tongue lapping at his scrotum. Catching their reflection in an oval floor mirror, Jude saw Doxie's head buried between his legs.

"Doxie!" Jude rolled off Chase.

"What happened?"

"I think Doxie wants to be part of a threesome."

"Doxie! Bad dog." Chase laughed, picking up Doxie and placing him on the floor before wrapping his arms around Jude's neck, saying, "I can't say that I blame him. Now, where were we?"

Resuming positions, this time, Chase on top and starting with Jude's mouth, worked his way down his body, licking the divide between his chest muscles and over one, two, three valleys of abs before ingesting Jude, whose eyes closed as he devoured a mouthful of air.

After several minutes, Jude aggressively rolled Chase over. With the expanse of his palms pushing his legs back, he eased into Chase, whose breath became heavy. He sucked in the air as if going for a deep dive, then letting out a guttural groan. Jude's hands held Chase by the wrists, pinning them to the bed beside his head.

Chase was rapt as he gazed into Jude's penetrating stare. Holding eye contact, Jude moved his hands to Chase's chest as he picked up his fevered pace like a runaway locomotive.

"I'd say your threshold is quite high."

Chase smiled, emitting audible grunts as Jude forced the air out of his lungs with each thrust. Letting out a throaty cry, Chase worked himself into a seismic orgasm. Jude's muscles tightened, and he barely had time to pull out before his volcanic eruption. Psychedelic colors exploded behind his closed eyes. He collapsed next to Chase. Turning his head, he laughed. "What *you* do to *me*, Chase Allgood."

They finished cleaning up when the doorbell rang.

"Who could that be?" Chase quickly pulled on his jeans. Shirtless, he headed downstairs.

A muffled voice traveled up to Jude. "Evan! What are you doing here?"

"Whose car is that in the driveway? It's not your parents' car."

Jude's heart jackhammered against his chest. Heat rose to his face, and his lungs compressed, making breathing difficult.

"Evan, you shouldn't have come."

"Who are you here with?"

Jude was at the top of the stairs.

"That's none of your business," Chase declared.

"Where is he?" Evan stepped forward, inches from Chase, his eyes scanning the open room.

"I'm right here," Jude said, tugging on his shirt as he descended the stairs to the foyer. Seeing Evan outside his bar, Jude saw his sharp, angular features, dark and menacing in this moment of pure jealousy.

Evan eyed Jude, then bare-chested Chase. "Oh, did I interrupt your fucking?"

Jude met Evan at the bottom of the stairs. "No. As a matter of fact, we just finished," Jude said. His smile was wicked.

Evan lunged toward Jude; Chase intervened.

Evan's black eyes squinted. "I've seen you before."

"Your bar. You saw me at your bar."

"You've got a lot of nerve showing up at my bar while fucking my boyfriend." A vein in his neck throbbed.

"He told me you broke up."

"Oh, did he?" Evan turned to Chase. "So you start fucking the first piece of trash that shows an interest in you?"

Jude stepped forward in protest before Evan aggressively pressed a hand on his chest and turned back to Chase.

"And to think I came here to talk some sense into you, to come back home. You realize all you're giving up, don't you? You'll have nothing. I know you're not used to living like that, are you?" Evan said.

Chase dropped his head into his hands in frustration. "Yes, I know. You keep reminding me."

"And what's he got to offer you?" Evan crooked his head toward Jude. "You're going to sacrifice everything? For *him?* What's he got, a big dick?" Evan gestured jacking off.

Jude stepped forward again. "I think you need to leave now." He pushed Evan towards the door.

"Get your hands off me. Stay out of this." He turned to Chase. "Please reconsider and come home. I miss you." His voice was begging, desperate. Evan attempted to embrace him, but Chase resisted.

"I can't do this now. I want you to go."

Evan dug the heels of his palms into his eyes. Switching emotions, he looked Chase in the eyes. "You'll regret this." Turning to Jude, he said, "And you. Stay out of my bar."

"Don't worry, I wouldn't give you the business."

Evan glared at Jude for several seconds before heading for the door.

"Oh, and Evan, for the record, I do have a big dick." He put his arm around Chase, displaying a smug smile.

Fury burst onto Evan's face as his fist struck Jude's eye. Jude fell to the floor.

"Evan!" Chase screamed. "What the hell is wrong with you? Leave. *Now!*" He grabbed at Evan's shirt and shoved him. Evan stumbled through the doorway. With a look of regret, he gave Chase a last glance before heading to his car.

***

"You're going to look so butch with a black eye," Chase said as they sat in the spacious kitchen. He handed Jude a plastic bag of ice to place on his emerging bruise.

"Yeah? I didn't feel so butch flat on my ass." Jude winced, placing the cold pack on his eye. "I guess I went too far with the *big dick* remark."

"It doesn't take much to push Evan."

Later, they sat at the coffee table, which was littered with containers of Thai food. Basia hummed low from the sound system. Chase crunched a pomelo; Jude plucked a prawn with his chopsticks. Chase wrapped his mouth around the morsel Jude held out for him. In return, Chase grasped a Kimchi Udon noodle, putting one end in his mouth, draping the other over his chopsticks, and holding it out to Jude.

"What is this our *Lady and the Tramp* moment?"

Chase nodded, sporting a sexy grin.

"Which one of us is Lady, and who's the tramp?"

Chase uttered a closed-mouth laugh.

Jude took the end of the noodle in his mouth, and they worked their way to the middle, where he grasped Chase by the back of his head. Lips merged. Tongues clashed in a coconut cream-flavored kiss, escalating to the point where they abandoned their chopsticks, clothes strewn like detritus around the Persian rug, and they engaged in a brief but intense round of sex.

After, they lay naked on the leather sofa. Chase was on his back, leaning against Jude, whose arm rested across Chase's smooth chest.

"When did you know you were gay?" Chase ran his hand up and down Jude's forearm.

"I don't think there was a specific moment when I said, 'Oh, I'm gay.' I mean, when I became sexually aware that I was attracted to guys, I just thought it was natural, so I didn't think anything of it. I liked the uniqueness of it. I had girlfriends in high school, but it was non-sexual, though I loved making out."

"I noticed, and you're quite good at it." He kissed Jude's hand. "What did your parents say?"

"Nothing. I didn't feel the need to tell them."

"They don't know about you?" Chase turned his head to look up at Jude.

"I'm sure they have a clue. I mean, I'm thirty, and besides Francine, there weren't any girls in my life other than casual friends. What about you? Do your folks know?" Jude combed his fingers through Chase's locks.

"Yeah, they know. Mine worried about AIDS, and since I'm the only child, it bummed my dad that the Allgood name ends with me. But they came around eventually. Neither are ready to have some guy put a ring on my finger and walk me down the aisle, but—"

"Oh, that reminds me." Jude jostled Chase and got up. "Close your eyes."

"I've already seen you naked."

"Not that. I have a surprise for you, and I forgot about it with all the Evan drama." He dug the thick silver link bracelet out of his jeans pocket. "Hold out your hand."

"Are you going to put a ring on me?" Chase cracked a laugh and held his smile.

Jude clasped the bracelet on Chase's wrist. He opened his eyes.

"Oh my God! Just like yours. You are too adorable."

"Now we're officially going steady." A smile spread East to West on Jude's lips.

Chase draped his arms around Jude's shoulders, giving him a thankful kiss.

"I love it."

I think I love you. *I sound like the Partridge Family.*

Chapter Sixty
A Black Eye for a Black Eye

A few days later, Chase traveled down to Jude's apartment. Seeing Chase at his door, Jude's face brightened with floodlight wattage.

"I need a drink."

"What's wrong?"

Chase gave Jude a quick kiss as he entered the apartment.

"I spoke to Evan at Eight Balls." He clenched his fists, pacing back and forth. "He cut me off from our accounts and told me I should have considered what I would live on before leaving him. I have to do something quick. My resources are running low," Chase admitted.

"How can he do that? Isn't your name on anything?"

Chase looked hopelessly at Jude.

He took Chase in his arms. "You'll get something. I can help you until then."

Chase pulled away. "Thanks, but no thanks. I have to fend for myself and make my way in this world. I don't want to always depend on people for survival."

Concern crossed Jude's face, watching Chase zigzag across the floor.

Chase inhaled as if he surfaced after a lap underwater.

"How's your eye?" He touched Jude's face.

"Still black," he said, kissing Chase's palm.

"You look sexy."

Jude locked his hands around Chase's lower back and said, "I know a great remedy for tension."

Their mouths connected as they stumbled to the bedroom, falling to the mattress. Their naked bodies, like two sticks rubbing together, ignited a spark, causing an all-out sexual inferno that engulfed them.

***

Nocturnal insects buzzed harmoniously, flying around the hum of neon signs along Lark Street. Entering Margarita's Mexican

Restaurant, a waiter led them to a table on the patio. Jude relished the intimate coziness shared with Chase, sipping margaritas, sitting among the tall shrubbery lining the terrace, white lights above outlining the deck. The magic of the moment eventually evaporated faster than a droplet on a scorched pavement.

"Shit. Don't look now, but Lawrence Gillespie and his posse are here." The last thing Jude wanted was a desultory encounter with him.

"I can't stand Lawrence. He sucks up to Evan every chance he gets like Evan is some celebrity because he owns a bar and has money," Chase said.

"He hates me because I went out with Connor McCracken for like five minutes."

Chase arched his eyebrows. "You did? I hope I can compete." Chase smiled; Jude melted.

"Please! He's a caterpillar; you're the butterfly. Anyway," Jude leaned in, "I ran into Adam Blanchard, Connor's ex, in San Francisco. He told me Lawrence loves Connor. He hates me because he was jealous." Jude glanced over at Lawrence. He displayed a cheeky, arrogant smile as he spoke in a hushed voice, which gave Jude the impression they were the topic of conversation. Lawrence's moon face displayed nothing but contempt. His eyes zeroed in on Jude.

Jude tensed but did not let it show. He wasn't going to give Lawrence the satisfaction.

Lawrence's whispering and snickering continued.

"Do you mind if we get out of here?" Jude asked.

Chase looked in Lawrence's direction and understood. "Not at all."

They downed the last of their drinks, but there was no way to avoid Lawrence.

"Hello, Chase." Lawrence's greeting was not cordial. "Nice shiner, Jude. I wonder who gave it to you." He turned to his crew and let out a Vincent Price maniacal "Thriller" laugh.

"Oh, you like it, do you? Well, here, have one of your own." Jude slammed his fist into Lawrence's left eye. Lawrence and his posse screamed like Howler monkeys, shattering the patio's quietude and their pretentious veneer.

"Ice! Ice! Get me some ice before I swell!" Lawrence shrieked as Jude pulled Chase by the hand. Inside, Jude quickly paid for the drinks, and they laughed as they exited Margarita's in a half-run.

They walked through Washington Park, a few blocks away, passing the statue of Moses and the boathouse near the pond.

"I'm sorry if I was a little on edge tonight," Chase said.

Jude put an arm around Chase and pulled him close. "It's fine. I understand what you're going through."

"I admit I'm scared. I've never been in this situation before, and struggling between my financial well-being and my emotional health is a real battle."

Jude gave Chase a reassuring kiss on his temple.

They walked in the moon's ghostly glow.

"You're going to be okay. I'm here for you."

Walking over an open field, Jude stopped near a swing set with a jungle gym and a slide. He tightened his locked hold on Chase. Jude sat him down at the bottom of the slide and leaned him back. Hot-blooded kisses ensued; jeans were unbuttoned. Jude held Chase down on the metal surface as he pressed their exposed groins against each other.

Chase held Jude tightly, feverishly running his lips over every inch of Jude's face. The friction between their bodies reached a boiling point, ending in orgasmic eruptions. Jude's semen shot off to the side, landing on the smooth steel. He collapsed, his arms outstretched over Chase's head. Jude joked when their labored breathing regained regular rhythm, "The first one down will have more glide to their slide."

Chase pulled Jude down; their mouths connected with a force that made their teeth click. His eyes glowed in the moon like two green lanterns in the dark. Jude noticed a tortured look in them. With faces still close, their warm breath was like little zephyrs comingling with the night air.

They walked back through the grassy field to Chase's car, parked near Jude's apartment. Chase hooked his fingers in the waist of Jude's jeans. The silence between them gave Jude an uneasy feeling that, for now, he kept to himself.

"I wish you could stay," Jude said, leaning against Chase's '64 Mustang.

"I do, too, but Doxie awaits."

"Ah, yes. Your parents' pervy little dog."

"Hey, he's got good taste in men."

Jude took Chase in his arms. "Drive safely."

"I will. The margaritas have worn off."

"Since I can't be with you tonight, let's switch shirts. I want to sleep with yours, so your scent is with me tonight."

"Are you serious?"

"Nevermore. Come on, switch."

"You are so romantic."

Chase unbuttoned his sleeveless shirt while Jude pulled his Abercrombie and Fitch T-shirt over his head. Their naked torsos were dully phosphorescent under the moon.

"Cover up quickly before I get the urge to attack you again," Jude said, buttoning Chase's shirt.

After switching tops, Jude pressed Chase against his car and stared into his eyes with mesmerizing focus. He leaned in, lightly brushing his lips against Chase's, who returned the kiss before getting in his car. Jude watched as the red Mustang disappeared into the night.

Jude held Chase's shirt in bed, realizing he was in deep, over-his-head, out-of-his-mind in love. It pleased and pained him. It pleased him because he never experienced such intense love for another man—not with Michael Antonnuci, Mickey Flynn, and certainly not with Connor.

Yet it pained him because it was frightening to love someone so deeply, leaving him defenseless and vulnerable. It was like wandering through the desert half-dead, vultures circling above, waiting to feast on his helpless carcass. The guardian of his heart was AWOL. Jude now knew what it was like to be in love for the first time. *Connor was right.*

He clung to Chase's shirt, inhaling his musky scent as he drifted into a euphoric dream about the guy he now loved.

Chapter Sixty-One
Replacements

The day before Labor Day, Jude and Chase planned to go to Saratoga Racetrack with Michael Antonucci and his new boyfriend, Dean Pratt. While Chase was in the shower, Jude called Augie to see how he was doing. Dolores handed the phone to him.

"Hello, son."

Upon hearing his father, Jude swallowed hard. Though his tone was cheery, his voice was weak and raspy, like he dragged his words across rough gravel.

"Hi, Aug. How're you doing?"

"Hanging in there, son."

On the one hand, it comforted Jude throughout his father's illness that Augie always remained upbeat as if he was being strong for the rest of the family, and it helped Jude deal with it mentally. On the other hand, Jude knew it was just a Band-Aid trying to cover up a hemorrhaging gash.

"I'm going to the track today with some friends, but I wanted to call to check in with you."

"Thanks, son. Win big."

Jude hung up, frozen by a chill brought on by the call. Jude did not have a good feeling about his father's fate. The sight of Chase emerging from the bathroom wrapped in a towel warmed Jude.

"How's your dad?"

"He sounds terrible."

Chase strapped his arms around Jude and gave him a comforting kiss.

"Thank you. I needed that." Jude went to the bathroom to splash cold water on his face to stimulate the color that bled out after speaking to his father.

A knock on the door signaled Michael and Dean's arrival. Jude beckoned them in as he was applying moisturizer.

If anyone was as obsessed about youth as Jude, it was Michael. When they were together, they spent hours riffling through magazines, checking out hot guys, comparing facial products, and debating the virtues of vitamin E vs. Retinol to determine which moisturizer was best for preserving youthful skin.

Jude finished smoothing in the moisturizer as he emerged from the bathroom.

"What are you using these days, girl?" Michael asked.

"Derma Plus with Retinol."

Since it was the first Jude met Dean, Michael did the introductions. "This is Dean Pratt, your replacement."

"My condolences," Jude said, shaking Dean's hand. "It's nice to meet you." Turning to Michael he asked, "And you? What are you using these days, sheep sperm?"

Michael laughed. "L'Oreal for me. Is my face glowing?"

"You're positively radioactive." Jude patted Michael's face.

"And if your face were any tighter, your ears would be fins at the back of your head," Michael countered.

Hearing their friendly sparring, Dean said, "You two sound like a gay version of *Death Becomes Her*."

Just then, Chase emerged wearing a red crew-neck T-shirt and faded jeans, looking sexy and adorable. Jude beamed.

"Guys, this is Chase." Looking at Michael with a playful smirk, he said, "*Your* replacement."

Chapter Sixty-Two
The Aunts

Early the following morning, Jude and Chase slumbered, limbs entwined like braided hair, when the jarring ring from the telephone fractured their blissful peace. Jude untangled himself and dragged his naked body out of bed.

He uttered a drowsy *hello* into the receiver.

"You better come to Mom's. Dad's not doing well."

"Shit." Jude rubbed his brow. "I'll be there as soon as I can."

Jude returned to bed, caressing Chase's feathery hair. "Hey," he whispered.

"Mmm," Chase purred. "Ravage my body," his sleepy voice begged. He stretched, pulling Jude down on him. He kissed Chase.

"I'd love to, but I have to go. Augie's not doing well."

Chase sat up. "Do you want me to come with you?"

"Thanks, but you stay and sleep. I'll call you later." Kissing Chase once more, Jude dressed and was on his way to his parents' house.

Anthony greeted Jude at the door. Katie was having coffee with Dolores, Teresa, and Zig Zyskowski in the kitchen.

Jude went to the bedroom where Augie was in and out of consciousness. A numbing sense of finality overcame Jude as a tidal wave of emotion washed over him. Seeing his father on the precipice of death made his insides bottom out. The hands of death had a stranglehold on the room, on Augie, on Jude. He left to compose himself and headed to the kitchen.

Shortly after, Father Clark stopped to administer last rites. His dark eyes behind black-framed glasses trumpeted a message of resolve and sadness as he spoke. "I suggest you each take a moment to say your goodbyes."

Jude went last.

He lay down beside Augie and put his arm across his father's chest. It felt like a sheath of flesh stretched over his bones.

"What can I say to sum up thirty years of being my dad? There aren't enough words to express my feelings. I admire you and am jealous of your ability to see the good in everyone. I wish I inherited that trait from you, but I got Dolores' cynicism instead."

Augie's chest heaved; a rattling wheeze followed. Jude waited a moment before continuing.

"I'm jealous of your ability to see the joy in life and who loves life as much as you, and it's crushing to see your life ending. I never told you I was gay. I didn't feel the need, mostly because I knew you wouldn't care. Your love is unconditional. But being gay doesn't define me. How you and Dolores raised me gives meaning to who I am. I'm proud to be your son."

Augie's hand squeezed Jude's forearm.

"Thank you for being my dad. I love you, Aug." A single tear rolled down Augie's cheek.

"Father Clark said we should say goodbye, but I'm not going to do that because you'll continue to live through Anthony and me." Jude kissed his dad. He was sure Augie wanted to return his kiss.

***

Augie lingered. He was tough. "Stubborn," Dolores argued.

All that changed two days later when he slipped into a coma. Dolores called her children, who arrived shortly after.

"It's a miracle that he hung on all this time," Katie said.

"He was always so determined, always overcoming obstacles," Anthony added.

"Yeah, like learning to bowl left-handed when he couldn't bowl with his right hand anymore because of his wrist injury," Jude recalled. The family laughed.

"And joined two leagues to boot. I was a bowling widow long before he's making me a real widow." Dolores kneaded her rosaries.

After several hours passed, Dolores announced, "Go home. It's been an exhausting week. You must be tired. I'll call you when it happens."

"You must be exhausted more than all of us combined, Dolores," Katie offered.

I'm fine. Teresa and Ziggy are coming over to stay with me for a while." Dolores stood up. "Go home before I put you to work."

"Are you sure?"

"I'm more than sure. Now go."

***

Jude got in bed beside Chase but barely slept. Up until now, praying for Augie's death would have been a sacrilege. Now, it was an act of mercy. He looked at his watch: one a.m. It was the last thing he remembered before the welcomed arrival of sleep.

Just as fast as he fell asleep, a muffled jangle seeped into his subconscious, dreamlike. The second ring was a blaring jolt of reality. He lay motionless until the third peal from the telephone, knowing Dolores would be the harbinger of sad news. He hesitated, then, on the fourth chime, he picked up.

"Your father's gone, honey."

Jude went to sit in his purple suede chair and hung his head. Chase came out to the living room.

"Augie died." Though his voice was melancholy, there was a hint of relief as well.

Chase hugged Jude for several minutes.

Jude was traveling back to his parent's house for the second time in hours, his mood as desolate as the deserted thruway.

When he arrived, his aunts were seated at the kitchen table having coffee, except Bridget, who was at the sink cleaning a chicken.

"Aunt Bridg…" Jude said, kissing her on the cheek. "Why are you cleaning a chicken at four in the morning?"

Bridget, the oldest sister, pushed her cat's eyeglasses up with her wrist. "I'm going to roast it," she said.

"For dinner," Dolores clarified.

Jude poured a cup of coffee. "Dinner is, like, fourteen hours away."

She continued to give what amounted to a *Silkwood* scrub down to the chicken carcass.

"I'm nervous. I have to keep busy."

"She's been cleaning that damn thing since we got here," Esther, the second oldest, said.

"The chicken's already dead, Bridg." Eve dipped a Stella D'Oro into her coffee.

"It looks plastic," Anita, the youngest, commented.

"Poultry's dirty!" Bridget turned to address her critics. "You want to eat unsanitary chicken?" Her high-pitched voice pierced the quiet.

"For Christ's sake, Bridget. It's after four in the morning. You're going to wake the dead." There was a moment of silence before Jude led in the laughter, realizing what his Aunt Maria said—even sensitive Eve joined in the laughs.

"You're terrible, Maria," Eve said, going in for another dunk of her Stella D'Oro.

Maria tried to hide her embarrassment but couldn't stifle her giggles. "I didn't mean anything by it. It just came out." Her face turned the shade of her perfectly-coiffed-at-four-in-the-morning auburn hair.

Eve reached for another biscotti. "Geez, Dee, don't you think you should put a blanket over Augie? He's probably cold." Her concern was heartfelt.

"He's dead, Eve. He's already cold." Realizing what *she* said, Anita looked around the table, waiting for someone to say something about her unintentional insensitivity. Instead, for the second time, the family burst into laughter.

"Jesus, I didn't mean to be so…" Her embarrassment brought on rapid blinking as if to erase her words.

"Don't worry," Dolores said, wiping up the coffee she spilled from laughing.

"You know Augie, he'd be the first to laugh," Maria said, getting up to refill her cup.

Hugging his Aunt Anita, Jude concurred. "You're absolutely right, Aunt Maria."

Eddie and Albert Rizzo, undertaker cousins of the family, showed up in dark suits as if it was the middle of the day instead of heading towards 5 a.m. to take Augie's body. Despite being relatives, they addressed the family in a very mortician, business-like manner as they hugged and offered professional condolences. After declining coffee, Dolores showed them to the bedroom.

Everyone gathered in the living room as they wheeled Augie out. Eve wiped a stray tear from her cheek as she sucked in her lower lip. Even Bridget stopped abusing the chicken and made the sign of the cross, watching the Rizzo brothers roll Augie away.

After several more cups of coffee, Dolores told Jude to go home. "Get some sleep. Your brother will be here later. We have to pick out a coffin."

"Okay, Dolores. I'll come back later." Jude hugged his mother and said goodbye to his aunts.

What a difference a few hours made. Now, the sun was a fireball in the sky, and the thruway—a ghost road earlier—was an energy-charged expressway, a conduit delivering morning commuters to work and Jude, a mourning traveler, back home for much-needed rest.

When Jude got home, it was just after seven o'clock. Jude laid down with Chase, putting an arm around him. Chase kissed Jude.

"Try to get some sleep," Chase said.

Despite his deadly fatigue, Chase's kiss sent sparks through him, hot-wiring him back to life.

Jude couldn't help but think of Francine. Chase, who only knew Jude for a few months and didn't even know his parents, was there to comfort him. Yet Francine, a dear friend since college, didn't even know Augie died. He knew how much she loved his parents and wondered if she would ever know about his father. Her absence at this time added to the remorse holding Jude captive in its relentless grip.

Thinking about the last few months, he was glad Augie was out of misery. But the next few days were going to bring more emotional weight—first the wake, then the funeral. Though it was nice having the relatives that the family only saw at wakes and weddings, Jude wondered, as a *co-host* of his father's, if it would be the same. Augie would want it to be a celebration.

Exhaustion fueled Jude's desire for sleep, and in minutes drifted into slumber from the emotionally arduous week.

Chapter Sixty-Three
Francine Returns

Jude, dressed in a charcoal gray linen suit, entered Rizzo's Funeral Parlor through the heavy oak door with the stained-glass window. He saw Augie from a distance in a supine position. He could have been on the couch watching the Yankees, except he was in a coffin.

"It's not even five o'clock, and people are gathering out front." He kissed Dolores on the cheek, then shook Anthony's hand. Katie embraced Jude.

The late afternoon sun's bright rays pierced the parlor's stained-glass windows, painting the floral carpet with a colorful palette. Like sentinels at each end of the casket were floor lamps with pink tulip-shaped glass shades. They illuminated Augie's casket with a soft glow.

Jude positioned himself on the kneeler before the bronze and mahogany coffin. He said his prayer. "Rest in Peace, Aug. I'll miss you." Then Jude rejoined his family, where they would begin to receive those coming to pay respect.

A flurry of activity and loud whispering at the front door signaled the aunts' arrival. Eve and Bridget bickered in hushed tones that would cause a librarian to scowl. Seeing Augie laid out, Eve's eyes teared up. Esther pulled out a Kleenex and handed it to her weepy sister.

After paying their respects and greeting the family, the aunts took their seats in the first of several perfectly aligned rows of wooden chairs cushioned with burgundy velvet.

The people began to pour into the funeral home to say their final goodbyes to Augie and to give condolences to the family.

Leading the line of mourners were Teresa and Zig Zyskowski. They embraced Dolores and the rest of the family, their presence a comforting balm.

Following them were Lorenzo and Gilda Cornelli, their grief palpable. Gilda, dressed in a flowing black crêpe de chine dress, held out her arms in a gesture of shared sorrow. A single tear traced a path down her cheek. Dolores, taken aback by Gilda's unexpected display of emotion, could only nod in response.

"Dolores, we are just heartbroken," Gilda said, her voice cracking.

With surprise, Dolores' eyes widened at Gilda's sincere embrace.

"We lost our favorite customer," Lorenzo added, gently kissing Dolores.

"But you…and Jude will still come for dinner, won't you?" Gilda held Dolores' hands.

"Of course we will." Dolores realized Gilda's lacquered nails were digging into her palms, but she ignored it, touched by Gilda's sympathy. The phony Jilda with a J gave way to a genuine and sincere Gilda with a G.

The mourners stretched the entire length of the funeral parlor and out the door.

Among the early guests was Chase. Spotting him, Jude's heart galloped. He introduced Chase to Dolores, though it was not the appropriate time to announce him as his boyfriend.

"Very nice to meet you, Mrs. Giacolone…"

"Call me Dolores."

"*Dolores.* I'm sorry it's under these conditions."

"Perhaps in happier times, we'll meet again." Dolores locked eyes with Jude. She returned her attention to Chase. "Thank you for coming. I'm sure it means a lot to my son."

Before Chase left, he hugged Jude.

The family greeted the cavalcade of Augie's customers, bowling and golf buddies, Elks members, people he grew up with, and guys he served in the army with. There was no end in sight.

Jude leaned into Anthony. "It's like *This Is Your Life* on steroids." When Jude returned to focus on the line, his heart sledgehammered against his ribs. His eyes welled up. Standing in the queue was Francine. He barely heard Charles Abernathy, a long-time customer of Augie's, ask, "Who's going to cut my hair now?"

Francine kneeled at Augie's casket. After a brief prayer, she approached Dolores, and the two embraced.

"Dolores. I am so sorry about Augie. I wish I had been around to see him one more time."

Dolores hugged Francine. "I know. We missed you, Frannie. I hope you and Jude have patched up whatever nonsense separated you two."

Francine nodded, fighting back tears.

"Good. Because you see?" Dolores nodded at Augie. "Life is too short to let things get in the way of friendships."

"I know that now."

Francine stood in front of Jude. An awkward second passed before they embraced with lobster claw grips. Together, they burst into tears.

"Let's go talk for a few minutes. There are a bunch of people I don't recognize, so no one will miss me," Jude said.

Jude and Francine accepted the Kleenex Esther held out like an automatic tissue dispenser as they passed.

They hugged again before sitting in the back row.

"Fran, I am so sorry about Dakota. Had I known—"

"I know. It was a mistake not to tell you about meeting him, but the son of a bitch made me keep it a secret. I broke our golden rule of sharing all the sordid details of our lives. I was so upset seeing you and Dakota together that I wasn't thinking straight. Then things got so heated between us at the café, and when you said you were going to San Francisco, I realized I might lose you forever. I froze. Panicked. I didn't know what to say."

"It's okay. You're here now. We're here." He squeezed her hand. "Together again. How did you find out about Augie?"

"The obituaries."

"I tried calling you from San Francisco to tell you he was sick," Jude confessed. "But your phone was disconnected."

"I moved to a bigger apartment. A place on River Street in downtown Troy."

"You lightened your hair, I see."

"Yeah, what do you think?" Francine fluffed her hair.

"Take it from Augie. The only thing permanent is death."

"Oh, you."

"I'm kidding. It's nice. It softens your face." Jude inhaled. "I think I'm in love with someone. His name is Chase. He was here earlier, but you'll meet him tomorrow."

"Really? Oh, honey!" Francine cradled Jude. "I'm so happy for you. How ironic. I think I am, too. His name is Douglas de Chambeau. I met him during the summer in the Hamptons. I can't wait to compare notes." Francine giggled like a love-struck schoolgirl.

The aunts in the front row shuffled, causing a commotion.

"Psst! Jude!" Anita's attempt at whispering shattered the low-speaking voices like a sudden clap of thunder. "Someone's here to see you. Get up here."

"Oh shit. Don't go anywhere." Jude crawled over Francine and rushed to his family. Jude saw Dominick and Michael standing to the side. Seeing his best gay friends touched him deeply. He hugged them and thanked them for coming. They chatted for several minutes before Jude had to greet other mourners.

Just after nine o'clock, the last people paying their respects were gone. Despite the physical and emotional exhaustion that suddenly seeped into every cell in his body, Jude was elated that Fran was finally back in his life.

Chapter Sixty-Four
Always a Pallbearer, Never the Corpse

As Jude dressed for his father's funeral, Chase was leaving a voice message.

Jude picked up. "Hi. What's up?" Jude clutched the phone between his ear and shoulder as he knotted his tie.

Chase coughed the words out. "I'm so sorry, but I won't be able to attend your dad's service."

"What? Why?" Jude felt heartsick.

"I have to go with Evan to our financial advisor. I couldn't get out of it. I'm so sorry."

Evan!

"I hope you're not too mad at me."

"I'm not mad." Disappointment flooded Jude's words.

Chase said he had to do some work with his dad over the next week and would call Jude when he could. He suggested going to dinner at the end of the week when he finished with the construction job he was helping his dad with.

"Yeah. Sure. Dinner." Dazed and dispirited, there was a sinkhole where Jude's heart was. He hung up and wondered if Evan would be a constant albatross around his neck.

***

Augie was laid in his grave at Saint Anthony's cemetery under a cerulean sky as florets of cumulus clouds slowly drifted by. A slight breeze fanned the overpowering scent of the abundance of flower arrangements from which mourners plucked and tossed a single bloom on Augie's coffin as Father Clark ended the graveside ritual.

Family and friends walked to their cars lining the narrow road, wreathing through the cemetery's meticulously carpeted landscape. Francine looped her arm through Jude's while Bridget was sandwiched between him and Anthony for support as they walked over the unstable ground.

The procession of cars exited through the cemetery's arched, wrought iron gate en route to Dolores' home.

As her sisters helped her put out trays of eggplant Parmesan, baked ziti, roasted chicken, and potatoes, catered by Cornelli's Restaurant, they mumbled about the beautiful service.

People queued around the dining room table.

Shultzie, a bowling brother, recalled to Wally Hubbard about the night Augie almost bowled a perfect game left-handed.

"Aw, let's not talk about it anymore." Wally's eyes were water balloons about to burst.

Jude and Francine sat with martinis in hand, slouched on the couch under the *Jesus in the Garden of Gethsemane* painting.

"There were so many times these past months I wanted to reach out to you to discuss all my surreal adventures I had in San Francisco. But I especially wanted to tell you about Augie's diagnosis."

"I hated being separated from you. You were the first person I thought of the night I met Douglas."

"Oh God. Here comes my stoner cousin, Carl," Jude said to Francine.

Carl was the oldest of several cousins.

"He's like a character in a *Twilight Zone* episode—stuck in the 1970s," Jude whispered in Francine's ear. "Hi, Carl."

"Hey, man. Bummer about Uncle Aug." He tucked his long, stringy hair behind his ear. His tan corduroy sports jacket opened wide, exposing a paunch.

"Thanks for being a pallbearer."

"Dude, like, no problem. You know this was the seventh time I've been pallbearer for the family. It's an honor, man."

"Well, that's you, Carl. Always a pallbearer, never the corpse." Jude felt vibrations from Francine's repressed laughter. Carl's face stretched into a smile. As he walked away, his brow puckered, riddled with confusion at the remark.

"How I missed sharing moments of laughter like that with you." Francine snaked her arm around Jude's.

"How did you meet Douglas?"

"He bumped into me, spilling my wine, and insisted on buying me another. We ended up in conversation. He immediately swept me off my feet."

"But he lives in the Hamptons? Is this a long-distance thing?"

"No. Ironically, Douglas lives in Saratoga. He has a summer house in the Hamptons."

"Cha-ching."

"His family owns several jewelry stores."

"Chase owns a gay bar and a construction company. The only fly in the ointment is he owns those businesses with his ex."

Francine winced. "Ooh, sweetie."

"I know, but once he gets his finances settled with Evan—"

"Honey, I don't want to be discouraging, but money matters between exes are like Herpes. They never go away."

"I know. But I really love Chase, and I think he loves me. We'll make things work. He's with Evan now, discussing their finances. That's why he couldn't be here."

Francine locked fingers with Jude and smiled. Jude sensed her smile was an act of contrition.

"It'll be fine," he assured her as he finished his martini. Now, Jude had to convince himself.

Chapter Sixty-Five
Crabs: The Other STD

A few days later, Jude in much need of a relaxing drink after the emotional strain of Augie's death, sat with Francine on the Beverwyck's patio. The moon in the September sky played Peek-A-Boo with the clouds. A slight humidity clung to their skin like the T-shirt Jude wore.

I want you to meet Douglas, and I'm dying to meet Chase. We should have dinner sometime. Douglas is away a lot right now managing the four stores because his father's having some health issues."

"I'd like that."

After a few silent sips of their drinks, Jude fidgeted before breaking the tranquility.

"Something wrong?" Francine asked.

"Since we tell each other everything, there's something I didn't mention about San Francisco." Jude took a long pull of his martini. He walled his mouth with one hand: "I came back with Gonorrhea. I think I got it the last night I was there from some older hottie with a BMW motorcycle."

Her eyes widened. She let the words seep into her brain before reaching across the table and smacking Jude on the forehead. "Do I need to lecture you about sex? You're gambling with your health and life, mister."

Her action roused the attention of a middle-aged couple a few tables away.

Francine turned to them. "Mosquito," she said and smiled politely.

Jude continued in a hushed voice. "I didn't think we did anything risky."

"It's all risky, *I know.*" Her eyes avoided Jude. Suspicion crept into his thoughts. He squinted, staring Francine down.

Catching his leer, she asked defensively, "What?"

"You had an STD, didn't you?"

"Shhh!" She put a finger to her lips as she eyed the couple minding their business.

"I did not!" Francine was indignant. Lowering her voice, she repeated her denial.

"C'mon, I know you. You're hiding something."

Her voice went into whisper mode. "It wasn't an STD," she stressed. "It was—"

The waitress approached. "Can I get you folks another round?"

"We would love one…to accompany the juicy story I'm about to hear." Jude grinned and turned his eager eyes back to Francine.

Francine waited until the waitress was far enough away before continuing. "You really are an asshole." Francine inhaled, then paused. "Crabs. I had crabs," she whispered through ventriloquist's lips. "ONCE!" Her finger came up this time to emphasize it.

Jude's boisterous laugh caught the couple's attention yet again. He turned and smiled politely at them before turning his attention back to Francine.

"Cookies and milk compared to what I went through. And when, may I ask, did you have the vermin?"

"In college."

"And I'm just finding out about it *now?*"

"I was mortified. Chickie doesn't even know. Remember the guy I met through that campus book club?"

"Oh yeah. What was his name again? Winter? Spring?"

Francine grimaced. "Autumn, wise ass."

"His parents were hippies? Thought he was conceived at Woodstock?" Jude recalled.

"That's the one."

The waitress returned, balancing the martinis on the metal table's delicately perforated design. Francine sat silently, her eyes watching until the waitress was out of earshot.

"It was the most humiliating experience of my life."

Jude rotated the speared bleu cheese-stuffed olives in his martini. "You want to talk humiliation? Try having your doctor grab your dick, shriveled like a prune from embarrassment and anxiety, and twist a six-inch cotton swab down your urethra. It's the penis version of sword swallowing."

"Stop!" Francine held up her hands in protest. "You're making me squeamish." She took a hefty sip from her drink as if the vodka would dissolve the image in her mind and the entire conversation. "The whole thing makes you want to be celibate."

"That's what I said until my hormones kicked in ten minutes later," Jude said.

They laughed like hyenas. The middle-aged couple got up and left.

It felt good to laugh again with Francine after months apart, even if it was over crabs and STDs.

Chapter Sixty-Six
Jude Gets Pearl Harbored

Chase made plans with Jude to have dinner at six o'clock on Saturday after he finished the construction work with his dad. Five minutes after six, Jude spotted Chase's red '64 Mustang and entered Stone Ends Restaurant. The inside looked like a neatly organized quarry with its prevalence of slate and cobblestone. Though the massive fireplace in the center and mauve accents generated cozy warmth, it still reminded Jude of something from *The Flintstones.*

Chase was at the bar. He looked so innocent toying with the swizzle stick in his drink. His hair, tumbling down just below his collar, caught the light.

"Hey, sorry I'm a little late." He kissed Chase.

Chase's smile was somewhat cheerless. "I took the liberty and ordered you a scotch with lime." Chase gestured to the bartender, who was wearing a paisley vest and bowtie.

"How was your dad's service?"

"Oh, the usual funeral fanfare. Laughs, tears."

"I'm really sorry I couldn't be there."

The bartender brought Jude's drink over.

"You want to run a tab, Chase?"

"No, put it on the dinner bill."

"Cheers." Jude took a sip. "The one bright spot in the wake was Francine showed up."

Over dinner, Jude told Chase more details about his friendship with Francine and its demise.

Chase poked at his salmon. Pink flakes littered his dish. His face lit up momentarily with laughter when Jude explained how he chased after Francine, entering the gallery wrapped in a towel and was mistaken for a stripper.

Jude eyed Chase's behavior. "Something wrong? You seem a little nervous." He dreaded asking, but he had to know. "Does it have something to do with meeting with Evan?"

Chase hung his head. When he looked up, his eyes flooded. "I…I don't know how to tell you, but Evan and I worked things out."

"*Financially,* you mean, right?" Desperation filled Jude's voice.

Chase's hesitation increased the tension. "I'm going back with Evan."

The words hit Jude like a speeding locomotive. His heart hammered. Death-cold blood rushed through his veins. Ambiguity blanketed his face as his mind became a jungle of confusion. He wanted to speak, but the words were trapped in his throat.

"He promised to give me half of all of our assets, the bar, the construction business. Everything."

Jude's eyes glazed over with unshed tears.

Chase tried to ease the pain and explained, "It's all I have."

"I wasn't enough for you?" Jude's voice cracked.

Chase lowered his face, unable to look at Jude.

"And this is definite? You made up your mind?"

Chase nodded, his head was bowed. Moments passed. "I'm so sorry, I—" When he raised his eyes, Jude was out of his chair.

"Jude…Wait…Please…" Chase followed Jude.

Jude headed for the exit, fighting the urge to cry, and ran to his car. Unable to breathe, his lungs felt squeezed like an accordion.

Inside his car, the dams in his eyes burst, unleashing a floodgate. He threw his arms against the steering wheel and buried his head in them. An explosion went off in Jude's chest, lacerating every part of his insides with emotional shrapnel.

There was a knock on his window.

"Jude, please," Chase pleaded.

He didn't want to look at Chase. He turned the key, hit the gas, and sped through the parking lot. Cascading tears blurred his eyes as if looking through a rain-streaked windshield.

Jude remembered Francine's new address. Twenty minutes later he was in front of her apartment. When she opened the door, his eyes were still porous vessels, trails of tears mapping his face.

"Sweetie! What's the matter?" Francine arms wrapped around Jude. "Come in." They walked up a long, narrow stairwell to Francine's spacious apartment. They sat in a cozy collection of chairs and sofa in the otherwise airy, open loft.

"I just got dumped by Chase."

"*What?* He broke up with you? Honey! Why?"

Francine went to retrieve a box of tissues. There was a dull thud to his left. Cantaloupe jumped on the back of the floral chenille couch and placed a paw on Jude's shoulder. Cantaloupe's tiny, rough tongue licked at Jude's salty tears glazing his face. He thought of Doxie lapping his scrotum during sex with Chase. The memory turned on the tear duct faucet again. Francine returned with the box of tissues. Jude pulled out several tissues.

"He Pearl Harbored me." Jude's voice was waterlogged.

"What happened?"

"He went back to Evan. Apparently, money trumps love." Jude explained that Chase had nothing without Evan. Everything was in Evan's name. "The only thing Chase has is that stupid vintage Mustang. Evan must have put Chase's name on all the legal documents. That's why he couldn't go to Augie's funeral." Jude blew his nose. Cants jumped off his lap.

"Oh, sweetie, I'm so sorry. What a bastard." Francine reached out to hug Jude.

"Sorry, I'm getting tears all over your blouse." Jude pulled away. "You never even got to meet him."

"It's a good thing because if I knew what he looked like, I'd hunt him down and kill him." She wiped a tear from Jude's face with the pad of her thumb. "You'll survive this, just like the others."

"This one's going to take a lot longer to recover from. Right now…" Jude's eyes suffered a cloudburst. "…I'm hemorrhaging inside. He was the first guy I fell in love with."

Francine cradled him.

After an hour, when he was composed, and his face felt waterlogged, Jude stood up and arched his back. "There's something I need to do to stop the bleeding, and for that to happen, I need to confront Chase."

Francine rose. Concern filled her eyes. "Honey, you're so vulnerable. Do you think that's wise?"

"Probably not, and I may regret it tomorrow, but I have to do it." Jude hugged Francine and kissed her cheek. His watery eyes scanned the living room. "Nice place, by the way. I can't wait to see it through dry eyes."

Chapter Sixty-Seven
Jude's Confession

Jude parked not far from Eight Balls. He looked in the rearview mirror. "I'm a mess." His eyes were swollen like he was punched in the face along with his heart. He didn't care. It was now or never. Jude took a deep breath and walked the short distance to the bar. Grabbing the door handle, he hesitated and sucked the night air into his lungs; he yanked it open.

Clarence was seated near the door. "Hello, darlin'." His blue eyes sparkled, but his smile was dim. "I'm sorry about you and my nephew."

"Is…um…Evan here?" Jude remembered his warning about showing up at his bar.

"No, darlin', my nephew is. He's around here somewhere. Not to make you feel worse, but I think you're much better for Chase than Evan. I love my nephew, but he's a fool."

Though hard to hear, Jude thanked Clarence and strode to the bar.

"Hey, sweets. Whoa! You need some ice for those peepers?" Suzie asked.

"No, just my usual. A double."

When she returned with the scotch and lime, she said sympathetically, "It's on me, honey."

Jude took his drink and went to stand by a table in a darkened corner. He saw Chase coming out of the office.

After stocking some liquor on the shelves, he cleared empty beer bottles and glasses from nearby tables. Jude hid his face, looking down as Chase worked his way closer. When he sensed Chase was near enough, he spoke. "Hey."

Chase looked up. A moment passed before a dim smile struggled to light his face. "I didn't think I'd see you again. Jude I…"

"Don't say anything, you said enough already. I want you to know something. I don't know when I'll get to say this again to someone, so I want to say it now—to you. *I love you.* I fell in love with you."

The words flew out of his mouth with the airy naturalness of a butterfly in flight. "You're the only guy I ever said that to. And if I never say it again, at least I got to say it once in my life. Now I know what it feels like to be in love, and for that, I want to thank you and will always be grateful to you."

The corners of Chase's mouth curled brighter. There was a long pause.

"But I hate you for robbing me of the chance to let it flourish. I guess you can't say *I love you* back, but that's okay."

"It's not that I can't say it. I don't want to cause you any more pain."

"The knife can't cut any deeper, Chase."

Chase stepped closer, placing his hand on Jude's arm, causing his heart to thrash. *His touch!* He wanted to wrap his arms around Chase and kiss him one more time.

"You're the most amazing guy I ever met." Chase's sincerity filled Jude with a burning desire that ran through him like a raging fever.

"Just not amazing enough, right?"

"I will never forget you and hope that someday you will forgive me for what I put you through."

As if the moon pulled at the tides in his eyes, Jude felt an emotional swell begin to flow. A sad look veiled his face. He had to get out of there before tears poured from his eyes.

"Good luck, Chase. I hope all this keeps you warm at night." Jude's arm scanned the bar and then walked away. "See ya, Clarence."

"Take care, darlin'."

Jude bolted out the door just as heavy rain began. Not caring, he walked with a deliberate pace to his car.

"Jude!" Chase yelled through the torrential downpour. Catching up to Jude, he pulled him so close that Jude felt his warm breath through the cooling rain. Chase's eyes bore down on Jude like a crushing weight before savoring a final kiss as if it were the last bite from an exotic fruit. For Jude, it was a desperate, drowning kiss from which he did not want to come up for air.

Finally breaking away from Jude, Chase said, "I *do* love you, but sometimes love isn't enough. I know someday I'll regret it…fuck, I regret it already, but I can't give up the life I built with Evan. I'm so sorry." Chase backed away. He mouthed *I love you.* Their eyes remained attached like opposing magnetic forces before Chase turned and walked, then ran towards the bar. His admission did nothing to alleviate the pain he inflicted on Jude. If anything, it cut deeper to hear, frustrating Jude to think Chase chose financial security over love.

Jude stood at his car; his mixed emotions crashed together like thunderclouds. The rain camouflaged his tears as he got in his car.

At home, Jude fixed another scotch. He sat, mourning the physical death of his father and the emotional end of his relationship with Chase Allgood.

Chapter Sixty-Eight
Dolores' Superpower

A week after the breakup with Chase, it was still an ulcerating wound on Jude's heart. Thoughts of Chase only served to feed the gluttony of his depression. Meeting Dolores at Cornelli's, he knew he had to pull off an award-worthy, upbeat performance, knowing how perceptive she was. One frown or sulking face, and she'd interrogate him like the star witness in a murder trial.

"Hi, sweetie." Gilda, looking all pink, ruffle-y, and stiff-haired, kissed his cheek. "She's at the bar."

Jude spotted his mother in the denim jumper and white blouse he gave her for her birthday. He took a deep breath and forced a smile to bow his lips as the curtain went up on act one.

"Hello, Dolores." He hugged and kissed her.

"You look tired. You're not sleeping."

Damn her acute motherly instincts.

Sol, the bartender, came over. "The usual, Jude?"

Jude nodded. *You'd better line them up.*

"Yeah, I'm sleeping okay." Jude forced a fake smile.

"You're lying."

"It's been an exhausting few weeks, that's all. *Really.*"

"I've been going through your father's things. You should stop by and see if there's anything you want."

Taking a sip of his martini, Jude felt her eyes stripping away his fake veneer, like paint remover. Something in Jude wanted to unload the emotional boulder weighing upon him, but he didn't want to upset Dolores so soon after dealing with Augie.

At dinner, Jude barely finished his salad, and halfway through the shrimp scampi, Dolores' suspicions persisted. She studied him like a scientist viewing a microorganism. "Something is bothering you. I can tell."

Was he as diaphanous as dragonfly wings? Or was it her x-ray vision superpower that exposed his depression? He toyed with his silver bracelet. And it hit him. He remembered the one he gave Chase. Blood flushed from his face, and a sentimental tear rushed to his eye. It did not go unnoticed by Dolores.

"I was seeing someone I was serious about," Jude blurted out, blotting the tear away. "And now it's over."

Dolores reached across the table, taking Jude's hand. "Oh honey, I'm so sorry. Who was it? That handsome boy at your father's wake?"

"What? How…how did you…you know about me?"

"Of course, I know. I've known for years. A mother knows such things about her children. What I don't know is why you didn't tell me."

"I never thought I had to. It was just who I was. I didn't have a reason to tell you until Chase. I thought he was *the* one. The one I'd introduce to you, bring home for the holidays, and live happily ever after with."

"Life isn't a fairy tale, honey."

"Yeah, no kidding. It's more like a collection of Sylvia Plath poetry." Jude finished the last of his martini.

"Obviously, honey, this Chase wasn't *the* one after all. But someone out there is." Dolores swirled her drink with a speared olive. "Besides, you're friends again with Francine, right? Good friends are so much more important than...than, oh, what do you call them nowadays, *lovers?*"

"Oh God. That's as bad as calling sex *making love*. Partners, Dolores. They're called partners."

"Oh, Jude, that makes it sound so business-like. *Lovers…*" She wiggled her shoulders, "...is more romantic."

"Now, who's sounding like a fairy tale?" They both shared a hearty, well-deserved laugh.

After dinner, Jude walked his mother to her car. The slight chill in the September night was a bellwether that autumn was imminent.

"Drive safely," Jude said as Dolores got in her car.

"Don't settle for anyone less than who you deserve, honey. And for God's sake, don't waste another moment aching for that Chase. He's not worth it. What kind of a person breaks up with someone right after they lose a parent? Tell him to go shit in his hat." She followed that with her usual mantra: "Call me when you get home."

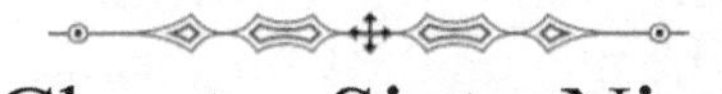

Chapter Sixty-Nine
Return To the Land of the Living

For weeks after the break-up with Chase, Jude went through his days like a somnambulant. Though his eyes were open, they were glazed over like a frozen lake, and he moved with the lethargy of a person pumped up with psychotropic drugs.

On the Sunday before his thirty-first birthday, Jude got out of bed to get a bottle of scotch and choose a CD to help him purge the ache his heart was pumping through his body. He chose Madonna's "Like A Virgin."

Flopping back down on his bed, he skipped to the track "Love Don't Live Here Anymore." With the remote in one hand and a scotch in the other, he kept hitting *replay* until he finished four more glasses of Johnny Walker Red.

As Chase ravaged his scotch-induced thoughts, Jude vacillated between pathos and anger. The more he dwelled on it, the boozy haze tipped the scales in favor of fury. Jude showered and went to Tea Dance at Eight Balls. He wanted to look alluring, so he wore his tan canvas Carhartt jacket, unbuttoned without a shirt, and his white NYU baseball cap.

Entering the club, he encountered Clarence at his post at the door.

"Hello, darlin'."

"Hey, Clarence." Forlornly, Jude's eyes scanned the bar hoping, and not hoping to see Chase.

"He's not working tonight." Clarence's face registered sympathy. "Is there something I can help you with, honey?"

"No. I don't know why I'm here.

"Get a drink and enjoy yourself, honey. For the record, though Chase is my nephew, he doesn't deserve you. He's a fool."

"Thanks. But I think I'm going to go. I'll see you, Clarence."

"Night, darlin'."

***

The following Saturday, Jude went out with Dominick and his new boyfriend, CJ, whom he met on the Confidential Connection Hotline. After a few drinks at Oh Bar, they ended up at Eight Balls since Waterworks had to shut down temporarily due to a health violation and lewd behavior. One of the Go-Go boys, Brody George, the owner hired to entertain the patrons, ejaculated into the crowd. When word got out, the police raided the bar and arrested Brody.

The three stitched their way to the bar. Clarence was helping Suzie bartend.

"Hello, darlin'. I have something for you from Chase."

Jude's heartbeat galloped in his chest. Clarence disappeared into the back office. For a moment, Jude was optimistic that Chase had changed his mind. Clarence returned with an envelope.

"Here you go, honey." He went back to tending bar.

When Jude opened the envelope, it contained the silver bracelet he gave Chase with a note saying, *I don't deserve this. Love Chase.*

Jude felt like his heart stopped and his life drained from him. "Well, that's it," Jude said, taking a deep breath. "That's the end. My last connection to Chase." A lone tear trickled down his face. "For a moment, I thought he changed his mind about our relationship. But quoting the Munchkin coroner, it's not only merely dead, it's really most sincerely dead."

"I'm so sorry." Dominick hugged Jude.

"He sounds like a douchebag," CJ said.

"Do you want to go?" Dominick asked.

Taking another deep breath and dabbing away the solitary droplet rolling down his cheek, Jude said, "Hell no. It's time I returned to the land of the living. Let's get some drinks and have some fun."

Chapter Seventy
Mr. GQ

Between his lingering depression and Douglas' busy schedule, it was the weekend before Thanksgiving when Jude finally joined Francine and Douglas for dinner at Sperry's in Saratoga. He walked into the restaurant a little dressy but still comfortable wearing jeans, a wool indigo sports coat over a white shirt, and a navy and white striped silk tie. He figured it was not appropriate to wear a baseball cap.

In the interior's dimly lit glow, he handed Simone his overcoat. Simone returned and handed Jude a small, hexagon-shaped chip.

Francine spotted Jude, got off the leather barstool, and went to greet him wearing a form-fitting black dress and shiny metallic high heels. Her smiling face lit up the restaurant's dimness like a luminous orb.

"Jude! How handsome you look." Their arms commingled as she led him to Douglas, who stood as they approached. He appeared to be the same height as Jude, but his impeccable posture made him seem taller. Jude caught himself before letting his jaw drop. Douglas was the most distinguished-looking older man he ever saw, a sight that filled him with admiration and awe. He was the epitome of the word *gentleman*. His meticulously groomed, argentine hair framed his sun-bronzed face.

Douglas extended his hand. "Well, hello, Jude. We finally meet." His smile revealed teeth as bleached as his white Eton shirt.

Veneers, probably.

Douglas wrapped his thick fingers around Jude's hand and squeezed with Python-like strength. The other hand patted Jude's upper arm, his fingers kneading his bicep. "Well, someone goes to the gym," Douglas said.

Jude blushed, simultaneously flattered and embarrassed, aware of Douglas' physique. His muscles strained against his plaid, vicuña sports coat.

Douglas' ice-blue eyes were glued to Jude, making him a little self-conscious.

"Can I get you a drink?" Douglas' eyes still stared.

"Sure. Grey Goose martini. Straight up. Olives."

Douglas looked away—*finally*. His profile, like that of a Greek God, showcased a straight, angular nose, while the neatly trimmed landscape of pewter whiskers, which amounted to more like a seven o'clock shadow, blanketed his strong jaw.

"Maurice. Grey Goose martini." He gave a thumbs up, as in straight up.

Jude glanced at Francine, who beamed. She shrugged.

Once seated, Xavier, black-tied and vested, brought over the magazine-size menus. "Can I get anything for your party?"

"A bottle of Châteauneuf-du-Pape." Douglas said as if he asked for ordinary tap water.

Xavier bowed like he was royalty.

"I recommend the filet mignon au poivre. Chef Georgio is a master with steaks."

"Douglas likes his rare. The thing is practically mooing." Francine's smile turned into a grimace.

"You don't know what you're missing." Douglas smiled and winked.

"I'm sorry, I don't like eating cute little animals."

"You eat fish," Jude countered.

"Yes, but they're not cute."

Xavier arrived with the wine. "Shall I pour?"

"I'll do the honors, Xavier. Thanks. We'll order now."

After placing their selections, Francine filled Douglas in with more details about her friendship with Jude, leaving out the sordid details of trying to seduce Jude and *Dakotagate*. At one point, she excused herself to go to the ladies' room. Douglas watched as Francine walked away.

"She's quite a girl. Father is quite enamored with her. Says she'll make a good wife."

"Wow, so things are getting that serious with Fran?"

Douglas shrugged in a maybe-so gesture. He leaned forward, resting his elbows on the table, his fingertips steepled under his chin. "So, you're the gay friend." His crystalline eyes had a mischievous twinkle as he scrutinized Jude once again.

Jude noticed his meticulously manicured nails. They had a dull luster, like pearls.

"There are others," Jude smiled.

Douglas snickered. "I meant Fran's close gay friend."

"That would be me."

"And you're one hundred percent gay?"

"Purebred homo. Next time, I'll bring my papers." He sipped his wine.

"Well, I'm glad to know. Otherwise, a good-looking guy like you might make me jealous." Douglas grinned, his eyes lingering on Jude.

"And good that you're all straight. Otherwise, *Fran* would have reason to be jealous," Jude said without thinking. *I probably shouldn't have said that.* Jude felt the heat rise on his face. A big gulp of wine followed.

Douglas, mid-sip, choked on his wine. Xavier rushed over.

"Are you alright, Mr. de Chambeau?"

"I'm fine." Douglas dabbed at his mouth with the linen napkin. "Just went down the wrong pipe."

Xavier backed away as Douglas controlled his cough and asked, "And were you always gay?" Douglas asked.

"Since conception."

"So, you're of the mind that sexual preference is determined at birth?"

"It's not a state of mind. It's a biological fact."

"Fair enough." A long pause. "What do your parents say? Are they okay with your being gay?"

"My parents didn't say anything. Just like they didn't have to say anything about my brother being straight." Jude's tone was a little defensive. *Where is this line of questioning going?*

Douglas ran a hand through his silver hair before locking his hands behind his head. His broad chest tested the resiliency of his shirt. Further pressure and the buttons—each a different color—would surely pop off and fall like ivory confetti.

"I'm sorry. I'm being a jerk."

Francine returned. "What did I miss?"

"I was just telling Jude I'd be jealous if he weren't your *gay* friend."

"The straight world's loss is the gay world's gain." She smiled and patted Jude's hand.

Douglas lifted his glass. "Here's to diversity."

Their glasses met in the middle, causing an echoing *ping.*

Francine sipped her wine. "As I was saying, Jude and I lost touch when he went to San Francisco—"

Douglas arched his eyebrows. "Oh, San Francisco. Beautiful city."

"But he came back because his father was sick and died in September, and we reconnected then."

"I'm very sorry to hear that. I'll bet your dad was a fine man."

Over dinner, Douglas discussed his family business. "Coming from a modest upbringing, my father worked his way up in the New York Diamond District. By nineteen sixty, he had enough money to invest with his then-partner to open a jewelry store in downtown Saratoga. My father wanted to start small and thought he could do well here, especially during racing season, and he did." Douglas motioned for another bottle of wine.

Xavier snapped to attention.

"Gained quite a reputation before expanding to other locations. Over the years, his clientele included Miss Saratoga, herself, Mary Lou Whitney, Kitty Carlisle, and Doris Duke."

"His father gave Douglas more responsibilities. He oversees the four stores. That's why I hardly get to see him." Francine's mouth curved downward. "And why it took so long for us to get together," she said, finishing her wine.

"Where are the other stores?" Jude asked.

"Outside Saratoga, there's one in New York City, Manchester, and Newport."

"He sure knew where to follow the money." Jude cut into his filet mignon.

"Yes, indeed. My father's a shrewd businessman—and a bit pompous. He added the *de* to Chambeau because he thought it made our name sound aristocratic. He always wanted to be part of the well-to-do crowd, so he was demanding in business and his personal life. He was tough on me, so I'd become the man *he* wanted me to be. 'Someday, you'll thank me,' he always said."

"And look how you turned out. A man of class and distinction." Francine beamed.

"He says he wants me to marry so I can produce an heir to inherit the business. He thinks Francine can make an honest man out of me."

Francine glanced at Jude, then looked down, blushing as a smile blossomed.

They finished their dinners as the conversation became informal.

Douglas wrung his hands. His shirt cuff, clasped by an orange button, shifted, exposing his gold Breitling watch.

"Ready for dessert?" Douglas asked.

They ordered lemon posset topped with Scottish raspberry coulis, whipped cream, and snifters of Courvoisier.

At the end of dinner, Douglas handed Simone their coat tokens. Thanking her, he stuffed a fifty into her tip jar.

Outside, Jude and Douglas shook hands.

"It was a pleasure to finally meet you, Jude." Douglas eyed Jude's herringbone Chesterfield coat.

"Snazzy coat." Douglas' fingers caressed the velvet collar. "Apparently, we have good taste in common."

Jude's mouth twitched into a semi-smile. "Thank you for dinner, Douglas. It was fabulous. Fran, I'll call you." He kissed her cheek and headed for his car. His breath hit the air creating a thick fog trailing behind him like smoke from a steam engine. Francine would no doubt ask Jude for his assessment of Douglas at some point tomorrow. Driving home, he wondered how in the hell he would tell her his suspicion about him.

Chapter Seventy-One
Jude's Gaydar

"What did you think about Douglas?" Francine asked on cue the next day.

"I enjoyed dinner very much. As for Douglas…" A long pause.

"Well?"

"I'm going to be perfectly honest with you, Fran. I think he's gay."

Francine choked into her phone. "What? What are you talking about?"

"Fran, the man has more style than a stack of GQs. No straight man has that much panache."

"You're stereotyping."

"If the Gucci loafer fits."

"Lots of straight men have class and style."

"Yes, of course they do. I'm going on my instinct. My gaydar is rarely off. I hope for your sake I'm wrong, but while you were in the ladies' room, he kept questioning me about being gay—"

"Oh, you think everyone is gay until proven straight."

"The jury is in. I think Douglas is a walk-in closet case." Jude downed his daily dose of vitamins and supplements with seltzer. As he talked, Jude paced around his apartment, filtered in the morning sunlight, knowing he was probably right. He didn't want Francine to think he had any designs on Douglas, leading to another Dakota-like feud. "If I may get personal, what's the sex like with Douglas?"

"It's okay. I mean, when we do have sex. Frankly, I floss my teeth longer. But sex isn't everything."

"How frequently do you have sex?"

"Haley's Comet comes around more often, but he's always away on business." Silence. "Thinking about it, the first time I slept with Douglas, he said he was too drunk to have sex. When we did have sex, he *was* drunk. Oh my God, Jude. Do you really think he's gay? Jesus Christ! What is wrong with me? Always picking men with skeletons in their closets.”

“I’m afraid in Douglas’ case, his isn’t alone.”

Fran wailed. “Shit, I just spilled coffee on my robe.”

“Fran, I’m sorry. I know this is hard, but I sense there’s a gay heart beating beneath his Armani suit.”

Francine sniffed. “You’re bursting my bubble.”

“I’m inflating your ego. As rich, classy, and handsome as Douglas is, you can do better. You *deserve* better. You deserve the truth. I don’t mean to make light of the situation, but if my guess is right, you’re not playing on the same team.”

“And until now, my biggest fear was if I was even in his league.”

“Look, all joking aside, I hope I’m wrong. Call me later.” Jude’s brow creased. He didn’t mean to leave Francine cloaked in conflict.

***

“What do you mean you *still* haven’t asked him about his sexuality?” Jude met Francine at Justin’s for a holiday drink since she was spending Christmas with Douglas. “First, it was because of Thanksgiving. I’m surprised you didn’t cite the anniversary of Pearl Harbor as an excuse. Now, it’s Christmas.”

Francine shifted in her stool. The glow of white Christmas lights twined in evergreen cast a shadowy consternation on her face.

“I know. It’s just awkward bringing it up with someone I’ve been seeing for six months. And with the holidays, he’s been going back and forth between the stores. I haven’t seen him much.”

“You may as well wait till after Christmas to see what trinket Santa de Chambeau brings you from Daddy’s store.” Jude twisted the knotted end of the bamboo skewer with three impaled olives in his martini.

“Please don’t make jokes or pressure me. You have to handle these things delicately.”

“Okay, Wicked Witch of the West. But the longer you wait, the harder it will be when the truth comes out…of the closet.” Jude couldn’t resist a giddy chuckle. “I’m sorry. I don’t want to see you deceived. Start the New Year off on the right foot.” Jude reached out, took Francine’s hand, and kissed it. “I’m here for you, whatever the outcome.”

Chapter Seventy-Two
Out of the Shadows and Out of the Closet

Fran stood next to Douglas and snaked her arm through his, feeling the softness of his cashmere coat.

"Thank you, doctor." I'll make arrangements to have my father's body taken to the funeral parlor." Douglas's voice was stoic.

The Emergency Room physician gave condolences before heading to the nurse's station, draped in fake evergreen garland and threaded with twinkling-colored lights.

"Douglas, I'm so sorry. What a terrible thing to happen on Christmas day. Let's go home now," Francine said. They headed down the corridor, whitewashed in the harsh, blinding glare of the fluorescent lights. They walked in silence past a vacant gurney. Francine was glad to be outside despite the drizzle falling. She hated hospitals and despised the smell of disinfectant and sickness. Inhaling deeply, she filled her lungs as if she held her breath the entire time they tried to resuscitate Douglas' father from his heart attack.

"Are you alright to drive?" Francine asked as they approached Douglas' black BMW.

Douglas nodded.

On the short ride home, Douglas did not speak, and Francine remained quiet also, partly to honor his desire for silence and because she never knew what to say at times like this. The tranquility was awkward and a relief.

Douglas drove his BMW into the circular driveway. The Queen Anne-style home was as beautiful outside as its interior. The headlights swept across the terracotta brick gabled façade with its rounded towers. The stained glass atop the windows emitted a soft glow from the lights inside. The velvet drapes were pulled to the side, allowing a view of the giant Christmas tree in the center of the bay window. In a glib moment among the fallout of the toxic day, it crossed Francine's mind that Jude would compare the sight to a scene out of *Meet Me in St. Louis*.

Douglas undid his tie and the first few buttons of his starched, white shirt while heading to the dining area. He poured bourbon into a glass, downed it in one swallow, then poured another.

Francine declined his offer for one. He took the bottle to the living room and fell into a wingback chair. His glass dangled precariously from his fingers as his hand rested off the scrolled armrest. Francine followed. Douglas tossed back another drink before hanging his head down. Seeing his shoulders heaving, Francine knelt before Douglas.

"I know how sad you must feel, Douglas."

He lifted his head. His hair fell like silver threads around his face. "Sad? *Sad?* I'm actually relieved." A lone tear traveled down his cheek, disappearing in the forestry of his platinum beard. After slicking his hair back, he picked up the bottle and filled his glass.

"I...I don't understand. You're *relieved?* Why?"

"Because I'm finally free." Douglas' lips formed a wan smile.

"Douglas, I'm confused. What are you talking about?" Frustration crinkled Francine's brow.

"Fran, I'm so sorry."

"Douglas, you're not making any sense. First, you're relieved, now you're sorry? Sorry for what?" She stared at Douglas; her face was one big question.

"I'm relieved because I'm free." Douglas stood, pacing in short, erratic steps around the Isfahan Persian rug.

"Free from what? Your father?" Francine's face registered confusion.

"All my life, he held me prisoner with his intimidation and authority." His face contorted into a tightly pinched mask. "Threatening me at every turn. Giving me ultimatums."

Francine's stomach contracted, watching and listening to the tortured man she suddenly did not understand.

Douglas emptied his glass, refilling it. "I'm relieved because now I'm free to be *me,*" Douglas spoke in a weak, almost child-like voice, choking back tears. "All my life, I denied who I am because of my father. Listening to Jude that night at dinner, I was so envious and filled with questions because I wanted to vicariously hear what it was like to have the freedom to be who I am."

Francine stood, confronting Douglas. "And why are you sorry for me?" Her voice was flat with repressed anger.

Douglas wiped another stray tear with the cuff of his shirt."

Francine collapsed her arm over the other like a shuffled deck of cards and pressed them against her chest. "*Why. Are. You. Sorry. For. Me?*" Each word felt heavy, like bricks falling from her mouth, her world suddenly lying in ruins around her.

Douglas stared blank-faced, glassy-eyed at nothing in particular. Downing the contents of his glass, he spoke in hushed tones.

Francine wanting and not wanting to hear what Douglas had to say.

"I was twenty-one, naïve. After the raid four days earlier, I didn't think there'd be any more trouble. When I finished my evening class at NYU, I went to join some friends in the village for a drink. Things were peaceful for a while until the police burst in and I was caught in the riot that ensued. Naturally, I resisted."

Francine shifted her stance. "What riot?" Her voice was soft but demanding. She began piecing the time and events in her head.

Douglas turned to face Francine. "Stonewall."

Francine inhaled a deep breath as if feeling excruciating pain. She clutched her fists to her chest.

"I was arrested. My father saw my picture in the *New York Times*. He had to bail me out." Douglas' words rushed out. "After that, he swore he would disown me, cut me off if I came out, if I ever brought shame to the family name he worked so hard to build…and protect."

"Jude *was* right. You *are* gay."

"I suspected he knew. It takes one to know one, I guess." A puff of air, forming a light laugh, escaped Douglas' lips.

"You son of a bitch!" Francine shouted. "All this time, wasted on your deceit."

"I'm sorry, Fran…I didn't mean to deceive you. My father was a very controlling person. I would have lost everything."

"Oh, not you, too." Francine pressed her fists against her temples. "Just like Chase with Jude. It's all about the money."

"I *was* going to marry you." Douglas grabbed Francine's shoulders. She pulled away.

"Well, I guess I dodged that bullet. What kind of a marriage would it be, Douglas? Hmm?" She pounded his chest. "You going away on business trips hooking up with strange men? No thanks. All your money isn't worth living life with a fraudulent husband." She looked around, frantic. "I have to get out of here. I endured enough death tonight." She unclasped the diamond tennis bracelet Douglas gave her for Christmas.

"Please keep it, Fran. I gave it to you out of love, perhaps not the kind of love you hoped for, but I do care about you."

Francine looked at Douglas. Contempt shot from her eyes like bullets.

"No thanks. I don't want anything to remind me of you." She grabbed his hand and slapped the bracelet into his palm. "Goodbye, Douglas. It's been…disingenuous." Francine stormed out of the room. Her heels clacking on the Italian tile floor echoed through the foyer. Douglas followed. She grabbed her coat violently, causing it to whip the air. Her anger was the momentum carrying her out the door, back down the steps to her car parked along the hedges lining the driveway.

The drizzle turned to a steady rain.

Opening the car door, she threw her purse to the other side, spilling its contents. She pounded her fists against the steering wheel once, then a second time before wiping the rain from her face. Too angry to shed one tear, her lungs felt compressed, and she breathed in a staccato rhythm as if plunged into ice water. She let out a wail so loud it hurt her ears. Francine pressed her shoe to the gas pedal with such force that the tires squealed, spitting up gravel as she drove off. She turned at the end of the driveway and headed down North Broadway for the last time.

***

The day before New Year's Eve, Francine finally returned a call from Jude.

"You were right. Douglas is gay. I didn't have to confront him. He confessed after his father died."

"Frannie, I'm really sorry. I hoped I was wrong about Douglas. But now you know the truth, even though the truth hurts, for now. You will rebound." Jude walked with his phone to the couch.

"How long did it take for you to get over Chase?"

"I don't know if I am completely, but I'm getting there. It's like open-heart surgery. Everyone's recovery is different. I have days where the pain hurts a little more than others. It's a slow process, but in time, I'll mend. We'll mend completely. Time cures all." Jude kicked his feet, clad in thick wool socks, on the sofa.

Talking about Chase brought on a moment of melancholy that chilled Jude as if a cold wind blew through him. He didn't envy Francine, whose heartbreak was fresh, like an open gash risking emotional infection if she let it fester. Knowing the feeling, he shuddered at the painful memory it dredged up.

"I'm angrier than I am hurt. And I'm mad at myself for not being more sensible about men."

"Don't beat yourself up over it. We can't choose who we fall for."

"Yeah? Well, the new year is going to see a different Francine."

Jude wanted to make the conversation lighter. "So, he was at Stonewall, huh? The *New York Times* outed him to his father?"

"Yeah, and drove him back in the closet so far I should have smelled the mothballs and cedar through his Hermés cologne."

"Why don't you come over tomorrow night? We'll celebrate New Year's Eve. We can watch the fireworks from my deck. It's supposed to be a beautiful, warm night."

"It's December. It should be snowing…wait. You mean you don't have plans for New Year's Eve?"

"I planned to go out with Dominick and CJ, but I'm sure they won't miss me. They're still in that early, star-crossed, puppy love stage. Besides, it will do you good to get out."

"Maybe you're right. I feel like I'm going to explode if I stay holed up for another minute. The only time I've been out this week was to replenish my Merlot supply."

Jude heard a glass ping as if placed on a hard surface. "Are you drinking?"

"Yes. Wine."

"It's eleven in the morning! Girl, you better get your ass out of the house. I'll see you tomorrow night for New Year's Eve."

"I'll bring champagne."

Chapter Seventy-Three
The Last Single Couple in America

"Hi Dolores. I just called to wish you a happy New Year. Are you sure you don't mind being alone?"

"Yes, I'm sure. I'm going to make a martini and watch a Barbara Stanwyck film. I'll be fine."

"Remember to swish the vermouth around the ice, then throw it out."

"I lived with your father for forty-nine years. I think I know how to make a good martini. Happy New Year, honey. Be sure to wish Frannie the same. I hope the new year is better for you both. I lit my New Year's good luck candle beside the Virgin Mary, especially with you and Frannie in mind."

"You really could start a new religious cult. Anyway, the new year can't be any worse." The year's casualties crossed Jude's mind with a meteoric flash: Augie, Connor, Grady, Chase, Fran and Douglas, San Francisco. He inhaled. "Happy New Year, Dolores."

Jude hung up and wondered how different his New Year's celebration would be if he were still with Chase. They'd drink champagne, watch the fireworks display, and have New Year's Eve sex.

Jude always thought how he rang in the new year determined how well the next 365 days would be. He thought having great sex was an indicator of a good year ahead. But regardless of good sex, bad sex, or no sex, the years always turned out the same—good and bad blended into a bittersweet concoction you had no choice but to swallow. *That's life.* It was impossible, not to mention unrealistic, to expect a perfect year, but every December 31st, that's the hope on everyone's mind. Jude's thoughts were interrupted by a knock at his door.

"I brought two bottles of Prosecco. One didn't seem enough." Francine kissed Jude's unshaven cheek as she passed through the doorway.

"Maybe Fran's New Year's resolution should be to join a twelve-step program."

"Isn't this weather insane? It must be fifty degrees outside."

"Fifty-five to be exact. The perfect night to sit outside and watch fireworks."

"Yeah, well, perfect for now. Let's hope this isn't the year the earth disintegrates into molten lava."

"Fran's New Year's resolution number two—start the new year thinking positively." Jude started making martinis.

"What's with the forties music?" Jude was playing a collection of vintage New Year's Eve songs.

"I bought this CD at a flea market down in the city a few years ago, thinking one year, I'd throw a New Year's Eve party like the one in *Holiday Inn.* You know, guys in tuxes, girls in black evening gowns wearing pearls." Jude handed Francine a martini. They clicked glasses.

"To new beginnings," Fran said.

"Here! Here!"

They sipped their drinks as Dinah Washington sang "Resolution Blues."

"Any resolutions, Fran?"

"To become a nun. I'm through with men."

"I wish I could say the same. Maybe you should try women." Jude exaggerated a grin.

"Maybe *you* should." Fran arched her brow.

Oh no. I may have struck out with some guys, but the game ain't over till the final out."

"You're a glutton for punishment."

"Cut me open, and you could count the scars on my heart. I'm a masochistic romantic. What can I say?"

They finished their martinis to Guy Lombardo's melancholy "Auld Lang Syne." Jude zipped up a black, quilted vest over his heavy thermal shirt and gathered two champagne flutes.

"You want a jacket? It's almost time for the fireworks to begin," Jude asked Fran.

"Please, it's like spring. The champagne will keep me warm." Fran grabbed the two bottles of Prosecco.

They headed out to the patio deck where the white lights Jude strung along the brick and iron wall glowed like stationary fireflies.

Below, in Washington Park, a train of cars snaked along the road showcasing the annual holiday lights display while the Empire Plaza Towers stood bathed in blinding white spotlights, like a Hollywood premiere.

They settled in the Adirondack chairs. Jude opened the first bottle of champagne. He poured until the effervescent foam reached the rims.

"Cheers," Jude said as he tapped his glass against Francine's, creating the timbre of a tiny bell. "Here's to nineteen ninety-seven." Jude was hopeful. "Ahh." Jude took a long pull of champagne. "There's nothing like that first sip."

"Only to be outdone by the giddy feeling of the last." Francine let out a tiny hiccup after swallowing some of the sparkling wine. "Can you believe we spent most of the year not speaking?" Fran wrinkled her nose as she observed the lines of tiny bubbles rising and swaying back and forth like tiny cyclones in her glass.

"It was a fucked-up year, that's for sure. Yet here we are. Fate brought us together again, helping each other lick wounds and heal scars as we ring in the new year."

A whistling sound signaled the fireworks' first launch. Jude and Francine turned their attention to the plaza. A red fuse climbed above the towers, bursting into an enormous sphere of red glowing tentacles, burning bright and fizzling into dying embers. They watched silently as several explosions produced multi-colored sparkling streaks that arched and drooped like willow tree branches. A faint, whirling corkscrew-like fuse traveled upward before popping into chaotic sparks, haphazardly shooting out like metal dragged across the concrete. As the fireworks continued, they polished off the first bottle of Prosecco.

The last time Jude was out on his deck watching a fireworks display was with Chase, though they spent most of the time in his bedroom having incredible sex. The memory possessed Jude like an unwelcome demon. Fortunately, Francine's voice exorcised his mind from the otherworldly thought.

"Do you ever think we were too picky, that we found the right person but let them go because of some silly flaw?" Francine asked, continuing to watch the fireworks.

"Picky? I'm not picky."

Francine choked on the last of her glass of champagne. "Not picky?

Please! What about that hot guy from your gym you said sweated too much during sex?”

“I could deal with the sweat, even though it was like having sex with a porpoise. When he grew his nails to play guitar, that was, if you pardon the pun, the final nail in the coffin.”

“Seriously, how long could they have been?”

“Polish them, and he could have been Barbra Streisand’s hand double.”

Francine scoffed. “And what about the guy who was a bad dancer?”

“No rhythm on the floor, no rhythm in the bed.” Jude swallowed the last of his sparkling wine. “Seriously, I didn’t care about those things. There just wasn’t enough chemistry with those guys.

A boom, sounding like a cannon, resonated from the plaza.

“And what about *you?* That guy who sent you roses all the time?” Jude asked.

“You mean Jonathan? He was too needy. I was supposed to be a girlfriend, not mother and nursemaid.”

“Let’s face it, those people just weren’t *our* Mr. Rights.” Jude popped open the second bottle of Prosecco.

As the fireworks continued in a bombastic strobe of color, Jude filled their glasses with the newly opened bottle of champagne.

“Why do all our friends appear to have found their *Mr. Right* but us?” Francine’s inquisitive face was like a chameleon reflecting the fireworks’ changing hues. “You know, Chickie has been dating a chiropractor for several months.”

“A chiropractor? Really? She’s finally getting her life straightened out?”

“She says it’s getting serious.”

“Even Dominick, Mr. Unromantic, is serious about CJ. If he can find love, we can.”

“My sister and Dina are having a civil ceremony this summer. My parents have been borderline comatose since hearing the joyful news.” Fran sipped her champagne.

A nonstop series of detonations blossomed into a bouquet of rainbow pyrotechnics against the sky, signaling the fireworks finale. They reflected so brightly off the glass tower windows that it appeared to be daytime instead of minutes to midnight and a new year.

Down on the plaza, distant voices declared, *one minute to midnight.* The crowd burst into a cacophony of cheers.

"So, here's my New Year's resolution—I'm going to cherish and appreciate my friends, especially you, my dearest Frannie, and not go looking for love. I will let it find me and enjoy life to the fullest—let life unfold according to my destiny." He raised his glass. "Happy New Year, Madame Fortuna, wherever you are."

The voices on the plaza counted down, "Ten, nine, eight…"

Jude and Francine held up their glasses.

"…four, three, two, one. Happy New Year!" the choir of spectators shouted in unison, accompanied by a symphony of party horns and noisemakers. The raucous noise rose and echoed from the plaza.

Jude and Francine exchanged a kiss.

"Here's to the new year, Frannie. It's going to be a good one for us." Jude raised his glass again. They drained their flutes.

Jude reflected, "If there is one thing I learned from this past year, it's that no matter how much we yearn for love, friendships are more important." He reached out to Francine. She stretched her arm across the table and took Jude's hand. "You know what else I learned?" he added.

Francine shook her head and sipped her champagne.

"Age is just a number. Heading into my thirty-second year, I feel no different than when I was in my twenties. Silver crosses and bracelets don't matter, either. When I opened the envelope Clarence handed me with the bracelet I gave Chase, I felt my heart sink, like life was ending. It was my last connection to Chase. Even though I didn't have him, he could have had a piece of me to hold on to."

"If he loved you, he'll remember you."

"And then I realized I was being crazy, a drama queen, as you so affectionately call me. There will be another Chase in my life, only a better version of him."

"And a better version of Douglas for me?"

"Of course."

"We can't regret it when things don't turn out as expected or hoped, but we can learn not to let silly things come between us again. And we should not worry about stuff we can't change, like age or trinkets that don't enrich our lives. Only friendship and family matter. In the end, that's what we leave this earth with."

"Do you really think it will happen for us?" Francine contemplated.

Jude turned his attention from the smoky cloud hanging over the plaza to Francine. "Will what happen to us?"

"Love. Do you think we'll ever find it?"

"Of course, it will happen, sweetie. We'll find love. Despite what happened with Chase, Connor, and Grady, I haven't given up hope. Neither should you. In the words of Maya Angelou, have enough courage to trust love one more time and always one more time."

"Yeah? Well, didn't she also say love is like a virus?"

"Yes." Jude nodded reluctantly, acknowledging Francine's cynicism. "And it can happen to anybody at any time, is how the rest of the quote goes. As much as Chase broke my heart, in the end, I realized I was thankful and happy for what we had, brief as it was. Never taking a chance on love is worse than short-lived happiness. When we crave something like love and find it, and it doesn't last, it makes us want to find it again even more, and we will. The trick is not to force it. It has to happen naturally. Every relationship is unique and teaches us something different about human nature."

"We should be scholars by now." Francine sighed. "I guess you're right. But it doesn't seem fair. We're the last of our friends to find love." Fran said in a semi-buzzed state.

"As former Miss America-turned-chanteuse Vanessa Williams once sang, they save the best for last." Jude smiled at Francine. He looked out towards the park.

A breeze picked up.

"Somewhere out there, a couple of guys are waiting for us. Listen, if it can happen for everyone else, especially Dominick, it can happen to you and me," Jude encouraged. He looked at Francine. His eyes were lamps of optimism. Retaking her hand, he said, "We have to be patient. Until it happens, we'll have each other," he reassured Francine. "Until then, we'll be…we'll be the last single couple in America."

THE END

Acknowledgments

Writing may appear to be a solitary endeavor but on the road to publication, it becomes a collaborative effort between many people, so there are several that need to be acknowledged. First, I would like to thank Peg Aloi for her professional editorial skills, her keen eye, and thoughtful suggestions. A special thanks to Joyce Hunt-Bouyea, my fellow writer, with whom I shared many Friday afternoon critique sessions. Your friendship is invaluable. I am grateful to the many family members and friends who took the time to read the pre-published manuscript and reacted exactly the way I hoped readers would respond after reading my novel. So, heartfelt thanks especially to Linda Fiorella (another fellow writer), Paul Goscinski, Steve Rees, Jon Gray, Shawn Hunziker, David Murphy, Pam Fiano, Carrie Hewitt, Meredith Robson, and Kathy Colarossi, my biggest "fan," and to my brother, Rick whose own writing talent has always inspired me. A heartfelt thanks to Erica Hughes and her team at New Book Authors Publishing for making my dream of being a published author a reality. To my partner, David Tassone who makes every day a holiday and a reason to celebrate living. I'm so glad to share this happy moment in my life with you. And finally, to you, the readers. I hope you enjoyed reading *The Last Single Couple in America* as much as I took pleasure in writing it.

About the Author

Martin received a Bachelor's Degree in Communications with an emphasis in film and creative writing. He is an avid reader, has been to 24 countries (and counting), and is a staunch supporter of animal advocacy. He lives in upstate New York with his partner and the spirit of their two Italian Greyhounds, Caesar and Dante.